WITHDRAWN

LOSE YOU to FIND ME

Also by Erik J. Brown

All That's Left in the World

LOSE YOU to FIND ME

ERIK J. BROWN

BALZER + BRAY
An Imprint of HarperCollins*Publishers*

For My Grandparents

Margaret Keels   Ann Brown
Aaron Keels   John Brown

Balzer + Bray is an imprint of HarperCollins Publishers.

Lose You to Find Me

Library of Congress Control Number: 2022951848
ISBN 978-0-06-305502-5

Typography by Chris Kwon
23 24 25 26 27 LBC 5 4 3 2 1

First Edition

CHAPTER
ONE

SUNSET ESTATES SOUNDS LIKE A COOL NAME, until you realize it's an old folks' home and "sunset" represents their lives.

That's some dark shit.

Sorry, it's not an "old folks' home"—I shouldn't call it that. In fact, our manager, Natalie, yells at us if we do.

It's a *retirement* community. And not like those ones you always see in movies or TV where there are a bunch of hundred-plus-year-olds drooling in wheelchairs wishing for death. Most of the people who live here are in great health, somewhere between sixty and a hundred and one "years young"—yes, management says that to their faces, if you can believe it.

Some wake up early and live active lives outside the community; others haven't left the complex in years. There's a structure and routine to how things run at Sunset Estates. Saturday night is movie night, birthday night is the second Wednesday of every month, and dinner is always from four p.m. to seven p.m.

It's what I liked about the job. It was structured and everything made sense.

But then Gabe De La Hoya started working there and ruined it.

Wait, no, that's not when everything got messed up. It started way before then.

PROLOGUE

I MET GABRIEL DE LA HOYA IN day camp the summer between fifth and sixth grade. He came up to me on our first morning with his dimpled smile and an Avengers lunch bag. He pointed at the brown paper bag in my hand.

"What did you bring?" he asked.

He was taller than me, so I'd assumed he was going to beat me up and take my lunch.

I figured giving it to him would probably be less painful, so I handed it over. He tilted his head but took it, then sat down on the curb next to me and opened the paper bag. He removed everything, one by one, and as he held up each item I told him what it was—the smoked turkey salad sandwich on brioche with lettuce (no tomato), the plastic baggie of homemade potato chips sprinkled with Trader Joe's Everything but the Elote seasoning, a bruised peach, and a piece of raspberry chocolate chip banana bread wrapped in tinfoil.

"Whoa, is your mom, like, a super chef or something?"

"My dad."

His mouth quirked at that, and he looked back at his own lunch bag. "I was hoping you'd want to trade, but I don't really have anything good." He opened the bag and pulled out what looked like a PB&J on white bread—no way I was giving up my dad's turkey salad for that—an apple, a pudding cup, and . . . Oh.

"Are those Takis?" I asked.

"Yeah."

My mouth watered and my cheeks seemed to tighten as I remembered the spicy, sour taste of the Takis I'd had at Steven Simmons's ninth birthday party. I had been the only one who'd eaten them, but they were amazing.

"I'll trade you my chips for those."

He held up the potato chips, scrutinizing them, and I realized I still didn't know his name. "What's on them?" he asked.

"Everything but the Elote seasoning."

His eyebrows jumped up. I expected him to ask what that was, but he didn't. "How about the chips *and* the banana bread?"

I must have shown how much I wanted the Takis. My dad always tried to make everything in our house from scratch, so I rarely got to indulge in processed foods.

"Chips, half of the banana bread, and if you bring more Takis tomorrow I'll ask my dad to pack a second piece for you."

He jumped up, holding out his hand. "Deal! I'm Gabe, by the way."

"Tommy." We shook on it.

After that my dad packed a second dessert for Gabe every day. Eventually, we went from swapping lunches to just sharing them.

He picked me first when he got to be matball captain, knowing full well I sucked. When we had a camp field trip to see a new Pixar movie, he sat next to me and shared the popcorn, candy, and soda he'd bought with the money his parents had sent with him. We spent every second of every weekday together.

But when August arrived, his family took him on what was supposed to be a weeklong vacation, and he never came back. I pretended he got swept away by a riptide or eaten by a shark. The rest of the summer I threw away the second dessert because I didn't know how to tell my dad that my new friend was gone and never coming back. Or maybe I hoped he would come back, and I'd have that second dessert ready for him.

It wasn't until the next summer that I realized why I had been so sad. Gabe wasn't like the other friends that I had grown apart from or who'd transferred to Archbishop Murphy after kindergarten. He was my first crush. The first boy for whom I ever really felt those feelings that other boys were supposed to have for girls.

So of course he'd royally fuck up my life when he came waltzing back into it.

CHAPTER
ONE (again)

I'M NOT SURE WHAT I THOUGHT WHEN I saw Gabe's name next to mine on the lineup sheet—this time during the summer between eleventh and twelfth grade. I'm pretty certain I stared at it for a good five minutes before I noticed my floor manager, Natalie, waving from the other side of the office door.

After taking one more look at the lineup sheet—yep, it still said Gabriel De La Hoya—I pushed open the door.

"Tommy," Natalie said, smiling her wide, shark-mouth smile at me. I tried not to shudder. Natalie wasn't the nicest person in the world, and like a brightly colored tree frog warning its predators that it's toxic, her smile warned of similar danger.

"I got your email," she continued.

Shit. The email. I'd totally forgotten I'd sent it. I mean, I'd remembered up until I saw Gabe's name next to mine, with the word "shadow" in parentheses. The boy with dimples who I hadn't seen in six years. I wondered what he looked like now. I wondered if he was still cute.

Wait, Natalie's email first—that was more important right now.

I closed the office door—dulling the sounds of Dante the sous chef chopping onions—and sat down across from her desk. My stomach began to tie itself in knots like a pretzel. There was a reason I sent that request as an *email* and didn't ask her in person. I just wanted a no in writing; I didn't need for her to tell me to my face.

Natalie's smile remained in place as she sat in silence across from me. I wasn't sure if she expected me to start the conversation or what, but I had said everything I had to say in the email. So, instead of saying anything, I admired her makeup again.

Somehow, Natalie managed to use as much makeup as a drag queen, but in a way that actually worked for her. With her light brown contouring and foundation, I had no idea if she was thirty or fifty. Her smoky eye and dark lipstick were stylish, so I leaned more toward thirty, but her outfits—that day it was a beige pantsuit and white blouse—had me veering toward the fifty side again.

Finally she spoke. "You're planning to go to La Mère?"

I nodded. "My dad went there. I heard it's a great school." I was trying very hard to downplay it. I hadn't just heard that La Mère Labont was a great school; I *knew* it was. It was always listed at the top of the best culinary schools in the world, several famous chefs had graduated from there, and admissions were extremely selective.

But I didn't want to let on how much I wanted to go there. Not to Natalie. She seemed to take joy in the misery of her subordinates.

She raised her well-drawn eyebrows and her tone became very know-it-all. "Oh, it's more than just a great school. You know, when I started looking into schools and was deciding between restaurant management and . . ."

I started to zone out. I already knew all this. She had been deciding

7

between becoming a chef or going into hospitality management, and she chose management—I mean, clearly. That's why she wasn't in the kitchen right now.

It was also why I wanted *her* recommendation. Natalie wasn't shy about where she had worked before Sunset Estates. She brought up her experience managing one of Chef Louis LaGuard's New York restaurants as often as she could. And now here she was, in an old folks' home in southeastern Pennsylvania, managing a bunch of high schoolers.

My, how the mighty have fallen, Natalie.

Anyway, Chef Louis wasn't only one of the most well-regarded chefs in the world. He was also one of the faculty members *and* on the admissions committee at La Mère. So yes. I absolutely wanted to use my Natalie connection to try to get their attention. Among other things I was working on, like the required essay—which I was sure the inspiration would come for any day. The application also said I could include supplemental material, and I already had an idea for that.

I tuned back in to Natalie at the perfect time. "So I assume that's one of the reasons you asked *me* to write your letter of recommendation."

"I also asked George," I said. It was a risk, making her feel less special by bringing up our other manager, but maybe if she knew I would have asked her even without her connections she'd be more open to it? "La Mère requires two professional references as well as one educational. But, yes, I did specifically want to ask you because I know you worked with Chef Louis in the past and he's on the admissions committee."

She shook her head, and my heart sank. "There are no professional strings to be pulled when it comes to La Mère."

"I understand that, but I figured since Chef Louis knew what kind of management style you had and saw that I had been working here for—it'll be three years when I leave for La Mère . . ." I trailed off, letting her figure out how I would end that sentence on her own.

In reality, the answer was absolutely that I was trying to look impressive by having her name on my recommendation letter. It felt like the universe conspiring to make this happen. Why else would she be here? Chef Louis's New York restaurant was still open and one of the top in the country.

Natalie clasped her fingers together. "I make it a point *not* to write letters of recommendation."

Again, my heart sank.

"However," she continued. My heart rose . . . but just a bit, because the tone of her voice made me nervous. "I don't often get asked to write recommendations for La Mère. So I'm willing to make a deal with you."

A deal? What the hell was this Faustian bullshit? She probably wanted me to stay late every night—off the clock, no doubt—and clean the kitchen with the dish crew. She *should* agree to do the letter because I'm already a good employee, not as a way to get free labor out of me. I kept my face as neutral as possible, waiting for her to continue.

"I'll give you three tasks to complete to prove to me that you're above and beyond what La Mère is expecting. If you accomplish all three to my satisfaction, I'll write you the greatest, most effusive letter

9

of recommendation in the history of letters of recommendation."

Definitely a devil's bargain. "What kind of tasks? 'Cause I'm not great at spinning straw into gold."

Natalie, as always, was more annoyed than charmed by my jokes, but she kept her composure. "And I imagine if you were, you wouldn't even need to be here! But since you *are* here, I'll keep the tasks Sunset Estates–related. Now, for the first, and probably easiest: You saw I gave you a shadow this evening?"

Gabe De La Hoya. The hairs on my arms stood on end and my cheeks flushed with warmth. I nodded, unable to speak.

"You'll be his primary trainer. If you're not on the schedule, I'll find someone else, but on the days you both work, I'd like you to focus on training him as wonderfully as I've trained you."

How nice of her to take credit for training me when it had actually been a series of other servers. "You got it. What else?"

"The next task is to prove to me that you can totally handle yourself with the residents."

I smiled politely. "I do that every day."

She shook her head. "I mean that I'll task one of the residents with testing you. Something particularly difficult." Her voice went up a few octaves, making it sound overly saccharine. "Something you can't say no to."

That was Natalie's biggest rule: never tell the residents no. If one of them asked for something that seemed impossible, we had to fetch her and either she would make it happen or *she* would be the one to tell them no.

Natalie continued, "It will test how you deal with a difficult resident." She seemed particularly proud of herself as she said it.

"Okay, I'll be ready for something fun tonight."

She shook her head and clapped her hands together quietly. "That's the best part! It won't be tonight because I want it to be a surprise! You'll never know who it will be or when it will happen."

Which meant every single batshit request that every single resident had from now until that letter was in my hand was potential disaster. *Kill me.*

I kept my face neutral. "Got it. And the final task?"

"I'll have to think about that one." She pursed her lips. "I think we'll know when you complete it. But if I get the inspiration before then, I'll let you know."

So every possible misstep—and certainly not my triumphs—could be the potential dead end to my La Mère acceptance.

"Sounds fun," I said with as much sincerity as I could muster. She dismissed me, and I left the office, pulling the door closed behind me. And there was Gabe's name again, right next to mine.

I needed to tell Ava.

Without saying hi to anyone else, I left the kitchen and cut through the salad bar, where James—a scrawny, six-foot-tall white kid with an inane ability to create unwanted nicknames for everyone—was refilling the last of the dressings.

"Bahama Mama!" He did a little dance as he said the ridiculous nickname he'd come up with for me. "What's up?"

"Hey, James." I continued back to the rear service station as James played both sides of the conversation he imagined I was supposed to stop and have with him.

James lowered his voice. "I love that shirt—is it new?" Then in his own voice, "Aw, thanks for noticing, Bahama Mama, but nah, it's the same one—I just spilled French dressing on it."

I called Ava, but it went to voice mail. She was probably driving, since her shift started any minute. I texted her my location and told her to meet me as soon as she arrived.

Several minutes later, Ava rounded the corner of the rear service station, looking a little anxious.

"You're late!" I scolded.

Her eyes went wide. "What?"

I showed her the time on my phone, and her shoulders relaxed. "Two minutes, and it took those two minutes to walk from the time clock to here."

"A likely story! Guess wha . . ." I started to tell her about Gabe but realized she still seemed agitated. "Wait, what's wrong?"

She sighed. "What isn't wrong? I had to borrow my uncle's car to get to my nail appointment, and he made me fill up the tank as payment. I tried to go shopping for GJ's birthday but couldn't find anything—"

"Get your uncle to buy her bourbon for you." Ava's grandmother was legit life goals. Almost eighty years old, but you'd think she was sixty. She had a set routine and ended each day with a glass of bourbon with two ice cubes while she watched old TV shows on their family streaming plan.

Ava shook her head and held a finger up to me. "No, Grandma Jenkins buys her own bourbon. Anyway, I still have two weeks. Till her birthday, I mean."

"Let me know if you want help? Or at the very least a chauffeur— that way you don't have to fill up your uncle's car."

12

"Thank you, Tommy." The way she said it, though, made it seem like I'd just offered her a kidney. But before I could press the issue, she said, "Were you going to tell me something?"

"Oh, you will never guess what's happening," I said.

"Then you should probably save us some time and tell me." Ava used the camera app on her phone to double-check her appearance. Her hair was already pulled back and secured for the night. Ava liked to keep her hair natural, but the Sunset Estates employee handbook was vague—most likely on purpose—when it came to Black girls' hair. All it said was that long hair had to be in a bun or ponytail. So Ava kept hers pulled back and wore a series of jeweled hairnets to match her nails.

Today it was sparkly blue nails with a sapphire hairnet.

"So," I said. "Do you remember when I came out to you?"

She nodded but still seemed distracted as she used the camera to check her hairnet. "You mean on our third date, when I said you either needed to tell me you were gay or kiss me already?"

"Right, so remember the kid I had a crush on at camp, Gabe? I told you he was the first guy I ever realized I liked?"

She sighed and put away her phone. "Honey, I love you, but I really don't."

"Doesn't matter. What matters is he's starting work here. Today. And I'm training him!"

Ava still didn't seem impressed. "Wow."

I slumped, disappointed. I didn't expect Ava to feel the same amount of enthusiasm, but I thought she'd be a *little* excited. She was, after all, the one who kept trying to push me and my occasional drunken hookup, closeted hockey boy Brad Waldorf, together after she'd walked in on us making out at a party the previous summer.

My excitement dissipated, and I finally realized: something was definitely up with Ava. I could see it in her eyes. We knew everything about each other, and sometimes could even tell what the other was thinking.

"Excuse me?"

Before I could dig it out of her, I turned to see a tall guy with light brown skin and short black hair. He gave us an awkward wave. "Sorry. I'm looking for Thomas."

Gabe.

His cheeks were thinner, jaw more squared, and his hair wasn't messy with a cowlick in the back anymore. But I'd recognize him anywhere.

Ava cleared her throat and pushed past me, harder than she needed to. "Look at the time; lineup's about to start." When she was safely behind him, she turned back and dramatically fanned herself.

He held out a large hand. "I'm Gabe De La Hoya."

My stomach dropped. I stared at him, trying to figure out if he was being serious. Did he really not remember me? Was he really staring into my face and forgetting that summer between fifth and sixth grade when we spent almost every day together, even after just seeing my name on the lineup sheet?

CHAPTER
TWO

IS THERE A WORSE FEELING IN THE world than your first crush forgetting about you entirely? I mean, sure, maybe getting shot, stabbed, or electrocuted feels worse, but I wouldn't know. On my scale of pain, this was the worst. At least it felt like it at the time.

I remembered *everything* about him. I knew his dad's family was from Mexico and his mother's family from Venezuela, but he was third-generation. I knew he was closest with his grandmother on his mom's side because she would come pick him up sometimes and they'd walk home together. I knew he went to the movies with his dad every Saturday afternoon because he'd tell me on Monday what he had seen. I knew he preferred sweet food to salty food. And that he preferred pie over cake but cookies over pie.

Remembering all that about him, while he forgot about me, made me feel like an absolute dork.

I took his hand and tried to look polite again. "I'm Thomas. Nice to meet you."

It was just like that first day of summer camp. We shook hands, and I looked into his hazel eyes—the eyes that changed from mostly brown to mostly green depending on the light—and I waited for that moment of recognition. For some kind of magic to happen.

First, he doesn't recognize me, then we look into each other's eyes, add a dash of nostalgia, let it rest for three seconds, and suddenly he remembers a summer of games on the playground and desserts made by my dad.

But there was no recognition. Just the friendly, polite smile. And dimples that I just wanted to fall into and die.

To make it all even worse, just at that moment Natalie rounded the corner of the rear service station.

"Thomas," she said, putting her hands on her hips. "There you are! We've been looking for you."

Shit. Her tone sounded like she was warning me that I was about to lose the letter of recommendation. My mind scrambled for an excuse, something she would actually enjoy hearing.

"Sorry, I was just checking my section."

She almost seemed to deflate as she turned to look at my tables, trying to catch me in a lie. My stomach clenched, and I even felt sweat at the nape of my neck.

Please don't find a missing spoon. The last thing I needed was her scolding me in front of Gabe. I mean, how much embarrassment could I possibly suffer in the span of thirty seconds?

When she seemed satisfied, she turned back to me. "Well, I see you've met Gabriel."

"Yes. We just met." For the first time ever, because we never swapped food in summer camp or anything.

"Gabriel here parked his car out front," Natalie said.

Rookie mistake, Gabe. The front parking lot was reserved for residents—and the formal dining room host, Doris, who at the tender age of four hundred and eighty-seven *should* have been a resident—while the rest of the service staff parked in the back by the dumpsters.

"Would you mind quickly showing him around to the staff parking lot?"

"Of course," I said, taking any excuse to get away from her. "We'll be quick. This way, Gabe."

I led him through the kitchen, where Chef Roni and her sous chef, Dante, were finishing up their last round of prep work. The kitchen smelled like the white wine/lemon/butter sauce that Roni was stirring on the stovetop.

"Oh my God," Gabe whispered. I barely heard him over the hiss of water coming from the dish room. "Who is that?"

I followed his gaze to the tall Jamaican woman as she poured the butter sauce over white fish in a shallow chafing pan.

"Chef Roni. She's the head chef."

"She looks like Grace Jones," he said, as though I was supposed to know who that was. "I love her."

We continued toward the dark private dining room as Roni called out a checklist for the evening's dishes to Dante. I was nervous and silent the rest of the way, still a little rattled from Gabe not recognizing me. Like, how awful is that? To be a nobody to the person who was kind of the building block to me realizing I was gay?

"Why don't we use this room?" he asked when we got to the private dining room. What was up with the questions, and why were none of them *Where do I know you from?*

17

"It's for special occasions only," I said. I held open the door that led out to Sunset Estate's main hallway. The plush dark-green-and-gold paisley carpet beneath our feet looked like it was probably from the late nineties but was still pristine. Residents walked past us toward the dining rooms, some of them leaning on walkers, some spry and power walking.

"Good evening, Judge," I said as a tall, thin Black woman strode past.

"Hello, Thomas," Judge Fredericks said. "See you in there."

I waited for Judge Fredericks to get out of earshot—much farther than the other residents, because the judge, in her early eighties, had even better hearing than I did—before I whispered, "That's Judge Fredericks. She always sits in the formal dining room at table twelve. You'll probably get her on your first solo shift. Whatever you do, never let her water glass get more than half-empty. She'll get up and try to refill it herself at the service station." Telling him my learned knowledge of Sunset Estates made it easier to pretend I wasn't obsessing about how he had forgotten me.

We continued toward the front entrance, but to the right of the reception desk I saw that the lights in the social activities room were on. I tried to remember what was supposed to be happening tonight but couldn't.

A frazzled-looking white woman in her forties popped out, wearing a plaid button-down and jeans. I wrinkled my nose at her.

"Dressing down today, Mother?" I teased. That's something else you should know. Everyone who gets a job at Sunset Estates either knows someone who works here or is related to someone who works here.

My mom smiled and crossed her arms. "Try 'not even supposed to be here today.' Effing TV isn't working, and no one could figure it out."

Oh, right! Movie night. I feigned worry. "Oh no! What will they do if they can't watch *Casablanca* for the millionth time this decade?"

"It's actually *A Star Is Born* tonight!"

Gabe jumped in, "Judy, Barbra, or Gaga?"

My mom closed her eyes. "I really don't care." Gabe laughed, and she turned her smile to him. "Hi, I'm Tommy's mom, Sandra."

"Gabe."

"My mom's the activities director. You'll usually see her here trying to convince the residents to sign up for trips to Atlantic City or Pure Barre for the over-fifty crowd."

"First day, Gabe?" Mom asked.

"Yes, ma'am."

I saw my mom try hard not to take offense at being called "ma'am."

"Well, you have a great server to be training with. I mean, I think I can take the credit for how well he turned out as an individual, but—"

"We have to move Gabe's car," I interrupted. "Before they open the dining room doors. Great seeing you, Ma."

"Love you, honey," she called after me.

Once we were outside, I let Gabe lead me to his car, an expensive-looking silver Audi. Why the hell was he working here if he could afford this? I knew nothing about cars, but I knew enough to know Audis weren't cheap.

I got in and started directing him around the back of the building, pointing him to the spot behind my car—my dad's old Honda that my mom kept for me. And then I showed him back into the kitchen through the rear entrance.

We'd missed lineup, and Morgan, the casual dining room host, was already walking four residents to our section when we got onto the floor. We arrived at the rear service station to find Ava staring into the distance as she clipped on her bow tie.

Our uniforms were simple: white tuxedo shirt, black pants and apron, black slip-resistant shoes, and a maroon pre-tied bow tie.

I nudged her gently, and her eyes refocused on us. Smiling politely, she introduced herself to Gabe. For a brief, horrifying moment I was afraid she'd bring up Gabe and me knowing each other from summer camp, but she was still so distracted that she instead excused herself and went to pour water for a group of ladies who'd just sat down at one of her tables.

I pointed to the laminated section chart taped to the service station.

"If you ever get confused about which tables are yours or which tables you're running food to, this is the cheat sheet."

"How do you remember them all?" Gabe asked.

"If I'm not in T or Hell, I usually *can't* remember them." Gabe's brows furrowed. "Sorry . . ." I pointed to Luke's section on the laminated sheet, the six tables outlined in a T shape. There was one six-top and five four-tops. "This one is T section. So named because it's shaped like a T. It's the second-worst section in the dining rooms."

"And Hell section is the worst?"

I pointed to our section. "Correct." I showed him around the corner and pointed out the tables in real life. "T and Hell are the only two sections with six tables. In the FDR—the formal dining room—the max is four tables; you'll start soloing there. CDR—casual dining room—servers get five tables each. T and Hell are for the people who have been here awhile and can take the extra tables. Hell has four six-tops and two four-tops."

"Six-tops?"

"Six seats at a table is a six-top. There are two-tops, four-tops, and six-tops."

"Sounds like a party."

I almost passed out. Was that a gay joke? It absolutely was. Was Gabe gay? Did straight guys make jokes about tops and bottoms?

Before I could even react, he asked, "What if only three people sit at a four-top?"

I shrugged, still trying to recover from what he'd just said. "It's still a four-top. Oh, also I should have told you the most important thing. Rule number one. Never piss off the hosts. Otherwise they're going to seat multiple tables all at once to get back at you."

For the rest of the evening, I went through everything Gabe needed to know. It was a busy night, which was good because that meant I didn't have time to stare at him. Or continue to freak out about how he totally didn't remember me.

Or how I absolutely never forgot him.

CHAPTER
THREE

WHERE'S THE LINE BETWEEN SOCIAL MEDIA DEEP dive and full-on cyberstalking? Asking for a friend.

It was the Monday after Gabe's first day, and I was on hour seventeen of his social media review. It's not quite as creepy as it sounds because he did add me first, which means *he* sought *me* out. I mean, yes, I absolutely found his profile the second I got home from work that night. But I didn't follow him. I waited for him to follow me first like a normal human.

As I was looking at a picture of Gabe—on the beach with a bunch of Archbishop Murphy bros from over a year ago.

"You good with that, Tommy?"

I looked up from my phone at Becky Jackson's arched eyebrow.

"Yeah, no problem."

"Then what did I say?"

The same damn thing you said an hour ago when this meeting should have ended. "That we should have at least three people taking pictures at each major event. But I'm not one of the photographers, so . . ." I turned to a few of the other people on the yearbook committee who were on the photography crew, including Lara Guthrie next to me, who was trying very hard not to laugh.

With the wind out of Becky's sails, I locked my phone and attempted to pay a bit more attention to our inaugural yearbook meeting. School didn't start for another eight days. But Becky couldn't wait to get her power back as head of the committee. Yearbook was supposed to be a simple after-school activity that didn't take up that much time, but ever since Patti Salvatore graduated and left Becky in charge, she'd demanded meetings more often.

Thankfully, our faculty advisor, Ms. Novak, wouldn't let Becky kick anyone out for not attending meetings. So as long as I showed up every once in a while and made sure my assigned pages were all good, I could still list yearbook committee as an activity on my college applications.

Speaking of which, there was another, more important reason I'd showed up to this meeting, and if it didn't end soon, it all might be for nothing. I shot Lara a text.

Ask her if she can give us our assignments already so we can leave. If I do it she'll just drag things out longer.

Lara smirked at her phone before putting it away and raising her hand.

Becky glared but called on her.

"Can we talk assignments? I think the photographers are good with splitting the activities on our own, right?" She turned to the other five photography club members—including her girlfriend, Helen Fink—who had also signed up for yearbook. All of whom nodded.

Becky looked disappointed, but she flipped to another section of her five-subject notebook of death. "Fine. When I call your names, write down which pages you have so you don't forget." She gave Anna Wheeler a death glare, reminding her about the Faculty Page Faux Pas last year, when she had reviewed and verified the faculty pages instead of the after-school clubs, and Becky's first year as yearbook committee president went undocumented because we forgot to put our group photo in.

"Tommy and Lara," Becky said after giving out most of the good stuff to her friends. "You two are on athletics, and, Tommy, you're reviewing the freshman pages."

Great. Checking that the right names are next to the right freshmen took forever because there were always so many, and they were new, so I didn't know any of them. Maybe once classes started and some freshmen joined yearbook at the first official meeting, I could pawn it off on one of them.

I kept my mouth shut, and when Becky dismissed us almost a half hour later, I told Lara I had to do one more thing, then asked if she or Helen needed a ride.

"Nah, we'll walk," she said. "What do you have to do? Stalk that dude on your phone in *real* life?"

Okay, so I guess I know where that line on cyberstalking is after all.

I had spent most of my summer at work, but the days I wasn't working, Ava and I were brainstorming ways for my La Mère application to stand out. A lot of applicants had vo-tech courses or were lucky enough to go to schools that had cooking classes. Our school didn't, so

I needed something to put me on par with the other applicants, other than "passion for cooking."

Working at Sunset Estates would do that. And so would Ava's idea, which had come to her after I made her watch a few YouTube cooking channels. I'd make a supplemental video to submit with my application.

Problem was, video taken on my old phone camera didn't look professional enough. And while my school, Green Ridge High, didn't have cooking classes, they did manage to have film classes and a TV studio.

There's something about the school's TV studio that just creeps me out. Everyone in the studio is nice enough—except for Mr. Taylor, the school's tech guy/studio faculty advisor, who is very intense and gets pissed off at every minor inconvenience that us *children* bring him—so maybe the creep factor just comes from the lighting and how it always seems like someone is in there, regardless of the time of day.

Take Monday, August 30, eight days before school was officially back in session, for instance. There were four people in the TV studio, and Mr. Taylor wasn't one of them. Did he just give these students keys to let themselves in? I knocked politely on the doorjamb, and the four kids on the couch talking about whatever movie was on the TV turned, clearly surprised to see someone enter their lair.

"Sorry," I said. "Just looking for Mr. Taylor?"

One of them stood, a chubby white kid with light-brown hair. His name was Grant Feldman, I thought—I recognized him from a few classes we'd had together. "He's out at the elementary school fixing some network issue."

The other three on the couch went back to discussing whatever weird movie they were watching.

"What did you need?" Grant asked.

"Oh, so . . . I actually wanted to know what the process is for checking out the video equipment?" I pointed to the opposite side of the room—past the morning show set where the TV studio crew delivered announcements every morning—to the cameras and lights that could be checked out. They were packed into yellow plastic briefcases that looked like props from a political thriller movie set.

"Are you taking one of the film classes?" Grant asked.

"No, I just needed to film a supplemental thing for my college application. I want it to look better than what my phone can do." I held up my phone to show him that, yes, it was four years old.

Grant shook his head. "Only the film classes are allowed to check out the cameras. Two of them disappeared last year, and Mr. Taylor made the administration agree to only let film students use them."

Shit.

"And no way I could even bribe you to let me borrow one in your name if I promise to bring it back?"

"Sorry. You can probably still try to add a film class to your schedule."

And change all my electives around and possibly lose my free period? Hard pass. I'd just have to use my phone after all. Or borrow someone's better phone. Ava's was one generation ahead of mine, at least.

"Is that Bahama Mama?"

I leaned back out the doorway to see James at the end of the hall walking toward me. And behind him, carrying two hockey nets, Brad

Waldorf. Grant moved past me and stuck his head out to see what the commotion was.

"And Garantula! I didn't know you two were friends. Wait, you hang out without me?"

Grant laughed and ducked back into the studio. "Let me know if you end up taking a film class."

I thanked him and shut the door behind me.

"What are you guys doing here?" I asked, making sure to address James and not Brad. There was no way Brad would ever let James know we had hooked up. Even though James would never be homophobic and in fact would immediately start planning our wedding. Actually, maybe that was the first reason Brad *wouldn't* tell him.

James hiked a thumb over his shoulder. "Me and Waldorf Salad got hockey practice tonight. And did you know Ice Works doesn't let us use their nets?"

"I did not know that." I also had never given it even a millisecond of thought in my life.

"Yeah, so I'm always the one who has to truck them to and fro, you know, since I got a truck and all."

"Picked up on that, yeah."

James spun, pushed past one of the nets, and wrapped his arms around Brad's middle. Brad gave a groan as James squeezed him tight and planted a loud kiss on his cheek, which promptly glowed red.

"And Bee-Rad was such a sweetheart to offer to help me carry them!"

"Yes," I said. "I can see how much he's helping since you aren't carrying them at all."

James pushed away from Brad and held his hands out to me. "Don't want to mess up my manicure."

I gazed at his bitten-to-the-quick fingernails, then at Brad, who just shook his head and readjusted the nets on his shoulders.

"Well, break a leg . . . or don't break a leg, I guess. Since it's hockey and not a musical. Whatever you guys say to each other before you go on the ice that's not offensive."

James cupped his hands around his mouth and shouted to the ceiling, "Score a hat trick, baby!"

I gasped. "There's gonna be a magic show?"

Brad snorted and James spun around, his jaw dropping. "What the hell was that? What did you do? What was that sound you just made?"

"Nothing." Brad straightened his face back to its usual stoic expression and nudged James. "Come on, these are getting heavy."

I said goodbye and moved aside for them as they continued toward the double doors leading to the parking lot.

"You never laugh at *my* jokes, Bradley," James said.

"That's because you're not funny."

"You bitch!" James kicked the doors open and stormed out into the parking lot. Brad took the time to turn sideways—using the nets to hold the door open—to give me a goodbye nod and a smile.

That was . . . new? Brad was more the type who paid me attention when it was convenient for him—read: horny—and rarely acknowledged me otherwise. And definitely not in public. I knew part of the reason was that Brad just wasn't ready to be out—which was fine. I wasn't totally out to my mom, so I got that journey.

But I felt like another part of it was just that I wasn't cool or interesting enough for Brad. Like he actually didn't like me for anything other than what we did in secret. Which was also fine. Whatever. A wave, though? In public?

I waved back, but still waited for the doors to shut behind him before I followed.

CHAPTER
FOUR

WHEN I SAW GABE'S NAME NEXT TO mine on the lineup sheet again three days later, my stomach did an excited flip. I must have made a face, too, because Ava—who still seemed to be distracted on our drive in, but wouldn't tell me why—gave me The Look. The one that said she knew exactly what I was thinking.

The door behind me leading to the formal dining room swung open, and Doris appeared in the doorway.

Doris was seventy-eight, going on prehistoric. She was a white woman with gray eyes who wore too much blush on her thin cheeks and had a cloud of white hair like soft serve swirled atop her head and the voice of an angel in a blender.

I tensed, waiting for the harpy cry that was about to emit from her throat.

"Line up!" And with that, she turned and went back into the formal dining room, her hair on a two-second delay.

"What did she say?" I asked Ava.

"Not sure, I was too distracted by you drooling over some boy's name next to yours." She tapped the lineup sheet and walked past me. And, no, she was right. I definitely didn't need to be distracted by relationship shit—relationshit?—when I had more important things to focus on. Like my letters of recommendation and the supplemental video for my culinary school application. Especially when I had no idea if Gabe was even gay.

But, like making an éclair, that was so much easier in theory than in practice. Especially since tonight was a slow night, which meant there was nothing to distract us from the decidedly un-recommendation-letter duty of talking at the back service station.

It was a risk, standing there and talking between each step of the service. If Natalie came back to see us not actively working, she'd launch into an ever-changing list of duties we *could* be doing instead.

"So you were, what, fourteen when you started here?" Gabe asked.

"Fifteen," I corrected, checking around the corner that our residents were still eating their dinner and no new tables had snuck into our section. "They're strict about the hours that anyone under sixteen works." I glanced at my watch. "So by law I had to be clocked out by seven. Which I hated because I wanted to work in the kitchen."

"How come?"

"I'm applying to culinary school. I can do kitchen support right now—that's what James and Sean G. are doing in there."

Gabe nodded, showing he was paying attention. "Calling out the dinners and stuff."

"Yeah, but I'm not allowed to actually *cook* anything until I'm eighteen. Which doesn't happen until February. But I'm hoping Chef Roni will let me do some kitchen work then. I only get to use the good knives when I'm cutting up lemons for the KS—or Ms. Kitchen Support if you're nasty—opening jobs." I sighed, pretending to be forlorn. "The closest I'll get before February is being a caller."

"It's culinary school—why would they need you to work in a kitchen when they're going to *teach* you to work in a kitchen?"

"Because it's not just *any* culinary school; it's La Mère Labont."

Gabe frowned. "This is a good school?"

My eyes went wide. "It's, like, the Harvard of culinary schools."

"Sacré bleu!" he said in a shitty French accent that still managed to make me laugh and my cheeks burn. "What makes it so special?"

"So, this woman, Eugénie Brazier, was a super-famous French chef—she was the first person to ever get six Michelin stars."

"And that's impressive?"

"Absolutely. Her restaurant—La Mère Brazier—is still open in Lyon. Back in the eighties, one of the chefs, Élode Labont, couldn't find a sous-chef she felt was up to snuff, so she decided to start a school and named it La Mère Labont as an homage to the restaurant, La Mère Brazier, where she got her start."

"Oh, an *homage*, very French."

"Now there are six campuses, in Paris, Sydney, London, Tokyo, LA, and New York City."

"So why this place?"

"I mean, I have backup schools. Le Cordon Bleu is similar—but a little stuffier, if I'm being honest—"

"We love honesty, go off."

"—and there's Johnson & Wales, too. But my dad went to La Mère, and he always used to talk about what an amazing experience it was, seeing the instructors do all this stuff he had never imagined."

Gabe tilted his head, and the dimples indented his cheeks again. "Your dad's a chef?"

My heart sank as it always did when my dad came up. Four years after his death, and it still hurt.

"No," I said, trying to push the thoughts away. "He had to drop out his sophomore year. My uncle, his older brother, died, and my grandfather needed help with the family business." The family business that was now shuttered because my grandfather and dad were both dead. That was, I think, the worst part. He always talked about how sad he was that he never got to finish school. How he thought about selling the business when my grandfather wanted to retire and maybe he'd go back and finish his degree. Then he never got the chance.

"That sucks, I'm sorry." After a moment he pivoted the conversation. "So, anyway, you need kitchen training to stand out on your La Boner School application?"

I snorted. "Exactly."

"Ew, wait, you want to work in a kitchen *forever*?"

"Yes, even when I'm burning in hell. No, I *want* to be a pastry chef or baker. Kitchen stuff is stressful. Baking is soothing."

Baking was how I calmed my brain. Sometimes I could get overwhelmed and start worrying about school or work or my future. Basically spiral down about things that could go wrong—if I were still going to therapy, they'd say it was probably left over from the trauma of losing a parent. But baking, and trying new recipes or tweaking old ones, always calmed me. I knew that by the end I'd either have something that worked, or I'd have something that I could learn from.

It was easy to throw away a loaf of bread that didn't rise properly, or even turn it into something else, like bread pudding, croutons, or stuffing. When things went bad in life it was so much messier.

Life could take longer and hurt so much more.

"Are you going to college?" I asked.

He sighed. "Unfortunately. That's why I'm here."

"Clearly not culinary school."

"God, no! What kind of loser do you think I am?"

For half a second I thought he was serious, but then I saw that smirk. And those dimples. Then the worry—that he thought I was a loser—went away and was replaced by the warm fuzzies.

"No, I want to go to film school," he said. I liked that he was going to school for something artistic, too. And that one of the things I knew about him—the Saturday afternoon movies—was still something he enjoyed. But I tried to play it off like I wasn't getting the big-time feels and instead fell back on old faithful: solid gold cynicism.

"On twelve dollars an hour? Good luck with that."

"Hoping for a scholarship, too."

"Where at?"

"USC." Then, off my puzzled look, "University of Southern California—it's in LA. Well, there or NYU."

Wait. Those were both locations with La Mère campuses. This was all starting to feel a bit more fate-y than just the universe putting us back together for the first time in six years before we went our separate ways in college.

What if this was the start of something bigger? I let myself fantasize at a million miles a second: the two of us meeting here, kissing for the first time, our first date—where I would come clean and tell him *we've met before!*—sex, prom, getting into the schools we wanted to go to and still staying in the same city, becoming a gay power couple, opening my own restaurant, Gabe getting an Oscar and thanking me, our three kids and a dog.

Okay, that got out of hand quickly. And yet it still seemed like a possibility. Like all this could be possible, and the universe was conspiring to make it happen.

I realized I hadn't paid much attention to the dining room for a bit, so I stepped back again to check our section.

"Hold the school talk," I said to Gabe as I grabbed the water pitcher. "We have another table." I led him out from the service station just as Alvin Turner and Willa Vaughn sat at our final four-top.

"Evening, Al," I said. "Ms. Vaughn, I love that jacket."

She plucked at the jean jacket and waved away the compliment. "I got it at Goodwill."

"How you doin', kid?" Al asked. He pulled out the chair for Willa as she swatted at him. Then he saw Gabe and his eyes went wide. "Oh! Who's this, now?"

"Calm down," I whispered, flicking his arm. He gave me a firm handshake as I pulled out the chair for him and started filling their water glasses. "Al, Ms. Vaughn, this is Gabe. He just started."

"I'll be gentle, Gabe." Al batted his eyelashes at Gabe and gave him a pleasant smile while Ms. Vaughn rolled her eyes.

"Al," I warned.

"You need to cut that shit out," Ms. Vaughn said. I bit my lower lip, trying not to smile. I looked up at Gabe to see his eyebrows raised.

"Or they're gonna kick you outta here. Or put you on a list or something."

Al held out his hands. "What? I can't be friendly?"

"Not *that* friendly," she said, whipping her napkin and placing it on her lap. "It's not the eighties anymore."

Gabe let out a laugh that turned into a cough and I spoke over him. "And on that note! Ms. Vaughn, I'm going to grab your lemons, and I will send *Gabe* back with your bread." I locked eyes with Al as I said Gabe's name and he smiled and nodded.

"Did . . ." Gabe said when we were safely out of earshot and heading for the kitchen. "Did that woman's husband just hit on me?"

"Oh, he hit on you." I was eager to see how Gabe reacted to that. Maybe he would just freak out and run away and never come back. That would take care of all my stomach-soufflé issues. Plus one less distraction. I was a little uncomfortable about the easy way we had slipped into conversation. It was like there had been no lapse in our relationship and everything was exactly how it was when we were younger. Even though *he* still didn't remember that relationship. "That's not his wife, though. I think she's a lesbian, but I'm not sure. She might just be the only person here who can stand Al." Other than me.

I told him the first thing he needed to do with Ms. Vaughn was run into the kitchen and grab lemons because she always asked for lemons with her water. If he did that, she'd be nice. Ms. Vaughn was a terror to anyone who wasn't me.

Hell, she had been a terror to me at first. Al was always pleasant, but Ms. Vaughn was like the strictest teacher I'd ever had—on steroids. She corrected servers if they were serving incorrectly, then scolded them to speak up if they mumbled. If soup dripped onto a saucer on its journey from the kitchen, she would ask the server to take it away.

But without fail, the first thing she would say when approached was "Lemons for my water, please."

So after I served her on my own four whole times, terrified each time, the next evening that I saw her and Al sit at my table, I walked right into the kitchen and grabbed four lemon slices and put them on a serving dish. I even went a roundabout way so she couldn't see me approaching, then placed the lemons on the table—serving from the left because she had yelled at me about that twice—and said, "Here are your lemons, Ms. Vaughn."

She spun on me, her eyes wide, and I was afraid she was going to yell. To tell me I should never present something to a guest who hasn't first asked for it. Instead, she took one quick glance at my name tag and said, "Thank you, Thomas. Well done."

Across the table, Al beamed and waited for her to look down at her menu before giving me two enthusiastic thumbs up.

"And don't worry about Al," I said. "He's harmless."

"Isn't it a little creepy?" Gabe asked. "An old man flirting with you every time he sees you?"

Al's humor stemmed from trying to make people as uncomfortable as he could. He liked to test boundaries, see how far he could go before he finally backed off and became the Al I knew and loved. The one who dunks on Doris or goes out of his way to make Natalie as miserable as she likes to make us. The one who got into playful bitch-offs with our other manager, George.

George was always on his best behavior around other servers and residents. But when he found out I was on Al's good side, he let his walls down. And watching the two of them throw shade at each other is performance art. Even Ms. Vaughn almost smiles at it.

"You'll see what I mean," I said. "I'll even let you take their orders."

Gabe seemed nervous, but did pretty well, all things considered— *Al* things considered? The only joke Al made was when he asked about the chicken.

"I'm not much of a chicken hawk," he said. "But I can always make an exception."

"Al!"

"It's okay, Ms. Vaughn," I said. "Whatever that reference is, it's so old we have no clue what it means."

"What an awful thing to say!" Al scowled at me playfully, and I smiled right back.

We dropped off Al's and Ms. Vaughn's soups and salads and went back to the service station. Natalie had made her way across the formal dining room and was now checking up on the residents in the casual dining room. She held two coffeepots in her hands, one regular, one decaf.

"Coffee?" she asked my five-top. "Sanka?" Two people flipped their coffee cups and began talking as Natalie filled them.

"Ah, shit," I muttered.

"What?" Gabe asked.

I nodded quickly to the table. "They accepted her coffee, so she's

going to think we didn't ask if they wanted any. She'll be over in a bit."
I hoped that wasn't a ding against my letter request. .

I wiped the crumbs off the service station and checked that there
was no evidence of Ava, Gabe, or myself eating back there. Natalie
. rounded the corner.

"Keep an eye on their coffee cups, Tommy," she said, placing the
pots on the warmer. "Make sure they don't go past the halfway point
before you ask if they need a warm-up."

They wouldn't go past the halfway point because none of the residents at that table drink coffee this late. They flipped their cups over
because they wanted to talk to Natalie or complain about something.
And since all she said was make sure I watched their cups, it meant it
wasn't a complaint about me.

"You got it," I said, acting like I was peering over her shoulder to
look at the coffee cups. Of course, not one of the residents had touched
the coffee.

Natalie turned her attention to Gabe, and her polite smile grew
wide. "Gabriel, how is your third day going?"

"Wonderful, thank you. Tom's a really great teacher."

Tom. No one ever called me Tom. Always Thomas or Tommy.
And yes, I know Tommy sounds like I'm a little kid and Thomas
sounds like I'm an old man, but Tom just sounds unfinished.

Behind Natalie, Ava rounded the corner, saw us trapped there,
and promptly about-faced in the other direction. I tried not to smile.

"And I'm sure he already told you the most important rule I
have?" she asked.

Oh, shit. Had I told him? I raced through every memory I had of

Gabe since last Saturday. Why did so many of those memories have to be of his *smile*!

Gabe nodded and opened his mouth. And I knew exactly what he'd say.

At one point on our first day I had pointed over to Luke's section, which was full when ours only had two tables occupied, and I'd reiterated my own personal rule number one: never piss off the hosts. Luke had broken up with Morgan at the beginning of summer, and ever since, she had been on a revenge mission, seating two or three tables at a time in Luke's section.

Before Gabe could speak I jumped in. "Yep, never say no."

I turned to him to see if he'd hold up his end of the bluff, and to my surprise, he did. He nodded quickly and smiled at Natalie. "That's the one."

She didn't seem entirely convinced. "Well, there's more to it than just 'never say no.' If the residents ask for something, you smile and say yes and make it happen. If you're concerned you can't make it happen, you come see me and *I* will make it happen, or *I* will be the one to tell them no."

This rule worked for big asks, but the little ones always bit you in the ass.

"Last April," Natalie said, and I already knew where the story was going, "a resident wanted baked Alaska, but dessert that night was pineapple upside-down cake. So I went to Chef Roni and asked her to whip up some meringue, then cut the pineapple upside-down part of the cake off, throw on some Neapolitan ice cream, put the meringue on top, and toast it with a torch!"

She clapped her hands like it was the easiest thing in the world.

The part of the story she always left out was that after a resident at another table saw it, *they* then asked for baked Alaska. By the end of the night it was full-tilt *Give a Mouse a Cookie* madness. We had over a hundred leftover tops of pineapple upside-down cake, and the dinners were coming out too slow because Dante was off whipping meringue into stiff peaks. And now, when Chef Roni plans the menus for the month, she won't make pineapple upside-down cake *or* baked Alaska.

My favorite part was when I brought out six of the new baked Alaskas and all the residents scrunched up their faces and said, "That's not baked Alaska."

"Never say no." Gabe nodded. "Got it."

"We should go check for our dinners before we take table fifty's dessert orders," I said to Gabe.

Natalie held up a hand. "Gabe, why don't you do that while I have a talk with Tommy."

Shit, maybe we didn't get away with it after all.

Gabe moved around me, shooting a quick *sorry* glance over Natalie's shoulder. When he was gone, she gave me that polite but devilish grin.

"Next time, I'd rather hear from Gabe directly when I'm quizzing him on what you're training."

"I'll be honest, I was worried he forgot. I told him on his first day and it's been a while since, and no one has really asked for anything not on the menu while I've been training him. I've noticed that people retain things better when they come up during the shift instead of me explaining it ahead of time." That was total bullshit, but it sounded good enough, right?

"The residents pay a lot of money to live here."

Great. So this was becoming a "teachable moment."

"And if we tell them no, they wonder *why* they pay so much money—"

I know that, too.

"And if they wonder why they're paying so much money, they may want to find ways to save money in order to *get* the things they want. And I don't want to lose my job. Do you want to lose yours?"

"No." Though I'm not entirely sure that logic tracks.

"And I'm certain Doris doesn't want to lose her job, or George his, or Roni hers, for that matter. So we have the most important rule for a reason. This is even more important because it's one of your tasks. Have you gotten any requests today?"

Was this a trap? Did she send someone in here to try to catch me up already? There were plenty of residents who didn't like Natalie. I knew they would give me a heads-up if she asked them to do something that seemed like a test or a way to trip me up.

"Not yet. But if I do I'll be sure to handle it."

"And remember, our jobs depend on it."

Our jobs rely solely on me saying yes if Mrs. Harrington asks for salmon when it's not on the menu? Got it.

"Absolutely. You're right. And I will make sure it's the first thing I tell new staff going forward. I'll also ask A—Mr. Turner to request something outlandish specifically as a test for Gabe."

Natalie's spine stiffened at that. "Maybe have Ms. Vaughn do it instead."

"Good point."

I moved to step around her when she stopped me again. "Oh, and I've started working on your letter of recommendation."

Of course. Because I only asked her five days ago. Then, as if she thought I didn't understand the subtext:

"I'd hate to have to write that you're a bit of a rebel when it comes to rule following. La Mère is very strict with their rules."

I nodded and headed for the kitchen where Gabe was waiting for me.

He whispered, "You told me the other day that rule number one was don't piss off the hosts!"

"Sorry about that," I said.

"You totally set me up." Gabe was acting indignant, but I could see the hint of dimples.

I shrugged as James called out Al's table. "Everyone has different rule number ones." I grabbed the tray and turned to James. "James, what's rule number one?"

"Don't touch Roni's knives. She keeps them sharp as shit. I almost sliced a finger off once." He held up his hand and mimed cutting off his fingers and blood spewing everywhere.

Gabe's smile grew and we walked back toward the dining room. As Ava came in I stopped in the exit doorway.

"Ava, rule number one?"

She said without looking back, "Don't stand on Mr. Gilbert's side of the table."

"I feel like I should be writing these down," Gabe said, grabbing a tray stand for me as one of the other servers, Bryce, entered the salad bar area.

"Bryce, what's your rule number one?"

Without stopping he said, "Don't stand on Mrs. Wells's side of the table."

Gabe shot me a questioning look.

"Right . . . Mrs. Wells is a butt grabber."

CHAPTER
FIVE

AT THE END OF THE NIGHT, I had successfully managed not to get onto Natalie's radar any more than I already was, and Gabe and I had fallen back into the natural rapport we'd had at summer camp. It felt so easy to talk to him. And none of it felt like small talk. It was all big talk. Even the small stuff ended up feeling bigger than the original question that led to it.

Like when we were resetting our section. After he told me more about his film classes at Murphy, I finally asked, "What's your favorite movie?"

He looked like I had asked him to choose between cutting off his foot or cutting off a hand. "How can I pick one?"

"Then . . . favorite director?"

"Akira Kurosawa." He said it quickly, as if he knew the question was coming. I had never seen any of his movies. Don't think I had even heard of him.

"Was he the one who did *Parasite*?"

Again, the hand or foot question. "I'm going to ignore the casual racism of that question for a second, but we'll be circling back to that."

Oh, shit. Note to self, don't make assumptions about directors you know noth-ing about.

"I'm sorry, I really didn't mean it like that."

"I know you didn't. I'm only half-serious. But you don't know who Akira Kurosawa is?"

I shrugged. "Am I supposed to?"

"*Rashomon? Seven Samurai? Drunken Angel?*"

"Ohhhhh!" I said. "So you're *pretentious.*" Though that was rich coming from me and my food knowledge. But he didn't know that about me yet.

He smiled and threw a spoon at me and continued to explain Kurosawa to me as we reset our tables.

"Any other directors I might know?" I asked.

"Hitchcock?"

"Heard of him."

Gabe groaned. "Tarantino, Scorsese, De Palma?"

"Yes, yes, no."

"Didn't you say you and Ava went to a movie last Saturday? What did you even see?" He seemed shocked that I knew what movies were—which, okay, fair. I wasn't really a movie person. In fact, I only tagged along on Saturday because Ava wanted to see the movie and had a crush on the concession guy at the movie theater.

I stopped mid-fork placement and pretended to think. "There was . . . a woman in it. She had hair?"

Gabe flung the silverware on the table with a loud clang, then pulled out a chair and sat down. I laughed as he leaned back in the chair, putting his hands on his head. Sitting down while working was definitely a Natalie No Pas. I was about to scold him, but then I caught myself staring at his arms, flexing around the cuffed sleeves of his tux shirt.

"As your trainee, I feel a responsibility to give you a crash course in film theory."

I smiled brightly. "Wow. You would do that for me?"

"All right, enough."

"No, when you put it that way it doesn't sound pretentious at all."

"Give me your phone."

I imitated the proper, well-enunciated voice that Natalie used for scolding. "No phones on the floor."

Still he held out his hand in a *gimme* gesture.

"What for?" But I had a feeling I knew what for, and I was already reaching into my pocket. He took my phone and held it up to me. I tried to make a weird face to block the facial recognition, but it failed and unlocked anyway. I looked over his shoulder as he opened the contacts app and added himself to it.

My stomach twitched and the remaining embers of fondness that must have been latent there since we first met—that had been slowly growing since seeing him again—seemed to ignite and spread warmth throughout my body.

"There." He handed my phone back. "Now call me."

"Meh." I locked the phone and put it in my pocket.

Gabe playfully swatted my shoulder, and I pretended to be in pain. "Seriously, now, so I have your number." Ava—resetting her own section a couple tables over—gave me *What is going on?* eyes.

I called him.

"Got it." He sent me to voice mail and started typing, glancing over his shoulder for Natalie or a host, making sure he wasn't caught. I was a little nervous, too, truth be told. Maybe a little bit of it was the thought of getting caught and having Natalie refuse to write a good recommendation letter—would she write an anti-recommendation letter? Would she be vindictive enough to *block* me from getting into La Mère?

Yes. Absolutely she would.

But the exchange of phone numbers was making me more nervous, in an exciting way. In a stomach-at-a-low-simmer kind of way. If he disappeared again I could still find him. It wasn't just social media, which maybe he might not check, or he could delete. This was his phone number. If he quit Sunset Estates tomorrow, I could still text him.

"There, now you're saved." The contact form said, *First name: Thomas, Last name: Sunset Estates.* Then, in the *Company* field, it said, *General of the S.E. Allied Forces.*

"My last name is Dees," I said. "Not Sunset Estates."

"Too late, contacts are permanent. Wait, your mom's name is Sandra *Dees?*"

"Yes. Why not just put 'Sunset Estates' in the company field and leave the last name blank?"

He smirked and his dimples returned. "I make up fake company names for everyone in my phone. Here, look."

He started scrolling through his phone, clicking on names of people I didn't know. Anthony Saltz's company was *CEO of Salty Italian Meatballs Inc., German Branch.*

I arched an eyebrow at him.

"He's a frequently short-tempered German Italian."

"Oh, so there's a *lot* of thought put into these." Kind of like James and his nicknames.

Gabe snorted and scrolled down to click on *Mommy*. That was kind of cute. I had already seen his dad listed as *Father*. Under Mommy's company—no last name, by the way—it said, *Leader of the Free World*.

"You make these up for every person you meet?"

"Yep, and then I laugh every time I see their name with whatever company I made up scrolling beneath."

I tried to hide a smile and went to his contact in my phone. I quickly typed up something and saved it, turning it around to show him.

His smile dropped, and he rolled his eyes. "Ha ha."

CHAPTER
SIX

AT EIGHT FORTY-FIVE P.M., MY PHONE BUZZED on the kitchen table. I wiped my hands on a dish towel and laughed at the name scrolling across the screen: *Gabe De La WHORE-a, President and CEO of De La Whore-a Phone-Sex Hotline.*

"'Ello?"

"Hi. What are you doing right now?"

"Wondering why a phone-sex line is calling me. I mean, I support sex workers' right to a living wage, but how much is this costing me?"

"Your film education starts tonight. If you're watching something, turn it off. If you're not watching something, bring up Netflix."

"I'm in the middle of baking bread."

Gabe groaned on the other end of the phone. "You can *buy* bread. This is more important."

"If you knew how my bread tasted, you wouldn't be saying that."

"Well, you'll just have to bring me some another time. Netflix, now!"

"I don't have Netflix."

Dead silence on the other end.

"Are you broken?" I asked. "Did you have a stroke? Should I call nine-one-one?"

"You're watching something," he finally said. "I can hear it. So I know you have a computer or TV you can watch it on."

"Computer." I paused the Food Network episode that was up on my dad's old laptop. It was just a cookie competition show.

"Okay, then go to Netflix's website. I'm sending you a text with my log-in info."

I glanced at the bowl of bread dough I had just been stretching. I could probably put it in the fridge and pick up tomorrow right where I left off.

As if making my decision for me, my phone buzzed. "Seriously? You're giving me your password?"

"It's a Netflix password, not my social security, which is 078-05-1120."

"One . . . one . . . two . . . zero . . ." I pretended I was writing it down as I covered the bowl with the dish towel and put it in the fridge. I opened the text and logged into Netflix with Gabe's username and password—Picklechips19! Cute.

"How do you know I'm not just going to use your Netflix account to watch *Great British Baking Show* episodes?" Because, yes, I absolutely wanted to do that.

"You're free to do so. Besides, you're general of the Sunset Estates Allied Forces. If I need help from you, we'll need a secret code. We can use movies."

"Why does the code have to be *your* thing?"

"Because we work in a dining room, Thomas. If you start talking flan around the old folks, they're going to ask for flan, and then Natalie is going to have to ask Roni to whip up a two-minute flan for every person in the dining room."

I snorted. "Say 'flan' again."

"Flan!"

Just then my mom entered the kitchen. "Hold on a sec," I said into the phone, then muted my side.

"What's that look for?" Mom smirked at me as she pulled open the fridge and grabbed a can of store-brand seltzer. Her smirk dropped to a frown when she saw the dough in the fridge. "No breakfast bread?"

I was more than happy to pounce on that question and not the first. While I was out at school and to my friends, I still hadn't managed to tell my mom. So she didn't need to know that a boy had created that look just by saying the word "flan."

"Dinner bread tomorrow," I said. "I thought I could power through, but I'm beat."

Her eyes went wide. "Grilled cheese for dinner?"

My mouth watered. "With bacon and heirloom tomatoes."

"Text me the cheeses you want. I can stop on my way home."

I nodded. "I'm going to clean up here and head to bed."

"Okay, good night, pumpkin." She kissed me on the cheek, and I blushed and said good night back, thanking God I had muted the phone so Gabe didn't hear her nickname for me. As soon as she went back upstairs, I unmuted him.

"All right, I'm logged in."

"Go to my list. I already put the most important movies you'll need to see at the top. Let me know which ones you've seen."

I told him a few as I wiped down the kitchen table: *Jurassic Park*, *Forrest Gump*—we had watched it in American History sophomore year—*Inception*, and *The Matrix*. But that was about it. He asked about my tastes—nothing scary but nothing boring—and my attention span.

"I make bread from scratch, which takes about eighteen hours."

"Jesus."

"Just don't make it a boring one."

"Even *Citizen Kane* is more interesting than watching bread rise."

Not when you're not sure if the house is warm enough or your starter was active or any number of other things that could go wrong, and then you suddenly see some movement. But bread baking certainly didn't have any explosions. If you were doing it right.

"How about . . ." I heard a soft blip of scrolling through choices on his end of the phone. "Wait! You've never seen *Back to the Future*?"

"I have not."

"Then we're watching *Back to the Future*. It's one of my all-time favorites. Okay, click on it, and when it loads, pause it so we can synch up."

I followed his instructions. "You know, there's a Chrome extension that does all this for you."

"I don't watch on a computer. You do you—I'm not gonna yuck your yum—but I still think film should be enjoyed on the biggest screen possible."

Then he'd probably be even more disgusted that my laptop screen was cracked.

I cough-said, "Nerd!"

"Shut up, sourdough. And hit play in three . . . two . . . one . . ."

I hit play. "Wait, do I hit play on one or after one?"

"I hate you. You'd better be synched up properly."

Judging by the ticking clock sounds from his side of the phone, we were. "So, what is this movie about?"

"Oh my God, shut up and just watch it."

I watched the screen. "So we're going to sit in silence this whole time? We could hang up and I could just call you when it's over."

"I don't trust you'll watch it all the way through if I'm not here to keep you focused. And we can talk, but when there's an important scene I'll tell you."

"So this is one of the movies you deem essential but you have to *tell* me when an important scene is coming up?"

"Shut up, this scene's important."

"It's the first scene."

"Yes!"

I shut up and watched. Every once in a while I broke in with a stupid question or comment I *knew* was going to piss Gabe off—"Why is this thirty-year-old teenager friends with a nuclear scientist?" "It's very convenient that he goes back to the *one week* he can actually use the power of lightning to get home." "Oh! So he's going to have sex with his mother and become his own dad? The eighties, man, wild times, amirite?"—but then I actually started to get into it.

By the time Doc Brown was hanging from the clock tower I was completely silent. When the DeLorean hit the wire at the precise moment it needed to, I squirmed with the laptop in my hands as Marty made the jump back to 1985.

Did I also make an excited noise? Maybe. Hopefully Gabe didn't hear it.

"What did you think?" he asked when the credits began to roll.

"It was actually really good. But what the hell was with that ending? Why would they end it with a cliffhanger?"

"You do know there's two sequels?"

"Of course, but did *they* know that at the time?"

Silence from the other side of the phone for a moment. "Do you want to watch the second one?"

It was ten forty-five. It was summer. I didn't have work at Sunset Estates until three thirty. "Sure."

Gabe counted down from three and we hit play together.

CHAPTER
SEVEN

THE FOLLOWING MONDAY WAS LABOR DAY, AND Ava and
I were both working. She sent me a text that morning asking me to
come over a couple hours early so we could hang out.

Usually, hanging out in Ava's basement bedroom entailed eating
junk food while I watched Ava play video games. I'm not a gamer, but
Ava is. She especially enjoys anything where she can beat other people in the world, so I expected another day of teabagging killers at the
exit gate during *Dead by Daylight* or shooting people while dressed as
Ariana Grande in *Fortnite*. Usually, I would find this boring, but there
is something about Ava's competitive nature and gaming ability that
just really gets me invested.

But when I arrived, Ava wasn't in her gaming chair. Instead, she
was pacing around the basement, putting her hand to her mouth, only
to realize she *stopped* the nail-biting habit years ago.

To be honest, I had never seen her like this before, so I just sat
down on the couch and was right up-front. "What's wrong?"

I secretly hoped it was just that her PlayStation had crashed, but if
that were the case, I would have seen her down here with the console

in pieces while watching a YouTube on how to fix it.

"Remember the other day when you were all excited about Gabe starting at work and you asked me if I was okay and I just said I was distracted by GJ's birthday?"

"Among other things, yes. Is this really about struggling to find GJ a good gift? GJ is the most gracious human being in the world. You could buy her socks and she would show them off to the guy at Wawa every time she wore them out."

Ava shook her head. "No, it's not that. And I already bought her these dessert plates from West Elm that have animals in people clothes. They're being delivered tomorrow."

"Aw, that's cute!"

"Tommy."

"Right, you were saying?"

She took a deep breath. "I wasn't stressing because of that. So when Jeremy and I . . . you know."

"Broke up."

Ava decided to break up with her boyfriend of over two years about three weeks ago. Something I thought would be short-lived, but they genuinely seemed to be done. She said it was a mutual decision, but I felt like Jeremy just said that because he was trying to save face. How could you not love Ava? I'm gay, and even I tried to make it work.

She nodded. "Right, that. Well, before that, we—for old times' sake . . ."

I waited for her to continue, but when she didn't, I started to do the mental math myself. *Oh no.* "Ava."

"Yeah." But she said it like she was confirming my suspicion. And then, to make it clearer: "I'm late."

"Wait," I said. "How do you know?"

Ava rolled her eyes. "How do I know? Because it's *not here*!"

Now I was kind of freaking out. Why did she wait so long before telling me? "Sorry, no, I mean how many days late are you?"

"Only ten. But I've never been late before."

"So it could be something else. Are you stressed?"

"Hmm, let's see, I'm a Black woman in America, I broke up with my boyfriend of two years, I'm about to submit my application for early decision to Johns Hopkins, and I'm ten days late. Yeah, Tommy, I'm fucking stressed."

"That's it, then," I said, hoping that was it. "You and Jeremy broke up—maybe it's just the stress from that. I mean, you're on the pill."

"The pill isn't one hundred percent effective."

"Right, I know. Sorry, I'm just freaking out." She looked like she was ready to hit me, so I quickly added, "I know you're freaking out, too. We're both allowed to freak out."

"Okay, that's what we need. Ten-second freak-out break." She told her phone to start a timer for ten seconds, and we spent the time pacing back and forth, fake crying, shaking our hands, crossing ourselves, whining, and finally just groaning unintelligibly, before the timer went off. "Freak-out over."

"Right, so we're good. Now that freak-out time is over, how long before you can take a pregnancy test?"

"Internet says to wait a week after a missed period."

"Okay, so you're at ten. We go get one and you pee on a stick, it says you're not, and we laugh about it."

"Best-case scenario."

We didn't need to talk about the worst-case scenario. Especially because I knew that despite our timed freak-out session, she was still freaking out. I mean, I would be, too. Ava and I were both type A people. Only, Ava was kind of a genius, and I didn't understand anything about bioengineering, yet she managed to make 3D-printed human tissue sound less sci-fi-y than it probably was.

Her application for early decision at Johns Hopkins was due in October. Then she'd be accepted, she'd go to Baltimore, and she'd major in bioengineering before going into a doctorate program. At least, that was her plan. Nowhere in that plan were kids. She always said she wouldn't think about that until her thirties. But what would a baby do to those plans? Ava couldn't have a newborn *and* go to a school like Johns Hopkins.

But that was later.

Ava looked like she was going to have an unscheduled freak-out. Maybe she was thinking all the same things I was. I pulled her into a hug.

"It's okay," I said. "Whatever happens, I'm here, and we'll figure it out." I knew it was actually Ava who would be figuring it out, but I'd support her and be there for her regardless.

"Okay, let's go get a test. But we have to drive down to Wilmington or into Philly."

"Why?"

She frowned. "If someone we know is working at Walgreens and you walk up to buy a pregnancy test, they're going to know who it's for."

Point taken. And with our school's limited and stereotypical mindset, it meant Ava would go from "nerdy Black girl" to "slutty Black girl." They wouldn't care that she and her boyfriend were together for over two years before this even happened. They would pounce on it as a way to take her down a peg.

No way in hell was that happening. "Okay, we find a drugstore in either city, get the test, and get to Sunset Estates before our shift starts."

"You really think I'm going to work if that test is positive?"

The idea of calling out when Natalie was holding the letter of recommendation over my head made me nervous, but Ava was right. There was no way we could work if it was positive.

"We'll burn that bridge when we come to it," I said.

Step one was to get a pregnancy test.

CHAPTER
EIGHT

"WHY ARE WE DOING THIS HERE?" I asked, handing Ava the plastic pee stick. The Sunset Estates employee ladies' room was not the first place I had in mind when it came to taking pregnancy tests. But we'd hit traffic on the way into Philly and had to take back roads to get here even close to on time for our shift.

"I know your ass isn't calling out if I'm pregnant."

"I would absolutely do that." It wasn't a lie. I would try to convince her that working would help keep her mind off it, but if she really wanted me to, I would. Even if we were getting double-time holiday pay for this sham holiday.

"Oh, so you'd rather do it at your house?" She pulled the stall door shut behind her. "Or *mine*? And then what? We leave everything in the trash can for my uncle to find?"

"No, we take it to the Taco Bell and throw it in their dumpster, then we eat Doritos Locos Tacos in the parking lot." Whether they were celebration or commiseration tacos, time would tell.

"Just tell me what I have to do."

"You pee on it."

"Read the directions, Tommy!"

I flipped the box over. "Take off the cap . . ." I waited until I heard the plastic cap click off. "Hold the absorbent test strip down and place under the stream of urine for five seconds."

Ava counted to five aloud.

"Okay, now don't—"

The bathroom door opened, and I jumped, hiding the box behind me.

Morgan yelped when she realized I was standing by the sink. "Tommy, what the hell are you doing in here? Get out!"

"He's with me!" Ava called from the stall. Morgan was in our class at school. We occasionally hung out with her outside work in a group setting or at parties, but she wasn't exactly in our inner circle.

At least not usually. But Ava seemed to be allowing her in now.

Once Morgan shut the door behind her—now more interested in what we were doing than in using the bathroom—I finished what I was saying. "Don't hold the absorbent side up, keep it down until you cap it, then it has to stay flat."

There was another plastic click. "Can one of you hold this for me?" Ava held the pregnancy test under the stall.

Morgan took it, gently, and placed it on the counter next to the sink. I set a timer on my phone for five minutes. Morgan gave me a concerned look, then turned to the stall as Ava flushed and joined us. I stepped aside as she washed her hands.

"I'm ten days late," Ava said, matter-of-factly.

Morgan nodded, not seeming all that shocked. "Have you thought about what you're going to do if that stick says you're pregnant?"

This was something Ava and I had talked around on the drive without getting specific. I didn't want to pressure her one way or the other, so I told her she would have my support no matter what happened. But I knew how she was—she had to figure out *this* before we could plan what was going to happen after. She looked at me as she leaned against the wall.

"I can't do adoption," she said. "I know I can't. I'll tell myself I can, but then I know as soon as that baby is here . . ." She let her voice trail off, shaking her head. "But you have to be eighteen to get an abortion without a parent in PA."

I didn't know that. But Morgan nodded like she did. "You can go across the state line to Delaware. There's a place in Wilmington, about thirty minutes away."

Ava turned to her with a questioning look.

Morgan glanced at me, then shrugged. "Screw it. I had an abortion last December, when Luke and I were still together."

Ava swatted her arm. "Why didn't you tell me? I would have gone with you for support."

"It was Luke's fault; the least he could do was sit there and watch daytime TV in the waiting room and drive me home after. That being said, if you want me to come with you—if you have to go—I'm in."

Ava looked over at me. I frowned. "What, you think *I'm* just in here because I like listening to you pee before I serve old people food for three hours? Yes, I'm going with you."

We waited in silence for another minute; three down, two to go. Ava and Morgan weren't looking at the test, but I kept sneaking glances. Trying to stop a second purple line from appearing by sheer force of will.

"How did you feel after?" Ava asked. And that seemed like my cue to leave.

"I'll give you guys a minute."

But Morgan stopped me. "You don't have to leave; it's fine. I know you're not going to go blabbing around school that I had an abortion—Ava would kick your ass if you did."

Ava cracked her knuckles like she was getting ready to fight me. She wouldn't actually beat me up, but she would stop being my friend. And she knew plenty more of my secrets than I knew of Morgan's.

"Cramping the first day, but after that, nothing of note."

Ava rubbed at her own stomach like she was feeling sympathy cramps. "No, I mean . . . like, how did you *feel*?"

"Oh." Morgan shrugged. "Honestly . . . relieved. I don't know how else to say it. I didn't have to worry about what I was going to do anymore."

The timer on my phone went off, and I suddenly didn't want to look at the test on the bathroom counter. The bathroom door popped open, and the second Emma, Emma C., walked in, tying up her blonde hair into a ponytail. She saw me and stopped in the doorway. I stepped in front of the pregnancy test, blocking her view.

"Occupied," Morgan said.

"What are you doing in here?" Emma C. asked.

"Playing hockey," I said.

Without saying another word, Emma C. turned and left. Ava laughed, and I turned to see tears in her eyes. She was shaking her head. "Why *did* we do this in here?"

"I think you just like the drama," Morgan said.

"Absolutely," Ava and I said at the same time. Ava wiped the tears from her eyes and let out a sigh.

Morgan nodded to the test. "You going to look at it?"

"Okay," Ava said. "Full disclosure, I've been having cramps, and when I woke up this morning my boobs were sore, so I think I'm getting my period. I probably don't need to look, right?"

"Are you kidding?" I asked. It was absolutely a joke she would take this moment to tell, but *was* she kidding? After all this? But I also wasn't ready to look at it, either, so maybe it really was just her nerves getting to her.

"Sore boobs are *also* a sign of pregnancy, you know," Morgan said.

Ava turned to Morgan. "Hey, maybe you can be nice when you're seating my section tonight?"

Morgan reached behind me and picked up the test. "If you were pregnant, maybe I would have, but since you're not . . ." She shrugged and handed the test to me. It was in fact missing the second purple line. Thank fucking God! It felt like a weight off my chest, so I could only imagine how much of a relief it was for Ava.

But as I watched her focus on the test in my hand, it looked like she was still concerned about something. Before I could ask her what was wrong, Morgan spoke up.

"Now get out of the girls' room, Tommy." She pushed me out the door, pregnancy test still in hand.

And right into Gabe arriving for his shift.

He gave me a bright smile and a "Hey," before his eyes drifted to the bathroom door behind me. And then to the test in my hand. He quirked an eyebrow.

"Something you need to tell me?"

My face burned with embarrassment. I held up the test to him. "I'm . . . not . . . pregnant?"

He laughed and it reminded me how much I loved that sound. How infectious it was. I wasn't just laughing because I was relieved for Ava, though I absolutely was.

"Good to know. Because usually a positive pregnancy test from a guy means testicular cancer."

My laughter stopped. "Wait, what?"

CHAPTER
NINE

OUR FIRST WEEK BACK AT SCHOOL WAS surprisingly uneventful. I worked at Sunset Estates that Tuesday, Thursday, and Friday, but Gabe wasn't there any of those days, so we must have been on opposite schedules for the week. The only good thing about not working with Gabe was that it meant Natalie wasn't constantly watching me for a mistake she could exploit.

In the two weeks since striking our deal, she had managed to find other ways for me to prove I was deserving of a lukewarm recommendation letter I had yet to see. On Tuesday she asked me to pull double duty, doing sick trays—delivering food directly to the apartments of residents who couldn't make it down to the dining room—and also taking a section when I returned. Thursday, she had me take a special table in the formal dining room; a resident brought her family to dinner, and even though I also had the T in the casual dining room, she "knew I could handle it." It was inconvenient, but, yes, I could. At least none of the residents I served asked for anything special or off menu. The downside was that this meant part of Natalie's challenge was still to come.

Thankfully, on Friday, George was the only manager on duty. But still no Gabe.

It wasn't until the following Monday that I walked into the kitchen and saw his name next to mine on the lineup sheet again. My stomach did a loop-de-loop. Ava must have gotten a psychic twinge next to me because all she said was "Mm-hmm" before we went out to the formal dining room.

Gabe was already there, waiting for lineup to start. When he saw me, his eyes brightened and his dimples showed up again. I really did like those dimples.

"I was starting to think you were avoiding me!" he said as I sat down next to him. Ava pulled out a chair on my other side.

"I am. You didn't get the hint from all the texts I've sent you, or when we watched *Eternal Sunshine* over the phone last Thursday after you said you were in the mood for a depressing comedy?"

"I mean, did I deliver or what?"

"You did."

I could feel Ava's eyes on me, so I turned to meet them, giving her a *What? I don't know what you're talking about* look. And was thankfully saved when Natalie came out to start lineup.

Gabe and I were in Hell again, but at least Morgan had been nice to us, seating all our tables perfectly timed out—but I think that was also just the natural flow of residents, because she only double-sat her ex, Luke, once.

Toward the end of the night I told Gabe to grab some linens for our tables while I headed back to get a fresh tray of silverware. Our closing duty was polishing the silverware anyway, so I'd get a jump on that for everyone.

When I emerged from the kitchen, seafoam-green silverware holder in hand, Connor—a tall brown-haired server who was in the same grade as us—was yelling at Gabe.

"I put those there for *my* section," Connor was saying. The service station cabinets were open, and there weren't any more tablecloths inside.

"All right, sorry." Gabe held out the white tablecloths, but I stepped forward before Connor could take them, blocking his hand.

"Hold up," I said. "You *didn't* put them there for your section. You just don't want to go back to the laundry room and get more."

"No, they're mine."

"Then why didn't you put them in the front station near your section? This is where all the linens are kept, and you know the rule: if there's none for your section, you need to go grab them from laundry."

Connor took a step toward me. He was barely an inch taller than me but still tried to make me feel small. I made my shoulders broader and held my ground.

"And what if I say I don't agree?" he asked.

"Then you know the rules for that, too." I'll be perfectly honest, I was hoping to call Connor's bluff.

"Fine." He took a step back. "Loading dock. Seven forty-five."

I held my ground. "Splendid. See you then." But now I was nervous. This was *super* against the rules and not only grounds for Natalie to deny my letter of recommendation, but also to be fired. Connor opened the door to the kitchen, and Roni's voice from the other side of the line filled the tense silence.

"I see a bunch of y'all standing around out there!" she said. "Come run these dinners!"

The others went to check if their dinners were up, but our tables were all finished, so I turned and motioned for Gabe to follow me back to our service station, past James dismantling the salad bar.

"Bahama, I hear a gauntlet was thrown?" he asked as we passed.

"Seven forty-five if you want to come by."

"Sweet!" He flipped a dressing ladle and caught it, getting ranch all over his hands. "I'll make sure my car is out of the way."

Gabe slung the tablecloths over the chairbacks for the tables he was changing. "What's the big deal with the linens?"

I shrugged. "It's just an annoying trip back to the laundry room, and you have to grab enough for everyone."

"I can do it; it's not a big deal."

"I know it isn't, and Connor does, too. Doesn't mean we want to go. You grabbed them, there was enough for our section, you win." I began polishing the silverware as Ava arrived, holding two cardboard boxes.

"I heard and came right over." She dropped the boxes on the service station.

"Has Connor gotten them yet?" I asked, reaching into the boxes and feeling the hard plastic of the individually packaged butter. Room temperature—perfect.

"No, he went right for the laundry room."

"Seriously, Thomas . . ." Gabe had started calling me Thomas. I wasn't sure why, since the only people who called me "Thomas" were the managers and residents. But I liked the way he said my name. Though Ava didn't seem to, because she made a face. "You don't have to fight him over this. It's ridiculous."

Ava snorted, and I smiled and patted Gabe on the shoulder. "It'll be fine."

As long as we didn't get caught. I hoped.

I grabbed a handful of butters and shoved them in my left apron pocket. Then I took two handfuls of the margarines and put them in the right pocket. Ava grabbed a handful of each and stuffed them in her own apron, giving me a wink.

"Gimme your keys," Ava said. "I'll move your car." I handed them over, and she left.

Gabe still looked nervous.

"It's going to be fine." But I think I was saying that for my own benefit.

I was taking a risk, getting into it with Connor when Natalie seemed to have her eyes on me at all times, just waiting for me to step out of line. But I still felt like I had to stand up for Gabe. Even if it was in a ridiculous way. I knew Connor was just lazy and trying to intimidate him, but I also wanted Gabe to know I would stand up for him if I had to.

Once in summer camp, while we were playing tag with a big group of kids, two guys who liked to be jerks for the sake of being jerks decided to gang up on me. One of them—Marcus Everhart—tripped me as I was running for home base. I landed on the asphalt between the rubber mats of the jungle gym and swing sets, skinning my hands and knees.

Gabe was there in an instant. He said he had seen the whole thing and told them off. He bent down next to me and put his hands on my forearm. "Come on, let's go clean you up."

"He's fine," Marcus said. "Stop babying him."

Gabe didn't bother arguing with them. He just walked me over to the counselor, Ms. Louis, who looked up from her phone and winced when she saw my skinned knees and palms.

"What happened?"

I didn't speak, expecting Gabe to tell her everything, but he didn't. Instead, he said, "He tripped while we were playing tag." Then he let me go inside with Ms. Louis, and she tended my wounds with burning antiseptic wipes and large bandages. Just as she was finishing, Marcus Everhart was brought in by another counselor, Mr. Harris. Marcus's eye was swollen, and he had a cut just above his eyebrow. He managed a scowl at me before wincing and putting a hand to his bad eye.

"What now?" Ms. Louis asked.

"He says he ran into a swing during tag," Mr. Harris said, getting an instant ice pack and popping it.

"No more tag!" Ms. Louis led me back outside, where she berated the rest of the campers and told them to play something else.

"What did you do to Marcus?" I asked Gabe.

"Nothing." He shrugged. "He ran into a swing."

I knew that wasn't true. Especially since Marcus decided to up his tormenting as soon as Gabe left in August. But at the time it gave me a squiggly feeling all over. My palms and knees throbbed with pain, but the rest of me radiated with warm fuzziness.

This thing with Connor was much lower-stakes, but even if Gabe didn't remember how he'd stuck up for me when we were kids, I'd show him how we did it at Sunset Estates.

CHAPTER
TEN

BY 7:35, EVERYONE KNEW WHAT WAS ABOUT to happen between Connor and me. Well, everyone except Gabe, who still seemed to think we were going to throw punches at one another. The cars had been moved a safe distance from the loading dock up front—except for Natalie's white Cadillac.

The garbage smell was especially rank this evening and drifted over us as Connor rolled up his sleeves. Ava was standing behind him along with the others who'd decided to hang around and watch the brawl. James, the night's KS, stood in only his undershirt and black pants. A box of baking soda he'd nabbed from the pantry was at his feet.

"Thought I was going up against the new kid," Connor said, glancing back at Gabe.

"New kid is new. He gets a freebie until he knows the rules."

"New kid has a name!" Gabe shouted from beside Ava.

"Enough talking, New Kid!" James said. "Let's get this going before Natalie comes out." He picked up the box of baking soda and popped it open.

I reached into the front of my apron and held a butter packet between my thumb and index finger, feeling for the air bubble. Behind Connor, Ava put two fingers into her mouth, raised her eyebrows at me, and whistled hard and loud.

In a flash, my hand was out of my apron, and I pointed the butter right at Connor, squeezing as hard as I could.

The packet gave a little pop, and the butter burst out, a greasy projectile headed right at his chest. He jumped out of the way, fumbling with his own apron. He finally pulled his hand out and popped a butter in my direction.

I could tell immediately that his wasn't room temperature when it burst out of the wrapping and plopped to the ground at my feet.

That's the mistake rookies make in a butter fight. They go right for the walk-in fridge and fill up their apron, hoping their body heat is enough to warm up the butter to make it a projectile. But the pros, people like Ava, James, and myself, we know to only use the butter that was left over on the tables.

I grabbed two more packets, popping them in quick succession, before discarding the empty plastic, like an action hero from one of Gabe's movies dropping a spent gun and pulling out another.

I dodged as Connor spun and jumped and lunged, trying to get closer so one of his butter bullets could finally hit me. One of my own shots went wide, and Morgan and the Emmas had to separate to avoid getting hit. After that Morgan took a few steps back, unwilling to get butter stains on her host blouse.

I reached into the right pocket of my apron and saw the glint in Ava's eyes.

Butter brawl pro tip number two: margarine is a better projectile.

The butter packets are small and packed tightly; also the Mylar wrapping makes a satisfying pop. Margarine's paper top sounds less satisfying, but there's more air in the packets.

I squeezed hard, and the margarine burst out in a fast-flying wad. It landed right in the middle of Connor's tuxedo shirt.

My hands went up, and I cheered. The other servers clapped and gave Morgan just enough time to run away in her heels before Ava let out a warrior yell and popped a butter at the Emmas. They shrieked and reached into their own aprons and popped butter back at Ava.

James took a butter out of his pocket and popped it in my direction, shouting out my silly nickname as he did.

Everyone was butter brawling. Except for Gabe, who had no idea this was how a butter brawl ended. When a victor was declared, it became an all-out war.

Connor finally got two butters to pop, and both hit me, one in the apron and the other on my pants.

I ran across the butter field—slipping and almost eating it—to Gabe's side. I reached into my pocket and gave him a handful of butter, which he accepted with a smirk, then popped one right at me.

"Allies!" I shouted.

"You should have warned me ahead of time." He popped another one, and I squeezed a margarine packet. It splattered on his shoulder, and he acted like he'd been shot.

Ava popped two packets at us, before we jumped in with everyone else. Morgan got in her car and left.

When all of us were butter spent, we started picking up the plastic packets from the ground while James walked around with the baking

75

soda, sprinkling it over the smeared butter puddles. Horace, the last guy out of the dish room, would come out and spray everything down before he left. If Natalie asked why the ground was covered in baking soda, he would also be the one to cover for us and say it was just a spot treatment to make sure the parking lot was clean and to deter rodents.

We passed around disposable wipes and a bucket of warm water and dish soap to wipe ourselves down.

"Good brawl, Tommy," Connor said before he left. He bumped my fist and got into his car, probably smelling like dish soap and margarine.

"So this is how we settle disputes here?" Gabe asked.

"It's tradition," Ava said.

"But rule number one is *don't* tell Natalie," I warned. I didn't need a repeat of the *don't piss off the hosts* near-miss. "I have a feeling George knows about it, but he turns a blind eye. Doris would have a conniption if she found out, but she parks out front with the residents, so she'll never know. Natalie would happily fire us all." I was also risking my recommendation letter, doing this. But if the butter brawl happened anyway and I wasn't here, she'd just tell me I should have done something to stop it or refuse to believe I didn't take part. Maybe she'd fire me anyway to set an example.

"Oh," Ava said, looking past me. "Especially if she saw that." She pointed at Natalie's Cadillac, which had five splatters of butter across the hood.

"Shit." James bolted up the loading dock stairs. It was almost eight, and Natalie would be leaving shortly.

Ava, Gabe, the Emmas, Luke, and I began wiping down the

front. First with dry disposable rags and then with a little bit of soap to get rid of the oily residue. Ava sprinkled some baking soda across the remaining oil slicks, and we waited a moment before wiping it away.

It looked fine, but there was clearly a large section of the Cadillac that had been recently cleaned. The other side of the hood was dry and pollen-covered.

James was on it. He emerged from the loading dock with Horace and the pressure washer. Horace sprayed down some of the dock and parking lot, washing clumps of baking-soda-butter into the grass, and "accidentally" sprayed down the front of the Cadillac.

James gave him a quick thanks and Horace went back inside, where, James informed us, he would tell Natalie he had accidentally over-sprayed and cleaned the front of her car.

"We should get out of here before she comes out, though," James said. "See you guys tomorrow?"

"I'm off tomorrow," I said. "I'm Wednesday, Thursday, and Friday this week."

"Aw man," Gabe said. "I'm Tuesday and Saturday."

"Sunday brunch?" I asked. He shook his head.

Ava gave the two of us a look only I seemed to catch.

"Guess I won't see you till next week," I said.

"See you next week, then." Gabe got into his car and drove off, Ava and I waving to him as he went.

"What the fuckity-duck was all that there?" Ava asked, waving her hand at me as we got in my car.

"Shut up."

"No." She buckled her seat belt and then sniffed. "Wait. What is that?" She scrunched her nose and sniffed again. She took the scarf she had tied around her hair to protect it during the butter brawl and sniffed it and her hair. Her armpits, the dashboard. Then she leaned across the center console and sniffed me. "Oh God! It's you!"

"What?" I sniffed myself. I did smell like butter and soap, but it wasn't rank.

"It smells like—oh my God!" She held her nose. "Gay *hormones*!"

I shifted into drive. "Oh, shut up!"

"No, it smells like . . . cold brew and the way Dua Lipa looks." She rolled down her window and held her head out. "Oh God, it's so *gay*!"

"Screw you!" But I was still laughing.

"It's like if you baked a cake, had sex with the cake, taught the cake how to walk in heels, and denied the cake its civil liberties for centuries."

"All right, that's enough." I was laughing so hard tears were coming to my eyes. We stopped at the guard shack, saying goodbye to the night watchman, Danny.

"Danny!" Ava shouted over me. "Do you know what gay love smells like?"

He raised an eyebrow. "Latex?"

"Daniel!" Ava sounded scandalized as he laughed and raised the gate for us.

We pulled out of the Sunset Estates complex and headed back toward Ava's house.

"So what's the deal?" Ava asked. "Does he even remember you two had a summer fling?"

"It wasn't a summer fling; we were eleven." But, no, Gabe still didn't remember me and I was way too embarrassed and hurt to remind him of our summer camp friendship. And how he'd ended up being the first boy I ever possibly fell in love with. And the one I started comparing other boys to.

"Do you want me to find out if he's gay?"

"I don't want you to do anything." All this was way too much to deal with right now anyway. Ava had only just found out last week that she wasn't pregnant, and I still had the sword of Natalie hanging over my head. It made work more stressful than it needed to be. Or maybe that was her entire point.

Having Gabe there was bad enough—him not remembering who I was and my damn stomach flipping every time he laughed or smiled. It was distracting!

No, I didn't want to date Gabe.

That's a lie—I absolutely wanted to. But not as much as I wanted Natalie's letter of recommendation. If I wasn't going to be able to make a high-production-value video to go with my application, a letter from Natalie—a former colleague of the most famous faculty member at La Mère—was the next best thing.

I just needed to keep telling myself that, and soon I wouldn't even be thinking about Gabe. It was bound to work eventually.

I stopped lying to myself the following Saturday. Amber Gallo—a girl from our class who Ava had been friends with since middle school— was throwing a party, and Ava said she wanted to celebrate *not* being pregnant. And what better way to do that than by drinking shitty beer at a secret house party with no parental supervision?

Since Ava wasn't pregnant and it was her celebration, I agreed to be designated driver. As I pulled onto Amber's street, I asked Ava something that had been on my mind for a few days.

"Have you thought about whether you'd go farther away for school if you had to?"

When I glanced at her, Ava looked deep in thought. Or maybe she was just confused because, yes, this was 100 percent coming out of nowhere. At least to her.

For me, it was part of those rare moments when I wasn't lying to myself about Gabe. When those little nanoseconds between lies grew into fantasies where we were both in LA. Or New York. It changed depending on the day.

And I knew full well that deciding my future based on a boy was a dumb move—something best saved for teen shows about girls who give up on Harvard to go to Ohio State. I mean, no offense, Ohio State, but Harvard, you ain't.

"Yeah," she finally said. "But early decision is binding, so I wouldn't be able to go anywhere else."

"Right," I said. "But say Johns Hopkins had another campus, like in Lo—" No, she'd see right through me if I said "Los Angeles." "Louisiana."

"Hard pass on the red states, honey. Purple is difficult enough."

"California, then." Generic enough. "Or Washington State."

Ava paused. And when she finally did speak, she seemed a little more unsure. "I don't know. Yeah. Probably. I've actually been looking into Johns Hopkins's study abroad programs lately, just to see what they're like. Sure, going away for one semester is different from four years, but . . ."

She let her voice trail off. And she seemed to be thinking about something else.

"What is it?" I asked.

She shook her head. "Wait, why are *you* asking this? Are you . . . thinking of going somewhere other than La Mère?"

"No! I'm just . . . wondering. Is all."

"Mm-hmm." But she still side-eyed me as I parked the car a little ways down the block from Amber's house.

Around eight—unattractively on time—we rounded the Gallos' McMansion to the backyard and said our friendly hellos to all the people we had seen sporadically throughout the summer and then every day since starting school last Tuesday.

I spotted Brad Waldorf in the middle of a group by the keg. After I'd seen him and James the other week, he had been even more distant than usual. Which was awkward since we shared European History and biology classes together. But tonight he seemed a little looser, and when he saw me from across the yard he gave me a wave, though it moved no higher than his waist.

Then when Ava and I passed him on the way to the house he tried to shove a can of aforementioned shitty beer into my hand, but I politely waved him away. Ava shot me a knowing look, which I took care to ignore. She'd caught Brad and me making out more than twice in the past year.

Ava and I posed for selfies, danced, and finally, after she went to get another drink, Brad Waldorf approached me.

"Hey," he said. I could tell the beer can in his hand was practically empty when he put it to his lips.

"How are you?" I asked. He said he was fine, then went quiet again, as if he wasn't sure what the next part of our conversation was supposed to be. I looked around the yard, where the other people from our school milled about, along with some guys from Archbishop Murphy. No one was paying attention to us, but Brad still stood in a defensive way. His shoulders were slightly slumped, and his arms looked like they were trying to cradle his chest.

This was also strange because he usually just sent me a text to ask if I wanted to go somewhere and hook up. And it was a little early— that didn't happen until after eleven most nights.

"Thomas?"

But that wasn't Brad's voice. I looked past Brad, and he spun to see who had noticed us talking. Then he took another sip of his empty beer and left without another word. Leaving me gazing across the lawn at Gabe De La Hoya.

"Hey," I said, trying to play it cool. But inside, I was screaming with joy.

CHAPTER
ELEVEN

I WAITED AS GABE TOLD HIS FRIENDS he'd be right back. He had a drink in his hand, and a bit sloshed out as he walked toward me. He held the cup out and pulled me in for a hug with his right arm.

"What are you doing here?" he asked.

"What are *you* doing here?"

He threw a thumb over his shoulder. "Amber's dating one of my friends." I had met the guy in question a few months back at her last party here. But Gabe hadn't been here, or if he had been, I'd missed him.

Doubtful. Gabe stood out.

I asked him how work was. He said it was great but then launched into complaining about the "creepy guy at table sixteen"—Mr. Gilbert—who wouldn't let his wife speak. I told him Mr. and Mrs. Gilbert always sat there and he always ordered for her.

"Gabriel!" Ava's shout drifted down the hill, and she came trotting down after it, Morgan following close behind her in clothes more fitting her age than the mom suits and blouses she wore as a host at work. The four of us sat by the fire and talked work for a bit before

Gabe told us to come meet his friends.

They were the typical straight white guys I expected from Archbishop Murphy—Gabe's all-boys Catholic school. Most Murphy boys came complete with fade haircuts, and when they weren't in their blazers and ties, they wore activewear and sweats. Gabe seemed to be the only exception among his friends. He wore jeans—which made me realize Sunset Estates' black pants did *nothing* for his butt and should be outlawed on him—and a plaid button-down with the sleeves rolled up. And there were those arms again.

The guy dating Amber was named Fred Shaughnessy, and though he had his arm around her shoulders, he kept looking down at Ava's chest.

The rest of them just kept saying and doing bro-y shit—shotgunning the cheap beer, talking about kicking each other's asses in video games *and* real life, whispering about the girls around them when Ava wasn't paying attention—like they were trying to one-up each other on their asshole-ish manliness. The only one of Gabe's friends who seemed less than insufferable was Kevin Wheeler, though he seemed to be flirting an awful lot with Ava. Who also seemed to be flirting right back. Or they were just talking video games—it was hard to tell.

Seeing Gabe with people like this—people he called his friends—was uncomfortable, and suddenly it felt like in summer camp, when Gabe seemed to get along with everyone and I was the awkward loser next to him.

It was something I hadn't really felt in a long time. I had a good group of friends at school, most of whom I had made over the years.

The Sunset Estates friends were made by necessity. We were all different but were joined together by this weird mutual job. At Sunset Estates, Gabe was part of us, but at school he must have been a completely different person.

For the first time in years that nagging voice in my head, telling me I was the loser and Gabe was too nice to tell me otherwise, was coming back. When we were kids, Gabe's mere presence and smile had been enough to silence it, but when I went to middle school that fall, the voice got louder. It took years, and my friends constantly encouraging me, for me to feel better about myself.

"Excuse me." I turned and headed for Amber's house. All the fun and excitement at seeing Gabe had dissolved. Those were the people he hung out with. Which meant he was one of those people, too.

I felt stupid that I had ever crushed on him.

I stayed in the downstairs powder room longer than I should have. It was the only room on the first floor with a door I could lock, and I just wanted to be alone for a bit.

There was a knock, and I checked my face in the mirror before opening the door. My stomach clenched.

It was Gabe.

He smiled. "I wondered where you went."

"Too much toxic masculinity." I tried to push past him, but he was still in the way. "Excuse me."

"Wait here for me." He stepped aside, and I opened my mouth to argue but instead just walked out into the hallway. When he shut the door, I went into the kitchen. Luke was there, mixing himself another drink. He nodded at me, and I gave him a raised-eyebrow "hey" on my way outside.

I stood on the back deck, scanning the yard. The party was starting to pick up, but I wanted to find Ava so I could tell her I was going home and ask if she could get a ride with Morgan. I don't know why I felt so weird, but all I wanted was to curl up and watch a cooking show. Maybe I would find a difficult recipe and bake my feelings away.

"Hey." Gabe was back. He pulled the sliding glass door closed behind him. "Can I get you a drink?" He leaned against the deck railing next to me.

"I'm heading out."

He tilted his head. "What's up?"

I took a couple of seconds to weigh the pros and cons of telling him the truth, then decided I didn't care if he didn't want to hear it. He was asking, so I'd answer.

"Your friends aren't really my speed."

He laughed. "I know, typical straight bro dudes."

"Yeah, and that's not really me."

"Straight? Bro? Dude?" Then he quirked his head. "Typical?"

Again he made me laugh. I don't know what it was about him that made me feel so comfortable when it was just the two of us. I also wanted to ask him if *he* was one of those three things. I already knew he wasn't typical.

"I should get going."

"Where to?" Gabe asked.

"Home."

He looked disappointed. "No chance of us being friends?" I didn't know what to say. He pounced on my hesitation and pouted. "Please. My only other friends are assholes."

I tried not to laugh. His friends *were* kind of assholes, but somehow he wasn't. Was that even possible? Didn't hanging out with assholes make him an asshole by association? But he was nice to me. To everyone I'd seen him interact with, really. Something in my chest betrayed me and told me to let it go. But not entirely.

"Maybe on a probational basis."

He nodded. "I can handle that."

Together we walked back down to Ava and his friends. I told Ava I was going to head home—there was no use pushing our luck when I had just decided I'd give Gabe the chance to prove he was different from his friends. Morgan said she'd drive Ava home.

Ava pulled me into a hug and whispered, "Smells like Gaga's key change in 'Shallow' and Tom Daley's surrogacy contract."

I almost laughed but whispered back, "Better than Acqua di Gio and wall art that says *It's Wine O'Clock Somewhere*."

"You're really just going home?" Gabe asked as he followed me out to my car. "I can't convince you to hang out somewhere else?"

With Gabe? Alone?

Those stubborn embers in my chest were still buzzing. What the hell was wrong with me? "Where did you have in mind?"

CHAPTER
TWELVE

"HOLY SHIT, YOU'RE RICH."

I pulled to a stop behind Gabe's parked car, looking up at the house—no, *mansion*—he lived in.

"We are not rich."

"Your house isn't connected to several other houses," I said. I pointed at the massive field to the left of the driveway. "And you own what appears to be three football fields. You're rich."

He seemed embarrassed. We got out of the car, and I took a better look at it all. It was an old stone house, three stories and what looked like a little attic window above the third floor. There was a wooden porch that wrapped around the front, all the way along the side of the house to the back deck. There was also a roundabout in front of the house, where we had parked, that led back to a stone carriage house that looked like a garage with maybe a guesthouse on the second floor.

The house also felt familiar, like it reminded me of one from a TV show or movie that I couldn't place but maybe Gabe could. Hell, maybe they had even filmed a movie here. It felt like I'd seen it somewhere before. The property had to be several acres, because we'd had to take a darkened, hilly back road to get here, and I couldn't see another house anywhere through the trees surrounding the property line.

The rowhome I lived in was probably smaller than his carriage house. Also, I had no front yard and just a concrete patio in the back-yard.

I'd grown up in a house with a yard, but when my dad died, we'd had to downsize.

"Is this where you grew up?"

"No," he said. "We used to live somewhere else. This was my grandparents' house. When they passed away, they left it to my dad, and we sold our other place and moved in here."

"Oh, so you're an *heir*."

"It's not like that at all . . . Trust me."

I was still skeptical.

"Oh, shit, hold on," he said. He turned to the front door and called back over his shoulder. "Do you like dogs?"

"Of course. I'm not a monster."

He opened the front door to barking, and two massive beasts lunged onto the front porch. Gabe started to talk in baby-dog-talk as one jumped up on him and licked his face.

They were two Saint Bernards, and I couldn't figure out how Gabe was able to stay upright while the two—had to be almost two-hundred-pound—creatures jumped up on him.

But I was about to find out, because one saw me out of the corner of its eye, let out a "Bork!" and ran to me. I put my hands down for it to sniff me, but it jumped up, pushing its massive paws against my chest and knocking the wind out of me.

"Gertie! Down!" Gabe yelled. "She's nice, I promise!" The other Saint Bernard stayed back. Gabe finally gripped Gertie's collar and pulled her down. He told her to sit, and she did, her tail sweeping the driveway. "She's still a puppy." He turned and pointed to the other dog, whose tail slowly wagged back. "This is Arnold. He's old and a lot calmer around new people. Go say hi, Arnold."

Arnold looked up at Gabe, then took two tentative steps toward me, sniffed my hand, and gave me a lick. All the while, Gertie whined and groaned for attention.

"Okay, yes, I give you love, too," I said, turning to her. Arnold seemed happy to go back to hiding behind Gabe, and I patted Gertie's head. Her butt wiggled on the driveway, and her massive pink tongue hung from her mouth like a slobbery snake.

"See? Not *all* my friends are assholes," Gabe said.

"Dogs don't count." I changed to my dog-talking voice. "'Cause doggies are never assholes, isn't that right, Gertie?"

She tried her hardest to lick my face while still staying seated.

"All right, go potty, guys!" Gabe waved them off and they ran out into the field to do their business. I looked up at the old house again; it was massive. Gabe followed my look and nodded. "It's more work than it's worth. My parents have to sink another few thousand dollars into it every month or so."

A few *thousand*? A *month*? Our hot water heater broke in April, and my mom was still paying off the new one.

"Why are you working at Sunset Estates if you live in a house like this?" I asked. It wasn't until after I asked that I realized that sounded rude.

"Because it's my parents' house, not mine." The tone of his voice made it clear that, yes, it was a rude question.

"Sorry. I meant it a different way, and even now I don't know how to phrase it more politely."

"It's okay." He kicked a rock into the grass and lowered his voice. "My dad's a lawyer; my mom works for a regional bank. They do make a lot of money, but they want *me* to make a lot of money, too."

"So they made you get a job at an old folks' home?"

"No. They wanted me to focus more on school. The job thing is still a sore subject. They want me to go to Penn or Georgetown like they did and get a JD or master's in finance like they did and they want me to marry a nice girl and have two-point-five babies, and I want to do none of that."

None of that?

"You want to go to film school," I said.

"And they won't pay for it, so I've got to save up and take out loans and the whole shebang."

I narrowed my eyes. "I feel like your rich brain doesn't realize exactly how much film school is going to cost you."

"USC is going to cost eighty-five grand a year. NYU is seventy-seven."

I whistled. My Tommy-and-Gabe-in-the-same-city college fantasy returned. La Mère cost the same no matter which campus I went to. Though I had always kind of imagined going to the New York campus of La Mère because it was close to my mom—and it was the one my dad had gone to. But maybe I shouldn't have entirely written off the LA campus.

Would I be able to leave home and go that far?

"Like I said," Gabe said, bringing me back from my thoughts.

"Loans and whatever else I can save up. My grandmother left me some money, but I can't touch it without my parents' permission until I'm twenty-one."

"No permission without law school admission?"

He laughed. "Exactly."

"Sorry, that sucks." I wondered if it was the grandmother I had met. She had seemed so nice when she was picking Gabe up from summer camp. I bet she'd be angry at his parents for not letting him follow his dream.

I couldn't imagine being forced to learn something you didn't want to learn. Especially when it required seven years of schooling. At least culinary school was something I *wanted*.

My parents had started a college fund for me before my dad died, but I'd still be stuck with student loans. And when I told my mom I wanted to go to my dad's alma mater, she was all about it. Cooking had kind of been our thing, my dad and me. During the day, he was stuck doing administrative stuff at my grandfather's window and siding business. But when he got home every night, he'd start working on dinner and I'd help.

When I was just a kid, it was grabbing ingredients, learning to measure out stuff, setting timers. But slowly I got to do more. My dad taught me how to caramelize onions, what spices create what flavor profiles, and—his proudest achievement—how to make the perfect poached egg.

Some of my favorite memories were of cooking with him after work while my mom enjoyed a glass of wine at the kitchen table and watched us or read a book. Cooking and baking were the only things I could think of that I'd be happy doing for the rest of my life. I couldn't imagine my parents not supporting my dream.

But then again, it was probably easier to support that dream when part of it was creating my own test kitchen on my days off where my mom got to eat whatever fun new treat I was making. And it was nice that it also honored who my dad was.

"Anyway . . ." Gabe put his hand down to pet Gertie and Arnold, who had joined us once again. "Still want to hang out? Even though I'm rich and have asshole friends and love movies when you have zero interest in them?"

That was a lot of strikes against our already burgeoning relationship—I mean friendship.

"No," I said. I waited for his smirk to drop before I bent down and held out my hands to Gertie, speaking in my doggie voice. "But I'll hang out because you have these puppers!"

Gertie lunged at me, knocking me off my feet. She licked my face as I shouted for help, pinning me under two hundred pounds of fluff and slobber.

Gabe grinned down at me. "You deserve that."

There *was* an apartment above the carriage-house garage. And it was Gabe's. Well, not technically his, but it was set up as a guesthouse, and ever since he'd told his parents he was going to film school, he had been hiding out there most days.

I dropped onto the leather couch. "So they just let you live on your own?"

"Not totally." He filled up a dog bowl at the sink and set it down on the kitchen floor for Gertie and Arnold to share. "My mom gets annoyed if I'm out here too many days in a row and demands that I come back into the house."

I glanced around. It was basically a studio apartment. There was a doorway leading to a bathroom next to a king-size bed. The couch was in the middle of the room, facing a large TV. The side door entered at a kitchenette, where Gabe was looking into a fridge.

"Do you want a drink?" he asked.

"Sure. Whatever you're having."

He took two sodas and tossed one to me. I popped the tab and took a sip as Gabe plopped down on the couch next to me. He leaned back against the armrest and pulled his bare feet up onto the couch.

"Should we continue your education?" he asked with a smirk.

"How many more *Back to the Future* movies can there be?"

"Oh no, we'll be moving on to something else." He set his soda down and scrambled for the remotes—there were three of them.

"Is this where you were watching with me?"

He shook his head. "There's a movie theater room in the house."

Of course there is. I tried to hide my smile behind the soda can, but he caught it.

"Show me your favorite movie," I said. "The one that made you decide you wanted to make movies."

"Those are two different movies."

"How? Shouldn't your favorite movie be the one that made you realize your dream?"

"No, because my dad took me to see *The Avengers* when I was six, and *that* was the movie that made me want to make movies. It was the first time I had ever seen anything like that spectacle. It's a great movie, but it's not my favorite movie by any means. It's a popcorn blockbuster."

"Oh, right, you're a *pretentious* film nerd."

He flicked his soda can at me, splashing me a bit while he tried not to grin. "Shut it."

"All right, well, even *I* have seen the Avengers movies. So what's your all-time favorite?"

He blushed, and I realized something. When he talked about *The Avengers*, his eyes gleamed for just a second. Like he was feeling that excitement of being a six-year-old watching aliens invade New York City for the first time. But then as soon as he dismissed it as a "popcorn blockbuster," that gleam went away. And then returned just now, making my heart skip.

"I don't want to show you."

I leaned forward. "Oh my God, is it porn?"

"No!"

"Because I won't judge you if it's porn. Well, depending on the kind of porn."

"It's not porn!" His smile grew and his cheeks flushed. "It's the polar opposite of porn, actually."

"So it's an educational video about abstinence."

"I just mean it's very chaste. Also . . ." He sighed. "It's a foreign-language film, so there's subtitles."

"Shit, you really are a pretentious film nerd."

"See, this is why I didn't want to show it to you."

I chewed the inside of my cheek. That glint in his eye was gone again, and I felt a little guilty. I also wanted to see it again. Feel my heart skip again.

"I'm just kidding," I said. "Show me. I promise I'll give it the same amount of respect I would *The Avengers*."

He narrowed his eyes at me. "That doesn't give me much confidence."

"Come on, what's the movie?"

He sighed, then turned on the Apple TV and went into his movie library. Before he scrolled down to the *Foreign* section, I saw the number listed under *All Titles*.

"You have over a *thousand* movies?"

"I haven't seen all of them. Some I just buy when they're on sale if I know I'll want to watch them someday."

I laughed. "Your parents want you to hoard money, but you hoard films."

"You should change my company contact to 'De La Hoard-a.'"

"'De La WHORE-a' sounds better."

"Ass."

He came to a stop on a movie called *In the Mood for Love*. My stomach did a little flip. The movie poster image on the screen had an Asian woman wearing a red dress.

"Oh my." I put my hands to my cheeks. "*In the Mood for Love*! So it's a *romance*!"

"Okay, now I'm not even sure I want to show you this!" he teased.

"You mean you're . . . not . . ." I couldn't get it out without smiling, trying to stifle my laughter.

He took the chance to cut me off. "Don't say it."

"In the mood . . ."

"Thomas." Again with the way he said my name.

"For *In the Mood* . . ." I giggled.

"I hate you."

"*For Love?*"

He reached across me, putting his hand on my chest, and grabbed my soda. "You're cut off. Get out of my house."

"No! You talked up this movie so much, I have to see it now." He pulled the soda to his chest, looking at me like he wasn't sure he trusted me. "Please."

He sighed. "You gonna talk through the whole thing?"

"I'll be as quiet as Arnold." I pointed across the room, where Arnold had already lain down by the door. Meanwhile, Gertie was pacing around, waiting for us to figure out what we were going to do.

He gave me back my soda and said, "Fine." He took out his phone, and with a few taps the lights began to dim.

"Oh!" I said, looking around the room. "You *are* in the moo—"

"I swear to God, Thomas." His voice was stern, but his face betrayed him, the dimples in his cheeks peeking at me, making my chest tighten.

"Right. Quiet as Arnold."

He pressed play, and Gertie—unable to read the room—jumped up on the couch, separating us.

"Gertie!" Gabe yelled. She flung her tongue at him, then plopped down with a grunt, splaying across both of our feet.

I reached down and scratched behind her ears, smiling across her. Gabe rolled his eyes and the movie started.

CHAPTER
THIRTEEN

WATCHING *IN THE MOOD FOR LOVE* WITH Gabe was different from watching *Back to the Future*. I didn't make jokes or ask questions. Mainly because I was too busy reading the subtitles, but also because it felt so much more personal. It felt like this was Gabe unlocking his phone without clearing his browser history and letting me do a deep dive for as long as I wanted.

It wasn't a fun time-travel adventure; it was an artistic display of love and relationships. If you, like me, had no idea this movie existed, here are the spoilers: It's about these sexy Chinese folks in Hong Kong in the sixties. The main guy and the main girl—both married to other people—become secret friends because in the sixties mixed-sex friendships in China were a faux pas. *Then* they find out each of their spouses is having an affair *with the other's spouse*. So they meet up in a hotel to do the deed, to show their spouses four can play at that game, or whatever.

But they can't do it—they don't want to stoop to their level. But the guy is in love with the girl and has to move, but he wants her to leave with him. Of course she just misses catching him before he's gone for good and it's too late. Years pass and they have these near-misses where they almost get to find each other again, but they never do.

And at the end of the movie the guy is telling his friend about a tradition where you're supposed to whisper a secret into a hole in a tree and cover it with mud. So we see the dude doing that, only into a hole in a temple wall in Cambodia.

I was glad the lights were dimmed, because the end credits started to blur. I pretended to sip at my empty can of soda and surreptitiously wiped at my eye.

"Want to watch something else?" Gabe asked.

I did. I wanted to stay and watch anything with him, but something more exciting maybe, and less emotionally devastating. I looked at my phone; it was almost eleven thirty. I had already texted my mom to let her know I was watching a movie at a friend's house. She didn't press me about who the friend was or remind me of my curfew, but I knew if I wasn't home by midnight I'd be in trouble. My mom rarely grounded me, but she had a way of scolding that made me feel awful.

"I want to, but I have to get home."

He reached over Gertie's snoring mass and took my empty soda can. "Come on, I'll walk you out."

I petted Gertie, but she kept snoring on the couch. Arnold was splayed out as well, and stayed put, watching Gabe leave.

We walked down the wooden staircase mounted on the side of the carriage house back to my car.

"Thanks for coming over," Gabe said. "And indulging me. I don't show many people that movie."

I could tell. Just watching it in silence with him felt like . . . well, it felt like I was the wall at the end of the movie. Like he was whispering his secrets into me and I'd hold them forever.

"It was really good. Sad, but . . ."

He nodded. "I know. One of the reasons I don't show it to people, but you did ask for it."

"I did."

"So . . ." He dragged out the word and avoided my gaze. "Now that I showed you that. And we've been friendly for the past few weeks . . ."

My mouth went dry. Which was not good if this was going the way I thought it was. Was this our moment? Was I actually *not* reading all this wrong, and was Gabe about to ask if he could kiss me, and was the object of all my adolescent desires finally going to—

"Maybe we can be honest and talk about how awkward I made it when I pretended we hadn't been friends before this?"

WHAT?

My mouth hung open. My mind went blank, and I just stared at his face in the moonlight. I didn't know what to say. Then it came to me.

"You *remembered* me?"

He bit his lip. "Yeah. Sorry. And I know you did, too, because I saw it on your face when I 'introduced' myself."

I crossed my arms, my cheeks burning. "What an ass! And you just let me be mortified."

"*I* was mortified, too!" He put a hand on his chest, and I could see he was trying not to laugh. "I just . . . assumed you wouldn't remember me, so I pretended I didn't remember you, and you were *supposed* to tell me we knew each other——"

"Oh, so it's my fault you manipulated me into thinking you completely forgot about me."

He laughed. "You could have said something!"

"And add a whole new flaky layer of mortification to my awkward croissant? No, thank you!" I gave him a playful shove, still pretending to be angry when I was actually burning with excitement. He did remember me! "So tell me what happened to you. You went away for a two-week vacation that turned into forever."

He motioned back at the house behind him. "This happened. My grandfather died in the middle of the vacation."

"Oh no. I'm sorry."

"It's fine. We came home to help my grandmother take care of his estate, and family came in from out of town for the funeral, and afterward it ended up being this whole big thing."

"I pretended a shark ate you," I said, without realizing how it sounded.

He chuckled and his eyes went wide. "We did buy a bigger boat after my grandfather died!" Then, seeing my shocked face, he said, "Kidding. I'll explain the joke to you another time. But three weeks ago wasn't the first time we've seen each other since day camp—you know that, right?"

Huh? My mind raced, trying to figure out what he could be talking about. When did we cross paths? I tried playing soccer for a season in middle school, but quickly realized it wasn't fun when the other guys on my team threw hissy fits and started screaming and crying when we lost a game. But the public schools and the parochial schools never played each other, so that couldn't have been it.

"You were at a party maybe a year ago. I was there too and we saw each other, but you didn't seem to recognize me."

"What? When? What party?"

"It was one of Amber's."

My cheeks burned a bit more. If I didn't recognize him, maybe it was Ava's turn to be DD and I'd had too much to drink. Shit, what if it was the night Brad and I first hooked up? What must he think of me if he saw me sneaking away with a closeted hockey player?

"So you just assumed I didn't remember you?" I asked. He nodded. He was trying to pretend he didn't recognize me when he first started because . . . because why? Because he would be embarrassed if I didn't remember him?

Or because, like me, it would crush him?

"Do you want to call me when you're home?" he asked, shaking me from my thoughts. "We can sync up something on Netflix."

I did, but I sighed. "I have brunch shift tomorrow morning. And I'm doing setup and sick trays, so I have to be there at ten."

"Maybe tomorrow night."

"Okay."

I leaned against my car, wringing my hands behind my back. My heartbeat quickened in my chest. The longer we stood in silence, the more nervous I got. Should I lean forward and kiss him? Or was he just showing me a movie because we were friends? Telling me he remembered me from day camp as a friend?

Everything felt more confusing than it had been just a few hours ago, when I told him his friends were assholes.

But he'd showed me his movie, the movie that was most important to him, and it was about love and two characters *not* doing what they really wanted and not realizing it until it was too late.

I tried not to smile for a few seconds before realizing it was too dark for him to really see it. I could barely make out his face in the light of the moon, but I could see his eyes on me. I shivered and my teeth chattered, but I wasn't sure if it was the cold. He put his hands on my arms, rubbing them to try to warm me up.

I chuckled and took a tiny tumble-step toward him. Our body heat bounced back and forth between us. His hands stopped rubbing my arms, and I felt one move around to my back, just resting there. I stepped closer, lifting my head to him.

His eyes were closed. We were silent.

My teeth stopped chattering, and we didn't speak. The only sound was the low croak of a toad somewhere in the trees.

I closed my eyes and leaned into him. His lips were warm, and he opened them to mine. I felt him apply more pressure to my back, and I wrapped my arms around him, pulling him close. He gasped into me, and his other hand cupped behind my ear and neck.

My chest was tight, and my heart raced.

The kiss was just a moment that felt like forever. Because he pulled his lips away. He put his forehead to mine, and I opened my eyes to see his were still closed.

"I should tell you something," he said. He chuckled, but it sounded sad.

"Don't tell me you're straight." I mean, did I have a type or what?

He laughed again, and his hands were back to rubbing my upper arms. "No. The complete opposite." His hands went down to mine, and he squeezed them. "I . . . have a boyfriend."

And the world came crashing down.

CHAPTER
FOURTEEN

THERE'S A SIMPLE RECIPE FOR GETTING OVER someone who is in a relationship. Step one, wipe them from your mind entirely. Just stop thinking about them; it's that easy. Like a buttery, flaky, perfect croissant, anyone—who happens to be a professional—can do it. And I am absolutely a professional when it comes to repressing emotions!

Step two, avoid them at all costs.

Unfortunately, my luck avoiding Gabe ended four days after I kissed him. Thankfully, I wasn't training him; he was in the formal dining room, training with another server named Katie, so at least we didn't have to do the awkward thing where we pretended we hadn't kissed as I showed him the correct way to fold napkins. Which would have been even more awkward because I hadn't answered the seven texts he had sent me over the past four days.

Al and Willa were my last table to leave, and I reset my section around them as they gossiped with me. I wanted to sit down and join them—Al had even told me to once or twice—but that was a major no-no. If there was one thing Natalie *would* allow us to say "no" to, it was sitting with the residents. Even if that was part of her tasks, it would be a trick task to gauge if I could say no when I should.

"And get this, kid," Al said, slinging his arm over the back of his chair. "She says she gets to choose because she's been here longer than me."

I frowned. "So she chooses every movie because she's had more time to develop bad taste?"

Al cackled and even Willa almost smiled as she took another sip of her coffee. Without asking, I walked to the service station and grabbed the coffeepot to freshen her cup.

"Last one," she whispered as Al continued.

"Seriously, so anyway, I stood up and I told the old bitch—"

"Al!" Willa scolded.

"If I have to sit through goddamned *Casablanca* one more god-damned time, I'm going to hire a bunch of tired drag queens to come give a running commentary through the whole fuckin' thing."

I turned to Willa. "You didn't scold him for that one?"

She shrugged. "It's a direct quote. He really did say it, so what am I going to do, scold him again?"

"You said all this?" I asked, keeping my voice low. "To Dictator Dowling?" Helga Dowling had a history of authoritarian rule over the Sunset Estates clubs she was a part of. Even my mom referred to her as Dictator Dowling when telling me about her own run-ins with her.

"I did, and you know what?"

"You get to choose the next movie?"

"No. But I do have Daisy Chain and Jenna Fluid on retainer, so she'll see who she's messing with at the end of the month."

I laughed and set the coffeepot back at the service station, turning off the warmers. "I would actually *pay* to come watch that."

"What are we watching?" Gabe had emerged from the salad bar doorway. Seeing him standing there, smiling his fake residents-only smile—very different from the real wide, handsome grin he gave me—was like a punch in the gut. Didn't he know this was *my* area? I still wasn't prepared to hash things out with him. In fact, I just wanted it all to go away. It was so much easier for me to be pissed off at him for never telling me about his boyfriend than for him to apologize and force me to actually be cordial.

"Al, Ms. Vaughn, you remember our new hire, Gabe?" I tried to hide the icy tone in my voice but must not have done it well enough, because Ms. Vaughn looked at me instead of Gabe. She held eye contact, arching an eyebrow. I gave up the staring contest first and looked away.

Meanwhile, Al was too distracted by Gabe. "How could we forget? How are you adjusting, Gabriel?"

Ms. Vaughn rolled her eyes.

"Fine, thank you."

"Al was just telling me he was hiring a couple of drag queens to do a running commentary on *Casablanca* for movie night."

Gabe's eyes widened. "I'll pay triple whatever Thomas is paying,"

"*Casablanca* fan?" I asked.

Gabe frowned. "Hell . . . er . . . sorry." He blushed and looked at Ms. Vaughn. "No. I mean, it's fine, but there's way better movies out there."

"My point exactly!" Al pointed at him. "Now try telling that to the old bitches in charge."

"Al!"

Gabe was less embarrassed now that Ms. Vaughn had scolded Al and not him. "But *Casablanca* with drag queen RiffTrax? I'm in there like swimwear."

"Great!" Al clapped his hands. "So you boys won't mind chipping in. I think a thousand bucks from each of you should be enough."

"A thousand bucks? For that money *I'll* put on a dress."

Al shook a finger at me. "No, no, honey. Drag is far more than just putting on a dress."

"I should have known all this shrill cackling and dress talk was you." I turned to see our senior manager, George, standing in the doorway, arms crossed.

Shade-off!

Gabe looked like he was scared he'd finally get the scolding he deserved for dropping a "hell" in front of a resident.

George—a white man in his fifties with rosy cheeks and wire-framed glasses—rarely set foot in the dining room unless Natalie wasn't there. He was more the administrative manager, making sure people and invoices were paid on time and being the liaison between the dining room, kitchen, building facilities, and the rest of the Sunset Estates higher-ups.

Al groaned. "I don't remember looking into a mirror and saying 'rug-rashed knees' three times."

Oh, shit! One point for Al. I bit my lip as I tried not to laugh. Gabe, new to the shade-off, let out a guffaw and clamped his hands over his mouth. I hated that I loved that sound.

George ignored it and approached Al's table. He put a light finger on Al's shoulder. "I love this shirt. My mother was buried in one just like it." Solid comeback from George.

Al brushed the space on his red-and-white striped shirt where George's hand had been. "Well, at least *she* had taste." Another point for Al.

"I chose it. I wanted the sadistic old broad to be sent to her maker looking like a blind lesbian candy striper."

"Did you get a haircut recently?" Al asked, looking up at George's thinning hair and brushing back his own thick gray hair. "Your head looks smaller than usual."

"Your hair looks whiter than it usually does—has it needlessly called the police lately?"

"All right, enough, you two." Ms. Vaughn sipped at her coffee.

"Yes, Mother," Al said. "Georgie, you'll be taking care of the bill, yes?"

"Naturally. I know you can't afford much these days."

"Thank you, dear. I'll let you get back to your *work* now." He waved his hand, and George turned away from them, wishing them a good evening and giving Gabe and me a devilish grin.

Gabe followed me back to the service station.

"What. The hell. Was *that*?"

"They always do that. I think George spends most of his free time coming up with reads for Al. But I'm pretty sure Al wings it every time."

"We're leaving you now, boys." Al and Willa had approached the service station. "It was a wonderful meal as always. And wonderful seeing you again, Gabe." Al batted his eyelashes.

"Enough, Al. Let them clean up so they can go home." Willa pulled at his arm.

"Wait," Gabe said. "What movie would you want to watch instead of *Casablanca*?"

Al rolled his eyes. "Honestly, anything. But I was pitching *Pink Flamingos*." Gabe let out a laugh that brought a smile to Al's face. "I just wanted them all to watch Divine eat dog shit."

Gabe laughed so hard he had to hold on to the side of the service station while Al joined in. Willa and I just gave each other puzzled looks. Gabe immediately launched into a conversation about the movie, which I couldn't follow.

I started clearing their table while Willa stood there, bored and waiting for Al and Gabe to run out of steam. I didn't have the heart to tell her I didn't think it was going to happen.

Ms. Vaughn was finally able to drag Al away, and Gabe jumped in to help reset my section.

"You don't have to help me," I said.

"You've been avoiding me."

"Correct. And your helping me out is directly interfering with that."

"You also haven't answered my texts."

Also correct, and yes, that may have been more childish than avoiding him. But it didn't mean I wanted to have this conversation *in person*! Step three in the recipe for getting over someone who is in a relationship: repeat steps one and two until you die.

"I'm sorry," he said, following me and placing butter knives next to my place settings. "I know I should have told you before we . . ." His voice trailed off.

I helped him. "Kissed."

"Yeah."

"Oh, good, you *do* know what kissing is." I let out a huge, sarcastic breath. "Because I was starting to worry you didn't know the word for it."

He stared at the knife in his hands. "I just . . . I didn't know what to say."

"Well, let's revisit our first interaction. You come up to me, pretend you don't know me at all, and say, 'Hey, I'm Gabe, blah, blah, blah.' Then, literally anywhere in the three weeks after, drop the words 'my boyfriend' into our conversations. Anywhere. Anytime, with zero context, would have been fine."

"I know that. It's just complicated."

I paused, looking up from my own silverware. Complicated how? Did that mean their relationship was complicated? Or maybe, like me, he wasn't out to everyone. My friends all knew, the servers at Sunset Estates and the yearbook staff at school. But my mom didn't. Maybe that was his complication, too.

He still hadn't gone any further, so I shrugged when he looked at me. "What's complicated about it?"

"Our relationship. Him and me. It's . . . I don't know."

I helped. "Complicated."

He smirked, and it nearly killed me. "You're *so* intuitive."

I went back to the service station to grab more silverware and he followed. "And I'm also upset. Because it seemed like you were into

111

me, but you actually had a boyfriend the entire time. Like, why would you spend so much time alone with me, talking about our interests? Watching movies over the phone? Why would you invite me back to your house and show me that movie? This is manipulative behavior." Ava helped me realize that when I told her what had happened.

His face fell, and he became as serious as I'd ever seen him. "I really wasn't trying to be manipulative. I'm sorry. I . . . Ugh, now this is going to sound manipulative, too."

"Then just say it." I crossed my arms. "I mean, I'm used to it by now."

He sighed and walked past me to check and make sure no one else was coming back to the service station. Then he came back, keeping his voice low. "Because you're cute."

My face burned all the way down to my chest, which ached from my suddenly pounding heart.

"And you're funny, and I love it when you talk about food because I can see how passionate you are and it becomes infectious. And before I know it, you have me wanting to . . . I don't know, fucking bake a cake or something. When I have no talent in the kitchen *at all*."

"There's a difference between liking someone as a person and kissing them."

"I know that! I'm saying it was a mistake. But I'm allowed to be attracted to you and like who you are as a person and have a boyfriend who I also am very attracted to and like as a person. We're human! We can't just turn off our brains when we're in a relationship."

Jesus, all this was only making me feel worse. I also wasn't so sure about that. If you liked the person you were with that much, wouldn't your brain naturally keep you from developing those more-than-friends feelings for someone else?

"You don't need to turn off your brain, but one way to respect your relationship and the people around you is to actually talk about it."

His shoulders slumped again, and when he spoke, he was very quiet. "I know. It's just been . . . hard to do. Talking about it."

"Are you not out? It's okay if you aren't, and I understand why you'd want to keep it a secret. I mean, I'm out to my friends and at school, but I haven't told my mom yet."

"No, it's not that. I'm out. But it didn't exactly go the best."

My stomach clenched. Bad coming-out stories were exactly why I was scared to tell my mom. She was the only family I had left, and I didn't want to lose her, too. But I had a grotesque need to know about Gabe's experience. Like another mental layer of protection to help me prepare in case the same happened to me. I could see how he handled it and then come up with other methods to avoid the end result. Like watching a cooking fail video and seeing exactly the moment the fail started—then figuring out how to avoid that when I did it.

"What happened?" I asked.

"I was dating someone before. Back when we were sophomores. His name was Quinn. It was a secret because neither of us was out, but we would go on dates and then pretend we weren't in love when we were around other people. But we got outed. Remember my friend Kevin?"

"Kevin outed you?" I was outraged. But Gabe shook his head.

"His brother did. I told Kevin, and his brother—he was a senior—overheard. So he waited a day or so, then asked to borrow my phone

113

the next time I was at Kevin's house. He screencapped Quinn's and my texts and emailed them to himself. Printed them out. Posted them around the school."

"Are you just an asshole magnet?"

He threw his arms up. "I must have been a war criminal in a past life or some shit. Everyone at school was making fun of us. Quinn got attacked a few times. It was hell for a few weeks."

"Holy shit. I'm so sorry." I thought, once again, about the Gabe I knew before. The protective Gabe. *That's* who Quinn would have known. I pictured Gabe putting on a brave face and walking through the hallways with his head held high, protecting his boyfriend. My heart warmed, but then I remembered that this was a story with an unhappy ending. "What happened?"

Sadness clouded his face again. "Quinn tried to kill himself. He failed, thankfully. His parents came home early, and right as they opened the door, he regretted it and ran to them and told them everything. They pulled him out of school and . . . slapped my parents with a lawsuit."

"What?"

"Yeah. That's how they outed me to my family. They said that I was emotionally manipulative in the texts and that *I* was the one who printed them out and posted them all over school. The texts were us kind of having a fight after I told Kevin. Quinn got pissed at me for telling, but I said I didn't want to lie to my best friend, and I needed someone other than Quinn to talk to. His parents said that I was retaliating for him getting mad, and they sued my parents for the medical bills, his therapy, emotional trauma, and pain and suffering."

"That's bullshit."

"Of course it's bullshit. And if it had gone to trial, Quinn would have never let it go forward. I know he wouldn't." But the look on Gabe's face told me he wasn't so sure. That it was more of a hope than knowing. "My parents settled out of court at the beginning of the summer, and that's when they took away my college fund and said I couldn't go to film school."

I wanted to know why he hadn't told me any of this before. I couldn't believe it. But the more I thought about it, the more I realized he didn't tell me because he was embarrassed. He was still upset from the whole thing.

"What happened to Quinn?" I asked.

He shrugged. "Part of the settlement was that I would have no contact with him ever again. I think my parents negotiated that portion. His parents put him in the CAPA school in the city, so he doesn't go to Murphy anymore."

"I'm so sorry."

Gabe shrugged, but his eyes were glassy, like he was about to cry. "So all of a sudden film studies became 'that gay stuff.' So I stopped talking about it at home. They stopped mentioning anything to do with me being gay, and now it's just this thing we pretend never happened. I think a small part of that silence carried over into . . . me and you, getting reacquainted. Because I'm just not used to talking about my boyfriend to anyone."

"But this is someone you met since Quinn?" I just wanted to be sure. But I also didn't want to ask the boyfriend's name. I honestly just wasn't ready for that.

"I met him at the beginning of the summer. We clicked. He kind of understood what I was going through and it was nice to be able to talk to someone else about it. Someone who wasn't Kevin. He means well, but he is still a Kevin."

I laughed.

"Can we . . . start over? As friends?"

Friends. That word also nearly killed me. Disappointment spread from my stomach up through my chest, making everything shrivel like radioactive fallout. This was the first boy I had ever liked. After he left camp, I had fantasies where he returned or transferred to my school and we picked up right where we left off, eventually becoming something more. When I realized I was gay, I had daydreams about the two of us becoming a couple. Being each other's first kiss. First other things.

Then it became reality with Hank Dyer, my first . . . well, I wouldn't say "boyfriend." He was just one of the only openly gay, single guys at my school, so we went on a few dates. But we never had enough chemistry. And then there was Brad Waldorf, who I absolutely had chemistry with but who couldn't be out or in a relationship. But I was still comparing both of them to the boy I first crushed on in summer camp. The boy with the beautiful smile and the kind, protective heart.

I think I managed to get away from the emotions with Brad because he wasn't able to be out.

Brad was the first guy I had ever been with, which is whatever—it was fun and we seemed to have good chemistry, at least. But he only paid attention to me when he was drunk or when he knew we could be alone and no one would know. At first, I went along with it, but then it started to hurt. Pretending we didn't even talk in school or at parties. So I quarantined him into the physical-stuff-only section of my brain, where the emotional side couldn't reach. Eventually, that helped me clear my head and realize that things could be good in different ways. Secretive, yes, but different.

But maybe Gabe and I could be friends. I just had to cordon him off from the physical side of my brain and keep him in the emotional— no, *friend* side. The friend-al lobe of my brain, if you will. No, actually, don't, that's dumb. Just keep it the friend side of my brain.

That was what this was supposed to be from the start, wasn't it? My fake company in his phone was the Sunset Estates Allied Forces. "Allied" from "Allies." Which comes from the Latin root phrase "sans-kissing, sans-cuddling," which comes from the caveman: "Aw, shit."

Yay, friends.

"Yeah," I said. "Just . . . if you're going to be my friend, can we pretend the kiss never happened? I don't walk around kissing Ava." In fact, a lack of kissing is what gave me away as a gay to her in the first place.

"What kiss?"

Ow. I forced the best fake laugh I could muster.

CHAPTER
FIFTEEN

I SPENT THE NEXT WEEK AND A half moping after that. I mean, I wasn't really moping, because I think moping has to have some self-awareness involved. I didn't realize I had been moping until the final Saturday of September, when Ava, Morgan, and I were at the pool hall waiting for a table to open up and Ava finally kicked me.

"Why are you moping?"

"I'm not moping."

Morgan laughed. "You're absolutely moping." Ever since our bathroom pregnancy heart-to-heart, we had started hanging out with Morgan more. It benefitted us in two ways. One, she was much nicer when seating our sections—making sure everyone was spaced out timewise and helping us when we got in the weeds. But two, she was actually fun. I'd liked hanging out with her outside work before, but I'd assumed it had just been because she was at a party and finally letting loose.

At Sunset Estates she took her job more seriously than I did. And that was only because I would rather be in the kitchen. Serving the residents, I was on autopilot. I knew how to smile politely even when

I was in a bad mood; I knew the general time between courses and how to do closing chores. But I'd only been taking it *seriously* since Natalie said she was testing me. Something that still hadn't happened in practice yet.

There had been a close call where I thought she made Ms. Masters ask for lime sherbet instead of rainbow, which was the sherbet of the week. She was extra pushy about ensuring I only got it from the actual container of full lime and not the lime stripe out of the rainbow sherbet because "You can still taste the orange and raspberry flavor in the lime when it's all in the same container!"

When I asked Natalie about it, she said that wasn't one of her tests, but she assured me it was coming. I was starting to think it was all a lie, though. A carrot she dangled in front of me to torture me, only to have my application deadline come and go without a letter from her.

"I'm depressed, not mopey," I said.

Morgan leaned onto the high-top table between us, resting her chin on her hand. "Situational or clinical depression?" Oh, right. I forgot Morgan wanted to go to school for psychology.

"What's the difference?" I asked.

"Situational depression is triggered by an event," she said. "Clinical is a chemical imbalance."

Ava said before I could, "The first one."

"Excuse you, please don't speak for me. But yeah, she's right—it's the first one."

"Talking about it can help," Morgan said.

"What if I don't want to talk about it?" I asked.

Ava raised her hand. "Uh, what if I don't want to *hear* him talk about it?" I swatted her hand down, and she flicked me. "No, just because Morgan wasn't there to hear you bemoan your Gabe drama before doesn't mean I have to listen to the replay."

"Wait, *work* Gabe? Now I *need* to know the drama."

But I *really* didn't want to talk about it. And Ava was being dramatic—I wasn't the one talking about it, *she* was the one talking about it because of my depression. Situationally. She kept saying, "Just forget about him! Who cares? He's not *that* cute! You can do better!" Which was easier said than done—*I* cared; yes, he was; and no, I probably couldn't.

"He and Gabe were friends back in the day, now they're both gay, and Gabe has an oyfriendbay. Sorry for the pig Latin—I just wanted it to rhyme."

"Pig Latin aside, that about covers it."

Ava held up another finger as a point of order. "And our Tommy— ever the universal spiritualist—thinks Gabe getting a job at Sunset Estates means they are fated to be together and is thinking of giving up all his dreams to go to school in Los Angeles, with Gabe."

"I never said that!" At least not out loud to Ava, I mean. How the hell did she even figure that out?

Morgan's eyes clouded. "Oh, that's not healthy."

"You didn't have to say it," Ava said to me. "I can read context clues—asking me if I'd ever thought about going to another campus if Johns Hopkins had another one. And I talk to Gabe at work, too. He's as hell-bent as you are on going to New York or LA."

"That doesn't mean I'm thinking of going to LA."

Ava arched her eyebrow at me. "Then why aren't you doing early decision?"

"Because . . ." Because I wasn't sure which campus I wanted to go to yet. "I still don't have my letter from Natalie. Which I need for the *New York* campus, by the way."

"Do you have a backup plan if she doesn't write you one?" Morgan asked. I had already filled her in on the bizarre deal I had going with Natalie, hoping she'd give me a heads-up if she saw Natalie talking to a resident before Morgan seated them.

As far as backups, I figured I could always ask Roni for a letter. But what would she write? *I haven't worked much with Tommy, but he comes to work on time and leaves on time?* Also, there was the slight problem with her being very intimidating. But it was more of a respectful intimidation. I respected Roni so much that having a mediocre letter of recommendation from her would be so much worse. I already expected a middle-of-the-road letter from Natalie.

"Hey, guys!" I looked up to see Brad Waldorf standing over us, pool cue in hand.

"Hey, Brad," Ava said. "I saw you kicking Terry's ass over there." She pointed to a pool table where a few of the other guys on the varsity hockey team—including James, who had shouted our nicknames across the pool hall to announce our arrival—were playing what looked like Cutthroat.

"Hey," I said when he turned to me expectantly. Then he turned back to Ava and raised his shoulders, putting on a cocky smile.

"There's a reason they made me a left winger."

Ava gave him a wide grin. "Not a clue what that means, hon. Y'all almost done with that table or what?"

"I think James and Terry are playing another round, but some of the other guys are leaving. Maybe you can jump in with them?" He turned his full attention to me. "Tommy, can I . . . talk to you for a sec?"

Talk? Brad Waldorf? Usually, when he came over to me, he wasn't using his tongue to *talk*. Was the hockey team having a bake sale? Maybe James told Brad to ask me to bake a few things for them like I did for the drama club when Hank Dyer and I were trying to force chemistry that wasn't there.

"Yeah, what's up?"

His eyes flicked to Ava and Morgan, then back at me. "Actually . . ." He turned to glance around the pool hall. "Can we take it outside?"

Oh, so it was the kind of "talk" that involved tongues in other ways.

Ava shot eyes at me and barely raised her eyebrows. "Go ahead."

I gave her a *You sure?* look, and she gave a slight nod. I really did have the best friend. She knew I didn't want to talk about Gabe, but there was something else I could do to forget about him.

"Sure." I grabbed my jacket as Brad handed his pool cue over to Ava and she and Morgan walked over to James's pool table.

"Euthan-Ava!" James shouted over the music. "Morganza!"

I followed Brad, and when he left me to grab his jacket at the table I continued to the door. I headed for my car and turned it on so the heater would warm up, then pulled out my phone to see a text from Ava telling me she and Morgan would get a ride home from James. Perfect. I could use a distraction from everything, and what better way to do that than getting handsy with your no-strings-attached straight-boy friend? Two separate words, of course—he was a boy, and we were friendly. Well, more than friendly.

One time last summer my mom had to take the Sunset Estates residents on a trip to some farm out in Lancaster. She left at seven in the morning and didn't come home till almost eight that night. I learned that sex in my own bed—even a twin bed—is much better than in the back seat of a car or in the dark of someone's basement while a party raged above. It was easier. It was actually nice. More enjoyable.

Although we could barely fit on my bed if one of us wasn't on top of the other. But even after that, I was kind of surprised to see him stay. I had expected him to come over at ten a.m., then leave by ten thirty. But we hung out, I made him lunch, and we watched TV and talked. Then we went back up and did it again. But he still didn't leave. He talked while we squeezed, sweaty and naked, onto my bed and he ran his finger up and down my back while I explained the process of baking the bread for the sandwiches we'd just had.

Thinking about it in the Ball Busters Billiards parking lot got me excited again. The pool hall door swung open, and Brad scanned the parking lot. I flashed my lights at him, and he waved and marched over.

"Hey," Brad said when he ducked into the passenger seat.

"I'm thinking Planet Fitness parking lot," I said. "Around the corner, where the staff usually parks. Plus, it's eight fifty on a Saturday, so chances are it will be pretty empty."

"Huh?"

"Where we're going," I said. "You said you wanted to 'talk,' but it's not like we can do that here." I pointed up at the bright shining lights of the pool hall parking lot. "Oh! We could also try the office park down the street."

There was a moment of hesitation before he nodded and put on his seat belt. "Yeah, the office park works."

I shifted into gear and pulled out of the parking lot.

Brad was quiet the whole ride. His legs bounced up and down as he wrung his hands between them. I smiled. He would always get nervous like this before we did anything. Like it took a few minutes of kissing before he finally realized he was safe and could relax. That was the Brad I liked, not this anxious, jumping-at-shadows—or pool hall doors—Brad. I enjoyed that confidence he finally got after he was comfortable.

Once—this was way back when I first entertained the idea of the two of us getting together after we had our second secret drunken make-out session—I went to one of his hockey games, and I saw that confident Brad skating around the ice. Of course, then he ignored me after the game when I waited outside the locker room for him.

I did hope he'd be able to be happy with himself someday. But for now, what we were doing was fine.

The office park was empty save for a few cars—their owners probably in the handful of offices that were still lit. I parked in the back of the lot near the trees. Ava had told me about this spot. It was always quiet since most of the offices were empty. And if the cops pulled into the parking lot, the entrance was far enough away, and had a concrete median with bushes and flowers the cops had to drive around, giving everyone enough time to get decent.

I unbuckled my seat belt, and Brad did the same, mirroring my movements.

"So . . ." Brad said. "Uh."

Something was up with him. I mean, he was always nervous—it was actually kind of adorable. Someone like Brad—tall, eastern-European-featured, stoic Brad Waldorf—who could check the hell out of someone in a hockey rink, all of a sudden became this awkward, anxious kid who was never sure what to do or how to do it.

"You okay?" I asked.

"Yeah. I'm okay. Sorry, just a lot going on up here." He pointed to his forehead. "Um . . . Can I . . ." His voice trailed off.

"Whatever it is, yes, you can. We don't have to talk."

He looked surprised, or was that disappointment? Nah, Brad was never comfortable—when he was sober—until I made the first move. So I figured I'd try to make it a little easier for him.

"Honestly," I continued, "I have a lot on my mind tonight that I'd like to forget for a bit, so I think it's even better if we don't talk."

"Are . . . are you sure?"

Was I sure that I didn't want to talk about the sheer embarrassment of the last guy I kissed having a boyfriend? At least Brad wasn't seeing any girls.

"Absofuckinglutely."

I leaned across the center console and kissed him. At first, he wasn't responsive—maybe he did need to talk and get comfortable? Then my mind started drifting to the kiss Gabe and I had shared. *Was* it shared? Or did I kiss Gabe and he didn't kiss me back?

Then, finally, as if he could sense my mind wandering to other places I didn't want it to go, Brad began to kiss me back. He reached across the console and hefted me by the waist of my jeans. After a brief tangle of limbs, I was straddling him in the passenger seat. I reached down and pulled the reclining lever and the seat fell backward.

Brad let out an "Oof!" then chuckled.

"Sorry," I said.

"It's fine." His lips were back on mine, his hands against my neck, then one slipping back to run through my hair while the other dipped under my T-shirt—past that sensitive part of my side that made me shudder—and to my back.

Yes. This was all so much better than thinking.

CHAPTER
SIXTEEN

"LET ME ASK YOU SOMETHING," JAMES SAID, handing me a dinner slip. It was a week later, and James and I were working kitchen support together.

Oh no. But at least a bizarre James musing would get my mind off the only thing that had been repeating for the past few weeks. *Gabe has a boyfriend. And we are just friends.* Unfortunately, my dalliance—I really don't think we as a society use that word enough—with Brad Waldorf had only made me forget for approximately nineteen minutes.

Thankfully, our theme of two ships passing in the night had been holding up, and I hadn't had to train Gabe recently. If I'd had to, Natalie would absolutely have to write *attempted to murder a trainee, needs to learn how to follow through with tasks* in my letter of recommendation.

"Do you think aliens know to only abduct people without any chill? Like, they never go after dudes like Neil Diggy-T—someone who'd actually know about space stuff and physics—but they'll abduct Randy Redneck nine times in a week."

Pretty tame for a random James question. I sprinkled some microgreens on the plate and put the metal topper on it to keep it warm.

"Table twenty-one!" I shouted, hoisting the tray up and walking around James to put it under the warmers. "I think they gave up on us," I said as I went back to the stack of dinner trays and flipped the next one over. "When's the last time you even heard of anyone being abducted?"

James nodded and called out three dinners.

Dante and Roni plated and put them up for me to wipe down, add fries to the chicken breast dish, microgreen it up, and call out the table again.

This was a completely unrealistic portrayal of a working kitchen, but it was nice. We were overstaffed compared to the kitchens from the stories my dad had told me or the ones I'd seen in TV shows. A lot of the food was prepared ahead of time and kept warm for just a few hours. It wasn't a quick-fire kitchen setup where burgers came in and all had to be cooked to temperature, or where a fish would have to be filleted fresh.

The kitchen at Sunset Estates was a well-oiled machine. Until—

"Chef Roni," Natalie came in from the FDR entrance. "I need a favor."

Roni stopped scooping green beans and looked up over her greasy teal glasses, her dark eyes clouding with fury.

"Oh, shit," James said under his breath. He tucked the slips into the front pocket of his white chef's jacket and crossed his arms. I think we were both getting baked Alaska vibes.

"What's going on?" Roni asked, her voice filled with authority.

"We have a resident who brought family for dinner."

"Uh-huh." She went back to plating, now paying less attention.

"That's not so much a favor, happens all the time. Tell them welcome and we hope they enjoy the meal!"

"It's a six-top, and they want six filets. All well-done."

I could tell Roni was trying not to cringe. The one thing Chef Roni hated making more than anything was a well-done filet mignon. But this was an old folks' home, and old folks were more susceptible to foodborne illness, so she did it for them anyway.

"Not a problem," she said through half-clenched teeth as Natalie handed the slip over to James. But I knew there was something else. Natalie hadn't actually asked Roni for a favor yet, just to do her job. Trying not to smile, James tilted the dinner slip to me.

Shit.

"They would also like A.1. steak sauce."

Roni slammed her spoon down on the line, and it bounced, clattering loudly to the floor. Everyone stopped what they were doing to watch the meltdown.

"Absolutely not!" she shouted. Roni never bought A.1. steak sauce, which meant Natalie was expecting her to stop serving on the line and *create* a gourmet version of it like she was Claire Saffitz. "I'm not stopping everything I'm doing so I can make a shitty steak sauce for them to slather over their expensive leather! They can use ketchup!"

"You have a half hour to cook the steaks—I'm sure you can whip it up in that time. We don't tell the residents no." With that, Natalie smiled and left the kitchen.

Roni mumbled under her breath and flipped off the door Natalie had just walked out. She picked up the spoon from the floor and tossed it to the dish room, then grabbed a fresh one.

"Dante!" She launched into demands. "Start the damn steak sauce."

"Yes, Chef."

Roni unwrapped each vacuum-sealed filet and began throwing them on the grill behind her.

"Tommy!" She threw the sixth and final filet on the grill. "Get back here and help me on the line."

I turned to James, both of us looking surprised. This happened every once in a while, but the hierarchy was that the caller—usually Sean G. because he was nineteen and old enough to be in the kitchen—went on the line and then I would take over calling. I wasn't supposed to *be* on the line.

James had *just* turned eighteen; he was supposed to be back there. Or, hell, *I* should be the one whipping up the steak sauce, and Dante should stay on the line.

"Come on!" Roni yelled, whipping off her rubber gloves and tossing them into the trash. "James, you keep us movin', all right?"

"You got it, Chef." James used his hip to bump me out of the way and get moving. I walked as fast as my slip-resistant shoes would allow and went to the other side of the line. My muscles felt tense, like they were about to pop from excitement. I glanced up at the rest of the serving staff, but none of them were paying attention anymore. To them, the excitement was over. They had their own shit to deal with, and none of them realized what a big deal this was.

James did; he gave me a toothy grin and two thumbs up as I put on two pairs of food-prep gloves Roni handed me.

"All right," she said, pulling on her own fresh gloves. "You know how it's done, right?"

"Yes, Chef."

Roni clapped her gloved hands together and said, "Let's keep it goin', keep it goin'!"

James started calling.

"Chicken, mashed, greens, peas."

I plated the chicken marsala—spooning a bit of mushroom marsala gravy over the top—and handed the plate off to Roni as James called out the next plate.

"Chicken, sweet, greens."

I plated the chicken as Roni threw an oven mitt toward me. "Go grab the sweet potatoes out of the oven and check how Dante's doing on that shit sauce."

"Yes, Chef." I passed the chicken plate to her and grabbed the oven mitt. I felt like I was buzzing. This was the most exciting day I'd ever had at Sunset Estates—even more exciting than the day Willard Humphries got drunk and started flirting with the female residents until a fight broke out.

I shuffle-walked back to the dish room, grabbing a fork as fast as I could, and passed the walk-in, where Dante emerged with jugs of Worcestershire, ketchup, and Dijon mustard. "How's it going, Dante?"

He smirked, probably seeing the excitement on my face. "Good, kid. I'll take as long as I need."

I opened the ovens and poked the sweet potatoes with the fork. It slid in easily. They were done. I grabbed a pair of tongs and put the oven mitt on, pulling out the sheet of sweet potatoes and hitting the oven door shut with my hip.

On my way past the grill, I noticed that the steaks were starting to drip into the flames below them.

"Behind," I called out. Roni moved out of the way as I put the tray down on the metal line and began transferring the sweet potatoes into the empty chafing dish. "Do you need to flip those, Chef?" I asked, flicking my head in the direction of the grill.

"Ah, shit. Yes. Here, let me do this—go flip those for me." Roni took the tray and tongs before I could argue. I glanced over to the servers again. Were they seeing this? This was wild! I grabbed the long tongs used for the grill and gently wiggled each filet before I flipped it, trying to match the grill marks to the other side.

I imagined doing this in a *real* restaurant during a *real* rush. Everything going so fast and chaotic. Yeah, it would be annoying after, like, the first week or whatever, but still. This was the exciting stuff. This was when I would be using all the tricks and techniques I'd learn from the faculty at La Mère.

But then my excitement deflated, like someone punching a bowl of rising dough. I *legally* wasn't supposed to be back here. There was a reason you had to be eighteen to work the kitchen, and it was because OSHA—Occupational Safety and Health Administration—made the rules for workplaces to follow. We had to have a whole two-day training session on it when we first started.

I mean, I didn't care about it. I did more dangerous stuff than flipping a steak at home.

But Natalie, the rule cop herself, would have a conniption if she came back and saw me working in the kitchen. There'd be another blowup between her and Roni. I'd have to sign some OSHA form while she reminded me I'm not allowed to work in the kitchen, and that would mean bye-bye to my letter of recommendation. Forget trying to please her after that.

If I impressed Roni in the short amount of time before Natalie came back, maybe she would write me a letter. But that wouldn't have the same clout as Natalie. Roni had never worked for Chef Louis.

Something on the other side of the line clattered, shaking me from my thoughts.

"Sorry!" Gabe was picking up a glass of spilled cranberry juice and mopping it up with a towel. Then he glanced up at me and gave me a wide-eyed look of *What are you doing back there?*

I returned it with a similar look that said, *I know, right?*

He just grinned. Damn him and those dimples.

Seeing Gabe there, watching me—smiling at me, *knowing* how big a deal this was for me—brought every awful, horrible, terrible, no-good, very bad, etcetera, feeling right back. And, dammit, it was not good. Because then I started thinking.

Roni's letter of recommendation might not hold the same weight as Natalie's, but maybe I could go back to my original idea of submitting a supplemental video with my La Mère application. I still didn't have the equipment or the wherewithal to make my own video. But I knew someone who did.

Gabe—Mr. "I Want an Oscar before I'm Thirty" De La Hoya—took one last look at me on the way out the door. He had said things were complicated with his boyfriend. And he'd also said I was cute and that he liked me. But maybe he just needed to be reminded of that some more. No, I didn't want him to cheat on his boyfriend—we'd

133

already kissed, and that was bad enough. But maybe if he realized there was someone else he could connect with, someone who wasn't complicated . . .

And maybe hanging out more often would make him realize that.

"Tommy!" Roni snapped me from my thoughts. "What's going on with them steaks?"

I flipped the last steak and joined her at the line. "All good, Chef."

Roni turned to check my work and said, "Great job, Tommy. James! Keep it goin'!"

We kept it going.

As it turned out, I wouldn't have to ask for a letter of recommendation from Roni—at least not yet. Dante finished the sauce as the steaks finished cooking, and we swapped back before Natalie was any the wiser. But for the rest of the dinner service I kept thinking about Gabe and his film projects. Once Roni dropped the last dinner under the heat lamp, she clapped her hands. "Great work tonight, everyone." We all thanked her. "Tommy, when you turn eighteen?"

"Uh, February."

"Remember to have George put you in the kitchen on a Sunday brunch when I'm here."

I tried my hardest not to smile. "Okay, thanks, Chef!" She gave me a thumbs-up as she and Dante went out to the loading dock for some fresh garbage air and to decompress.

So she *did* like me! If I screwed up Natalie's task list, Roni would be a great backup. Especially if I could get Gabe to agree to work a little movie magic for me.

James waited until they were gone before hitting my arm. "Look at you, Bahama Mama, getting a brunch shift four months out!"

"They're going to make you, me, and Sean G. fight over kitchen duties."

James shrugged. "Eh, you and *Seen* can swap off. I just hate old people. Keep me in here as KS and I'm cool."

I had to go find Ava in her section and tell her. Just about the working-on-the-line part. Not the Gabe part.

That part still needed a little finesse.

CHAPTER
SEVENTEEN

THE FOLLOWING WEDNESDAY WAS THE OCTOBER birthday night at Sunset Estates. I was in the private dining room showing Ava a meme on my phone when the door from the kitchen opened. I tucked my phone in my apron, and we both turned around to see who it was, pretending we were setting the table in front of us.

"I'm here to bribe you," Morgan said, closing the door behind her. Ava and I smirked at each other and pulled out two chairs to sit down, motioning for Morgan to take another.

"Please, step into our office."

Morgan sat down, giving a quick glance back. "How many other people have come to you so far?"

"You're the first," Ava lied.

"Bullshit. But I checked the schedule and you're both working days I'm hosting for the next *two* weeks."

"What do you propose?" I asked.

"If you have a section, I seat everyone else's tables twice before I seat you once. Then at the end of the night I help *only* you clear and reset your tables and I complete your chores for you."

Ava glanced at me, her eyebrows raised. Like me, she was impressed.

"Do we give her a chance to counter other offers, or are we doing silent auction rules?" I asked.

Morgan frowned and crossed her arms. "What better offer could you have gotten?"

"Mackenzie says she'll take every other table we get while we're working with her," Ava said.

I continued. "And she'll bread and water every table we have, get our linens, and presort the silverware for our section and hide it from everyone else."

Morgan seemed to be thinking. "For two weeks?"

"Three."

"She's off the whole last week of October," Morgan said.

"How do you know?" I asked. "The schedule for that week isn't even posted yet."

"She asked Natalie for time off because she's on the Halloween dance committee."

"That sneaky witch," Ava said.

"So her offer's off the table," Morgan said with confidence. "Who else?"

"That's still a pretty cushy two weeks of work," I said. But she was right. There was no way Ava and I would go for that. But she could be a close second-place contender.

"Bryce offered us twenty bucks each," Ava said.

Morgan rolled her eyes.

"Henry offered a couple of assorted gift cards. Connor said he would let Ava punch him in the jaw."

"Twice," Ava interrupted, a little too giddily.

"And . . . I think that's it." I stopped myself from telling Morgan that her ex, Luke, said he would give us the remainder of his current vape cartridge. There was a little over a third left, and I was definitely leaning more toward that one than the others. Ava and I had a tradition that was going on two years now. Each Halloween we would get a little tipsy—either share a bottle of prosecco she nabbed from her uncle or split a gummy we would buy from Luke—and eat candy we were supposed to be giving out while watching the worst Halloween-themed cooking tutorials or episodes of *UNHhhh* on YouTube.

Morgan seemed to detect a hesitation, figure out what it was, and let it go. "So I'm at least near the top?"

Ava bobbed her head back and forth. "You're up there. First or second."

"All right, I can deal with that."

Before we could discuss any more, the door opened, and we all tensed, probably expecting it to be Natalie.

Gabe gave us a quick glance, then looked around the room. "I was starting to think you lied to me and I'd never see this room in use."

Oh, that's right. He hadn't worked a birthday night yet. Before I could say anything, Ava gasped.

"Is this Gabe-y-Waby's first b-day?"

"It is." He looked to me. "Birthday night?"

"Second Wednesday of every month is birthday night. Residents who have a birthday that month are invited to dine with us here, in the private dining room."

"Yes!" Ava jumped up and started channeling Kristen Wiig from the SNL Super Showcase Spokesmodels sketch—another YouTube Halloween night favorite. "In the lovely private dining room, you and your guests feast upon snapper soup, a surf and turf delight, and look! What's that in the corner?"

I lowered my voice and tried to sound like Bill Hader. "Well, it looks like birthday cake to me."

Gabe approached the massive sheet cake that Dante had spent the afternoon decorating. Instead of buttercream roses, Dante had fashioned buttercream pumpkins and fall leaves. Scrawled across the white buttercream in brown, red, and orange icing were the words *Happy Birthday, October Babies!*

"October *babies?*" Gabe asked.

Yes. Babies.

Gabe looked at the menu on each bread plate. "Holy shit, we're serving lobster tonight?"

Morgan snorted and pointed at Ava and me. "No. *They* are serving lobster tonight."

The menu had lobster and filet mignon as the main entrée with green beans almondine and roasted red bliss potatoes, no other choice—unless they asked, of course. Because rule number one is "never tell the residents no."

"So we get leftover lobster?" Gabe's eyes went wide. Morgan let out a loud laugh, and Ava bit her lip.

"Too late, new guy," Morgan said.

"They buy enough lobster tails for the residents who RSVP." Though that was kind of a lie. They bought enough for the residents and a few extras just in case one or two forgot to RSVP, showed up with an extra guest, or one of the lobster tails jumped off a plate and landed on the floor. "The only way there's leftovers is if they change their mind and don't show up."

"But if there are leftovers . . ." Ava said, knowing full well there would be.

I finished. "We get first dibs."

Morgan closed her eyes like she was in bliss. "And I don't know how she does it, but Roni makes the most perfect lobster. I ordered lobster from a nice place I made Luke take me to for Valentine's last year, and it was garbage. Roni makes her lobster tail so tender and delicate. You don't even need a knife." She fanned herself for good measure.

Ava shrugged. "And everyone else has already made their offers."

Gabe turned to me, pretending to be outraged. "So much for allies."

"Everyone for themselves on birthday night."

"And what do we serve?" Gabe asked.

"The other dining rooms get a . . ." I paused, trying to think of the perfect way to phrase it. "Knock-off birthday night dinner."

"But they do get the snapper soup!" Morgan added.

Just thinking about it gave me shivers. "Yes. They do get the snapper soup." Snapper soup—a southeastern Pennsylvania delicacy—is absolutely disgusting. It's thick, chunky, and stringy all at once. And made with real turtle meat. I always get sad seeing those shells being discarded when Dante strains them from the stock.

Morgan added, "It sucks for you guys in the regular dining rooms because Natalie is hounding the soup chafer to make sure none of you are sneaking nips of the sherry that's floated on top."

Ava pointed to the cake. "And instead of this cake, there's chocolate and vanilla sheet cake in the dessert fridge."

"It's arguably a better cake," Morgan said.

"It's better *cake*," Ava said. "But this one has better frosting."

Gabe sighed with disappointment. "So what are we serving for the entrée?"

"Monkfish," I said. I turned to Ava, pretending to think. "And . . . the second entrée option is . . . is it beef?"

Ava smiled and nodded, going right back into her Kristen Wiig impression and not taking her eyes away from Gabe. "It *could* be beef."

The PDR doors opened again; this time it was Natalie. She gave us a polite look as she gazed over the tables, probably looking for something to fault us on. But it didn't matter because one, there was nothing to fault us on. And two, the PDR during birthday night was George's domain.

Probably figuring that out, she just kept her eyebrows raised and her fake grin plastered on. "Gabe, Morgan, lineup is about to start." Morgan and Gabe left, and I followed Natalie out.

"Excuse me, Natalie." She stopped in front of the time clock and spun on her heels. "Sorry, I just wanted to check if our deal was still on. I haven't had any big requests come up from the residents." I mean, there had been a bunch of big requests—the September sherbet situation, Mrs. McMenamin asking for wasabi aioli for her tuna steak, Mr. Wynne sending back three cuts of prime rib because they were "undercooked"—but the fact that Natalie hadn't admitted to any of them meant they probably weren't hers. She liked to take credit for her torture. But if there was even a chance one of them was, maybe she'd be impressed that I thought they weren't difficult.

"Of course!" Her voice was saccharine. "Just making sure you're always on your toes!"

I turned up the charm and gave her a polite nod. "Thank you very much. I appreciate you."

"And I you!" She spun on her heels again and headed down the hall.

Early decision was clearly out if she wasn't going to write me a letter before January. Not that it had ever really been in. That all worked for Ava, but I still hadn't finished my essay. Early decision was too much pressure. When you applied for early decision at La Mère, you also had to choose the campus. And I still hadn't decided which campus I wanted to go to—which, yes, despite what I said to Ava and Morgan, might have been a newer development because the universe brought Gabe back into my life, and his number one school was USC.

If the universe had put us together again, after so much time, maybe it was for a good reason. Could all this mean we were supposed to be more than friends with complications?

I'd need to know sooner rather than later if there really could be more between me and Gabe. If he were to, say, help me with my video, it would be a nice, non-homewrecky way we could spend more time together. Besides, if Natalie was going to use the letter of recommendation as a way to get me to fall in line, I needed to figure out a backup plan. I had to take charge and not just rely on her or her connections.

But step one to getting all that together was getting Gabe on board.

CHAPTER
EIGHTEEN

BIRTHDAY NIGHT—AS LONG AS YOU'RE WORKING in the PDR—is amazing. Everyone comes in all at once. We double-check that no one has any shellfish or nut allergies, then put specialty breads—croissants, a cranberry walnut bread, and fresh sourdough—on the tables and give everyone Aqua Panna, so there's no need to refill water pitchers. After that, Ava and I split the room down the middle and start taking orders. Basically, it's just making sure that everyone is okay with the surf and turf and that there are no special requests—remember, rule number one: never tell a resident no.

Then it's grabbing the Caesar salads and snapper soups and waiting until Roni has the entrees ready.

Most of the time we sit in the hallway next to the time clock, talking and relaxing, with the occasional quick spin around the room to check on water and ask if anyone needs anything else.

After Gabe and Morgan left for lineup, George came in to do a quick glance over the tables before he opened the private dining room doors, smiling jovially. George was always in charge of birthday night—I think Natalie was jealous—so he always made sure his favorites were working it with him. And, yes, Ava and I were probably his favorite favorites.

"Looking great, gang," he said, moving one fork slightly to the left. "All set?"

"All set," I said. Ava gave a thumbs-up and an enthusiastic smile.

George opened the doors, and the line of residents began to drift in to find their seats. The place cards were massive and written in dark Sharpie, but that didn't stop them from picking up each one, glancing at it, and then putting it facedown before continuing to the next.

If we let them do that to every setting, we wouldn't serve dinner till nine, so George began telling them where their seats were while Ava and I helped the residents we knew by name.

After I helped Greta Von Schmitt and her friend Cheryl DeWitt find their seats, I turned to see Ms. Vaughn and Al whispering back and forth with less-than-impressed looks on their faces.

I walked over to them. "How can you be complaining already?"

Al's face brightened, and he flicked a hand in George's direction. "Did he bathe in cologne today?"

"Follow me. You guys are over here on my side of the room." I had already seen Al's and Willa's names on the table and told Ava which side was mine. I pulled out the chair for Willa—her lemons already placed next to her water glass—as Al whispered into my ear, "I have something for you. Don't let me forget when we leave."

I shook my head. "Whatever it is, you know I can't accept it."

Batting the words away with a wave of his hand, he sat down. I knew exactly what he was giving me. He was early—Halloween wasn't for a few more weeks. Every holiday, Al would pass a card to me when no one was looking. I would always pretend I couldn't pos-sibly accept it—because we weren't supposed to accept any kind of gifts or tips from the residents—even though I appreciated it so much. Every card, without fail, had two crisp hundred-dollar bills in it.

It didn't matter the holiday. One Memorial Day I took his hand and tried to push the card back to him.

"It's too much," I had said. "I really can't accept it."

"Bullshit, you're underpaid and I can't take it with me when I go." He pushed the card back at me, slipping it into my apron. "You're a good kid, and you put up with my shit. I'd say you've earned it."

I still pretend I can't accept it, because I shouldn't, but I don't argue as much anymore.

"Ms. Vaughn," I said, pouring water into their goblets. "Are you a Libra or a Scorpio?" I knew Al's birthday was in March.

"Scorpio," she said, putting her napkin in her lap and reaching for one of the lemon slices.

"She's the definition of a Scorpio, kid."

"Look who's talking, you old ram," I whispered. Willa snickered, and Al gave her a sassy look.

Halfway through the shift, we pulled all the servers in from the other dining rooms to sing "Happy Birthday." I moved back to stand next to Gabe.

"Can I talk to you after work?" I whispered.

"Oh no. Am I in trouble?" He raised his eyebrows at me in a way I would have considered flirtatious if we hadn't already had the just-friends talk.

"The most." Okay, maybe I was the one being flirty.

He smirked as everyone started singing. "I love that for me."

After we sang, the rest of the servers went back to their dining rooms and George played the game where he asked the birthday people to raise their hands. Then "Lower your hand if you were born after [date]," always starting with the current year to a smattering of forced laughter before going on to 1970 and back from there.

Mrs. Donnelly was the last hand up, born on October 13, 1929. She then shuffled her little walker over to the cake, made the ceremonial cut, and George served.

Meanwhile, Ava and I ducked out to take stock of the lobster and filet. Filets were on the menu every day, but they were made to order. On birthday night, Roni had a general idea of how many needed to be made, so she made just as many filets as lobster tails.

There were three filets and three lobster tails left.

James took a filet, but Sean G. didn't want anything and left everything else for us. We plated two lobster tails on one plate and wrapped it up, writing Morgan's name on it. Then we put a lobster tail and a filet on another plate and wrote Luke's name on it.

Neither of us wanted the last filet, so we decided to give it to Mackenzie because we knew Bryce wasn't good for the money, and even with two weeks of helping instead of three, it was a better deal for us.

Once the cake was eaten, Ava and I stepped back into the private dining room, waiting for the residents to leave so we could clean up. We didn't have to reset the tables because they wouldn't be set again until the next private party or birthday night.

Al and Willa were the last two at their table, waiting for the table closest to the door to get up and leave so Al could slip me the Halloween card without drawing attention.

"Did you behave?" I asked.

Al acted offended for half a second before Willa said, "He went off on Reagan to Mary-Sue Humphries."

Al's offense turned quickly to glee as I shook my head.

"He's dead," I said, keeping my voice low. "Why do you always antagonize her over it?"

He didn't bother to keep his voice down. "That bastard let thousands of my friends die—"

"*You* had *thousands* of friends?" Willa interrupted with a sly grin.

"You're right. That bastard let *hundreds* of thousands of my *family* die. I can drag his filthy dead corpse as often as I want."

"He also told her that when Mitch McConnell dies, he's going to move close to wherever he gets buried and urinate on his grave every morning."

Al shrugged. "I am."

"And I'll be sad to see you go, Al," I said.

He pointed a finger at me, and his eyebrows pinched together. "You'd better not be here longer than you need to. You're better than this shithole."

I took a glance at the table by the door; they were all standing up. Al knew what he was doing. The more he cursed and talked down on conservative Republicans, the more everyone wanted to avoid him.

I lowered my voice and bent closer between him and Willa. "Hey, as far as shitholes go, this is a pretty nice one."

Al laughed and Willa almost smirked. "For us. Not for you. You gotta go out and start a bakery or open up your own restaurant."

"I'll get right on that, Al."

He gave a quick glance back as the last table left and pulled a wrinkled orange envelope out of his pocket. "To get you started."

"Thanks, Al." I tucked the card into my apron as George came back into the private dining room.

"Oh!" Al stood, acting scared. "Little early for Halloween masks, isn't it, George?"

"You don't like it?" George touched his cheek. "I had the shop special-make it to look like you."

While Ava collected our payment from Luke, I went to Gabe's car. He stood by the passenger side, waiting for me. His sleeves were rolled up, and the first four buttons of his tux shirt were unbuttoned. It was extremely unfair for me to like such an attractive person and not be able to kiss him.

"I would like your help with something," I said.

"Shoot."

"How good are you at making movies?"

He wiggled his eyebrows at me. "What *kind* of movies?"

Very unfair. "Not *those* kinds. Remember the school I'm applying to?"

"Boner school."

"Sure. I want to make a video to submit with my application." Gabe tilted his head at that, suddenly very interested. "My plan is to have it be a little like some of my favorite cooking channels on You-Tube, maybe five minutes tops? Do you think you could help me?"

I had two reasons for this. One, he wanted to go to film school, so maybe this would be a fun challenge for him that would make me look even more professional when I submitted it to La Mère. Two, it would force us to spend time together. Outside of work. The two of us, sharing something we both loved together. What better way to get him to see that I might be someone he could like more than his "complicated" boyfriend? If it went smoothly, maybe he'd see how *un*complicated I could be. Basically, I just wanted him to think of me the next time he heard Taylor Swift's "You Belong with Me."

You know, as one does.

"Absolutely," he said, beaming. "I'd love to help! When does it need to be done by?"

"End of January?" The deadline for my La Mère application was the end of February, so the longer we dragged it out, the more time we'd have to spend together.

"Perfect. I'll need to see some of the videos you're talking about so I can get storyboards going."

"I don't know what that means, but I can pick some videos. Then we can get together and watch them." I could have just sent him some links, but what would be the fun in that? This way, we'd be watching them and analyzing them alone in the carriage-house studio.

I promised I'd get working on them when I got home, then went back to my car, where Ava was waiting with a look of suspicion.

"What?" I asked as I ducked in, avoiding her gaze. I was doing nothing untoward. I was only giving Gabe more opportunity to see me be passionate about food. And maybe have him thinking more about what *else* I could be passionate about?

CHAPTER
NINETEEN

I HAD JUST FINISHED WRAPPING THE FINAL salad dressing when Gabe rounded the corner with a tray of cleared plates and utensils from one of his tables. Here we were in the last week of October, and he was already in the casual dining room. That usually didn't happen until halfway through your first year.

"First day in CDR on your own," I said. "Check out the fast mover."

I hoped Natalie was taking note of how well he'd been doing since his training ended.

"Actually . . ." He set the tray down and moved around the salad bar toward me. "This is my *second*. Jake had to call out on Sunday brunch, and I took his section."

I raised my eyebrows, impressed, as he peeled the plastic wrap off the cucumbers and used tongs to snatch one out.

"What are your Halloween plans?" he asked.

"Ava and I hang out and watch Halloween-themed cooking and music videos on YouTube. It's a fun time. You should come by. We can finally watch the videos you promised to rip off for me." I'd pushed hard for the first week or so, trying to schedule a time for us to get together and watch the videos I'd chosen, but Gabe had been busy with a school film project. He offered to watch over the phone, but I said I'd rather explain some of what I wanted in person. Which, yes, is a total lie—Gabe probably knows more about the film techniques the YouTube cooking folks use than I do. It had been a while since we'd hung out, just the two of us.

"Your video will *not* be a rip-off—it will be an original with plenty of homage! Not going to the Halloween dance at your school?"

"No." I tightened the plastic wrap on the cukes and gave him a death stare. "*I* don't have a *boyfriend* to go with."

Gabe pretended to be annoyed, but his ears turned red. He went back to his tray but didn't pick it up. "We're actually having a party at my place tonight. My parents are out of town. You and Ava should come."

A party? Tonight? Why didn't he invite me sooner? I may have been more proactive in trying to get Gabe to hang out outside of work these past couple weeks, but so far we still hadn't met the elusive boyfriend. Ava would occasionally ask when we were going to meet him, but Gabe would say he was working or he had something due for school.

Sometimes we would hang out as a group—Ava, me, Morgan, Gabe, and his best friend, Kevin—but Kevin was tediously straight. He flirted nonstop with Ava, and if I wasn't wrong, Ava seemed to be enjoying the attention. I'd asked her about it on our way home one night and she just shrugged and said, "I have a type, and it's dorky white boys who are bound to disappoint me. It's how I keep myself humble until I find Mr. Right."

Gabe also didn't change his Netflix password on me, so one night I'd texted him that I was looking for a movie and asked which one to watch.

We texted through the movie *Chef*, which was absolutely amazing.

At work I was a little flirtatious, doing what Ava and a few other people said he had been doing to me. We texted more than we spoke on the phone, and when we did text, there was a definite undercurrent of sex. At least from me there was. Our social media interactions were pretty tame, but I did notice he never posted pictures of his boyfriend. He would use the word "we" when talking about something, but never a name. He never tagged a guy in his posts, other than his friends, and he never posted pictures of him and another guy.

What did that mean?

Maybe the guy wasn't out, so Gabe couldn't post pictures of them together. But if there's one thing I know about homophobes, it's that their brains will make major leaps to create a narrative where two guys *aren't* boyfriends. Look at all the historical "bachelors" who lived with "good friends." So why couldn't Gabe post pictures of another guy who was just his "good friend"?

My first thought: Maybe Gabe didn't like him that much? He never talked about him—which, yes, that could be because it would create awkwardness with me. But even Kevin didn't talk about him. Though that could be because he was too busy flirting with Ava.

It was extremely frustrating. Ava and I had done a fair amount of cybersleuthing to try to figure out who it could be, but had gotten nowhere.

"Anyone else from Sunset going to the party?" I asked. Ava

thought maybe the boyfriend was someone from Sunset Estates.

But everyone knew everyone else's secrets in Sunset Estates. Except for the big stuff.

"I invited Morgan," he said. "And Mackenzie and Connor said they were coming." Mackenzie and Connor were dating, so it wasn't them. "Then just you, Ava, and Luke."

Ava walked into the salad bar with a tub of napkins to fold.

"You want to go to Gabe's Halloween bash tonight?" I asked her, trying to keep my voice calm.

She looked at Gabe. "Costume party?"

He shrugged. "If you want."

"Are *you* dressing up?" she asked.

"I have to. I'm the host."

"Then it's a costume party. And yes. We're in."

Gabe perked up. "Awesome! See you guys then." He picked up his tray and his face dropped. "Oh . . . and, uh, every time I pass through here on the way back to my section for the next forty minutes."

I laughed as he fled.

"Think we'll finally meet the boyfriend tonight?" she asked.

"I do." If Gabe's boyfriend *wasn't* there, what kind of boyfriend would he be? What was even the purpose of having a boyfriend if he wasn't going to spend time with you?

Plus, it was time for me to figure out who I was up against, and why it was so complicated.

CHAPTER
TWENTY

AFTER WORK, AVA AND I THREW TOGETHER a quick couples' costume—full disclosure, it was a recycled costume from Sophie Farnsworth's Spring Fling–themed birthday party last summer. Ava and I had both won the Goodwill search the afternoon before the party, just as panic began to set in. As soon as we walked through the doors, there they were: two mannequins, one wearing a polyester seafoam-green three-piece tuxedo with black piping, a frilly shirt, and a matching seafoam-green bow tie, and the other wearing a dark-green lamé dress with an alternating lime-and-hunter-green mermaid skirt.

We looked hideous. It was perfect. And even more perfect tonight with the new Halloween spin we put on it.

Morgan—dressed as a witch—offered to drive us so we could drink, and we got to Gabe's around nine. We were worried about being early, but based on the number of cars in the driveway, and those lining the dark street along his property, we had nothing to worry about.

The carriage-house doors were wide open, and orange and purple lights ran from the wraparound porch to the carriage house and back. There were jack-o'-lanterns of assorted sizes along the drive, and the front porch was decorated like a house of horrors—scarecrows, skeletons, three witch dummies surrounding a bubbling cauldron, bats hanging from the ceiling. The windows on the second floor were all lit by strobe lights while "Riboflavin-Flavored, Non-Carbonated, Polyunsaturated Blood" drifted from speakers hidden all over the front yard.

"Holy shit," Ava said. "Gabe's rich."

"And really into Halloween," Morgan said.

We stood on the drive for a bit, scanning the people in costumes and looking for Gabe or anyone else we might know.

"Should we get a drink?" I asked, pointing to the carriage house. Ava led the way, and I locked eyes with everyone I passed, trying to recognize Gabe.

There was a keg in the center of the empty garage with a line that led out the carriage-house doorway. To the left was a small bar with a pirate mixing drinks. *Expensive* drinks. I noticed all the liquor was actual brand names, which meant they weren't the Russian-inspired off-brand vodka served at most of the parties I'd been to. None of the bottles even had handles.

We skipped the beer line and went to the pirate.

"These aren't for everyone," the pirate said, before we even got within three feet of him. "VIPs only." He took a sip from his own Solo cup just to be a dick about it.

"Oh, right." Ava hit my arm. "Told you we should have splurged for the VIP meet and greet."

I hit my forehead. "Curse my frugality!"

"We're friends of Gabe's, dude," Ava said, stepping forward and snatching a cup from the table. "He owns the house."

He scrunched up the eye that wasn't behind a patch. "Yeah, *dude*, I know who he is." He grabbed for the cup, but Ava pulled it back.

Then someone called Ava's name from across the room. The three of us turned to see Kevin waving from the keg. He turned back to the guy he'd been talking to and excused himself to join us. He had smeared black-and-white paint on his face and a wavy black wig. He also wore obscenely tight leather pants and platform boots.

"What are you supposed to be?" Ava asked.

"I'm Sloppy Kiss!" He smirked and motioned to his ratty T-shirt and messy makeup.

"That's promising," Ava said, just loud enough for me and Morgan to hear. Then Kevin turned his attention back to the pirate.

"They're cool, Vic. Gabe works with them."

Vic the Pirate didn't seem impressed, but he still handed cups to me and Morgan—who refused it. "Ice is over there. Make your own drinks." With that, he left and Kevin moved around the bar to watch over the cups.

Ava and I smiled politely at Vic as he left the carriage house. Ava and Kevin started their heavy flirting, and I took Ava's cup to the bar.

"I'm starting to be happy that Gabe has a boyfriend," I told Morgan as I mixed a stronger drink than I probably needed to. "He doesn't have one friend who isn't a dick."

Morgan shrugged, looking over at Ava and Kevin. "Kevin's all right."

"Gabe told me he had to *train* him not to use 'gay' as an insult."

Morgan smirked. "Oh, train him how?"

I retched while she laughed.

"Teenage boys are stupid and say very stupid things. We hung out with them at Amber's last month after you guys left, and they weren't so bad. I've met a lot worse Murphy boys than Gabe's friends."

I brought Ava her drink, and she—ever the room reader—asked Kevin where Gabe was. Kevin spun, scanning the garage and drive-way, but I spotted him first. Gabe was heading toward us from the house, wearing a well-fitted astronaut suit.

"Whoa," I said, loud enough only for Ava to hear. She nudged me.

Gabe's eyes went wide as he gave us an up-and-down. "Wow, you guys look great."

"Thanks!" Ava curtsied in her mermaid dress.

"Eighties slasher movie victims?" he asked. "*Prom Night II?*"

"You *would* think it's a movie," I said. "We're just a dead prom king and queen." Ava had done our makeup, putting a little blood spilling from our mouths and noses, but the crown and tiara from our eight-ies prom king and queen costumes came from winning the costume contest at Sophie's party.

"Well, you look great either way," he said, holding out a cup to toast us. We clinked our plastic Solo cups together. "And Morgan, I love your—"

"You don't have to pretend I put in any more effort than throwing on a black dress and a witch hat." She shrugged and spun the witch hat around. "I'm not big on Halloween."

"Gabe sure is," Ava said, looking up at the skeleton and pumpkin lights hanging from the carriage-house rafters.

"Our kind usually is," I said.

"Right, but this . . ."

"Yeah." Gabe looked up at the lights with pride. "You guys should come by on Halloween *night*. My family goes all out. We decorate the front yard, and we turn the porch into a haunted house walk-through. All my uncles, aunts, and cousins come over and play different roles."

I looked at the porch, already half-decorated for the haunted house. Then everything clicked into place. Why this place had looked familiar when Gabe first brought me here.

"Holy shit!" I said. "I've been here!"

Gabe frowned. "Yeah . . . You've come over before."

"No, no, for Halloween."

I walked out of the carriage house to the driveway, taking it all in. Gabe, Morgan, and Ava followed. It had looked familiar when we first pulled up, but I had been too distracted by how big the house and its property was.

"My dad took me here when I was . . . I don't know, six? Seven, maybe?" I turned back to Gabe and gave him a smirk. "It scared the shit out of me."

Gabe pumped a fist in celebration. "Your dad has good taste."

I didn't correct the present tense.

"Oh my God," Ava said, jumping on the moment—probably knowing full well that I was spiraling into Sad Nostalgia Land about my dad. "That means the two of you were probably seven-year-old ghost ships passing in the haunted night."

"We were!" Gabe did an adorable little dance in his space suit and beckoned for us to follow him as he walked up onto the porch. He pointed to a small stand in front of a pillar. "Do you remember a kid vampire who popped out from this corner?"

Holy shit, I did. My heart raced at the memory. The stand was painted black and hid most of the white support column that was a real architectural feature of the porch. And when Gabe stood on top of it, hiding behind a black cape, trick-or-treaters wouldn't see him. Until he opened the cape and hissed through his plastic fangs.

"And you were tied to that pole." I pointed. "So it looked like you were going to lunge out at us, but the rope stopped you from falling."

Gabe jumped up and down, excited, reminding me again of that spooky kid vampire. "Yes!"

Ava bit her cup, trying to hide a smile as she gently kicked me. Thank God I was wearing a layer of white makeup. No one could see me blush.

"Anyway, my little cousin Amelia gets to be the vampire now." Gabe's eyes went wide again as he looked behind us. "Oh! Babe! Come meet my friends from work!"

Babe.

My heart stopped racing, and the excitement in my belly evaporated—like a vampire bursting to ashes in the sunlight. I followed Gabe's eyes as a guy pushed between Ava and me and put his arm around Gabe's shoulders. "Guys, this is my boyfriend, Victor."

"We've met, actually," the pirate said.

Gabe gave us a confused look. Ava put out her hand. "Not officially. Ava."

"Vic, nice to meet you." He shook her hand and then put one out to me, finally cordial.

"Tommy," I said, fully numb. Morgan introduced herself, but I barely heard any of it.

Vic tried on a charming smile. "Sorry about before. You know how these parties get."

"No problem," Ava said.

"He was *supposed* to be the Dread Pirate Roberts, but he misunderstood the assignment," said Gabe.

"No," Vic said, his fake smile dropping. "You didn't tell me it was a specific pirate from a specific movie."

"*Princess Bride*!" Morgan pointed.

"Yes!" Gabe said. "Thank you! And I was going to be Inigo Montoya, but . . . he showed up like this." He motioned to Vic, who, in addition to the eye patch that was now on his forehead—above his eye—wore a white shirt, raggedy vest, and cutoff khakis. He also had stubble that I was pretty sure wasn't makeup. "Thank God I had this backup astronaut costume."

Ava groaned. "That would have been so good. Way to suck, Vic." Ava does this thing where she says what she really means but makes it sound like a joke. I love my friends.

Vic actually smiled, probably not even realizing Ava would pluck his eyes out if I asked her to. "Well, I think you look cuter as an astronaut anyway." He took Gabe's chin between his thumb and forefinger and kissed him.

"Shit," Ava said, turning to me and coming up with an excuse on the fly. "We were supposed to go find that girl we were talking to.

Would you boys excuse us real quick? Can we get you a drink?"

Gabe held up his cup. "I'm good, thanks."

"We'll come find you," she said, pulling me away from them as they kissed again. When we were halfway to the carriage house, she asked, "You good?"

"Fine."

She slung her arm around my shoulder. "Finish that. We need to get you another drink."

I did as she said.

CHAPTER
TWENTY-ONE

I HAD BEEN SPEAKING TO GABE'S FRIEND Kevin for the better part of an hour. Despite my original dislike for him, Ava seemed to enjoy him, so while she and Morgan used the bathroom and mingled, I was stuck entertaining him.

"Where even are his parents?" I asked over the loud music, which was still playing well after midnight. Though since we were so far from the closest house, there wasn't anyone to call the cops.

"Apparently," Kevin said, "his dad had some work thing in Miami this week and his mom went down last night to make it a short weekend getaway. They'll fly back up Sunday morning for the whole House of Horrors thing they do."

"Who bought the alcohol?"

"That would be me."

I turned to match a face to the voice behind me. It was the Dreadful Pirate Vic. I took a sip of my drink to hide my lack of desire to talk to him.

Vic moved past Kevin to the bar to make another drink. Kevin gave me a wide-eyed *better you than me* look and left.

"Thanks. What do I owe you?"

"Don't worry about it. Gabe paid for it. I just did the purchasing."

So he was at least twenty-one. And dating a seventeen-year-old *and* buying that seventeen-year-old and his seventeen-year-old friends alcohol. Kind of skeevy. Vic mixed himself a drink, then came around to my side of the bar.

"So," he said. "I wanted to say sorry again. I feel like we got off on the wrong foot."

"It's cool, I get it." Though he had been so protective over the bar before, I was curious to know what had changed.

"So you all work at the old folks' home. Gabe tells me a lot of crazy stories."

"It's a retirement community. 'Old folks' home' is an offensive term."

He chuckled. "To who? Old folks? Meh, the way he tells it, they can be offensive themselves. Apparently, he gets asked 'where are you from?' on a daily basis."

Again, my face burned. That was true. It had happened several times when I was training him, and he always did a great job pivoting. He'd say, "Oh, I live off Route 202. Would you like soup or salad this evening?"

"They can be . . ."

"Racist? Spoiled? Entitled?"

God help me, I actually laughed. "Yeah, all of that, actually. I mean, not all of them. A large number of them, yes, but there's a few who are polite and nice enough to tolerate."

Vic's eyes lit up. "Yeah, he told me about his favorite, some dude named Al."

For a moment I felt a weird sense of possessiveness. Al was *my* favorite. How often had Gabe even served Al and Willa?

"I feel kind of bad for him, though, you know?" I said.

"For Al?"

"Yeah. Like, it must suck to be one of the only gay dudes in the place." I thought about that frequently. And how lucky Al and Willa were to have each other as friends.

Vic smiled again. "But imagine how different it'll be in an old folks'—er, *retirement community*—"

"Thank you."

"—when we're older, and how many openly queer folks will be in there then. That's a pretty cool thought."

That *was* a cool thought. And one I had never really imagined on my own. Maybe it was working at Sunset Estates that made me think I'd never live in an old folks' home (it was okay when I said it).

"Oh!" I said. "What if there are even whole entire retirement homes that cater only to queer folks—and I guess allies, because you couldn't discriminate against the poor straights."

"Right, it's not their fault they were born that way."

"Totally!" I laughed. Shit. Was I enjoying talking to Gabe's boyfriend? After I had asked Gabe for his help on my video, just to get him to see I was better than Vic? A wave of guilt hit me. This was absolutely not the Taylor Swift fantasy I was trying to serve.

I was still chuckling when Vic turned serious. "So, listen," he said. "He told me, you know. That you kissed him."

My throat felt like it was closing up, and my face got so warm I was worried it would bake the makeup and make it flake, exposing red specks of my embarrassed flesh. Gabe told his boyfriend we kissed. Wait, he told his boyfriend that *I* kissed *him*—which, yes I did, but he *did* kiss me back.

I ran through my memories of the night. He did kiss back, right? I wasn't making that up.

"Don't worry." Vic put his hand on my shoulder. "I don't care. It was just one kiss—it doesn't mean anything."

Maybe not to Vic, but it meant a whole lot to me. At least I'd thought it did. Now all the power behind it seemed soiled. Anything good about the kiss was gone because Vic knew. Because Gabe had told him. And they probably had laughed about it. Laughed about me.

Stinging tears threatened my eyes, but I refused to cry in front of Vic. I wasn't going to give him something else to laugh at.

"I get it," he said. "He's sweet, he's adorable. Just don't do it again. Once was enough, and he's not interested."

Vic's smile returned, and his eyes drifted behind me.

"Here he comes. Play along—we don't need to make it awkward."

Gabe walked up beside me, putting an arm around my shoulders. My body tried not to cringe away from him as I caught Vic's eyes on the touch. His smile dropped a bit.

"What are you guys talking about?" Gabe asked.

"The decorations," Vic said. "You did an amazing job, babe." He planted a kiss on Gabe's lips. Gabe's eyes darted to me for a second—gauging my reaction?—before returning to the decor.

"Thanks! I still have a lot to do, though, and it'd be better if my parents were around to actually help."

I forced the sad muscles in my face to smile and held my cup up. "But then we wouldn't be here having this party."

"Hear, hear," Vic said. We toasted and drank.

"I'm going to find Ava and Morgan," I said, waving as I went back out around the side of the carriage house. But I didn't get far. When I took out my phone to text them, I saw that Ava had sent a message to the group chat saying that she and Kevin were going to make out in Morgan's car. That thought conjured the image of Vic and Gabe kissing in the darkness. Removing their costumes. Hushed whispers and gasps.

My stomach rolled, and now the tears really started coming. I ran down the side of the carriage house, around the back, away from prying eyes. The music had faded, blocked by the structure. I was at the bottom steps of the carriage house's apartment.

I took a deep breath, held it, then let it out until the pounding in my ears subsided. I took out my phone and brought up the self-facing camera. My makeup was smeared from my tears. I used the sleeve of my seafoam-green polyester jacket to wipe off as much as I could.

Thank God for wash-and-wear.

When most of it was gone, I checked my phone again. Morgan's text said she was hanging with some other girls from school, so I didn't feel bad just staying by myself for a bit. But then I heard footsteps. Someone was coming. Anxiety filled my stomach as I imagined Gabe and Vic sneaking away to the carriage-house apartment. I didn't want to see that, so I got up and patted my face to make sure any tears were gone, just as the person rounded the corner.

Thankfully, it wasn't Gabe or Vic. It was someone else. Tall and broad-shouldered, wearing sunglasses and a blue FBI windbreaker.

"Hey, Tommy!" Brad Waldorf. My chest lightened a bit. "I thought I recognized that prom getup."

He would, because the last time he had seen me in it he was taking it off me in Sophie Farnsworth's third-floor bathroom.

"Hey, Brad. Or . . . Agent Waldorf, I guess?"

"No, no, it's . . ." He did some kind of kung fu move, sloshing his drink into the grass as he kicked. "Burt Macklin, FBI." He gave me a goofy grin as he stood straight.

I shook my head. "Sorry. Is it from a movie?" Gabe would probably get it.

Brad took off his sunglasses and tucked them away in the jacket. "Nah, *Parks and Rec*. It's a show. Chris Pratt played him."

Why did Brad have to choose to be the worst Marvel Chris?

"Chris Pratt was an FBI agent in a TV show?"

Brad waved his hand. "He wasn't *actually* FBI . . ." I sat on the step, and he gave me a quick rundown of how Andy Dwyer role-played as Burt Macklin. It made me laugh, and I felt a little better.

"Can I get you a drink?" he offered.

"No, thanks. I think I've had enough." I poured out my drink onto the grass.

"Cool, cool . . ." He got fidgety and took a sip from his own cup. Still shy Brad, trying not to seem too eager. Or maybe he was trying to respect my boundaries. But I didn't want him to respect my boundaries tonight. Screw boundaries.

"Brad, do you want to make out?"

He grinned and said quietly, "Hell yeah."

* * *

This is better, I thought. My head was swimmy, and Brad's hands were all over me. Groping and caressing, a potent blend of soft and hard. His tongue moved somewhat overzealously, but I was feeling better. He tasted like Sprite and the almost gasoline flavor of the weed pen he had been smoking. And despite everything that had happened earlier, my heart still managed to race with excitement. Probably because— among other things—Brad was a fantastic kisser.

He pressed his body to mine and pushed me up against the back of the carriage house. His lips moved down to my neck, raking his teeth against my skin but not biting down, and I shuddered, biting back a moan.

This was how it should have gone with Gabe. If Vic wasn't around, this is how it all could have happened. Instead, it was Brad. Brad, who ignored me at school but searched me out at parties in hopes of this fleeting moment where he could be himself.

I felt bad for him. I felt bad for me.

But this was better than nothing. And it was better than wishing it were Gabe.

I didn't wish that anymore, because what Brad and I were doing was an exorcism. We were expelling the demons and memories from this place. The kiss where I know Gabe kissed back. I *know* he kissed back, and this is how it *should* have gone.

My phone vibrated in the inside pocket of my jacket.

"Do you need to get that?" Brad asked. But he kissed me again before I could answer, grabbing at my ass through my poly-blend pants.

"It's probably just Ava."

It vibrated again. A text. She most likely wanted to leave and was

168

wondering where I was.

"I'll text her back in a second." I pulled Brad back onto my lips, and he laughed through his nose.

Another vibration.

Then another.

And another.

"Jesus." I put a hand against Brad's chest, pushing him away, and took out my phone.

But it wasn't Ava. The notification said *Gabe De La WHORE-a*.

I didn't smile.

"One sec." I pushed Brad back a bit farther. There were five messages. Each one a different knife in a different part of my body.

Did you leave?

Sorry I miss you.

*missed

But I do that, too. Miss you.

Oof. That's definitely an embarrassing drunk text to send. UNDO! UNDO! DELETE!

Another was delivered as I was reading.

Drunk Thomas if you're reading these delete them before sober Thomas comes back! Drunk Gabe will owe you ice cream!

"Everything all right?" Brad asked.

"Yeah," I said. Drunk Thomas took Drunk Gabe's advice and started deleting the messages. "I have to find Ava. She's puking and wants to head home."

"I can drive you guys if you want." He seemed nervous. And it took me a second to realize that it was because he was probably anxious that Ava would think we were doing more than just making out every once in a while. He knew she could keep a secret, since she had already walked in on us, but it probably still worried him.

I deleted every single text except the one that said *But I do that, too. Miss you.* My finger hovered over the red rectangle that screamed *DELETE.*

"No, that's all right. Morgan drove us. She hasn't been drinking."

"I can take *you* home, if you want." He quirked his eyebrows in the moonlight. That still managed to make my stomach twist, but not enough.

"I should get going." I gave him a friendly smile back and grabbed his disheveled tie, pulling him to me. "One for the road?"

This kiss was sweet. Neither of us lost in the musk of horny hormonalness. Brad's lips were soft and gentle, and he pressed his large hand to the small of my back.

"Maybe next time?" I offered. And maybe next time I wouldn't have the memory of Gabe's kiss hovering over me.

"Yeah, definitely." He kissed me one final time, and I left. The text from Gabe was still on the screen. The one demon that Brad couldn't exorcise seemed to latch on and dig in its heels. Because I didn't delete it.

I called Ava as I cut across the lawn, hoping Gabe wouldn't see me. But also hoping he would.

CHAPTER
TWENTY-TWO

WHEN I SAW GABE THE WEEK AFTER his party, the first thing I said to him was sorry I didn't say bye when I left and that I didn't remember much after getting in Morgan's car. He smiled a crooked, teeth-hiding smile and nodded, telling me he was glad I had come and that I'd had fun.

In the two weeks since his party we had managed to avoid working the same shifts most days. Including Veterans Day.

Al and Willa were the last people in my section for the night. Most of the residents had come in right at four p.m., some in their old military uniforms if they still fit, some in VFW hats and shirts. Thank God it was Thursday, because Veterans Day on the weekends was like New Year's Eve for most of these old vets—90 percent of whom were male.

Yes, even though the residents are all retired, they still have weekday vibes and weekend vibes. The weekdays are for running errands, volunteering, and doctors' appointments, while the weekends are for golfing, lunches with the ladies/fellas, seeing family, or church.

Usually on weekend Veterans Days, they sat in the common areas drinking whiskey or beer and swapping war stories. By the time the brunch shift rolled around at noon, at least a third of them would be drunk. By the time we left, the second third would be drunk—despite us not serving alcohol in the dining rooms—and the final third drank so much normally that they either didn't get drunk anymore or they just always were.

On a weeknight, they drink, but they all arrive at once when the dining room doors open. And most aren't hungry because they've gotten their free veterans' meal from Applebee's at lunchtime.

"What the hell's with you, kid?" Al finally said after I refilled his coffee for the second time. He pointed at the other two cups he hadn't drunk and had just moved over to an empty place setting.

"Sorry, Al, but why did you go and dirty the other two mugs?"

"To test if you were paying attention. Which you aren't."

"Of course I'm not," I said. "I never pay attention to you."

"That's bullshit. I'm captivating."

I laughed—he had me there. I turned to Ms. Vaughn. "And you encourage this behavior?"

She shrugged. "I was curious where your mind was at, too." *She* actually drank her coffee.

"Spill, kid. You freaking out about school? Guys?" He frowned. "Gals? You need money?" He reached into his jacket and whipped out a red envelope, holding it where no one else in the dining room could see.

I pushed it away. "Stop it. No. I'm fine."

"Just take it."

"Al, I'm not even a veteran."

He pushed past my hand and dropped the card in my apron. "I just watched you serve with a forced smile as Ted Hinman told Korean War stories with his full racism on display. You're an honorary vet."

"Well, I can't very well scold the old bastard, can I?" In the past, staff had threatened lawsuits a number of times for being reprimanded when they spoke out against racist residents. Now we were told to smile, pretend we didn't hear it, and let a manager know immediately so they could talk to the resident with their well-practiced sensitivity training on how to "defuse and educate."

Surprisingly, a few residents had learned and changed. But Natalie had already politely asked Ted Hinman not to say the things he said multiple times, so now I only told her if I passed her while it was happening.

I thanked Al for the card and took two of the coffee cups off the table. "Can I ask you for advice on something, Al?"

Al's college know-how was probably about forty years out of date, so I didn't need to bother him with my anxiety around that. I had also decided not to go the early acceptance route. For one thing, I was still waiting on Natalie's hoops. Earlier that night, one of the residents asked me for a milkshake, which of course wasn't on the menu. I *knew* it had to be Natalie's test. So I went back, scooped the ice cream of the day into a bowl, mushed it with a fork until it was soft enough to mix with milk, and poured it into a glass—and then very carefully hid it from all the other residents in my section so they wouldn't ask for one, too, when I dropped it off. Still, Natalie didn't fess up.

Meanwhile, Ava had submitted all her early decision stuff for Johns Hopkins and didn't have to worry about anything school related ever again. Lucky. Though she still seemed nervous. I had no clue why, but whenever I brought up celebration plans for when she got her acceptance, she would go quiet. The only way Ava wasn't getting in was if there was some clerical error.

Al held his hands out. "I didn't survive this long to *not* pass on my wisdom. Why the hell do you think I talk to you so much?"

"That's you passing *wisdom*?"

Ms. Vaughn snorted. He pointed a stern finger and said, "Cut the wise shit and ask what you're gonna ask before I change my mind."

"All right, don't stroke out on me, old man. Did you ever . . . crush, I guess? On someone who was already seeing someone else."

Al and Ms. Vaughn both groaned.

"Ah! Don't bother." He waved his hand and turned his attention to his coffee. "No one is worth that hassle."

My heart shriveled, the last of my hope dying out. Al frowned at me over his coffee cup.

"What? You thought I was going to tell you how to break them up and get him to go after you instead? Kid, that's such a waste of *time*. And if there's one thing I know about time, you don't get any of it back. You're young, you're going off to school next year, why put all that time into trying to get someone who likes someone else to like you instead?"

But Gabe *does* like me. He misses me, even.

To answer Al's question of *Why?*: Because it was Gabe. Because he was special and different and he had always been in the back of my mind. He was sweet and so quick to be my friend. Twice! I just knew that if he was single this time around—knowing what we know about

174

ourselves now—things would be different. So if I could remove that one variable, the one thing keeping us from being together, I was sure it would be worth it.

"Who could be so important that you spend weeks and months trying to break up their relationship so you maybe get a shot?"

I sighed. No point in hiding it, and Gabe wasn't here anyway. "Gabe."

Al's eyes brightened. "*My* Gabe?"

I scoffed. "Okay, sure."

"So he *is* a friend of Dorothy, then."

"I . . . don't know what that means."

He blew a raspberry and rolled his eyes. "That's because you kids all have the Grindr stuff, so you don't have to cruise like we used to."

"Ew. And I do *not* have Grindr, and I'm kicking you out now. Go cruise your pillow or something."

"You're so abusive to me." He stood, feigning offense. "I really oughta write management about your attitude."

I lowered my voice. "You already did, you senile old bastard. And they gave me a raise."

Ms. Vaughn chuckled, and Al laughed hard until his laughter turned into a hoarse cough. I patted him gently on the back and he laughed some more.

"Thanks for the card, Al."

"You're not going to take my advice, are you?" he asked, wiping a tear from the corner of his eye and getting serious again.

"No, I will."

"Well," Ms. Vaughn said, still seated at the table, "considering it's

Al, and advice from him should be taken with a grain of salt, I want to tell you a story."

"Oh, Willa's got a story!" Al sat back down and held his coffee cup up to me. I refilled it.

"When I was in college, this was . . . gosh, 1968." She put a hand to her cheek, like she couldn't believe how much time had passed, then waved away the thought. "I met a girl named Phyllis."

"Typical lesbian name."

"Al," I scolded. But inside, I was shaking with excitement. *Lesbian!* I knew it! Ms. Vaughn was telling me about her personal life, and I don't think I could have been more excited.

She stared daggers at him. "Would you mind keeping your mouth shut for five minutes?"

Al zipped it.

"We grew close in the spring of sixty-nine, and I wrote her letters all summer while she was back home and I still lived in the city. But then fall rolled around and she didn't come back to school. I later found out through a friend of hers that she had dropped out and gotten married."

Ms. Vaughn moved her water goblet, not drinking from it, before sitting up a little straighter. "Anyway, about seven years later, I'm at the supermarket with my girl at the time and there's Phyl. Standing at the butcher counter buying roast for Easter dinner. It was as if . . ." She shook her head. "The world imploded. She looked fantastic, and all those old emotions came flooding back—the ones I'd thought I'd dealt with. Turns out *that* was wrong."

"What did you do?" I asked, needing to hear what happened next.

"I went over to her and said hello. I was about to ask if she remembered me, but, my God, the way the woman blanched you'd have thought I was a ghost. She had her daughter sitting in the cart, and she introduced me as a friend from school. I'm not proud to say I took a little joy in introducing her to my girl, seeing the look on her face. I'm glad her husband wasn't there, because I probably would have had that same look. I saw pictures of him later—he was one of those beefy football types. Looked like a real dummy. You know, your type, Al."

Al laughed into his coffee, spilling a bit on his lap.

"Join the club," I whispered to him. Willa shook her head, like she thought we were hopeless, and I turned my attention back to her. "Did you . . . get her number or something?" I asked.

Ms. Vaughn looked scandalized. "God, no. I was with someone, and she was married with children. I'm not a homewrecker."

My own stomach filled with familiar guilt at the word.

"Anyway, jump ahead again to 1988. I went to an ACT UP meeting, and wouldn't you know it, there she was."

Al turned to me. "Do you know what ACT UP is?"

I shook my head and Willa groaned, but Al looked unsurprised. He said, "It's an AIDS political activism group."

I raised my eyebrows in surprise. "She was at an AIDS activist group?"

Ms. Vaughn nodded. "She was. Her baby brother had died from AIDS the year before—she didn't even know he was gay. She was the only one of her siblings who went to the funeral. Awful. I learned about all this over coffee after the meeting. And . . . that she had also gotten a divorce."

My jaw dropped. "And you two started dating?"

"We did not. She was dating another woman at the time."

"This is a terrible story, Willa," Al said. It was reminding me of Gabe's movie, *In the Mood for Love*. How those characters never had their chance to be together.

Willa held up a hand. "It's not over, calm down. Despite that we stayed friendly, saw each other out at the bars, I went to parties at their apartment. Then finally one day in 1998, she was single, I was single. So we went out on a date, and eventually we moved in together."

"You mean on the second date?" Al asked.

"Of course—we're lesbians, not Catholics."

Al and I laughed. It seemed like that could be the happy ending to the story, and we could leave it at that; Willa had gone quiet, so she seemed to think it could end there. But Phyl wasn't sitting with us. And I couldn't leave well enough alone.

"What happened then?"

Willa smiled like she was happy I'd chosen to know the real ending. "She lives in California with her wife now. They own a vineyard near Los Olivos, and she's a big old hippie with a hippie blended family. It's wonderful. Also they ship me cases of wine every December."

Al pointed at her. "That's the stuff we drank last New Year's?" Willa nodded. "Oh! It's *fabulous*. Do you have any more bottles? I want a nightcap."

"Of course, dear."

I held up my hand. "But hold on—you guys waited all that time and nothing happened."

Willa seemed annoyed. "First off, neither of us was *waiting* for anything. She had a family. She was living her life and I lived mine.

Second, plenty happened. Just because it didn't work out and we aren't still together doesn't mean nothing happened. That's my point, hon."

Hon. Willa Vaughn called me "hon."

"I know you're young, and young people don't listen to older people who know better, but my point is, forcing things to work out doesn't usually help. What would have happened if I'd disrespected her wishes and shown up at her house or interrupted her wedding? I would have pushed her away, and when I saw her again at the ACT UP meeting we might not have even spoken. And I still resent you saying I was *waiting* for her my whole life. There were times I thought about her, yes, as one does. But to not live your life because you like someone . . . that's just silly."

She took a sip of her lemon water, then placed it back on the table. She turned to me and looked directly into my eyes.

"All I'm saying is, find the person who gives you what you want. Don't wait for the person you want to finally figure out what that is. We'll leave you with that." She patted my hand and put her napkin on the table. "Al, shall we take our nightcap?"

"Great idea."

"Hold on," I said as they both stood. "Was this just . . . a gay intervention?"

Willa rolled her eyes. "Yes, honey."

Al nodded. "You needed it, Mary."

I laughed as they wished me a good night, then went back to the service station and took out my phone, staring at the text I couldn't bring myself to delete.

But I do that, too. Miss you.

And that's what kept sticking. Ms. Vau—*Willa*—said not to wait around for the person who I liked to figure out what I wanted. But Gabe seemed to want it, too. Vic hadn't seemed all that bad when I met him on Halloween. Maybe the *complicated* part was that Gabe had needed him during that rough time when he came out, and now he didn't. But Vic was too nice to him. Maybe Gabe couldn't figure out a way to break up with him without getting hurt.

I started and deleted four different texts before putting my phone away. I wanted to just ask him outright, but I couldn't figure out how. What do you say to someone you like when you think they don't actually like the person they're with? Because what if I was wrong? What if he really did like Vic?

And he also liked me? And that was the only complication?

After I dropped Ava off at her house, I idled out front, staring at the text some more. Right above his message was another from Brad, who had texted me when he got home that night around two a.m.

Brad's message was innocuous, saying it was great seeing me and to text him sometime.

I opened up Gabe's messages and sent: **Have you ever watched Parks and Rec?**

I stared at the blue bubble of my text. He answered in less than a minute.

Of course! Why?

I heard it was good. I've never seen it . . . is it on Netflix?

No, but it's on another streamer I can give you my password to. Want to watch an episode or ten later? 😵 **You can get**

through the first season in less than three hours and tell me how work was without me (terrible, obviously).

Sure. Call you after I get home and shower.

And yes. I brought up the shower so he would automatically think of me *in* the shower. I'm not proud.

CHAPTER
TWENTY-THREE

"WHY ARE YOU ALL DRESSED UP?" MY mom asked when I entered the kitchen.

"I am not dressed up." I grabbed a can of tangerine-flavored sparkling water from the fridge. I was only wearing jeans and a button-down shirt, and yes, the button-down was new and these were absolutely the jeans that made me look least like a frog wearing pants, but I wasn't dressed up. At least, I hoped Gabe wouldn't think I was.

It was the Saturday after Al and Willa's gay intervention, and while I'd never tell them, it didn't work. In fact, when Gabe texted me Friday afternoon to suggest I come over to show him the cooking videos I was trying to emulate in my La Mère video, I had absolutely zero chill and said yes within seconds.

"Well, then, where are you going all not dressed up?" my mom asked.

"I'm legit going to hang out with Ava and a few others from Sunset. It's not a big deal."

"Sure, fine, whatever." She got up and went into the dining room. "Before you go, I wanted to ask you something."

"Something clothing related?" I called out.

"Actually, yeah." She came back into the kitchen with a white piece of clothing in her arms. "I was going through some old boxes in the basement and found this. Figured I'd ask if you wanted it."

She handed it to me. It was a jacket, and it looked perfectly clean and pressed. I held it up and my heart leaped. It was a double-breasted chef's coat with navy piping. Stitched into the left side was the La Mère Labont name and logo. And under that was my dad's name in the same navy stitching.

When I didn't say anything, my mom spoke. "I thought he threw it away or donated it when it was clear he wasn't going back. But it was with a few of his books and some old stuff from his dorm."

"What stuff?"

"Old bedsheets, a surge protector, nothing interesting. But I thought it might be nice for you to have the coat."

I tried it on. It was big around the middle, but the sleeve length was good. "Did you wash it?" I asked, looking at the cleanliness of the sleeves. White was a terrible idea for a chef's coat—gray and black hid the stains more easily.

My mom shook her head. "He never got to do the hands-on stuff in the classroom. And why bother wearing that at home to practice what he'd learned, when he could wear street clothes?"

That's right. La Mère was strict about their lesson plans. The chefs took time off from their busy schedules to come in and show techniques and explain certain methods. Students were expected to return to the dorms to practice afterward. It was pretty cool to have an industrial kitchen in the dorms. But also it seemed a little counterintuitive to just *watch* your professors do things instead of doing them and having them give feedback.

"Did Dad like going to La Mère?" I asked. I had always assumed he did. He talked about it enough when he was showing me what he learned.

My mom tilted her head as if she was trying to figure out why I'd ask. But instead of asking me, she said, "I think so. He never said otherwise, and I know how sad he was to leave. He also said he felt guilty because he took someone else's spot, then couldn't finish."

"But he said he wanted to go back, right? If he had the chance, he'd try to finish."

My mom nodded. "I mean, not specifically La Mère. We talked about him doing some night classes at the community college to get his associate's. But he was worried if he spent more of his free time in school and less with us, he wouldn't like cooking as much. I think he just enjoyed cooking with you and seeing how excited you got when you were both in there baking or making dinner together."

I'd liked that, too. Making pizza from scratch on Saturdays, starting with the dough in the morning—even though in the winter the dough took a little longer to rise because of the cold, which meant we might not eat until nine at night. "We're eating like the Spanish tonight!" he used to say when our recipes ran late.

My dad also never seemed daunted by anything. He loved trying new foods, and if the recipe didn't work, he'd try it again. I looked at the stitching of my dad's name once more, rubbing my fingers across it. My mom finding this now—years after my dad's death—felt even more like the universe telling me I was doing everything right. That this was how the plan was supposed to go. But how did the choice between the New York and LA campuses play into the universe's plan?

"Let me ask you a question," I said. "Did Dad ever talk about going to another campus other than the New York one?"

"Nope. Why?"

I shrugged. "Just curious. What about you? Would you be sad if I went to the LA campus?"

Her face answered before she did. She looked as though I had just told her I had an incurable, deadly disease. She probably realized that and adjusted it to a more neutral one and then swallowed before answering. "If . . . that's what you wanted to do. I would be sad, sure, but only because I'd miss you. A six-hour flight is a little more difficult than a two-hour drive. Is there a reason you want to go there instead?"

Definitely not the cute boy who just reentered my life. "I'm not saying I *want* to. Just trying to figure out which campus I should apply for."

"Well, I vote New York, but it's for entirely selfish reasons. If there's someone out in LA you want to learn from instead and you think it will be better for you, I fully support that." I could tell when she was trying to just be a supportive mom, though. She definitely didn't want me going that far.

And I wasn't even sure if *I* wanted to go. Why was I even still considering this? Because of Gabe. Because everything that was happening—Gabe coming back into my life just in time to help me with a video that I was struggling with, his "complicated" relationship with his boyfriend, Natalie requiring me to train Gabe as part of my letter requirement, Gabe deciding between two schools that happened to be in the same cities as the school I wanted to attend, my mom finding this coat—it all felt like I was reading the universe's secret recipe. Like the path was ahead of me, I just had to follow it.

"What's wrong?" my mom asked.

"Nothing."

"Doesn't look like nothing. Looks like you're noodling."

I smiled at her. "I'm trying to figure out what recipe I want to bake first to try to make a mess of this coat."

She snorted as I handed it off to her. "Whatever it is, that shouldn't be an issue."

Yes, I was absolutely a sloppy baker. But I think that just meant I was good at it.

When I got to Gabe's, the lights were already on in the apartment above the garage. I took the stairs two at a time and opened it to find a screen saver on the TV—a school of fish in the ocean—but Gabe and the dogs were nowhere to be found. I went back down the stairs, thinking about going to the front door and knocking, but I didn't want him to get into trouble if he wasn't supposed to have strange boys over to his house. Especially not in the apartment outside the house, where his parents couldn't keep an eye on him.

Not that *we* were going to be doing anything as long as things were still "complicated" with Vic. But they didn't know that. Also, it sounded like they didn't even know about Vic.

I went back to my car and sent Gabe a quick text telling him I was here and asking if I should wait in the apartment.

His car wasn't in the driveway like it normally was. I was parked on the opposite side of the garage—where he told me to—but there were a few other cars in the little asphalt roundabout that I hadn't seen before.

Including a white Cadillac that looked chillingly like Natalie's. I laughed to myself and went over to it to take a picture. My plan was to send it to Ava with the message: *This is at Gabe's house. Do you think he and Natalie are an item, too?!*

"Thomas?"

I turned to see Natalie on Gabe's side porch. Watching me hold my phone up to her car. Oh my God, I was hallucinating.

I blinked a few times, but the hallucination wasn't going away. Natalie was still there, wearing not her normal workday suit, but a T-shirt and jeans. Like a human and not a poison tree frog in a pant-suit.

"Natalie? What are you doing here?"

She crossed her arms and arched an eyebrow at me. "Seeing my family. What are *you* doing here?"

Gabe appeared from the doorway behind her. "He's here to see me, Aunt Natalie."

Aunt.

Fucking.

Natalie!

CHAPTER
TWENTY-FOUR

WHEN I SAID EVERYONE WHO WORKS AT Sunset Estates knows someone who either lives or works there, I didn't mean it like that!

The boy I like isn't supposed to be *related* to one of my managers. Especially not the manager who prides herself on being a sadist and who blackmails teens into behaving in exchange for letters of recommendation.

Also, why wouldn't she tell me Gabe was her nephew when he was hired?

Also-also, why the hell didn't Gabe tell me Natalie was his *aunt Natalie*?

Also-also-also, why was I still holding up my phone to take a picture of her car?

I looked at it, then swiped the camera away and held it up to the sky, then down toward the ground.

"Sorry," I said, trying to keep my voice as normal as possible. "I sent you a text, Gabe, not sure if it went through. I have sh—really crappy service out here."

I locked my phone and put it away.

"I got it," Gabe said. He had the self-awareness to be very clearly embarrassed, so thank God for that. It meant he knew he'd done something wrong. "You can go up. I'll be right there."

I nodded. "See you at work, Natalie."

Where I hope to only see you ever again.

She waved and turned back to Gabe, who she started speaking to quietly. I couldn't catch much of what they were saying, but I did hear Gabe say, "I'm friends with a lot of people from Sunset Estates. If you didn't want me making friends, maybe getting me the job there wasn't—"

At that point I was far enough away that I couldn't hear him.

Also, he was calling me his friend, which for my own personal well-being I'd like to hear as infrequently as possible.

I waited on the couch, mind reeling. My face burned. What would this mean for me? Natalie clearly didn't like her nephew hanging out with the gay know-it-all from Sunset Estates. Would she start treating me like crap? No, of course not—she already did that.

A wave of nausea numbed the heat on my skin. What if she decided not to write me my letter of recommendation after all? Maybe this was just the thing she needed to disqualify herself from having to write it entirely. Of course, she'd let me complete the second task and whatever the third mystery challenge was, but right after that she'd give me that smile that looked like she was going to unhinge her jaw and swallow me whole, and then say, *I don't think it's appropriate for me to write a letter of recommendation for one of my nephew's friends. Conflict of interest and all that, you understand.*

The door to the apartment opened, and Gabe entered, his shoulders slumped. Thank God he didn't bring Gertie and Arnold, because I wouldn't be able to fake the doggie talk, which I just wasn't in the mood for.

"Natalie is your *aunt*?"

"Yeah."

"You couldn't have said that three months ago when you first started?"

He hopped up onto the counter, still keeping his distance from me. "I was afraid you'd treat me different."

"Of course I'd fucking treat you different! My boss is your aunt!"

"*Our* boss."

I thought about all the times I had talked shit about Natalie—about his aunt. How many times I gave him shortcuts that accomplished exactly what she wanted, just not the way she wanted it done. How many times I'd called her "Shat-alie" around him—which, fine, was only once because it still needed some workshopping.

But this was way too much to deal with.

Then it hit me. It was *another* thing Gabe had lied to me about. No, I'd never asked him if Natalie was his aunt—because why would I?—so it was lying by omission, but still lying.

"Why are you so secretive?" I asked.

He crossed his arms. "I'm not secretive."

"You didn't tell me you had a boyfriend until I made an ass of myself and kissed you. You didn't tell me Natalie was your aunt until I showed up to your house and she was here. What else aren't you telling me?"

"Maybe I didn't want to tell you because I knew this is how you'd react."

He clearly meant about Natalie, but I didn't know if he meant that about Vic, too. Did he not tell me about Vic because he thought I'd back off and he didn't want me to? At least I *should* have backed off. But I was still here.

Gabe shrugged. "I just . . . I know how she can be, and I knew she had to be even *worse* at work. So I asked her not to tell anyone I was her nephew. And honestly, I think she was happy about that."

"Because she had a spy."

His eyes clouded, and he actually seemed pissed. "You don't really believe that, do you?"

"I don't know what I'm supposed to believe. This is bad. You said it yourself: you *know* how she is. She could put me on weekend-only shifts. She could ice me out completely from the kitchen when I turn eighteen. She could watch me every second of our shifts until I mess up one thing and fire me."

"Sure, let's make it all about you."

"Oh, okay, so what would she do to you?"

He didn't bother to answer and jumped on my last point instead. "She can't fire you for being my friend. She'd have to fire half the staff."

"Half the staff aren't *gay*. You said your family wasn't cool with you being gay, and I'm assuming she's part of that?"

He didn't answer, which I took to mean yes.

"So, yeah, if she thinks we're in here hooking up, she might see that as a good reason to find an excuse to fire me."

"She wouldn't do that." Judging by his voice, he didn't seem so sure. Which made it all feel much worse. I thought about my dad's chef's coat at home. His name stitched onto it.

I thought about how if I didn't get into La Mère, that would be the only version of that coat I'd have.

"I should go," I said.

"You don't have to."

"I know, but I should." I didn't want my car to still be here when Natalie finally did leave.

"This is going to be a weird thing between us now, isn't it?"

"I don't know." It didn't need to be. I needed to see how she treated me after this. "Maybe not. But just—don't bring me up to her. And please downplay our friendship if she asks you anything."

He smirked at me, and goddamn him for flashing those dimples. "Oh, so it's okay for *you* to hide our relationship from other people, but when I do it to you—"

"You admit it! You *were* hiding it!"

He laughed with me. Was I overreacting to him hiding that Natalie was his aunt? I was still uncomfortable, so I didn't think so. But maybe it all stemmed from the way he hid Vic, too. Doing it once, I could make an excuse for him. He was newly out and nervous about telling people who he was seeing. Fine.

But we were supposed to be closer than that. He should have been able to tell me by now that we worked with his aunt.

I don't know if I would still react the same way if he had been the one to tell me or not. Probably I would.

I said goodbye, my supplemental video—the one that was supposed to be a backup plan if Natalie refused to write my letter—the last thing on my mind. Even someone like Brad was more forthcoming with his life. There had been a few times when we were in our cool-down phase and just talking before going our separate ways, and he always seemed fairly open.

Yes, he was hiding *me* from his life. But he never hid his life from me. With Gabe, it seemed like he was going out of his way to hide his life from me.

And me from his life.

When I got home I had a text from Gabe: Sorry. I promise I'm an open book now. Anything you want to know, I'll tell you.

I stared at the screen for a moment before typing out: The night of your Halloween party, why did you say you missed me?

But reason got the better of me, and I deleted it before hitting send.

I didn't know what to do. I wanted Gabe to like me, but I also wanted to get into La Mère. And I wasn't sure I could stand out without Natalie's letter. This was also the second thing Gabe had hidden from me.

I finally wrote back: I get it, you were worried you'd be treated differently. But you don't have to hide things from me.

I'd have to see if Natalie treated *me* differently after this. School was more important than Gabe. Especially since Gabe had a boyfriend.

A boyfriend he wasn't spending his Saturday night with, because he was supposed to be spending it with me.

Why did this suck so much? And why wasn't there a better metaphor out there than having your cake and eating it, too?

CHAPTER
TWENTY-FIVE

BEST PART ABOUT WORKING THANKSGIVING: DOUBLE-TIME pay. Second-best part about working Thanksgiving and other major holidays: it's an early brunch shift only, no dinner service, so we're usually out by two p.m. Third-best thing about working Thanksgiving: buffet!

There's no order taking other than drinks and dessert. So even when I saw my name listed on a section after running sick trays, I couldn't be annoyed.

After I returned the sick tray cart to its normal spot by the dish room, I pulled my sleeves down and put on my maroon bow tie as Dante carved more turkey in the kitchen.

"How is it out there?" I asked.

"Fantastic. There was a big rush at the start, but it's slowing down. We might all be out of here early. Oh . . ." He gave a cursory glance around the empty kitchen. "Can you do me a favor?"

"Yeah, what's up?"

"Pies." He nodded in the direction of the ovens. I moved before he even finished talking. "See if they're done. Roni insists they need an hour, but I say fifty minutes."

I pulled the oven open, blasted by the heat. The apple pies inside were browned perfectly. "Yeah, they're done. Want me to grab them or just turn the oven off?"

"Can you grab 'em for me?"

I put on an oven mitt and reached for the first sheet with five pies on it. The weight of the sheet pulled my wrist down and the pies shifted. I spun quickly to a work surface before the pies could tumble off and, letting out a relieved sigh, placed the sheet onto the metal tabletop. It was a lot heavier than I thought.

Something smelled off, though. Like plastic burning. I looked into the oven at the other pies. No smoke. I turned back to the ones I had taken out and saw the pink cutting board, its upper left corner tucked under the hot metal sheet.

"Oh, shit!" I pulled the cutting board out from under the sheet, but it was already melting. A string of liquid plastic pulling from the sheet to the cutting board. Without even thinking, I reached out to break the molten plastic. With my bare fingers. "Ahh!"

"What's wrong?" Dante asked.

The pink plastic had stuck to my thumb and forefinger. I rubbed them on the metal work surface, trying to peel the melted mess off. It cooled and fell to the table, but my thumb and forefinger burned, throbbing with my heartbeat.

"Nothing," I said. "I put it down on the cutting board and burned myself trying to get it off."

"Shit." Dante walked over and took my hand to look at the burn. His voice turned dark, annoyed. "We're going to have to fill out an

OSHA form. And now *I'm* in trouble 'cause I let you back here."

"It's just a burn," I said. "I've had worse at home." I showed him a burn scar on the outside of my pinky from when I once tried rolling out pizza dough onto a preheated stone. "I'll run it under the cold water for a bit, pop the blister when I'm home, and put on some anti-biotic ointment."

Dante gave me a skeptical look as I grabbed another oven mitt, making sure there was enough clear space to put the other pies down, and finished unloading them.

"See?" I said when I was done. "It's like you've never been burned."

"No one can know about this, Tommy!"

"Know about what?"

I walked over to the sink and ran my fingers under the cold water. It throbbed with pain, and I could already see the blisters rising.

Burns hurt like hell, but in a kitchen they were inevitable.

"My, how the mighty have fallen." I turned away from my blistered fingers to see Gabe approaching my service station. He dropped his tray on the counter, shaking his head. "In the *formal* dining room with the other children. Wait, is the formal dining room like the Sunset Estates kids' table?"

Natalie had spent the last few weeks pretending she and Gabe weren't related, but I looked around to make sure she was otherwise occupied anyway. I could take the not-so-subtle hint of our being assigned opposite sides of the dining room. And yes, maybe my being in the FDR on Thanksgiving was another way for her to keep us separate.

"It's because I had to run sick trays and they knew it didn't matter where they put me when it's *buffet* day."

"Oh man, right? A revelation! Why can't it always be buffet day?"

"Because these old bastards pay a lot to be waited on hand and foot, not to get up with their walkers and mosey to the converted salad bar. Also, the café is usually buffet style, so if you want it that way, go join those degens. But you have to get into heavy metal."

It was a commonly known fact that the Sunset Estates Café crew were the staff members who were best kept to limited interaction with the residents.

"Is this how every holiday is?"

"No, Christmas is sit-down service again. Same with New Year's Day, Mother's Day, and Father's Day. Fourth of July is outside— unless it's raining, then, yes, the barbecue is inside, like this."

I peeked around the corner at my section. Only two tables, and all of them had enough water and drinks.

"So what's your Thanksgiving family tradition?" Gabe asked.

"My mom is making the turkey now, we'll eat when I get home, and afterward we shop online Black Friday deals and watch the Food Network *Ultimate Thanksgiving Challenge*. You?" This year I also had to find time to work on my college application essay, but every time I sat down to work on it my mind seemed to go blank.

"My aunt and uncle host—on my dad's side." Not Natalie, then. "So I'm changing here and driving right over. Usually, they have this massive spread, and dinner isn't over until almost six, when I just want to be teleported home so I can pass out into a food coma until I'm ready to raid the fridge for leftovers around ten."

I tried not to smile. I always saved the turkey leg to eat cold from the fridge after my mom went to bed. Though that wasn't so much a family tradition. At least not anymore.

"I expected you to make everything," Gabe said. "Like some teen Iron Chef."

"Not when I'm here making double time. No, I do the bread and pies, and I made all of them last night."

"How many pies do you guys eat?"

"It's just an apple and a pumpkin, and we have leftovers for days. I'll bring you some. The apple pie is great, but my pumpkin . . ." I rolled my eyes into the back of my head and let my tongue hang out.

"Charming! Is it just you and your mom and dad, or do you have extended family over?"

My smile dropped. "No, just my mom and me."

"Oh. Sorry." Gabe picked at the peeling layer of rubber on the corner of his serving tray. "Are your parents divorced?"

"My dad died. And grandparents on his side are dead, too. I have an aunt in Georgia, but she doesn't travel north often. My mom is from California, and her parents are out there, but none of them really get along, so it's just us."

The caring, protective Gabe—the one from summer camp—was back. His voice was low and full of genuine concern. "How did he die?"

"Not to be rude, but can we not discuss my dead family members on Thanksgiving? Maybe save that for Memorial Day." I tried to fake a smile, but Gabe seemed able to tell I wasn't joking. I took the throbbing in my burnt fingers as an excuse to look away from him.

"Sorry, Thomas."

"It's fine. What about Vic? What does he do for Thanksgiving?" I asked. I didn't actually want to know, but I couldn't help it. I had a morbid curiosity about how Vic fit into Gabe's life. We had been watching *Parks and Rec* over the phone a few times a week, and Vic never seemed to be over. I didn't get it.

"He has his family thing, too. They're kind of like mine in that they don't approve of his lifestyle 'choices.'"

"*Choices.* Got it."

"Yes, because it's a choice. Clearly."

"Clearly!"

Maybe that was why things were complicated with Vic, and it had never even had anything to do with me. I wanted to know more. I wanted Vic's story and how it compared to Gabe's. Maybe it was similar and that was their only connection? Maybe they were together—when they possibly didn't like each other like that— because they both needed someone on their side.

I still hadn't told my mom because she was all I had left. She had gay friends, but having gay friends and having a gay son are two totally different things. There was the tiniest part of me that thought, every time I considered telling her, *What if that makes her hate you?*

I imagined getting kicked out and told never to come back. I didn't know where I would go. To Ava's, probably, but I couldn't stay forever. Then the nightmare daydream spiraled into an Orville Peck music video montage where I'm traveling across wood-paneled Middle America searching for meaning and a home.

But Gabe hadn't been kicked out. If his parents just ignored it, how was that? Was it better that way?

"Holy shit." Ava popped up between us. Today her hairnet had topaz gems to match her copper-colored nails. "The energy here is *very* dark."

Gabe and I both tried to laugh, but we knew she was right. "I should go check on my tables," he said. "Be right back."

It was nice being able to use the tables as an excuse to defuse a situation. As soon as the awkwardness was gone, anyone could jump right back and talk about anything and it was like the depressing conversation had never happened.

"What did I interrupt, and do I get a *thank you* or a *hate you*?"

"It can't be both?" I asked. I grabbed a tray and went to check on my tables. I spun around and pointed at her. "Thank you."

"Hate you." She blew me a kiss.

While resetting my final table, I heard a knock from across the room. I turned to see Al at the formal dining room door. He waved an envelope through the window. I rolled my eyes and laughed as I went out into the salon.

"How were the old turkeys?" he asked. He smelled like whiskey. Jim Beam, specifically. I knew because my pop-pop used to be a Jim Beam fan, too. Every time I smelled it, my brain immediately grasped for the tobacco smell from his pipe, reminding me that it should accompany the whiskey, but not getting why it was missing.

"Gobbled everything up."

He snickered and handed me the envelope. "I didn't want to miss you."

"Thank you, Al." I took the envelope without arguing this time.

"You guys could have ordered sick trays; I was delivering today."

I knew where they were. Willa and Al had their own tradition. They got loaded and watched the Macy's Thanksgiving Day Parade. Then later, after a disco nap, they would order Indian and watch *It's a Wonderful Life*, the first of their Christmas movie nights, which moved to Friday nights leading up to Christmas Eve.

Al patted his belly. "Saving room for the saag paneer I'm going to demolish later."

"I've got to tell my mom we should do Indian for Thanksgiving one of these days."

"You'll never go back to dry-ass turkey again." Al waved at someone behind me, and I turned to see Gabe waving back from the casual dining room. "How are things with him?"

I bit my lip, trying not to look too embarrassed.

Al rolled his eyes and flicked his hand at me as he started to walk away. "You're hopeless."

"Happy Thanksgiving, Al!"

"I'm thankful I'm not a teenager anymore."

"Tell me that again when you break a hip." He flipped me off, and I laughed.

CHAPTER
TWENTY-SIX

"I THINK JOHN'S THE ONE FOR ME," my mom said from the couch across the room.

"Huh?"

She pointed at the TV. "The Asian guy making his sweet potato pie leftovers into a scallion pancake and the cranberry sauce into a sweet-and-sour reduction to dip it in."

"Oh yeah. He's definitely resourceful." I was barely paying attention to the show. I was too busy texting Gabe.

He'd sent me a bunch of pictures of his family meal—it really was huge. And now he was back at home watching some HBO show. I sent him a picture of the food on the TV, and he responded by asking what it was and how soon I could make it.

I chuckled to myself.

"Who are you talking to over there?" my mom asked.

"Friend from work."

"A friend or a . . . 'friend'?" I saw her do bunny quotes out of the corner of my eye.

"Friend, Mother." My chest tightened a bit. I wondered how bad it would be if I gave her a small hint that I wanted him to be more than a friend. Or even just the sex of the friend. "You've met him."

I turned to check her face. To see if she looked surprised. But she looked like she was running the pictures of everyone I worked with through her head.

"Not that burnout Luke?" I laughed and said no. "Oh, the one I met on his first day."

"Gabe, yes. That's the one."

She smiled brightly. "Tell him I said hi!"

"I will."

My mom says hi.

Hi Mom!

"He asked if you're single and wants your number."

My mom groaned and sat up on the couch. "You're a wretched child, you know that? I'm heading up. Record the rest of this for me. From tomorrow on, it's all holiday cookie challenges."

I grabbed the remote from the coffee table and started recording the show. There were only fifteen minutes left.

"Good night, sweetie." She kissed me on the forehead and headed for the stairs. "Great job on the pie as always."

"Pumpkin crust wasn't flaky enough. I need to put more vodka in it next time."

She stopped halfway up the stairs, pointing at me. "I marked that bottle, by the way."

"Ew, Mom. You know I don't drink that cheap stuff. It's Belvedere or nothing for moi."

She stared at me, trying to figure out if I was joking or not.

"Yes, it was a joke." I'd drink the cheap stuff in a pinch. "Good night."

I asked Gabe how much longer his HBO show was, and if he

wanted to watch *Parks and Rec* together.

Thought you and your mom were watching some Food Network thing.

We were. She went up to bed and asked me to record the rest for her.

My phone buzzed in my hand, informing me that Gabriel De La WHORE-a, President and CEO of De La Whore-a Phone-Sex Hotline was calling me. I chuckled again at the words scrolling across the screen before answering.

"Let's watch this Food Network thing. I've never seen it before."

"It's just a low-stakes cooking competition show."

"I need low-stakes. I just spent six hours with my extended family and followed it up by watching a bunch of robots take over the world. Now tell me what this dude is doing with the pumpkin pie."

I stifled a yawn and told him it was sweet potato pie, then walked him through everything the chef had done so far. After the episode was over, another started up, and I set a recording so the DVR saved it for my mom. We talked through the episode and into the next until finally I said what I'd been working up to over the past hour and a half. What I had been wondering for weeks but wasn't sure how to say.

"Do you think it's weird we watch TV together more than we see each other?"

He was silent for a minute. "Probably."

"Like, how many other people are you watching TV shows or movies with?"

"Well, to be fair, it started as an education in an area where you were severely lacking!"

Then what is it now?

I wanted to know if he watched TV with Vic like this. Or Kevin. Was it a boyfriend thing, too, or just a friend thing? Or was it just a *me* thing?

I yawned for the eighth time in the past five minutes, only this time I didn't stifle it. "I should probably get to bed before I fall asleep like you did when we watched the episode where Leslie forced Ron to let the Parks and Rec women go on the hunting trip."

"Hunting is boring, Thomas!"

I laughed. "You working tomorrow?"

"No, Saturday. You?"

"Tomorrow and Sunday brunch."

"Two ships passing, huh?"

It was a theme for us, after all. "Good night, Gabe." He said good night and I hung up. But I didn't go to bed yet—I went into the kitchen and unwrapped a turkey leg from its tinfoil. I stood at the kitchen sink and started picking at it.

The Thanksgiving when I was five, I snuck down to the kitchen after hearing noises. My dad was in there, my mom asleep on the couch. He had a glass of red wine sitting on the counter and he was standing at the sink, pulling at the turkey leg in his hand.

He jumped when he saw me at the doorway, then laughed and held out the turkey leg for me. I pulled off a piece, despite the fact that I didn't like dark meat. Dad was the only one who liked it. He sat on the kitchen floor, letting me pull meat off the drumstick with him. I wish I remembered what else we talked about that night, but the only thing that stuck was how to eat a turkey drumstick.

They always have those cartilage spikes in the meat that make it impossible to bite right in. So it was best to just peel it apart with your fingers, bit by bit.

"That's why," he said, "I always wait till Mommy falls asleep and eat it standing over the kitchen sink. So she doesn't have to see me looking like a vicious monster." He growled and ripped off another piece of turkey and scarfed it down, making gross snorting noises that made me laugh.

The next year, my mom fell asleep before I did, and while we were watching TV he said, "Pssst!" then pointed at the kitchen and mimed eating a drumstick the *wrong* way. I nodded, and we shared the leftover drumstick again.

When I turned ten, I got my own drumstick, and I was finally tall enough to stand over the kitchen sink like he did. The last couple years before Dad died, we would talk about school and he'd ask if I liked any girls in my class and I would always say no and play it off like I just hadn't met anyone. We talked about the baking my grammy was teaching me, his memories of her teaching him when he was a kid, and his favorite things that I had made recently and what he wanted me to make again. Sometimes he'd tell me stories about watching a professional chef make consommé or béarnaise sauce in the kitchen at La Mère.

Our last Thanksgiving, I fell asleep in the chair I had been watching TV in. He ate without me but put a sticky note on my forehead saying he'd left the last drumstick for me.

Now I always left the last one for him.

I sniffed and tried not to cry as I ate.

CHAPTER
TWENTY-SEVEN

THE FOLLOWING WEEK I WAS AT THE ice rink where our high school's hockey team plays. Lara Guthrie and I had scheduled the yearbook photo shoot at the absolute last possible minute. It was my job to get all the names of the players so it matched when we finalized the page layout.

The other athletic teams were easy; their photos could be done almost any day after school in the gymnasium or on one of the fields—though we did have to walk to the middle school on the other side of the football field for the swim team. Why they'd put the pool in the middle school when the middle school didn't have a swim team, I will never know.

For the hockey team, we had to travel to Ice Works, and they had to be in uniform, so the shoot had to be either during practice or before a game. This would be the last home game of the season, so it was our last chance to schedule the photo. The coach was annoyed that we were taking time away from their warm-up practice, but that was his problem. Also, truth be told, I had kinda dropped the ball and forgotten to schedule it until late in the season.

I was still too distracted by Gabe, and by my La Mère application. Though recently Gabe had been more of a distraction than the application, which definitely wasn't helpful, since I still had to write my personal essay and Natalie never said more than three to four words at a time when I was at work, so I had no idea where I stood on her letter of recommendation.

Gabe and I had been talking a little more regularly, and now when we watched something over the phone it was usually YouTube cooking channels like Food52 or Babish Culinary Universe instead of Netflix. He had great taste in chef personalities; all his favorites—Rick Martinez, Sohla El-Waylly, and Claire Saffitz—were my favorites, too.

He also seemed to be getting more and more excited about the La Mère video, judging by the text I received while at the ice rink.

I can't wait to show you my storyboards!!!!!

I smirked at my phone as Lara continued to adjust her camera to compensate for the harsh ice rink lighting. I didn't really have an idea what storyboards were, but it still made my stomach tingle.

We were meeting tonight at the Blue Comet Diner so he could give me his ideas for the video. Ava was tagging along because she "wanted to watch our chemistry in action." That was bullshit. She was just hoping that Kevin would be there, which, yes, she asked Gabe to invite him.

"Tommy?"

I looked up to see Lara Guthrie looking at me expectantly. "Yeah, yeah, I'm ready." Lara and I wobbled on our ice skates out to the area where the goal usually sat. The hockey coach, Mr. Garrity, had already moved it out of the way for the varsity team's yearbook picture.

Thankfully, Ice Works had agreed to let Lara and me use their rental skates without paying for them.

Why the varsity ice hockey team needed to take their picture *on* the ice was beyond our pay grade. I assumed it was Becky Jackson's doing.

"All right!" Lara shouted. She let out an ear-piercing whistle. "Tallest players in the back. Shorter guys, you're up front and taking a knee. Coaches, you're flanking. Right here." She pointed straight in front of her.

The team moved quickly, a few of the shorter players arguing that they should be allowed to stand in the back. Lara let them argue for a bit before she started telling people where to go. While she did that, I snapped a quick picture on my phone and opened up the Notes app.

Starting from the left, I wrote Coach Garrity's name, then moved to the next player.

"Bahama Mama!"

"Spell your first and last name," I told James. I knew his first and last name, but this was the yearbook, and Becky would murder me if I spelled it wrong. It was easier to double-check my Notes app once the page formatting was finished than to hunt down their pictures one by one.

"James Borrero. *J* like James, *A* like ames, *M* like mes, *E* like es, *S* like ess." He continued to spell his last name the same way before I went to the next-tallest player.

"Brad Waldorf. *B* like Brad, *R* like rad . . ."

I gave him a death glare, and he let out an adorable laugh I think I had been lucky to hear three times in my life. It was a sweet laugh that gave me a pang in my chest. Probably because I hadn't heard it often. I imagined Brad probably hid things that could be considered "adorable" because adorable was so very close to gay. Straight men weren't adorable. Though, yes, you could make a case for himbo golden retriever straight-guy boyfriends being adorable. But Brad was a manly sports guy who had to *pretend* he wasn't adorable. He was handsome and rugged.

I remembered being like that. Not that I had ever been handsome and rugged, but I *had* felt that fear of being too soft because then people would see that I was gay.

James scrunched up his face. "You just made that noise again, Waldorf Salad. What is that? Are you sick?"

I knew James didn't have a mean bone in his body and was just trying to be funny and—Oh my God! *James* was the adorable himbo golden retriever straight guy! But James was touching on the exact nerve that *made* Brad hide that sweet side of him. Before James could ask anything else, I spoke over him.

"Spell it for me for real, please?"

"*B-R-A-D-W-A-L-D-O-R-F.*"

"Thank you, Brad," I said.

I moved on to Steven Whalen—oops, I mean Stephen "PH" Whalen—while James continued to tease Brad for laughing. I wanted to punch James and tell him to lay off, but I also didn't want to bring any extra attention to it. This was how straight dudes were. They always teased each other over dumb stuff. I just hoped Brad could figure out sooner rather than later that he might not have to hide every part of himself. Every time I glanced back at him, he would look away from me and his cheeks would flush. Or maybe that was just the cold of the rink.

Once all their names were noted and Lara got enough pictures, she and I headed back to the edge of the rink to take our skates off. As I started to tie my shoes, I heard someone skate to a stop at the rink door. I looked up, expecting to see James, but found Brad instead.

"Hey, Tommy. Are you . . . doing anything tonight?"

My stomach dropped, and I instinctively looked to my right at Lara. She had slipped her shoes on and was scrolling through the images on her camera. But I could see her eyes go slightly wider. Not at the pictures—at what Brad had just said. Because it sounded like he was asking me to hang out. And Lara knew Brad and I didn't really hang in the same circles. Lara also had never been at one of the parties at which Brad and I hooked up in secret.

Keeping her nose down at the camera, she quickly grabbed her skates and left without saying anything.

I turned back to Brad, my words failing me. "I . . . No."

He smiled. "Cool. I actually was wondering—"

"I mean, yes! Sorry. Yeah, I forgot I have a school thing tonight." It sounded vague, I know, but I'd never told him about the video, and why bother with all that backstory?

His smile dropped. "A school thing?"

"Yeah. I have to do—"

"Waldorf!" Coach Garrity's voice echoed through the rink, and he waved Brad back to practice. "Talk about picture touch-ups on your own time."

Again, my face warmed. How fucking much toxic masculinity did

Brad have to deal with on a daily basis?

"Sorry," Brad mumbled. He put his helmet back on and skated away.

Lara was waiting for me by the vending machines in the ice rink lobby, no longer paying attention to her camera. I handed my skates back to the attendant, and we walked quietly to my car.

"So . . ." Lara said.

Thankfully, I'd had enough time to think of an excuse. "He wanted me to bake something for his cousin's birthday on Sunday, but I couldn't." I said I'd had enough time to think of an excuse, not that it was a good one.

"Oh. Right."

Lara didn't ask me anything else, but I could tell she knew. And because she was queer herself, she knew it wasn't for me to say anything. If Brad wanted anyone to know, he would tell them.

So did that mean he wanted Lara to know?

CHAPTER
TWENTY-EIGHT

"SO USING THE BABISH FRAMING WON'T WORK," Gabe said. He was sitting in the booth next to me while Ava sat across from us—visibly bored and annoyed that Kevin hadn't shown up for her to flirt with. Gabe moved our drinks out of the way to make space to put down the papers he'd brought with him.

Ava smirked at me from across the table. As usual, I knew that look. It said, *It's kind of adorable how much work he's done-slash-how excited he is.*

Gabe pointed at the printout of one of the videos from the Binging with Babish YouTube series. It was just a picture of Andrew Rea's hands holding a sandwich cross section in front of his torso.

He continued. "Because it's your application, you know? We have to see your face."

"Right."

"Show off the moneymaker," Ava said.

Gabe pointed at her. "Which brings me to my next point." He reached over and took my hand. Ava's eyebrows shot up. "The money-maker is these. We need to see it's *you* making this stuff, but we also need to see close-ups and your techniques. So . . ."

He moved all the papers aside and grabbed his backpack from under the table. Again, Ava gave me a look. Only this time it said, *This is all far too much.* I felt bad; she had to be so bored by this. I decided to make it up to her by playing some co-op game together later. No matter how horrible I might be at it.

Gabe withdrew a spiral-bound sketchbook and flipped it open. The page was broken into framed quadrants, and each frame had what looked like a poorly drawn cartoon chef in it.

"Ignore my bad drawing skills. I promise I'm a pro behind the camera." He nudged me with his elbow, and my cheeks flushed.

He drew these? And they were me? Each of the frames had some kind of stage direction, or I guess it would be a camera direction. And some of them had arrows pointing toward or away from the camera.

Gabe explained the setup for the video: me, in the guesthouse kitchen. He'd do something called a Steadicam shot—whatever that meant—for the moments I'd be talking to the camera, and he'd move in to focus on my hands while I explained what I was doing. Then for the steps where I'd be doing more mundane things, he'd edit the shots all together into something he called an "Edgar Wright Crash Zoom Montage," and every time I completed a step in the recipe, we'd do a "match cut"?

It was overwhelming, but the more Gabe talked about it, the more exciting everything got. He put so much passion into something he didn't even need to put it into. This was just a video to supplement my application, and he was talking about choreographing transitions and editing tricks.

Was he doing this because he loved making movies? Or was he

doing this because he . . . liked me? Maybe it was both, but let's be real here, he even watched Claire Saffitz's croquembouche video to get an idea of what my recipe would involve, so it had to be because he liked me. Right?

By the time our mountain of fries came out, my stomach was at a full rolling boil. I couldn't even eat yet.

Ava excused herself to the bathroom to wash her hands.

"What do you think?" he asked when he was finished.

"I think it's . . ." I didn't have words.

"Sorry," he said. "I got a little intense, huh?"

I grabbed his forearm. "No! I mean, yes, but also no. Intense in a good way. Like it's *really* exciting. Do you do this for every project?"

"Of course."

Well, shit. I had thought I was special.

"We have to go in prepared," he said. "Otherwise time is wasted and you don't get the shots you want or your talent gets tired." His knee nudged mine under the table. "I'm going to do my best to keep you alert and on the whole time."

I laughed. *Oh yeah, no problem there.*

"Babe?"

I turned my gaze away from Gabe, expecting to see some dude meeting his girlfriend or something. But instead Vic was standing at our table. His eyes drifted down to my hand, still on Gabe's forearm.

"Hey!" Gabe pulled away and stood. He kissed Vic, and I took the time to drink my soda, my mouth suddenly very dry. "You done studying already?"

"We're taking a food break." Vic motioned to the group of college-aged students by the front door waiting to be seated. They all stared at the three of us. "What are you doing here? You said you had a film project you were working on."

"Yeah!" Gabe pointed at me. "You remember Tommy, right?"

"Of course." But there was more than that in his "of course." His voice made it sound like, *Of course, he's the guy who kissed my boyfriend.* But what he actually said was, "Nice to see you again."

That was clearly a lie, because his face definitely did *not* say he was very happy to see me again. When he had told me not to kiss his boyfriend, apparently he'd also meant *don't touch his arm and share the same booth with him, either.*

"Tommy is applying to culinary school, so I'm helping him make a video for his application."

Vic continued to stare at me. "What kind of culinary school requires a video application?"

I shook my head. "They don't require it. It's a hard school to get into, so I'm trying to stand out."

"I'm sure your grades will do that, too," Vic said. He gave a fake smile that would make even Natalie jealous.

Before I could say anything else, Ava returned.

"Vic!" She slung her arms over Vic's and Gabe's shoulders, pushing them apart. "Good to see you again!"

I turned my attention to the fries in front of us, taking one and biting into it. But it didn't help my nausea at all. Vic, Ava, and Gabe were talking, but all I heard was the pounding blood in my ears.

Finally, Vic said, "Oh, looks like we're being seated. Babe, are you done? Why don't you join us?"

"Um." Gabe looked at me as Ava took her seat across the table. He seemed to think for a moment. And it really was only a moment, but for that moment I thought he'd stay. I thought he'd tell Vic he'd meet up with him later and sit back down. But instead, he said, "Yeah, I think we're all set, right?"

"Yep, go ahead," I said. "I'll talk to you at work about when we can film."

"Okay." He grabbed his stuff, packing it all away in his backpack. Then he said goodbye—something Vic hadn't bothered doing—and joined Vic and his study buddies at another table.

"You good?" Ava asked.

"Not even a little bit."

"Yeah, let's get the check." She locked eyes with our server and nodded. I put cash on the table for the tip, and Ava went up to the counter to pay the bill.

For most of the car ride home we were completely silent, the music turned low. All that excitement was ruined by Vic. It was so easy to forget about him when he wasn't around because Gabe never talked about him. But then he was so quick to leave us and go hang out with Vic's friends.

Why did Vic have to show up?

Ava gasped in the passenger seat.

"What?" I asked.

But she didn't answer me. She was staring at her phone. My mind started to race with possibilities. Maybe Gabe texted her by mistake when he meant to text me—or it was an accidental group text—and he said he broke up with Vic after they got in a fight. Or maybe Vic went back to his studying and Gabe was asking to hang out again. Or maybe there was an alien attack on Moscow and we needed to get underground.

"What?" I yelled again. "Tell me—you're freaking me out." I was also not paying attention while I was driving, so when we reached a nursery on the side of the road I pulled into the empty parking lot.

Ava's eyes just kept darting back and forth across her phone. And that's when I started getting nervous. Maybe it was something worse. Worse than waking up one Sunday morning to her entire family in her house, except for her mom and dad. And her uncle telling her there'd been a car accident.

But when she spoke, the worry in my chest lifted immediately.

"Johns Hopkins. I got in."

I was silent for a moment, stunned. Then I cheered and she startled before giving me a smile. I reached across the center console and pulled her into a hug.

"Of course you did!" I said. Because, I mean, *of course* she did. We knew she would—she had the grades and the test scores, *and* she'd impressed the shit out of the head of the bioengineering department, who'd promptly written a letter of recommendation to the admissions board.

"Get out of the car." I opened her door. "We need to have a celebration dance."

"No, Tommy, wait—"

But it was too late. I was already switching to my party-hype playlist, and I turned up the music and jumped out. I knew Ava hated dancing, but I didn't care—this was a celebratory moment she would remember for the rest of her life.

I tried to pull her to her feet, but she was still buckled in.

"Tommy, stop. Just listen to me a second."

"Dance and listen," I said, dancing in place. "I can do two things at once."

Ava reached over and turned off the music. Then she got out and put her hands on both of my upper arms, trying to hold me still. "No dance. Only listen."

I stopped moving. "Oh no. You prepared a speech."

She laughed. "I really did not."

I didn't know what this was, why we weren't celebrating her win when this was something she had always wanted. Her parents had met at Johns Hopkins, and Ava had known since kindergarten that she was going to go there. Though she didn't figure out what for until seventh grade, when she entered the science fair with a project explaining an engineered E. coli that created reusable plastic. She got second place because the judges couldn't understand all of it.

But now there was something wrong, and I didn't know what. It scared me because I always knew what she was thinking, just like she always knew what I was thinking.

"I . . . don't think I want to go."

CHAPTER
TWENTY-NINE

I STOOD THERE IN SILENCE FOR A moment, my mouth hanging open. What was she talking about, she didn't want to go? Johns Hopkins had always been her plan. Johns Hopkins was basically in Ava's future from birth. She had always said she wanted to go, even before her parents died.

"Sorry." I finally blinked. "You . . . don't think you *want* to go to Johns Hopkins?"

"Correct."

"Your dream school."

"Yes."

"The one you've said you wanted to go to for as long as I've known you?"

She took an annoyed breath. "I feel like you need to choose an exit and get out of this roundabout, sweetie."

"Are you insane?"

"Oh, that's the one we're choosing, huh? No, I'm not insane. I just—I don't know. The last couple of months I've been thinking about my future a lot more. It was like, the moment I peed on that pregnancy test—when I thought that I'd go get an abortion and how all this wasn't part of my plan—it was the first time life seemed to slow down enough for me to actually rethink everything."

That was months ago. This was all coming out of nowhere. "Why didn't you tell me?"

She laughed, but it seemed joyless. "I really didn't know until I read the acceptance email." She looked again at her phone, locking it and tossing it onto the passenger seat of my car. "I had been thinking about it—not going, that is—and it all seemed crazy, but then I realized maybe it isn't. Maybe just me thinking it's crazy is all the evidence I needed."

"So what are you going to do? Apply somewhere else?" Applying early decision was a binding agreement, though. They couldn't *force* her to go, but if they found out Ava applied anywhere else, they would contact the school's admissions office.

She bit her lip and started to pace back and forth. "I don't know. I think I want to . . . just . . . take a gap year."

"A *gap* year?"

"Or two. Figure out what I really want to do."

I shook my head. "You've known what you wanted to do for *years*! How has all that changed in the last minute?"

She glared at me. "If you've been listening, you'll recall it's been more than a minute."

"You said since your pregnancy scare, but that's all it was. Just a scare."

"I know, and I thought it was just me being scared in the moment. Like *Holy shit, this was not supposed to happen!* You know? And I had to take that time thinking about all the possibilities—do I want to be a mom, now or ever? Do I want to get into this field that I happened to connect with when I was twelve? Do I want to take someone else's place at a school that I only really have set in my brain because my parents put it there?"

That last one resonated with me. But that wasn't what I was doing, right? Yes, I wanted to go to La Mère as a way to honor my dad, but also it was a *great* school. It had a great faculty, and it was prestigious and hard to get into. Sure, there were plenty of schools other than Johns Hopkins, but there weren't any better than La Mère.

"Also," she said, shrugging, "I think the idea for this existed way before the pregnancy scare. I think me stressing over not wanting to go was one of the things that made me late."

"So you're just gonna . . ." I shook my head. "I'm sorry, my brain is melting down."

"Welcome to the club."

"So what's your plan, then?" I asked. "You're just going to take a gap year or two and work at Sunset Estates?"

She gave me the glare again. "No, Tommy. The point of taking the gap year or two is to *figure out* the plan. My parents had life insurance that went to me in a trust. I just need to get my uncle to agree to let me use it for something that isn't school."

"Something like what?"

"I've been thinking I want to travel. Leave Pennsylvania and see other places, in the US and abroad. Figure out if there's anything else I want to do with my life."

"*Travel?*"

Ava laughed. "It's good enough for middle-aged white women

going through a divorce. If I have the means, why shouldn't I?"

"Because you're not middle-aged; you're seventeen."

"So I need to know right now how I want to *spend* my middle age? Fuck that!"

"But you're not going to figure that out through traveling. You can go to school and still travel."

"You're being reductive now. It's not about traveling; it's about me not wanting to go to school for what I thought I wanted to go for. And maybe I don't want to waste money and take up someone else's spot when the point is I *don't know* what I want." She crossed her arms. "Honestly, I thought you'd be more supportive."

"Supportive of you throwing your life away?"

"I really can't tell if you're being willfully dense or if you're just too consumed with yourself."

"I'm not worried about me right now. I'm worried about you regretting this decision later."

And what happened if the early-decision Scarlet Letter followed her after her gap year? Maybe that would keep her from ever being accepted to any school in the future.

"Then I'll deal with that then!" She sighed and shook her head. "But I don't think I will regret it. Even if I realize later that I'm delaying what I always wanted. I'd rather regret doing something than regret *not* doing something. I feel like even you can relate to that."

"How? I'm *going* to La Mère if I get in."

She gave me a *Girl, really?* look and crossed her arms. "I'm talking about Gabe."

What did Gabe have to do with college? Or even *her* choosing not to go to school? Ava was there ready with the answer.

"It's been four months of you following him around, trying to get his attention. Butter brawling for his honor. Flirting shamelessly. Having him help you with your video. But Gabe is still with his boyfriend and hasn't given you the time of day."

That wasn't true. We watched TV shows together over the phone. We texted all the time. He sent me clips of the short films he was making for his video production class at Murphy and asked my opinion on them.

But Ava wasn't finished. "You have this toxic nostalgia for him polluting your mind. He's not the same kid you fell for, and he's still not into you."

"We hang out all the time."

"You *work* together. You're chasing after him while he takes advantage and uses you for whatever he's not getting from Vic. You didn't even do the early decision for La Mère like we had talked about."

"Because I want to submit something to make me stand out!"

"And you haven't filmed any of that video yet. You aren't even serious about it; you're just using it as a way to keep hanging out with Gabe. Have you started writing your essay?"

Well, no. But I wasn't about to tell her that. Besides, there was more to the video than that. It had to be perfect, otherwise I'd stand out in all the wrong ways. *Oh, here you go, admissions committee, here's a boring, three-minute video you're forced to watch about me making some donuts.* Hell no. And Gabe was good at that stuff. It was just an added bonus that we got to hang out more while we were working on it.

"Listen," Ava said, trying to put calm in her voice. "I'm saying I get it. You regret that you weren't able to tell him back then what

224

you know now—and I don't want to make a mistake now that might make me unhappy later. And honestly, you really need to think about that, too. Because if you do want to go to La Mère, you need to get more serious about that than about trying to break up Gabe and his boyfriend."

"You know what?" I said. "This isn't about me. It's about *you* giving up everything you worked for because you had a pregnancy scare *months* ago! And you're absolutely making the wrong decision."

Shit. As soon as I said that I realized it was completely insensitive and wrong.

She narrowed her eyes. "So because it happened months ago, it means nothing? Is that it?"

"No, that's not what I mean."

"I think it *is* what you mean. *You* think it means nothing because it has nothing to do with you. And you know what, for once you're right about something. *That* had nothing to do with you. You didn't experience it; I did. But another thing that has nothing to do with you is my decision about my future. Let me say it again: it's my future! And yes, something that happened 'months ago' did change how I see my future. But you're equating what I want from my life, and the hard work I put in, to the work you did and what you want from your life. And it's not the same."

"I know it isn't, and I'm sorry I said that thing about the pregnancy scare. But you did work hard, and I am talking about you working hard. You just want to throw that away?"

"Tommy! This is what I'm talking about! *You* think I'm throwing my life away because you're still looking at it as what you, personally,

225

want with your future. I don't see it as me throwing my life away. Can you really not get that?"

I couldn't. If she didn't want to go to Johns Hopkins, then what had been the point of studying so hard? Why had she spent her limited free time learning all she could about bioengineering or spent hours a day for a whole week last summer on a virtual science summit for high schoolers?

She stared at me and shook her head. "Just take me home."

Without another word, she got in the car and slammed the door shut.

We didn't speak the entire ride home. But the longer the quiet lasted, the more frustrated I got. Mainly because we had always understood each other. But I couldn't understand this. When we reached Ava's house, she got out without saying goodbye. I rolled down the window and shouted.

"Okay, night! See you at school on Monday."

She flipped me off but didn't look back.

CHAPTER
THIRTY

"GOOD EVENING, EVERYONE!" I SAID TO MY new six-top, my
third in the first hour—thanks, Morgan. At first I was worried Ava
had told her about our argument, but everyone seemed to be getting
slammed tonight. It had been five days since our fight, and Ava was
still avoiding me. When I texted, she either responded with reactions
only or flat-out ignored me. At school she barely acknowledged me
with a raised-eyebrow "hey" in the hallway. The more she gave me
the cold shoulder, the angrier I got. I was at least trying to move past
the fight. She was still stewing about it.

"How are we all feeling?" I asked.

The woman directly across the table from me—Mrs. Murphy—
shrugged but didn't look up from her menu. "Woke up today, so I'm
feeling better than Marjorie Flanagan."

I cringed internally but kept my polite smile on. "Well, that's a
good way of looking at it."

RIP, Mrs. Flanagan.

It was always a risk asking how the residents were doing. Some of
them remained stoic and private, while others would tell you every

inappropriate thing that happened to their aging bodies. Still others didn't fear death and would make a joke about the most recent resident to die.

"Why do I work here?" I asked Gabe once I was safe in the kitchen.

"So you can see my smiling face every night."

My stomach, lungs, and heart all gathered in the center of my chest like they were whispering to each other, *Did you hear that? He knows! And he doesn't care! He likes us, too! *Squeal!* Whatever the verbal version of "UwU" is!*

I tried to hide my blushing face in a flurry of salad and soup gathering. We never talked about Vic showing up at the diner on Friday. In fact, when Gabe texted me a few soundtrack samples for the background music of my video—almost all from the *Ratatouille* film score and a movie called *Amélie*—he didn't even mention it.

When I got to my section, Natalie was leaving the table that had just been seated. My heart leaped as she smiled at me and went up to the front service station. This was it. This was the test she had been waiting to spring on me.

Seeing Judge Fredericks, a spry eighty-year-old Black woman with short, stylish gray hair, sitting at my table with her friends was a dead giveaway. Judge Fredericks only ever sat at table twelve in the formal dining room.

She would never request to sit in the casual dining room unless Natalie went to her and asked her to sit in my section. It made sense, too. Judge Fredericks was one of the few residents who didn't hate Natalie.

I quickly grabbed the water pitcher and headed over to fill her glass. "Good evening, Judge."

"Thomas, so nice to see you again."

"What brings you onto this side of the dining room tonight?"

"Just a change of scenery." But she gave me a wink. I greeted the other women at her table, then took their orders. But none of them asked for anything special or off menu. When I dropped off their salads and soups, I asked them if I could get them anything else, but they said no.

After I cleared that course, I watched the kitchen like a hawk, making sure I ran out their dinners as soon as they were up. Even then they didn't ask for anything.

I was starting to worry that the judge—or whoever at the table Natalie had told to ask me for something strange—had forgotten what it was, and that now Natalie's game was going to continue for *months*. I kept an eye on them while they ate, watching Judge Fredericks's water goblet to make sure it was always full. Then I cleared the table and went back to take their dessert orders.

Oh, please don't let them ask for baked Alaska.

"So," I said, approaching the table during a brief lull in the conversation. "For dessert tonight, we have mixed berry cobbler, the sugar-free dessert is angel food cake, and our ice cream flavors are chocolate, vanilla, butter pecan, sugar-free chocolate vanilla swirl, and lime sherbet."

"Just coffee tonight, Thomas," Judge Fredericks said with a smile.

I looked at the other ladies, all of whom nodded and flipped over their coffee cups.

What the hell?

I smiled and put my pad and pen away. "Coming right up."

Were they going to ask for a latte when I got back? Honestly, that wouldn't be so bad. We didn't have espresso, but I could just use the coffee and have Dante heat up milk. Warm milk wasn't exactly an odd request from the old folks.

But when I got back to the rear service station, the coffeepots were gone, and the burners had been turned off.

I headed for the casual dining room's front service station but stopped halfway there when I saw those burners were vacant, too.

No way. Natalie wouldn't do this.

I headed immediately for the formal dining room's service stations, but the burners at both stations were empty and turned off as well. I checked the dining rooms themselves to see if Doris or Natalie might be walking around with the pots, but neither of them was anywhere in sight.

This didn't make sense. Natalie was such a freak about making sure the residents had coffee if they wanted it, why would she take away all the coffeepots as a test for me, knowing more than just Judge Fredericks would be ordering it at the end of the night? I felt like I had fallen into some weird simulation where Natalie had turned off the coffee-craving button for all the resident robots except for Judge Fredericks.

Still, I wasn't too concerned. Even if she got rid of the pots in the dining rooms, there would be coffee in the giant maker in the kitchen.

But when I arrived, Emma G. was already dumping it down the drain. "No, no, wait!"

She flinched and dropped the stainless-steel drum into the sink.

All the coffee spilled out into it.

"What are you doing?" I asked.

Emma G. looked indignant. "My side chore. It's six forty-five and my sections all reset."

"Well, other people still have tables." I picked up the hot stainless-steel drum, hoping there would be some coffee that hadn't spilled down the drain. Barely enough for one cup. "Was this the decaf or regular?"

If it was regular, I could just give them decaf if there was any left. They wouldn't know the difference. And if I was going to give them one over the other, at least this way was safer. I'd never give regular to someone who ordered decaf, but the residents were going right back to their apartments, so it's not like they needed to stay up all night.

"It was regular," Emma G. said.

Thank God.

"I already dumped the decaf."

"Emma! You're killing me!"

"What? There're still two full pots out there!"

"No, there aren't." She looked confused, but I didn't have time to explain it to her. I went back to the dish room and asked one of the washers for the glass coffeepot. He handed me a clean one, and I went back to the coffee station as quickly as I could. There was no way I could brew an entire batch of coffee—our machines brewed a gallon at a time and it took fifteen minutes. But I could do a fake pour-over with the hot water spigot we used for tea.

I folded the filter—it was way too big—into a cone and stuck it in the top of the pot. Then I threw several heaping spoonfuls of coffee into the cone and poured the hot water over it until the water reached the top of the cone, and waited as it slowly dripped down.

"What are you doing?" I turned to see Gabe watching me.

"Making coffee. Can you watch this? I have to check on a table." I told him what to do when the coffee got low, then ran-walked back out to the casual dining room.

I tried my best not to look like I was stressing out—but I was. How the hell was it possible that my entire college career was riding on Natalie *hiding* coffeepots so I was forced to make some artisan pour-over bullshit?

The judge was laughing and telling a story as I approached. Her eyes dropped to my empty hands, and her smile waned.

When I reached the table, I smiled brightly. "I just wanted to check in and let you know coffee is coming right up. I had to make a fresh batch for you, but it shouldn't be much longer."

Her smile returned. "That sounds wonderful, thank you!"

"Of course! Has anyone changed their mind about dessert?" Maybe that was the test. But they all said no. "Okay, I'll be right back." Then I sped to the kitchen as naturally as possible.

Thankfully, Gabe was still helping me with the pour-over. "Thank you."

"Since when do we do this?"

I glared at Emma G. as she scrubbed the coffee drum. "Since Emma G. dumped all the coffee before the last table left."

"Dude, there are pots of coffee out there, or there were when I checked. I don't know what to tell you."

I took out the filter and threw it into the trash. As soon as I did, I realized it might not be enough. What if it didn't fill all four of their cups? The pot was only half-full—no, screw that, this was a half-empty situation.

And what if they asked for seconds?

Then I'd make more. But for now, I went out and poured the coffee, starting with the judge. The coffee was darker than usual. I started panicking. What if it was too strong? Shit, what if it gave one of them heart palpitations? I should have used the decaf just to be safe.

"Anything else I can get you this evening?" I asked, probably a little too loudly and anxiously.

The judge didn't answer. Instead, she put the coffee cup to her lips, took a sip . . .

And flinched.

My stomach dropped.

Sweat beaded at the nape of my neck. It was too strong. Too bitter.

But then her eyebrows popped up, and her smile returned. She looked at me. "Thomas, this is a great cup of coffee." She turned to the other women. "Try it, don't you think it's better than they usually make?"

The other ladies sipped their coffee and gave me plenty of compliments, asking if they'd changed the brand. I told them it was probably just because it was right out of the machine.

"Well," the judge said, "we'll have to make sure we ask for a fresh pot every night." They all laughed, and I laughed with them because if I didn't laugh, I would probably cry. Now they had something new to ask for. Baked Alaska 2.0.

I went to the rear service station and turned on the warmer, then placed the pot back on it. There was enough for one, maybe two cups. I'd check on them later and refill as many as I could before they were empty. Hopefully if they *watched* the coffeepot empty, they wouldn't ask for more.

Before I could get too comfortable, Natalie rounded the corner. Two full coffeepots in her hands. She gave me the same surprised expression that I gave her.

"Where did you get those?" I asked, motioning to the coffeepots.

"The warmer. Where is that pot from?" She seemed to be genuinely asking, as if she was surprised.

She didn't need to hear *how* I'd accomplished her task, especially since I didn't do it entirely correctly. "Judge Fredericks wanted some coffee, so I narrowly caught Emma G. before she dumped it. The other service stations were empty."

She dropped off the decaf on the other burner, turning it on and putting her free hand to her cheek. "Oh, sorry. I was going around but got distracted talking to Mrs. Murphy at the host stand. Marjorie Flanagan passed, apparently, and she's a little distraught, poor thing. But I talked to Judge Fredericks on the way back."

"Oh?"

"Yes. She said you passed your test with flying colors."

I pretended I didn't know what she was talking about. "Test? Wait! That was the test?"

Natalie gave me the smile that I imagine a female praying mantis gives before she bites the head off her mate. "Absolutely! I've been trying to tell her for years that she'd get the same wonderful service in the casual dining room as she receives in the formal dining room."

Huh?

"And you proved me right! She said she was very impressed that despite how many extra tables you have, nothing much changed."

"Wait, the test was just . . ." I looked at the coffeepots again. "Doing my job?"

"Yes!" Natalie continued. "You've completed the first two tasks, so when I have everything squared away on my end, we'll talk about your final task." She put a singsong lilt to her voice. "You're very nearly there!" And with that, she spun around and left.

So this whole task that I had been worried about—I could have done it easily, any day of the week, whenever I wanted. And I didn't even need to make this pour-over coffee?

What in the yellow-brick bullshit?

CHAPTER
THIRTY-ONE

ABOUT A WEEK AND A HALF LATER, a week before Christmas,
Gabe called me after dinner.

I had already seen him at work and told him I'd be working on my
recipe for my supplemental video. We even got a date down for our
first—and hopefully *only*—day of shooting: January 7.

"I've got puff pastries in the oven," I said as I answered. I decided
not to tell him I was also staring at my La Mère essay. Well, the blank
page that *should* have been the La Mère essay. "And I'm about to make
the cream base and see what kind of flavors I should add to make it
pop. So I can't watch anything until this is done."

I had decided to go with the croquembouche for the video. But
I wanted the cream in the puff pastries to be different colors and
flavors. The admissions people wouldn't be able to taste the flavor,
obviously, but I thought maybe if we recorded a few reaction videos
from my mom and friends they could explain how it stood out.

I was going to do a strawberry, blueberry, salted caramel, chocolate ganache, and a bananas Foster.

Gabe sounded weird when he spoke. "How much longer?"

I turned on the oven light. "About three minutes?" The timer said five, but they were starting to brown. I'd have to keep an eye on them.

"Want to take an ice cream break?"

I laughed. "It's twenty degrees tonight."

"The ice cream place I want to go to has seating inside."

"Are you okay?"

"Not really. Can I come pick you up? You can bring all the cream and pastries and keep working. I'll even help you fill them if you want. I just don't want to sit at a table like a sad sack eating ice cream alone."

Why wasn't he calling Vic? Or Kevin, or the whole crew of Murphy friends he had? He was calling me, for ice cream, at eight forty-five p.m. on a Monday night.

Maybe it was related to Vic and their relationship. Plus, the pastries could be stored for a day. Then I could do all the cream tomorrow when I got home from school, since I didn't have work, and Mom would taste test for me and help figure out which cream recipes to go with.

"Yeah," I said, looking back at the blank page on my laptop screen. "I can take a break."

He picked me up and we talked about work on the drive. After twenty minutes, Gabe pulled to a stop in a parking lot with a P.F. Chang's, a Fine Wine & Good Spirits, a Trader Joe's, and a handful of other smaller stores. I had been to the Trader Joe's a few times but not the others, so I followed him toward the place with the gold lit sign that said *Oscar's Ice Cream*.

He opened the door for me, and I ducked in quickly to get out of the cold.

And so he couldn't see me smile.

Oscar's had reclaimed wood lining the walls and uncomfortable-but-fashionable-looking wooden booths. We were the only people in there. Of course. Because it was a twenty-degree night in December.

I followed Gabe toward the counter, glancing at the framed pictures on the walls. Each one was a famous actress holding an Academy Award in her hands.

"Hey, Tommy." I turned to see Grant Feldman behind the counter in a black T-shirt with the poster for a movie called *Last Night in Soho* on it.

Grant, who had denied me the use of the film class equipment. I should probably thank him now that Gabe was helping me.

"Hey, Grant. This is my friend Gabe. He goes to Murphy."

"I've seen you in here before," Grant said. "What's up?"

I glanced at the board behind him with the ice cream flavors. It looked like a movie marquee, and I think it was in English, but it made no sense to me. *Rum Raisinette Bening. Reese's with a Spoon Sundae. Cake Blanchett.*

"What are these flavors?"

Grant sighed. "All the flavors are named after Oscar-winning or -nominated actresses. I can tell you what's in everything if you have any questions."

I turned to Gabe, tilting my head. He smiled broadly. "I love this place."

"You would." I laughed. "What's your favorite?"

"Can I do the Frances McDor-Mint Chocolate Chip?" he asked.

"Associate Producer, Producer, or Executive Producer?" said Grant.

"Producer." I gave him a face, and he smiled wider. "It means medium. And I think for you . . . the Scoop-ita Nyong'o or . . . Jodie Bananas Foster."

I burst out laughing.

"Go with Jodie," Grant said. "It's real banana and our house-made caramel swirl. Associ—"

"*Medium.* Please."

Grant stared at me, stone-faced. "What's 'medium'?"

I rolled my eyes. "I can't believe you're making me say this. Producer. Please."

Grant smirked and said, "Eleven fifty-six."

I went for my wallet, but Gabe pushed my hand away and handed Grant a card. "I got it. Plus, I get an extra punch on my Costar Card." He showed me the punch card, which said *Get Your 10th Ice Cream Free! You Like Us! You Really Like Us!* Gabe already had four stars punched out of the card when he handed it to Grant.

"I'll bring it over to you guys if you want to sit?"

"Thanks, Grant," I said.

We sat at a table, and I clasped my hands together.

"So what's going on with you?" I asked.

He faked a look of concern. I knew it was faked because I could read his face better than I could read my own. His dimples popped every time a genuine emotion came through. When he faked it, there were no dimples.

"I just wanted some ice cream."

"Don't bullshit me. Or I'm taking Jodie to go."

He laughed—dimples—and picked at the table. "It's just been . . . a week. You know?"

"It's Monday."

"I know." He sighed and sat back. He spoke as though he were typing his words and deleting them as he went along, pausing to make sure he got each word correct before it was said. "Are . . . I think we've become good friends. Right?"

Ew. Friends. "Right."

"So can I talk about stuff that friends talk about?"

I pretended like I was trying to catch the eye of other imaginary people sitting around us. "We don't already?"

"I mean, stuff queer friends talk about. Like . . . boyfriend stuff."

I felt myself slump but tried to correct it and failed.

"I'm sorry. Let's just get the ice cream to go." He scooted across the booth to tell Grant to pack it up, but I reached for his hand.

I didn't want to talk about Vic with Gabe. But I also didn't want to go home. What was it called when you had conflicting emotions and knew exactly what you should and shouldn't do but pretended you didn't? When you did what you shouldn't do and justified it in some Rube Goldberg logic machine in your head that only doesn't make sense years later?

Oh, right, it's called being a dipshit.

"We can talk about it," I said, dipshittily. I took my hand back and crossed my arms. "But I'm already biased. You know, because I kissed you that one time before I knew about him."

I tried to make it sound like a joke, and he laughed, so I must have tricked him. Or he tricked me.

"Can I ask why you don't ever post pictures of the two of you on social media?"

Gabe started fidgeting with his fingers, suddenly very focused on his cuticles. "I don't like posting a lot about my private life on socials. My family follows me, so as long as I'm only posting about family, friends, or film, they won't feel the need to comment with anything passive-aggressive. Or aggressive-aggressive."

Well, shit. Now I felt bad. I'd thought he was *hiding* Vic because he was embarrassed by him, not as self-preservation. My mom wasn't on social media, so I never had to worry about her. Plus, my profiles were private and I only approved people I knew. But also, I had slowly started subtly posting queer stuff and figured it would be an easy way to gauge my mom's feelings if I did make my profiles public and if she ever got curious and searched for me. If she didn't bring it up, maybe she didn't want to know about it. If she did, maybe she was okay with it.

But it seemed like Gabe's family brought it up even if they weren't okay with it.

He settled back in the booth, and Grant came over with the ice cream, setting it down in front of us with gold plastic spoons and a handful of napkins.

"Holy shit, that's a lot of ice cream." There were at least five scoops of ice cream in the plastic bowl.

"I gave you guys Executive. On me."

"Thanks!" Gabe said.

"Enjoy."

I took my spoon, unsure where to start on the giant mound of frozen dairy. I dug into the side and saw Gabe was watching me. "What?"

"You need to get a big scoop—"

"Scoop-*ita*."

"Yes, that."

I took a bite, and the banana ice cream really was pretty amazing. It didn't have that fake banana flavor most banana confections had. But the caramel was super overpowering. It was a thick ribbon but a little too sweet and not enough salt.

He pushed the Frances McDor-Mint over to me and took my Jodie Bananas Foster. "See if you like this one better."

I tasted it. And yes, it was less overwhelming. Much better. I gave him a thumbs-up.

"So what's going on?"

Gabe dug around in the ice cream before answering. "We got in a fight."

Yes!

"Or not a fight, I guess. An argument."

"What's the difference?"

He scrunched up his face. "I actually don't know? 'Argument' sounds a little softer."

"Was the fight soft?" *Please say no, please say no, please say no.* Oh, but not in a violent way.

He didn't say anything and just wiggled his shoulders like he wasn't sure. "It was stupid but also . . ." He let his voice fade out and took a bite of ice cream. I mirrored his movements, then swapped back with him.

"Have some Florence Mint-engale or whatever that's called. It'll cheer you up."

He smirked, and I felt like I was going to explode when I saw his dimples. "Frances McDor-Mint!"

"That's the one." Jodie was growing on me, anyway. The fresh banana, probably.

"He's not going to be around for Christmas, so I called him tonight and told him to come over so we could hang out and exchange gifts."

I took another bite of ice cream, not even tasting it anymore.

"He was all . . ." Gabe stuck his spoon in the ice cream and made a confused face. When he spoke, he did an impression of Vic that chilled me more than the ice cream did. "'Wha . . . wha . . . what do you mean? We didn't agree to exchange gifts.'"

"He didn't get you a Christmas gift? How long have you been together?"

"Six months, but it's not even that. He could have just said he didn't get me a gift. I don't *need* a gift from him, but when I said I could still give him his, he went off on me. Saying it wasn't fair that I'd bought him a gift—"

What?

"—and that I wasn't respecting his boundaries—"

Whaaaaaat?

"—and that I was just trying to manipulate him and make him feel bad because he was going away for the holiday without me."

If I didn't have a mouthful of ice cream, my mouth would be hanging open. I swallowed, feeling the cold glob freeze my insides on the way down. "Don't take this the wrong way—but there's something not right with his brain."

He laughed, but this time the dimples were nowhere to be seen. "I think he was just embarrassed. And . . . ugh, this sounds awful." He leaned back in the booth, no longer interested in his ice cream. I gave him a face that said, *Go on*. He finally did. "I *did* want him to get me a gift. It's not that I'm materialistic—"

"You're seventeen and you drive an *Audi*, sir."

"I said I wasn't materialistic, not that I didn't like nice cars." I scoffed but let him continue. "It didn't have to be expensive, just, like . . . remember the old holiday episode of *Sesame Street*, when Bert and Ernie did the whole *Gift of the Magi* thing?"

"Was that when Ernie traded his rubber ducky for a cigar box for Bert's paper clip collection?"

"Yeah! And Bert traded his paper clip collection for a soap dish that Ernie could put his rubber ducky in. Anyway, Vic didn't even need to give away something to get me something thoughtful. It could have cost a dollar, and as long as there was thought behind it, I would have loved it. All he had to give me was a soap dish."

My face burned hot. Not even the ice cream could cool me down. "Finish your ice cream," I said. "It will make you feel better."

And I knew something else that would, too.

CHAPTER
THIRTY-TWO

HE CAME TO A STOP IN FRONT of my house, and I told him to pull over and park for a second. I asked him to wait and hopped out of the car, running up the front steps as fast as I could. Once in the house I said hi to my mom, told her there was leftover Jodie Bananas Foster in the freezer if she wanted, and grabbed a little box from my room.

I was back in the passenger seat in under three minutes, out of breath. Gabe's eyes dropped to the box in my hands, then up to me again.

He closed his eyes, biting his lower lip. Did he not know how much that made me want to kiss him?

"I was going to give it to you on Christmas Eve after work, but . . ." I held it out to him. "Merry Christmas, Gabe De La Hoya."

He looked like he wasn't going to take it. And for a second I thought he wasn't going to. He shook his head, his smile growing. And then he got out of the car. I clutched the box against me, embarrassment blooming in my chest. He stood at the back of the car for a moment, then opened the trunk.

I laughed when he got back in holding a giant gift bag.

"I got you a gift, too."

We passed them over the center console and stared at each other.

"Open it!" he said. I told him to go first, but he refused.

I finally relented and opened the gift bag. Then I saw the name on the box and stopped immediately. Emile Henry was a cookware company. And not cheap.

"Holy shit, Gabe." I took out the box and gasped.

"It's a—"

"A bread cloche, no, I know!" He snorted. I had seen them online and actually wanted one. It was a Dutch oven that doubled as a bread box. It was also a hundred and fifty bucks. Way more than I'd spent on his gift. "This is too nice, Gabe. I can't accept it."

"You can, 'cause it was on clearance and all sales were final."

I didn't know what to say. "Was it really?"

"No. But I did just see your face, and you're not making me take that back. It's yours. All I ask is you bake me some bread in it."

"Hell yeah! You get free carbs for life."

He laughed. I wanted to bask more, but I saw him fidgeting with his gift. Oh, right! This was an *exchange*. And there was no way I was giving him the gift in that box now. I put the bread cloche in the gift bag and grabbed for the box in his lap.

He snatched it away, smiling. "No!"

"I just realized it's the wrong box."

"Oh, did I get Ava's present?"

That kind of hurt. I did have a gift for Ava, but we hadn't exactly spoken since our blowup, so I didn't know where we stood on gift giving at the moment.

Gabe pulled open the cardboard box. "Is it a—"

He stopped speaking. I bit my top lip and pulled at my fingers. I was so nervous. What if he thought it was stupid? It *was* stupid. Shit, and now it was too late. Pandora's box was opened.

He stared at it. I couldn't read his face. There were no dimples at all. My chest tightened, and I pulled at my finger harder, cracking a knuckle.

"I know it's silly. I just thought it was . . . I don't know." I chuckled. Now I felt super dumb. Even dumber, if that was possible, when he took it out. It was a little Hot Wheels DeLorean from *Back to the Future*. I saw it at an antique store with Ava a few weeks ago. It was just sitting there in a shoebox on top of all the other little Hot Wheels cars from who knows when.

It had seemed cute at the time. But that was before he gave me a $150 piece of bakeware.

He turned to me, and I could see the smile growing on his face. "I fucking . . . *love* this."

Dimples! YES!

"Seriously? It's a silly toy."

He shook his head and stared at it in his hands, his eyes turning glassy. "No, Thomas. It isn't." My face burned hot again.

But before I could get too embarrassed, he reached across the center console and pulled me to him. There was no question this time: *he* was kissing *me*. His hands went up to my hair, but he was still holding the Hot Wheels in one. It felt like he was trying to drive it across my scalp, and I laughed against his lips.

He must have known exactly what I was laughing at, because he laughed too and put the Hot Wheels back in the box in his lap. His hand then returned to the nape of my neck, and I breathed him into me.

Vic be damned.

Finally, after what felt like seconds yet also an hour but was probably ten minutes, I pulled away. When I spoke, it sounded like I was out of breath, even though I hadn't moved from my seat. "My mom's probably wondering where I ran out to."

"Probably."

Then we were making out again.

"I should go," I said, pulling back. Also, if anything else was going to happen—and *MY GOD*, did I want it to happen—I didn't want the cloud of Vic hanging over us. All that had to be over with if we were going to do anything else.

Gabe gently nipped at my neck. "Probably."

So why did I keep leaning back across the center console to kiss him more? Finally, I pulled myself away.

"I really should go." He said nothing. This bastard wanted me to kiss him again, didn't he? And I wanted to. I shook my head. "Good night, Gabe."

"Good night, Thomas." I kissed him. This time it was a simple, gentle kiss on the lips. A good night kiss. He reached for the DeLorean again. "Thank you for my soap dish."

Dimples again. Score.

Then something hit me. I tilted my head. "Why did you reference *Sesame Street* redoing *Gift of the Magi* and not just *Gift of the Magi*?"

He frowned. "Bitch, I never read *Gift of the Magi*; you get what I know." He drove the DeLorean across his dashboard, and I laughed.

Then I leaned back in and kissed him again.

CHAPTER
THIRTY-THREE

I PULLED MY FOURTH BATCH OF MACARONS out of the oven, and like two of the three batches before it, their feet were small and broken. I sighed and threw the tray on top of the stove to cool, not even bothering to move them onto a rack. I checked my phone again before returning to the chocolate ganache. Still nothing from Gabe.

It had been almost two weeks now. I'd left his car the week before Christmas feeling high. I was buzzing with so much excitement, I stayed up until almost two in the morning finishing my pastries. The next morning he sent me a picture of the DeLorean in his driveway, but he framed it so it looked the same size as his Audi.

We texted almost nonstop all day. He was off that week to study for midterm exams and only scheduled to work once winter break started. But then he had called out on Christmas Eve. I texted him, but he didn't answer, and I'd assumed it was just because of the holiday and he was busy. Of course, I didn't hear from him on Christmas, either.

That's when the high finally wore off and was replaced with dread. Had I done something wrong? Had something changed? I read and reread our text exchange, trying to figure out where I messed up or said something I shouldn't have, but I couldn't find it. He didn't answer texts—nor the picture of my Christmas bread using the bread cloche, and yes, it came out great—or my calls, until finally, on the twenty-sixth, I sent a text saying, Just let me know if you're alive, please. He didn't answer, but I saw him start to type.

And worst of all, I couldn't talk to Ava about it because I was getting the silent treatment from her.

Now here it was, New Year's Eve, and still nothing.

"Oh!" My mom entered the kitchen, plucking up one of the coconut pandan macarons. "These look good."

"Well, enjoy them," I said. "Because the rest suck."

She bit into the green cookie, then cringed and spit it out. "I think something might be wrong with these ones."

I took one and bit into it. And, yes, it was bitter. I spit it out and tried to retrace my steps. What had gone wron—oh no.

"I put in a tablespoon of the pandan extract."

"And you weren't supposed to use a tablespoon?"

"Teaspoon." I must have mixed up the recipe in my head. I was supposed to use a tablespoon of the vanilla bean paste in the vanilla buttercream, and a teaspoon of the pandan extract in the coconut buttercream.

My mom looked at the other batches of unassembled macarons I had been working on all day. "Well, these look good, too."

"Their feet are broken. The ones that puffed up, I undermixed, so I mixed a little longer on these . . ." I pointed to the larger cookies. "And now they're overmixed."

"Well, I'm sure they'll still taste good." But she didn't reach out and try any. Instead, she pulled out a chair and watched me mix the ganache. I was wearing my dad's chef's coat, and yes, there were new stains that actually made it look used. "What are you stressing about?"

"Nothing."

I didn't need to look at her because I could feel her eyes on me. I put down the ganache and went to the mixer to start working on the buttercream filling. As long as I didn't measure the paste wrong, I could still give out the imperfect macarons. At least they'd taste fine.

But the butter wasn't in the mixing bowl coming to room temperature, though I could have sworn I put it there. I spun around, looking for the sticks on the counter and the kitchen table. Finally I opened the fridge, and there they were. What the hell?

"Yes, that's the face you make when you're not stressed," my mom said.

"I'm stressed because these macarons aren't working!"

"You said they're hard to perfect."

"And I perfected them! Now they aren't perfected anymore, and I'm stressing."

"But you didn't stress when you were perfecting them before. So something is distracting you. What is it?"

I couldn't tell her that all I had thought about over the past few days was Gabe and why he was ignoring me. What was I supposed to say? *Oh, a boy I like kissed me, but he has a boyfriend, and even though it seemed like he was going to dump his shitty boyfriend for me—because, again, he's shitty—I haven't heard from him in days, and oh, by the way, I'm gay?*

"Are you on drugs?" she asked.

"No."

"Have you been smoking weed?"

"Mom! I'm not high!"

"That's not a no, so if you are smoking weed, at least lie to me!"

"I'm not smoking weed."

"Thank you." She let out a sigh of relief. "But . . . now I'm wondering if you really are lying."

"Mom!"

"Okay! So if you're not doing drugs, is it school?"

"Yes." It was easier to say it was just school, but it was everything. La Mère, Ava still not talking to me, Gabe now also not talking to me, and the uncertainty behind *why*. With Ava it was obvious—she was pissed because I didn't support her gap year idea. I understood it in theory, but what had been the point in her doing all that hard work over the past few years for nothing? *That's* what I didn't understand.

My mom folded her hands together. "Ava's uncle called me." I didn't say anything. "He told me she doesn't want to go to Johns Hopkins. He's worried about her." So she had told him. Which meant the "possible" gap year was officially a for-sure gap year. And she didn't even bother to let me know.

"So am I. She did all that work to just throw her life away."

My mom tilted her head. "Why do you think that?"

"Because she's not going to the school she worked so hard to get into!"

"That doesn't mean she's throwing her life away. Maybe something changed and she just needs time to figure it out."

"She can still do that *in* school."

My mom laughed, loud and harsh. "Yeah, well, it's fifty thousand bucks cheaper to do it outside of school. Take it from someone with a bachelor's in marketing who's a glorified event planner for a retirement community. It might be easier to take some time and figure out what you really like before you get buried in student loan debt. But is all this really about you worrying if you'll get into La Mère?" She motioned to the macarons. "They're not going to make you whip up a batch of these to prove you belong."

"I was going to make a video to show I belonged, remember? And the person who was supposed to help me backed out, and now I'm screwed and I have to figure it out myself."

That was completely secondary, though. Yes, I still had to get my video together, but I had time to do that. What I really needed *now* was to know how Gabe went from kissing me to completely ignoring me. Even after we first kissed and he told me he had a boyfriend, he still answered my texts.

She shook her head. "You don't have to figure it out yourself. I'll help you. Just tell me what you need, and I'll help you do it. Or if you don't want me, just text Ava an apology and ask her for help."

"I'll see her tonight," I said. "She'll be at the party."

"The party you're not going to be drinking at, right?"

"Right." That was actually true. I had no plans to spend tonight drinking at Amber Gallo's house because I didn't want to get all mopey when I had no one to kiss at midnight. I also wanted to see if Gabe would show up—if he did, it would be much better if I was sober for that conversation.

My mom stood and pointed to the coconut pandan cookies. "Maybe don't give her these, if you're trying to make up."

But Gabe wasn't there. Ava was, with Morgan, and even though I had been at the party for twenty minutes already I had yet to go over and say hi to her. I dropped off the bags of chocolate ganache and vanilla/strawberry macarons in the kitchen, not bothering to look for a plate to make them look presentable.

I went right out onto the back deck, where I could see Kevin and a couple of other Murphy bros smoking.

"Have you seen Gabe?" I asked Kevin.

"What's up, Tommy?" Then when I didn't answer, he shook his head. "Nah, he's not here."

"I know he isn't." I had looked inside. "I mean have you seen him recently? Is he alive?"

Kevin laughed. "Yeah, man, he's alive. What are you talking about?"

"He called out of work and hasn't answered my texts."

Kevin stepped away from the other Murphy bros and lowered his voice. "Look, I don't want to get into whatever y'all's drama is."

"We don't have drama. He just hasn't been answering me when I text him."

"Yeah. That's drama. He went skiing with Vic and his friends, man. If he's not answering, maybe he's busy. Or has shitty service. Or . . ."

Drama.

Vic. He went skiing with his boyfriend. After he kissed me. After he gave me an amazing gift and sold me on the one I gave him being some *Gift of the Magi* bullshit. My cheeks burned with embarrassment. Or frustration. Or both.

I nodded and headed back into the house, leaving Kevin and his friends. I made a beeline right to Ava and Morgan.

"Can you stop ignoring me now?" I asked Ava.

She tilted her head. "Are you going to lecture me again?"

"Guys," Morgan said, her tone warning us not to say something we'd regret.

"I wasn't lecturing you."

Ava's eyes went wide. "You said I was throwing my life away."

"That's not what this is abo—"

"I know it isn't," she snapped. She took a step closer to me. "It's about me wanting to figure out what *I* want to do with *my* life and my best friend not supporting me."

"I do support you. I always will, I just wanted you to think about it."

"You seriously think I would ever do anything without thinking about it? Without dissecting every possible avenue or misstep?"

"But you never even mentioned anything until you got accepted."

"I said I'd thought about it. I didn't say I needed your opinion or to talk it out with you. It's my decision, one that I absolutely *had* been thinking of—and way before you thought I started thinking about it!" Morgan tried to get our attention again, but Ava was already going, and she wasn't stopping. Her eyes were glassy as she yelled at me. "What gets me is you *know* the amount of pressure I'm under at home. You knew how important my family thinks me going to school is. I just needed you on my side in this because no one else is. They pulled a full-blown intervention on me Christmas morning."

"What?"

"My whole family. Aunts, uncles, cousins, my grandmother. All morning and half the afternoon spent bombarding me with what-ifs and cautionary tales of Black girls who don't get a college degree. How I'm squandering everything my parents gave me and all the sacrifices my uncle made to take me in and make sure I had all the best opportunities."

And now I understood everything. Of course they were worried. I was, too. And I got why she wanted me to be on her side. It was totally out of line for them to bring up her parents, but were they entirely wrong?

"I'm sorry. I get it, you want to be sure of what you're doing. But you can still go to schoo—"

"Stop it, Tommy!" she yelled. Tears streamed down her face, and this time everyone around us turned to look over. "You're doing it again. Just stop. I don't need you to solve anything. I don't need you to tell me what I need to do."

Morgan finally stepped between us. "Okay, I think that's enough. We're not going to solve any of this now, and I think we need to take a break."

Morgan was right. We needed to step back from this because we were just arguing in circles. Ava wasn't going to change her mind because of something I said. I knew she thought she was right. And, I don't know, maybe she was. She was smarter than me, after all. But I still didn't understand how giving everything up would make her happy. Ava loved learning new things and taking on new challenges.

It was why, when she got a new video game, she'd play it nonstop for almost twenty-four hours to figure it out. It was how she'd realized all the bioengineering stuff fascinated her. I couldn't see how she was going to be happy this way.

So, instead of continuing to argue, I nodded and said, "Okay." Then I left, heading out the front door into the cold. Unfortunately for the person sitting in the middle of the front steps blocking me, the porch lights were off, and I walked right into them.

I tumbled headfirst over their shoulders. They let out an "Oof!" and I heard their plastic cup tumble onto the stairs, spilling whatever drink they had. I grappled for the handrail to my right but couldn't get it. There was just enough time for me to think, *My skull is going to crack like an egg on this pavement*, before the person I'd walked into scooped me up in their arms.

"Sorry, are you okay?" they asked. I knew that voice. "Oh, hey, Tommy."

"Brad, you just saved my fucking life." I may not have been in the mood to see Brad—or really any guy—right now, but if I did have to run into someone, his friendly face wasn't a bad one to see.

Brad chuckled and helped steady me. "Well, I did almost end it, too. So . . . sorry about that."

"Why aren't you inside?" I asked. He pulled the hood of his sweatshirt down, and I could see his features in the dim light of the moon.

He shrugged. "I dunno. Why aren't you?"

"Because I'm leaving."

"Didn't you just get here?"

"I realized I'm not in the mood to party."

Brad looked down at his feet and nudged the now-empty cup with one. "Me neither. Can I . . . ask you something?"

Before he could finish his sentence, I shook my head. Making out with Brad might seem like a good idea, but it wasn't. Yes, it worked in the moment, but I immediately went back to pining for Gabe. Because Brad wasn't emotionally available. Gabe at least had told me he liked me, despite not being available. Brad had never really said those words to me. He was a closeted boy who wasn't ready to come out yet. Which was fine. But Brad wasn't out to any of his friends, either. Gabe was out, but he was in a relationship. There was some hope with Gabe. At least I'd thought there was.

"Sorry," I said. "I'm not really in the mental place for a make-out session right now."

Even in the dim light I could tell he was disappointed, which, yay me, I guess? But when he spoke, he didn't sound disappointed. He sounded concerned.

"What's wrong?"

"Trust me, you don't want to know."

"I wouldn't ask if I didn't, Tommy."

That was true, actually. Brad never really asked that much about me, but when he did—usually when we were alone and he was sober—he actually seemed interested. And I didn't really have anyone else to talk to about it. Ava was clearly still pissed at me, and I couldn't talk to my mom about it because I was still worried about coming out to her. Plus, Brad could absolutely relate to that part.

"You're sure?" I asked.

Without a word—and without going inside to get another

drink—he plopped down on the top step again. I paced back and forth as I explained everything to him, starting with meeting Gabe when we were kids and ending with him ghosting me after he kissed me. I also included the part about Ava and me getting into a fight. He listened, only stopping me to ask for clarification here and there.

Maybe that's what Ava meant. All she needed was someone to listen to her and understand her pain. And support her. Shit. I really just played myself, didn't I? But she was my friend. I wanted to help her. I also wanted to make sure she was happy with what she chose to do, which, of course she would know better than me what would make her happy.

Brad sat on the front steps the whole time, listening to me. After I was done, he asked, "So what are you going to do?" If I wasn't mistaken, he seemed bummed. As if me talking about another guy made him jealous. Of Gabe. Not in a possessive way, but in a way that he wished he could have, maybe?

"Nothing?" What could I do? Go to Gabe's house every day until he got home from his ski trip? First off, no. That would be beyond unhinged stalker behavior. Two, and risk Vic being there and seeing how upset I was? That would just give him more power.

I chuckled. "Maybe I'll get lucky and he'll just never come back to work. I can pretend he got eaten by a shark again. No, killed in an avalanche! I mean, I did it before, and it worked then."

"Mmm, yeah . . . totally." But he sounded skeptical.

I opened my mouth to ask what he meant by that, but shouts came from inside the house. "TEN! NINE! EIGHT!"

My phone confirmed it. 11:59. Brad turned and looked at the house.

"SEVEN! SIX! FIVE!"

He looked back at me and said quietly, "Four . . . three . . ."

I joined. "Two . . . one."

The shouts of "HAPPY NEW YEAR!" and cheers inside broke our own silence once midnight hit. Was he going to kiss me? I wasn't sure how I felt about that. He was still here; he didn't leap up and run inside to find his friends or anything. He stayed put, with me. But also he'd stayed put while I had just spent the last forty-five minutes or so talking about why a kiss with another guy went wrong. Would he even *want* to kiss me? *I* wouldn't want to kiss me.

He stood and closed the distance between us.

But instead of kissing me, he wrapped his arms around me in a warm hug. "Happy New Year, Tommy."

I was in an extremely vulnerable position, and if he *had* kissed me, I think I would have let him—and I'd also have enjoyed it. But he didn't. And I'll admit it, I respected the shit out of him for that. He probably knew I would have kissed him back, but he chose to give me a friendly, supportive hug instead. So maybe he wasn't jealous after all. I hugged him back. And it was a nice hug. "Happy New Year, Brad."

He stepped back. That was when I realized that he was out here all alone before I came out. And instead of going someplace more private, he'd stayed put and listened to me. Sure, no one had walked out and interrupted us—yet—but it was a possibility.

I remembered a month earlier, when he'd seemed to be asking me out in front of Lara. Maybe Brad was starting to feel more comfortable with himself. And maybe that meant he was more comfortable with me? I was a little curious. Usually, this was when I made things easier by making the first move so Brad didn't need to go through the moments of self-hate before giving in and actually kissing me.

Instead, here we were, talking. And Brad wasn't seeming all that uncomfortable. Hell, he'd even hugged me.

"So," I said. "Do you want to tell me why *you're* out here, listening to me talk about boy troubles, instead of inside with your friends?"

He shook his head and waved his hand. "It's a new year; leave it in the past."

"New year, new queer."

He snorted. "I like that. You going back in?" He pointed to the front door behind him.

"Nah. I have to apologize to Ava, and I want to make sure she and I are both sober for it so we can have a real talk."

We said goodbye and I went back to my car. I checked my phone for a text from Ava, but there was nothing. And that was fine. We'd make up in a day or two. I'd be lying if I said I didn't wish for a *Happy New Year* text from Gabe. But I'd also be lying if I said I expected to see one.

CHAPTER
THIRTY-FOUR

"WHAT THE FUCK!"

There was no one in the kitchen for me to exclaim to, but I did it anyway. I was staring at the lineup sheet posted on the office door right above the chores. I wanted to see where Gabe was stationed today, hoping I could convince Morgan to triple- or even quadruple-seat him. Yes, I had moved on to the anger stage of my Gabriel Grief Process. But imagine my surprise at seeing Morgan was in the dining room training a new girl, while Gabe's name was under *Host*.

He was the first boy host probably in Sunset Estates history.

James came up behind me. *Oh, good. Someone did hear my exclamation.*

"What're we lookin' at, Bahama Mama?" I pointed to Gabe's name. "Babe!" He seemed to be excited.

"You call him '*babe*'?"

"Yeah."

"Why?"

"'Cause he *is* a babe. Even I can see that. And I'm, like, a . . . which side of the Kinsey scale is the straight one?"

I shrugged and went back to my opening task duties.

"Well, I'm not the zero or the six, but I'm not a three, you know? Like a two or one. Or five or four, whichever is less gay but still kinda gay, where you can be like, *Yo, the Rock looks* good *in* Jumanji, you know? You ever see *Jumanji?*"

James continued talking about *Jumanji* for thirty minutes while I stacked glasses and fried up the frozen French fries. All the while thinking about Gabe.

Here I'd thought he might quit to avoid me, but he was back at work. As a host. Which meant that he was out in the formal dining room removing the Sunday brunch printouts from the leather-bound menus and inserting the new dinner printouts. And that he got to work before I did—even though I hadn't seen his Audi by the loading dock, which meant he'd probably parked out front to avoid me.

I glanced up at the clock when I emerged from the walk-in with a giant bowl of lemons. Everyone would be arriving shortly for the dinner shift. How much longer could he avoid seeing me? How much longer could *I* avoid talking to him?

The answer ended up being "forty more seconds," because as I grabbed one of Chef Roni's giant knives and a mint-green cutting board to slice the lemons, Gabe came through the kitchen doors, giving me a quick glance. Then he went to the lineup sheet to write on his laminated floor plan who was in which section.

Rookie mistake.

Rule number one when trying to avoid someone: if you don't have to step foot in the kitchen the whole shift, do all the kitchen work before the person you're avoiding arrives. Morgan was a professional at that; maybe she should have done some training with him.

I walked right past Gabe, put the cutting board on the metal counter next to the dinner trays, and started cutting my lemons.

His slip-resistant shoes squeaked as he approached me. "Hey."

I froze in the middle of throwing cut lemons into the shallow chafing dish I had set aside. I didn't even turn to look at him; I just dropped the lemons and went back to cutting.

"I'm sorry I haven't been in touch."

"Are you?" Dammit. I couldn't just keep ignoring him, could I? No, I couldn't. Because I deserved to know what was up. Why he was ignoring me.

But I knew why. It was Vic. I glanced at Gabe, and his face was red. I focused my attention back on the lemons. Thinking about them only. Slice one in half, then slice into thirds.

Slice. One-two-three. Into the chafing dish.

"I know. It's just complicated."

I put the knife down. I didn't want him scared when he heard how angry I was, and holding a super-sharp knife the size of a small machete might be intimidating.

"No," I said, keeping my voice down. "It's not that fucking complicated. You kissed me. *Twice*, by the way. And I know you told your boyfriend *I* kissed *you*, even though the first time—when I, maybe, started it—you did kiss me back. The second time, though, *you* kissed *me*. And then you ignored me. So no. I get it. It's not complicated. You're a user."

"I did not use you."

"Then where the hell have you been?"

He opened his mouth to answer but looked behind me. I knew

James was listening, but I didn't care. "Can we go to the PDR?"

"No. I have to finish my prep work." I went back to the lemons.

Gabe sighed and turned to leave the kitchen but came back. "No, you know what? It *is* complicated. Because I do have a boyfriend and . . . I also like you."

"How good for you."

"Vic and I have history. He was—he was there for me when I was having a rough time, and sometimes, yeah, he can be a dick, but then other times he's the sweetest, most charming person, and I remember why I fell in love with him to begin with."

Love. Ow. I chopped the lemons a little bit faster, kind of wishing they were onions so I could cry and not have it look like I was sobbing over Gabe.

"Did he end up giving you the soap dish you always wanted?" I asked, venom in my voice.

He was quiet just long enough for me to know I had struck a nerve. "He was getting me a surprise. He and his friends all rented a place up in the Poconos. And he was going to have me come up and meet him, then surprise me with a ski day."

"I didn't know you liked skiing."

He was quiet again for a second. Another nerve struck? I paused with the knife above the skin of the lemon.

"Didn't you say he was already going away?" I turned to see Gabe avoiding my gaze. "So he knew you were pissed and invited you on his friend trip. And what? Paid for your lift ticket? Did he even pay for that? Or ski rentals—no, you probably own skis already, even if you haven't ever skied before. But how about food? Or booze? Or the cabin itself. Did he pay for all that, or was that another thing you paid for, and he suddenly didn't care about not getting you a gift?"

Fury wiped the embarrassment from Gabe's face, and I realized I was right. And I felt bad for him.

He pointed a finger at me. "Fine, be petty and pissed off if you want. I just came to say it was a mistake."

"It *was* a mistake," I said. I turned back to the lemons and kept cutting, talking in frustration as I chopped. "And you *did* use me. Even if you don't realize it, I've had enough time over the past *two weeks* of radio silence to figure it out. You called me to vent about your boyfriend, and I think even if I didn't have a gift for you, you would have kissed me. Because you don't know what you want. You think you want him, but he's an asshole and you like being dumped on. Maybe you like me because I'm the nice guy who gives you the happy feelings while Vic is the asshole who makes you feel like dirt. 'Cause you think you deserve to feel like dirt."

Ava had been right all along about him. I was holding this ideal in my head from when we were kids, but that Ideal Gabe wasn't the Gabe before me now. The Gabe who I was in love with—because, yeah, I do think it was love, even though we were young—*that* Gabe wouldn't have dated an asshole. That Gabe would have stood up for himself because he stood up for other people. This definitely wasn't that Gabe. Tears stung my eyes. Maybe I could pretend lemons did that. Maybe no one else knew enough to know otherwise.

I glanced at Gabe, and his face was filled with sadness.

"And you know what?" I said, pouncing on his silence. "I'm glad you have someone like Vic to love, because if you really want to feel like garbage all the time, he's perfect for you. And my solace can be knowing you feel like shit with your shitty boyfriend. But I'm not going to be used by you anymore. I don't want to be your friend. I don't want to kiss you. Now get out of my kitchen. I have prep work to finish."

I chopped the last lemon wedge just as I said "finish"—it was timed perfectly. But my hand also slipped, and as I felt the blade bite my skin I hissed, dropping the knife.

"Ow! Shit." Then came the acid burn of the lemon juice. Oh, *that* was awful! Knife cuts always start with sharp pain, a quick wince, and then adrenaline numbing the pain. But the lemon juice added a whole other level of burning agony. But once I cleaned it, if it wasn't too bad, in an hour I wouldn't even notice. And hopefully I wouldn't have to fill out an OSHA form.

I lifted my fingers to my mouth to suck the blood but stopped halfway. My hand was already red, blood spilling down my palm and wrist.

"Holy shit," Gabe said.

"Tommy." James's voice was quiet, and he hadn't used my stupid nickname.

I glanced at the cutting board. There was a tiny pool of blood and lemon juice on the center of the board, spreading out from what looked like half of my ring finger and the top third of my pinkie.

My brain couldn't reconcile seeing those pieces of my body on the cutting board when they were supposed to be on my hand. I stared at them, flexing, but they didn't move. I turned back to my hand, blood spilling out of two clean-cut stumps of flesh.

"Gabe!" James shouted, still not using nicknames. He was pulling on a pair of food prep gloves. "Call nine-one-one!"

"It's okay." I held up my other hand, but I knew it wasn't okay. James launched toward me with a thick disposable towel. He shoved it over the two fingers I had cut off.

Oh my God, I had *cut off* my fingers.

I was shaking. I was nauseous. Gabe was speaking quickly into his phone, and Dante ran over with the first aid kit as James helped me sit on the floor. The towel was already red. There was blood on the floor, a trail of fat drops from the kitchen line all the way to me.

Dante shouted for me to hold my hand above my head, but I was starting to feel woozy. James lifted my arm for me.

I looked up for Gabe, but he was gone.

CHAPTER
THIRTY-FIVE

THE WHOLE EVENT WAS SO FUCKING EMBARRASSING.

I had felt so great for telling Gabe off, but then it was like the universe said, *Okay, Mr. High Horse, let's take you down a few pegs.* Only, in universe-speak, "pegs" translated to "fingers."

As if cutting my fingers off wasn't enough, my timing was perfect, because everyone had just started to arrive for their shifts. George and Natalie were clearly rattled but trying to pretend to be calm. Doris screamed her earsplitting harpy cry. Morgan freaked out when she saw me and started crying.

But why stop there? The paramedics—one of whom was devastatingly hot, by the way—then had to do a quick dress of my wound before they forced me onto a *stretcher* when I got a little wobbly standing up. They put my fingers into two separate ziplock bags—provided by Roni and Dante—then put the bags in a cooler—provided by the EMTs.

And of course, because there were only stairs at the loading dock, I had to be wheeled out through the PDR—like I was the sick trays—past every single resident on their way to dinner.

I even heard one old man I recognized whisper, "Hey, look! It's not one of us this time!"

Thankfully, the nurses and doctors at the hospital made this all seem normal. For them, maybe it was. My mom showed up shortly after I arrived, as they were cleaning the wounds and prepping me for surgery.

The doctor cleaning my severed fingers looked at them closely. "We shouldn't have too much trouble reattaching them. This is a really clean cut. What brand of knife was this?"

I sighed. "Wüsthof."

The doctor muttered the name under his breath like he was saving it to a mental shopping cart in his mind.

"How did this even happen?" my mom asked from across the room. She was behind the curtain, too squeamish to look.

"It was an accident." I said it too quickly.

"Did they not train you how to use a knife?"

"No, they didn't," I said. "I *know* how to use a knife, Mom. You've seen me use them a million times. It was an accident."

"Why weren't you doing the . . ." She waved her hands on the other side of the curtain. "What did you call it? Claw thingy?"

"It's just called the Claw. And I was. That's why only two fingers are off instead of all of them."

"What's the Claw?" the doctor asked. I bent my right fingers and put the knuckles against my left arm.

"You make a claw like this and hold the veggie you're chopping so you don't . . . cut your fingers off. Usually."

The doctor seemed impressed. "I don't really cook much. I'm

usually a hospital cafeteria or delivery kinda guy."

"I wanted to go to culinary school." I stared at my numbed, severed stumps. "Will I be able to use my hand again?"

He nodded. "Fifty percent get full use. You're young, and the cut was clean, so with physical therapy, your odds are good for a full recovery." He stood, taking my fingers with him. "I'm taking these to the OR. A nurse will be by to bring you up and I'll see you in a bit."

My mother thanked him and came to my side of the curtain, looking up so she wouldn't have to see my hand. Once it was just the two of us, I couldn't hold it in anymore. Tears started streaming down my face, and I began to sob. My mom's voice changed.

"You'll be okay, sweetie." She came over and kissed me on the forehead. "I know. I don't like hospitals, either." But I wasn't crying about my fingers. And I wasn't crying about the hospital. Something worse had happened to me, worse than Gabe not reciprocating the feelings I had for him. I had cut off my fingers and cut off my feelings for Gabe all at once. And now it all felt so much worse.

I cried again when I woke up from surgery. I was in a recovery room, alone. A nurse came over and told me not to worry and that my mom was on her way up now. Everything had gone well in surgery, and a doctor would come by after I was moved to my room.

When my mom got there, I was still crying. She asked what was wrong.

"It's okay," the nurse said. "Some people get weepy when they come out of anesthesia." My mom nodded but didn't look convinced. She stayed with me, holding my right hand until they came to wheel me into my room. The doctor gave us an update: The bad news was that apparently I had to stay in the ICU for a week. The worse news was that during that week they would be using leech therapy. Yes. They still do that. So leeches would be sucking on my fingers for a week.

Great.

Once he left, telling me a nurse would be bringing something for the pain, my mom shut the door.

"Tell me what's wrong."

I played dumb. "I . . . cut my fingers off." I held up the bandaged hand. My reattached fingers were splinted so I couldn't move them.

She sat down next to my bed and reached for my good hand. "I'm not talking about physically. You've been a mess for weeks. You burned a blueberry quick bread on Saturday, you messed up the macarons on New Year's Eve—and you said yourself that you had perfected that recipe. You barely paid attention when we were watching *Christmas Cookie Challenge*, and when I asked if you wanted to make pizza last night, you said you didn't *feel like* baking."

Shit. I really had been off. I should have seen this amputation coming a mile away.

"The last time I remember you being like this was when your father died."

That hurt even worse. And not because I was missing Gabe, but because my mom was equating the worst thing to ever happen to us with a relationship that never even got off the ground. I started to cry again, and it wasn't the anesthesia. When my mom put it that way, being this upset over Gabe felt cheap.

"Honey, please just talk to me. Whatever it is, I want to help."

And in that moment, for whatever reason, I wasn't scared anymore. I wasn't scared for her to know this part of me because I knew what scary was. Scary was saying goodbye to my dad for the day, thinking I'd see him again that night, but being called out of school just hours later and seeing my mom in the office with tears in her eyes. Her telling me in the car on the way to the hospital that my dad had an accident at work and hit his head. And, later, the slow realization after a whole week that he wasn't going to wake up.

And now, in the same hospital myself, I realized how stupid it all was. Because of course my mom would still love me. Like she always had.

I sniffed and wiped at my cheeks. "It's stupid."

"Then tell me so I can laugh at you and call you stupid."

That did make me laugh. "I was . . . sort of seeing someone. But not really. And now *really* not really."

She stared at me, her eyebrows scrunched in concern. "You cut your fingers off because you were sad that somebody didn't like you? Okay, yes, I admit it—you are stupid."

"No!" I laughed with her. "I swear it was an accident. But I was talking to them when it happened, and I may have gotten angry and . . . distracted."

She nodded. "And what is their name?"

There it was. Any anxiety lifted from my chest, and I smiled. She said "somebody," and she said "their." So she knew. And she didn't care.

"You met him. Gabe."

Her jaw dropped, and for a second I was scared I had misunderstood the signs. But then she said, "Oh yeah, he was cute. I might have cut a pinkie off for him back in the day."

I laughed. "Ew, please stop."

"Though not the ring finger, because *that's* some symbolism, kid."

I laughed again until I cried. Only this time the tears were happy. My mom had tears in her eyes, too. She squeezed my right hand.

"You know I'll always love you, right?" she said. "No matter what."

"Love you, too."

CHAPTER
THIRTY-SIX

WHEN THE DOOR TO MY ROOM OPENED, I looked away from the TV, expecting to see my mom returning from the cafeteria, but it was Ava.

"Ava Maria!" I put my good hand up as I shouted one of James's nicknames for her. "Euthan-Ava" was a little too close to home for an ICU patient.

Her eyes went wide as she shut the door. "Oh, yay! You're stoned! Making up is going to be so much easier."

"Hell yeah. I cut my fingers off. What are you doing here?"

"Visiting you, doofus. There's a few other people here, but apparently the ICU tyrants only allow one visitor at a time. Your mom said I could come in as our elected Sunset Estates representative."

"Aw man, I was hoping it would be Natalie!" Being stoned on pain meds also helped soften the blow when I realized I now wouldn't be getting a letter of recommendation from her. Cutting off my own fingers while scolding her nephew for being a coward was definitely disqualifying behavior.

Ava withdrew two cards from behind her back and held them out to me.

I recognized the handwriting on top, and my brain struggled to figure out why it was there. I held it up to her. "What holiday is it?"

She frowned. "How stoned are you? New Year's was two days ago."

"And I got Al's New Year's card four days ago, three days after his Christmas card." I held it out to her. "Open, please. I don't have the dexterity."

I held up my bandaged hand, and she opened the envelope and handed it to me. I laughed at the front—a handsome, shirtless beefcake lying in a hospital bed. I opened it and several bills fell out. A thousand dollars.

Al's handwriting read:

THOMAS, THANK YOU FOR BRINGING SOME EXCITEMENT TO THIS BLAND ROACH MOTEL. MORGAN HAS EXPLAINED WHAT HAPPENED AND I'VE SUCCESSFULLY MANAGED TO START SEVERAL RUMORS AS TO WHY YOU WERE WHEELED OUT OF HERE:

DORIS ATTACKED YOU WITH A BROKEN SANKA CARAFE.

THE KITCHEN RAN OUT OF BEEF AND YOU OFFERED YOUR HAND TO FEED US.

YOU'RE FAKING IT.

FEEL FREE TO RUN WITH WHICHEVER STRIKES YOUR FANCY. GET WELL SOON, YOU FAKER.

LOVE,

AL

Below that, in dignified, clean handwriting, it said:

Thomas, so sorry to hear about your accident. I will keep Al in line until your return. Wishing you a speedy recovery.
All the best,
Willa

Willa. Not Ms. Vaughn. I wondered if that meant I could call her by her first name aloud now, too. "How does he always have these cards at the ready?" I asked. Also, this was *way* too much. I had to pay him back.

"Well, sorry to say, we didn't give you a grand." Ava opened the other card and handed it over. Everyone had signed the card and written a little message telling me to get well soon. Gabe's was the only name missing. Before I could even ask, Ava had the answer for me.

"Gabe didn't want to sign it."

I don't know what I expected. Why *would* he want to sign it, after the scene I made telling him off? But still, I couldn't help feeling upset. Ava probably recognized the look on my face.

"I think he's embarrassed," she said.

"What for? I'm the one who cut my fingers off."

"No, I think it's because you spit a little too much truth for him to handle. You should have seen him: all night he was just walking around like a zombie."

Maybe something I said did get through to him, then.

I wasn't in the mood to talk about Gabe, though, so I changed the subject. I told Ava that I'd come out to my mom. We had talked and my mom said she was happy I felt comfortable enough to tell her.

She'd even pretended she hadn't known, but I finally got her to admit that she and my father had talked about it before he died.

It was nice to know he knew and still loved me, too.

"How about us?" Ava asked. "If I say I miss you and I'm sorry, are we good?"

"No," I said. Her eyes went wide, and if I'm not mistaken, she looked hurt. I quickly added, "You don't need to be sorry, I mean—*I'm* sorry. I should have just listened and been there for you. You were right: I should have supported you from the beginning. It's your life, and you know what's best for you."

She actually looked relieved. That was when I knew we'd be fine. It was exactly what she'd wanted to hear from me from the start. I should have known that she'd already done most of the thinking about her gap year for herself way before she'd even brought it up to me. That she knew it was what she wanted. It just kinda took a bit for me to get there.

"If you want to talk, I'm ready to listen now. And fully support you."

For a moment it looked like she didn't want to say anything, and I couldn't blame her. The last time she tried, I made it all about me and my worries for her future. But then she seemed to rethink and let out a sigh.

"I'm just not sure I want to do something so significantly specialized anymore. Like, yeah, I love learning about the groundbreaking biomedical stuff, and the idea of creating something that could legit save lives in the future is a wonderful boost to my ego."

"Naturally."

"But I'm not sure I want that anymore."

I nodded and started to think about how scary that must be. To rethink everything you thought you wanted. But also how freeing it is when you decide to change your path.

"So was it the pregnancy scare that started you thinking this way?"

"No. I'd thought it before, but it felt fleeting. Almost like I was just trying to save myself the embarrassment of getting rejected by Johns Hopkins by self-rejecting. The scare started to solidify things for me, though. I was looking into my options, and it's so damn difficult to get an abortion in this country. And on top of that, health care and childcare are both fucked. So I started thinking about all the other ways the world needs to be bettered before 3D-printed human tissue or diagnostic nanotech can even be a realistic thing. Someone's going to figure that out eventually—I just realized it doesn't need to be me. I want to figure out another way to make the world better. And I don't know what that is yet. But I know going to school and following my plan isn't the way I want to do it."

We were silent for a moment before I spoke.

"Shit."

"What's wrong?" Her eyes darted to my hand like she thought something had happened to my injury.

I shook my head. "I really did just need to listen to you." She snorted at that. "I'm sorry I didn't. And whatever you do, you're going to kick ass."

"Thank you, Tommy. Totally forgiven."

"And for what it's worth . . . You weren't wrong. You told me to get my shit together before I got hurt."

She rolled her eyes. "You're far too literal."

"I miss you and I'm sorry."

She kicked off her shoes and climbed up into the bed beside me, giving me a tight but gentle hug.

"I miss you and I'm sorry, too." She kissed my cheek and I kissed hers. "When are you coming back to work?"

More bad news from the doctor. "Six months."

Ava closed her eyes. "Shit, Tommy."

"Yeah. So much for getting some paid kitchen training time before college." Even if I was back in three months, it would be six to eight months before I got my full mobility back. If I got it back at all.

So now I'd have no kitchen time for my application, no letter of recommendation from one of Chef Louis's former managers, and no supplemental video. Maybe an essay on my amputation would be enough to stand out. But what culinary school would offer admission to a clumsy student who had cut off his own fingers in a kitchen?

"And of course . . ." I said aloud to Ava. "Since I will no longer speak to Gabe nor ask him for any help, that means no more supplemental video for my application."

"Forget that bitch," Ava said. "I'll help you do your video. I saw his little drawings on how it's supposed to look. How hard could it be?"

I hugged her again. I *knew* how hard it would be, and I knew I'd never get it done in time. But I also knew it felt good to have my best friend back.

CHAPTER
THIRTY-SEVEN

I WASN'T EVEN IN THE ICU A whole week before Natalie came to visit. I saw the manila envelope in her hand and knew right away she wasn't there to check up on me. In fact, she didn't really waste any time. After she said hello, she took out a sheet of paper and put it on the rolly table my food usually went on.

"I need you to review this," she said as she slid the table toward me.

I had just finished up my leech therapy for the day, which meant I hadn't been given any pain meds in a while, so maybe I was a bit short with her.

"This my termination paperwork?"

She gave me what could only be described as a half grin—not her usual wide, white-toothed smile. She still spoke with the trademarked singsong voice she used when she was pretending you weren't getting under her skin. "Unfortunately for you, no. It's just an OSHA incident form. When there's an accident, we're required to fill these out. I've filled out most of it, but you'll need to write down whatever you can remember and sign it."

"I have to do this now?"

"No." She took the paper away and put it on the counter next to the nurse's sink. Then she withdrew another form, this one several pages long. "I'll also need you to look over this and let me know if any amendments need to be made."

The form said *Supervisor Accident Investigation Form* and listed all my information, as well as the date and time and witnesses. Gabe's and James's names were both listed. The following page had a human figure with the left fingers circled and a box next to it marked *amputation*.

I scanned everything, but it all looked fine. There was no emotion in the form—she didn't mention that I had been arguing, just that I had become distracted while talking with a coworker. I handed it back to her and said it was fine.

"Do I need a lawyer?" I asked.

"Only if you're planning to sue, which you don't have to tell me if you are." She put the form back in her folder. "Your mother said you won't be back at work until July."

I nodded. Possibly sooner, but that was if I did well in physical therapy when I started that up in three months.

She pursed her lips and took another piece of paper out of her folder. "Well, guess I should hand this off to you now, then."

I took it from her. It was a letter printed on the Sunset Estates letterhead. I assumed it said I was being laid off. Maybe she didn't consider it a termination notice because I couldn't physically come back to work. I almost thanked her and put the paper down, but the salutation caught my eye.

To the Admissions Committee of La Mère Labont.

"What is this?"

"Your letter of recommendation."

I skimmed it, expecting some rude statements about my inability to use kitchen utensils or my failure to follow kitchen safety guidelines.

But it was a real recommendation. Sure, it didn't have the flowery praise that George's letter had; it was all business. Which was probably what she knew Chef Louis would be looking for. She didn't mention that she used to work at one of his restaurants—obviously unwilling to pull those strings—but she did say I showed "immense talent that would only be amplified by an education at a prestigious institution like La Mère."

I looked back up at her. "I don't get it. Was the third task cutting off my fingers?"

She frowned. "No. The third task was going to be a shift where you were on the line with Chef Roni all night."

My jaw dropped. "But I'm not allowed to work in the kitchen until I'm eighteen."

"You're not allowed to do *prep work* until you're eighteen—things involving the stand mixer, grill, ovens. *Knives*, now." I did see that she'd written *Knives only to be used after proper training and by employees of at least eighteen years of age* on the OSHA form under *Recommended preventive action to take in the future to prevent reoccurrence.*

"My plan," she continued, "was to have you work the line while Sean G. called. Then Roni would give me your performance evaluation."

I looked at the letter in my hand. I would have totally killed that if I'd been able to do it. So why had she written the letter anyway?

"Is this so I don't sue you?" I asked.

She sighed, frustration starting to rear its ugly head. "No, Thomas. You made a mistake. We don't punish well-performing employees because they make mistakes."

"But—"

"Fine, I'll take it back." Natalie opened her folder and held her hand out.

I clutched the letter to my chest, gently. "No, please. I'll keep it."

She closed the folder again. "You're welcome."

"Thank you."

With that, she turned and walked back toward the door. But she stopped herself. She turned her head slightly, looking at the wall to my left and not me.

"I heard you. Arguing with Gabriel."

Shit. Was the letter a bribe? Gabe's parents had paid off the last kid who was in love with their son and ended up in a hospital. Maybe Natalie told them she had a cheaper plan. I didn't say anything, just waited for her to speak. To threaten me and tell me to stay away from her nephew.

"Our family," she continued, "has a habit of holding each other to standards that can be difficult to reach, let alone maintain."

Okay? I'll be honest, that kind of made sense as far as why Natalie was the way she was—especially her management style.

"Some people, when faced with that kind of pressure, thrive. While others . . ." She paused and seemed to change her mind on what she was going to say. "I'm sorry things didn't work out between . . . the two of you. I think you might have been a good influence on him. He seemed happier when he was working with you. I thought it was just that he was making his own money. But after the night you came to my sister's house, I realized it might be more. I noticed a change in him when you were on the schedule together."

She opened her mouth as though she was going to say something else, but closed it. Then, without saying goodbye, she opened the door and left.

I said a lot of mean things to Gabe when I was telling him off, but maybe some of them weren't so far off the mark. Maybe he did think all he deserved was someone like Vic. I hoped he realized he deserved more.

But the throb of pain in my fingers reminded me that I wasn't the one who could give it to him. Not anymore.

CHAPTER
THIRTY-EIGHT

WHAT DO THE CULINARY ARTS MEAN TO YOU?

What a silly fucking question. How was it that the best culinary arts school in the world could come up with such an awful essay question for their applicants? And yet I'd been staring at my cracked computer screen for what felt like hours—not counting the literal months previously—unable to answer said awful question. At least I had the question of which campus I was applying to answered. Now I knew I didn't need to apply anywhere except New York.

My phone buzzed with another text from Ava.

You can still do the video. It was YOUR idea even before Gabe came into the pic, so I still think you can do it.

Instead of answering, I locked my phone and tossed it on the bed beside me. I didn't feel like writing back to her. That text would be a whole other essay on why Gabe's preproduction work just made *actually* doing the video seem daunting, and whatever I made would always disappoint me. I wanted it to be perfect, and doing it any way other than Gabe's vision—the way he'd explained it to me—would always be less than perfect.

So instead, I was focusing on—and overthinking—my essay. The letter Natalie wrote me wasn't going to push me to the top of the application pile, so my essay was my only hope.

But why couldn't the question be something easier? Why couldn't they ask for my pie crust recipe or the process through which I'd perfected it? I knew they'd be impressed with my use of brown butterfat–washed vodka.

What do the culinary arts mean to you?

I slammed the laptop shut and went down to the kitchen. It was almost one in the morning, and I probably should have been in bed, but I had been having trouble falling asleep in my own room for the past few weeks since being released from the ICU, nervous about rolling over onto my hand and ruining the healing process.

There had to be something I could bake one-handed. With a lot of care, I slipped my dad's old La Mère coat on—forgoing the buttons because they took forever with one of my hands only half-usable.

Cookies. I could do cookies with one hand. Simple ones—no macarons this time.

I opened the pantry and grabbed the sugar and flour. No chocolate chips, but we did have oatmeal and raisins. And before you come for me about oatmeal raisin cookies, you're wrong. Yes, chocolate chip cookies are superior, but oatmeal raisin—the way I make them—are amazing.

I grabbed the spices and set them out on the counter—including my secret ingredient, which I will never share. Never mind—I just made a whole stink about my oatmeal raisin being better, so I might as well share the knowledge:

Equal parts cardamom powder and cinnamon.

Then I set about preheating the oven and measuring out the ingredients into individual glass bowls. When it came to mixing, I should have used the stand mixer, but it was way too loud and I didn't want to wake my mom. So instead I sat on the kitchen floor and put the bowl between my legs while I mixed with my good hand.

The whole time I tried to think of something intelligent to write for my essay. What did these cookies mean to me? What did the fact that I baked away my feelings mean? Did any of that make the culinary arts mean anything to me?

The cookies were in the oven for four minutes before I heard my mom coming down the stairs. She looked at me, then the mess I'd made of the kitchen, then at the clock on the microwave.

"It's two in the morning."

"Sorry. I didn't mean to wake you. I couldn't sleep."

She frowned and sat down at the kitchen table. "When I can't sleep, I usually stay in bed and count my breathing. I feel like it helps a bit more than baking . . ." She leaned over to see what was in the oven. "Cookies."

"We all have our strategies, Mother."

"Well, now I'm up. So why don't you tell me why you can't sleep?"

I stopped hovering over the oven and joined her at the table. "What the culinary arts mean to me." She scrunched up her face, so I added for clarity, "It's my essay for La Mère."

"Is this really all about an essay?" she asked. "Because if so, it's a lot, sweetie."

That *almost* made me laugh. "Seriously, though. It's my last chance to stand out from everyone else, and they require answering the most generic essay question."

"It's generic on purpose. They want to see how you can wow them while giving you nothing. What happened to your video idea? I thought that was smart."

"I relied on someone else to help me, and they . . . aren't able to." I'm sure Gabe would still help me, but I didn't want to ask.

My mom chewed her cheek; she seemed to be choosing her next words carefully. "Is the only reason you want to go to this school so badly because your father went there?"

"No." That kind of felt like a lie—but there was more to it than just my dad going there. "I mean, I do want to go there because he did, too, but it's also a great school."

She reached out and took my uninjured hand in hers. "I'm not saying it isn't. But you seem to be putting a lot of pressure on yourself to get into *this* school. Your dad wished he could have finished school there and pursued the career he wanted, but the universe had other plans. We didn't decide to have you as some kind of proxy for us to fulfill our failed dreams. You don't have to go to the school your dad went to. He was always going to be proud of you no matter what you did with your life."

I didn't want to go to La Mère just because my dad went there. Baking did make me feel closer to him after he died, though. When I started going through each step of a recipe, I pretended to talk to him in my head. Explaining a video I saw online that gave me a new idea or a different way to do the recipe. And then sometimes it felt like a conversation, where I could almost hear his voice suggesting I use melted butter to see how the texture would change or add an extra egg yolk for more density.

"I know he would have been," I said. "But I want to go to La Mère because it's where the best go."

My mom shook her head. "No one goes to school already as the best. And a lot of people who go to school never become the best. Trust me. I know dudes who went to Yale and still suck at their jobs."

I didn't say anything. Of course there were people who went to great schools and coasted on their privilege or slightly elevated intellect. But that wasn't me.

She probably saw me thinking something along those lines, because then she said, "Think of it like one of your recipes. All the instructions are there, but if you don't have the best ingredients and the passion to make it . . ." She shrugged.

I tried not to smile as I crossed my arms. "I'm so mad at you for making this a baking metaphor."

"But it worked, right?" She threw up her hands.

I sighed, still trying to hide my growing smirk as the egg timer on the table went off. I stood and took the cookies out of the oven. But as I set up the cooling racks and grabbed the spatula, it hit me.

My dad was the reason I loved what La Mère referred to simply as *culinary arts* in all their informational packets. It was time we'd spent together; it was him passing down what he'd learned to me. Even wearing his chef's coat made me feel closer to him. That's what they were looking for in their stupid essay question. What the culinary arts meant to me was a connection to my family. A way to remember my dad and share that with my mom. And it was baking things for the people I loved and hopefully for the people in my future. There was something more there, but it was a great start.

"I'll be right back." I put the spatula on the table and raced up to my bedroom to get my computer. I also grabbed my phone and saw there was another text from Ava—probably taking a break from the video game she had been up playing. And this one more ominous.

If you aren't going to do it, I'll plan it myself!

I'd answer her later, but only when my essay was finished. I didn't want to lose the chance to get this done while it was fresh in my mind.

When I got back to the kitchen, my mom was gently tossing a cookie between her hands and blowing on it.

"That's what the cooling racks are for."

"*I'm* going up to bed. No time for cooling!" She took a bite of the cookie and rolled her eyes. "Wonderful, as always, pumpkin." Then she kissed me on the cheek as I sat down at the kitchen table. "Clean this place up before you go to bed."

"I will. Night."

With that she left. And I started writing my essay.

CHAPTER
THIRTY-NINE

"WHAT ARE YOU DOING?" I ASKED AS Ava pulled into the parking lot of the Super Save Lot. It was already nine thirty, and she'd been late picking me up. The party she said we were going to was bound to get messy by ten thirty.

It also wasn't supposed to take place in the Super Save Lot parking lot. She parked all the way in the back, next to some familiar cars.

Morgan's truck was there, next to a Buick Lucerne I didn't recognize. But the owners of the cars were missing.

"What is this?" I asked as Ava parked.

"A parking lot. Now get out." Before I could ask another question, she got out and popped the trunk of her uncle's car. She grabbed a flashlight and waited for me. "Off we go."

"Go where? What's going on?"

"A surprise."

I groaned. I didn't want a surprise. This was supposed to be my first night out since New Year's—watching TV at Ava's house didn't count. And instead we were going into the woods?

"Did the party get broken up?" I asked.

"Yes," she said, taking my arm and leading me into the woods. "Watch your step."

"So you guys are drinking in the Super Save Lot parking lot?"

"Clearly not, since it's now several paces behind us."

Drinking in the woods wasn't much better. I was not going to be partaking because the last thing I needed was to get drunk and fall on my healing fingers. Though that still seemed possible since we were traipsing through the woods at nine thirty at night. Ava held on to my arm as she pointed the giant flashlight ahead, reminding me to be careful as we stepped over fallen trees and branches.

The woods started to thin out a bit, and we came to an asphalt pathway. Every few yards of the path had a small blue emergency pole with a light and speaker. I knew exactly where we were now.

"Seriously?"

It was the Sunset Estates walking path.

"Why are you dragging me to work? And why wouldn't you just go through the front gates?"

"Because it's nine thirty at night, and that would look suspicious."

"Yes, much less suspicious than sneaking through the woods."

"As long as we don't get caught, yeah."

We emerged near the east wing's exit and went around the darkened windows of the casual dining room. The dumpsters by the loading dock were somehow still stinky, despite the cold weather.

Standing on the loading dock were four figures, three of them holding paper grocery bags. I could make out Morgan and Kevin in the darkness. But who—

"Bahama Mama!"

Kevin and Morgan shushed James.

He whispered again, "Bahama Mama!"

So that's one. Who was the last person? He stood off to the side of James, Morgan, and Kevin. Like an outsider. My stomach lurched as I wondered if it was Gabe. But the closer I got, the less he looked like Gabe. He was lit from behind with the bright white bulb over the rear door, so I could see he wore loose-fitting jeans and a hoodie. In his left hand he also held what looked like a giant yellow plastic suitcase. I held up my hand to block the light.

"Grant?"

"Hey, Tommy," Grant said. The last time I had seen him was at Oscar's Ice Cream the night Gabe and I kissed the second time. The thought somehow made my fingers ache and my stomach flip.

"Let's take this inside," Ava said. "Before we get caught on one of the cameras."

The four on the loading dock turned and opened the door, which should have been locked.

"What's going on?" I asked Ava.

"I promised Greg in the dish room he could look at my boobs if he left the door open before leaving tonight."

"Ava!"

She let out a huff. "I'm kidding. I paid him forty bucks. You need to calm down."

"But why are we here?" We went into the darkened rear hallways, passing the laundry and staff bathrooms, and headed into the kitchen. Only one fluorescent light above us was on, casting the kitchen in shadows. Natalie's office and the hallway leading to the PDR and

Roni's and George's offices were dark, too.

"Because your application to La Mère is due in nine days, and I know you haven't finished your video yet."

Grant placed the yellow case on one of the cleaned and sanitized metal countertops with a thud, and Morgan, Kevin, and James started unloading the paper bags. The bags were filled with groceries. Milk, eggs, flour, sugar, heavy cream. They unloaded spices and extracts, bananas and strawberries, and cold brew and energy drinks. Morgan handed one of the energy drinks to Grant, who popped the tab and opened the yellow case.

Inside, nestled in a foam cutout, were a camera and microphone.

"No way," I said. "Are you kidding me?"

They all looked at me.

"We can't break into Sunset Estates in the middle of the night—"

Kevin interrupted, "It's nine thirty."

"—and record an entire video. Do you have any idea how long it takes to make croquembouche?"

"Bahama, I don't even know what a croquembouche is. I just bought whatever Morganza and Ava Maria told me."

I glared at Ava, who held up her hands. "Don't look at me; this was Kevin's idea."

That was surprising. I looked at him, and he shrugged, giving me a grin. "I like breaking rules."

I sighed. "Listen. Thank you all, I really appreciate it, but . . . you also forget I can't really use my hand." I held up my bandaged hand.

"We didn't forget that," Morgan said. "Boys, hands out."

Kevin and James put their hands out next to each other. Morgan reached for my good hand and held it next to theirs.

Grant looked at them, then pointed to Kevin. "His looks most like Tommy's." Morgan let my hand go as James let out a sad-sounding "Aw man." Grant took out the camera and mounted the mic to the top. "We do all the medium-wide shots of you explaining the steps you're going to be doing, hiding your bad hand. Then on the closeup shots where you'd need that hand, we use Kevin's as a body double. I'll edit everything together so your voice-over continues to the close-up so it looks seamless."

"That's cheating," I said. "I can't just lie and say it's me."

Grant scrunched his nose at me. "It's not lying, it's movie magic."

James put up jazz hands and whispered loudly, "Maaaagiiic!"

Morgan turned away from us and walked into the rear hallway toward the laundry room and loading dock.

"We'll help do everything," Ava said. "You just tell us the steps, and we'll shoot enough footage to cut it all together. We'll make your three-minute video better than anything the Babish Culinary Universe could pull off with one hand and in one night."

She gave me an encouraging smile. I looked at the rest of them, my heart swelling with pride and excitement. I really loved these people. Before I could tell them, Morgan returned. She handed me a white chef's coat—the Sunset Estates logo was blocked out by a piece of white tape.

"Just tell us where we start, Tommy."

First, the pastry. I turned and set the ovens behind me to 425 degrees. Morgan and Ava helped me into the chef's coat, buttoning it for me while I thought. We'd need a large saucepan, and the mixer would have to be set up. My stomach turned with excitement. This was a *real* kitchen. The video was going to be so much better than I'd ever imagined.

I opened my mouth to tell James to set up the stand mixer, but another voice spoke.

A deep Jamaican accent.

And angry.

"What the hell are y'all doing in my kitchen!"

CHAPTER
FORTY

I SAT DOWN IN THE CHAIR ACROSS from Roni's desk. She slammed the door behind me and moved around as if to sit in her chair, but instead she kicked the chair backward and braced her hands against the desk.

"Do you have any idea how irresponsible this is?" she asked. I did, but I also hadn't known it was happening. Not that I was going to rat out the others. "What if something went wrong or there was a fire? What if you slipped and hurt your hand again? Do you have any idea of the repercussions that not only you but the kitchen staff could face?"

"That's why we wouldn't have involved you," I said, trying to act like this was partly my idea. "If something happened, *we'd* be in trouble, not you. You had no reason to think we would ever come in here after hours."

"What about Danny at the security gate? He could be in trouble if you got hurt. What if there was a fire and the alarm malfunctioned and people died?"

That was a lot of what-ifs. Also, if the alarm malfunctioned, that wouldn't be on us. Still, seeing the anger in Roni's face terrified me enough to keep quiet. I had seen Roni lose her temper on Dante or Natalie, but she usually never had reason to go off on servers. Being on the receiving end of it made me respect Natalie's cool calmness way more.

"I'm sorry," I said. "We weren't thinking."

Roni sighed and pulled the chair over to her desk. She sat and leaned back, shaking her head at me. "Why risk this, Tommy? Your job and your health? For what, a social media post?"

"It was for my culinary school application," I said. Her eyebrows twitched. "I want to go to La Mère Labont."

My eyes flicked up to the certifications behind Roni. One was her bachelor's degree in culinary arts from Johnson & Wales. The others were her certifications—Certified Executive Chef, a ServSafe food safety certification, and a pastry certification from the American Culinary Federation.

I continued, "I wanted to make a short video to show off the skills that . . ." I started to say *that my dad shared with me* but stopped myself. ". . . I have. Since I'm hurt, I asked the others to help me."

"You were going to make a video of you cooking?"

I nodded.

"What were you going to make?" She sounded intrigued.

"Croquembouche. But with different-flavored creams. Bananas Foster, strawberry, vanilla, and salted caramel."

She chuckled. "Why croquembouche?"

"It always came up when I searched most difficult pastries. I thought it would help me stand out."

"Plus, a tower of puff pastries held together with strands of caramel always looks impressive, yes?"

"I mean . . . yeah."

She nodded again. "Tommy, why do you want to go to La Mère?"

"Because it's the best?"

"Is it? You don't sound so sure. Was it the first one to pop up when you searched 'best culinary schools'?"

"Yeah." Was she joking? Did she know something about the school that I didn't?

She took a deep breath. "Just because things look flashy or seem to have clout, doesn't mean they're the best option for what you're looking for. So tell me again, do you just want to go to La Mère because it's ranked highly? Because if so, why not Le Cordon Bleu? Or Auguste Escoffier?"

I had looked at them as well. And I was going to apply to Auguste Escoffier School of Culinary Arts as well as the Culinary Institute of America as backups. Johnson & Wales was another I had been looking at as a backup. All three were listed among the best culinary schools in America.

"Because my dad went there," I admitted.

I wanted to finish because he couldn't.

"And of all the schools you looked at," Roni said, "that's the one that will fit you the best?"

Of course it would. It was always the one that I'd thought would fit me the best. It was the one my dad had gone to and the one I had grown up hearing stories about.

"I think so," I said.

"Do you have any backup schools? You know La Mère is extremely selective."

I nodded and counted them off on the fingers I hadn't sliced off. "CIA, Auguste Escoffier, and Johnson & Wales."

"Now, I do have friends who are instructors at CIA and Johnson & Wales. If you'd like, I can reach out to them as well."

"That would be amazing. Yes, please." My cheeks flushed, and I smiled wide.

"I am extraordinarily biased because I loved my time at Johnson & Wales, but it is an excellent school. If you haven't visited yet, let me know. I can have someone show you and your mother around."

"Thank you so much." Having Roni on my side seemed like such a win. And this was the most I had ever learned about her. She was always very focused when she was in her kitchen, so seeing this supportive side of her was something special.

"Can I ask you . . ." I said. "You're a really great chef."

"Not a question, but thank you, I know I am!" She flashed her perfect teeth at me, and I laughed.

"Just . . . why here? You could probably be head chef anywhere, even have your own restaurant if you impressed the right person. So why an old folks' home?"

Roni frowned. "What's that supposed to mean? An *old folks'* home. Like Dante and I don't turn out the best food these 'old folks' have ever had."

"No, no, that's not what I meant."

She nodded and gave me a sly grin. "I know what you meant, Tommy, I'm teasing you. Once I dreamed of owning my own place, but then I worked in the field and realized maybe that wasn't something I wanted after all. My mama lives here. When I heard they were looking for a head chef, I applied. I just want to be close to her and make sure she's eating right."

"Your mom?" I tried to run through all the residents I'd ever spoken to. None of them had Jamaican accents like Roni. Maybe Roni was adopted?

"Carol Fredericks."

For the millionth time that night, the world seemed to drop out from beneath my legs. "The *judge* is your mother?"

Told you. Everyone who works here either knows someone who works here, or someone who lives here.

Roni groaned. "The judge. No wonder she feels so self-important when I come see her. You all calling her the judge."

"I mean, she is, though. But . . . why doesn't she have an accent?"

"She was a Black woman in a white male profession, so she had to hide her accent. But, oh, you give that woman a couple glasses of cream sherry and you see how her accent comes out." She laughed—something Roni very rarely did. "That's why I was coming through tonight on my way out and found you all trying to mess up my kitchen!"

I had almost forgotten about why we were in the office in the first place. "Oh, but . . . Does that mean we're all fired?"

Roni frowned. "No. You're not fired. We can't just fire four of our senior staff, though you're lucky Natalie lives forty-five minutes away and hates to stay past eight. *She'd* fire you just because she could."

She stood, and I followed her as she went back out to the kitchen.

Grant had packed up his equipment and Morgan, Kevin, and James had put the groceries back in their bags. Roni put her hands on her hips and looked at all of them.

"And who are you?" She pointed at Grant.

Usually calm, cool Grant stuttered. "Um, I—uh, I'm the cam-camera guy?"

"Your *name*, camera guy."

"Grant. Ma'am."

"Grant, unpack your camera. And it's *chef.* Not *ma'am.*"

Grant nodded. "Yes, ma—erm, Chef." He spun and began unpacking his equipment. Ava and Morgan gave me a look of concern as Roni passed between them and reached into the paper bags.

"What y'all got in here, then?" She pulled things out one after the other, placing them on the counter. "Tommy!" she shouted over her shoulder.

"Yes, Chef?" I walked around to the other side of the counter.

Roni pursed her lips together. "You sure you want to do croquembouche?"

I glanced at Ava and Morgan on one side of her, then at James and Kevin. Was she really planning to help us?

Her words echoed in my mind: *Just because things look flashy or seem to have clout, doesn't mean they're the best option for what you're looking for.*

"Unless you had something better in mind, Chef?"

She smiled at me. "Right. Ava! Go get clean chef's coats for everyone."

"Heard." She turned and left.

"We're not doing croquembouche, Tommy. It's very pretty to look at, but it's still just a cream puff."

James turned to Kevin and whispered loud enough for everyone to hear, "What did she just call Bahama Mama?"

Roni turned to him. "James, you're on *my* side of the line tonight, so you cut the shit, you hear me?"

"Yes, Chef," James said, his cheeks turning pink.

"So what are we doing?" I asked. Ava returned and handed out chef's coats to everyone—including Grant, who put it on without question.

Roni buttoned hers up and smiled brightly. "Baked Alaska."

CHAPTER
FORTY-ONE

GRANT'S VIDEO TURNED OUT GREAT. SO WITH my letters of recommendation, an essay, and a supplemental video, I managed to get my La Mère application in a few weeks before the deadline. Unfortunately, I still had to wait until mid-to-late April to get my final answer.

The first Saturday night in April, Ava dragged me to a party at Charlie Matthews's house—Charlie being the captain of the hockey team. Apparently, the hockey team had won some big game that morning, and this was a celebration. Which explained why Ava hadn't planned for the party until after she had seen James at work.

James, who was over by the keg Charlie's brother had bought. The heteronormativity in the air was thicker than the smoke from the bonfire keeping me warm.

The anger was keeping me slightly warm as well. Ava had asked me to take her here because she wanted a sober ride home and knew I couldn't drink. It didn't matter that I hadn't taken one of my painkillers in two days. My mom's horror stories about the time she'd spent as a substance abuse counselor before moving on to the much more subdued job of Sunset Estates activities director kept me in check. I know it would probably take years of mixing drugs and alcohol before destroying my liver and bleeding internally, but I wasn't exactly prepared to risk it.

So Ava got to have fun while I sat by the bonfire wishing we were in her basement eating greasy pizza and watching reality TV like she'd originally promised me we would be doing. But since I was her DD tonight, I did manage to guilt her into being my prom date. She kept saying she didn't want to buy a dress for a dance when she didn't even like dancing. But she'd finally admitted that she'd have FOMO if we skipped it.

I took out my phone and scrolled through my social media, trying to find something more interesting than the third run-through of the hockey game James was shouting out.

"Hey."

I looked up to see Brad Waldorf standing above me. He wore a shearling-lined denim jacket that looked like it would burst at the seams if he bent an arm too quickly. Beer foam spilled over the top of his red Solo cup, and he switched hands, flicking it away.

"Hey, Brad. Congrats on the win."

"Thanks." He glanced around us, checking that we were pretty much alone. "Can I sit?"

"Yeah, go for it."

He took the chair to my left, probably so he could keep an eye on everyone else by the keg. Make sure he knew when to stop talking if someone came over. Brad sipped his beer, sucking the foam mustache away with his lower lip, then pointed at my hand.

"What happened?"

He hadn't heard by now? I had seen him eyeing the bandage in biology class and the hallways at school, but maybe he hadn't thought to ask James or anyone else he knew from Sunset. Maybe because that would open up the question of *Why do you want to know about Tommy?*

"I was at work. Sharp knife plus slippery lemons equals digit amputation."

His eyes went wide. "You cut them *off*?" I made a chopping motion with my arm. "Are you okay? Are you going to be able to use them anymore?"

"I started physical therapy last month. We'll know if everything is back to normal in a few months."

"I'm sorry, Tommy."

I shrugged.

"Do you want a beer?" he asked. "I can get you one."

"No, thanks. I'm Ava's DD." I turned, scanning the crowd on the back patio. Ava and Morgan were alone in the corner, talking conspiratorially.

Brad nodded and rubbed at his leg with his free hand, like he was nervous.

"You okay?" I asked.

He smiled, and I noticed his eyes looked a little glassy. "Yeah, just cold." He put his hands out to the fire. I decided to help him out. I knew why he was here, talking to me. New Year's hadn't really been the time to hook up, and he'd sensed that. But now that Gabe was far in my rearview, maybe all I needed was a good make-out-and-groping session to make me feel better.

"My car's out front," I said. "Do you want to . . . go . . ." I glanced back to make sure no one was coming over to us. "Hang out?"

For a second he looked surprised, and I regretted asking. Like maybe he really *hadn't* had enough to drink, and he was on a not-gay kick.

But then he smiled and nodded.

"Okay." I stood. "I'll act like I'm going to the bathroom inside and just go out the front door. Come whenever you're ready."

He took another sip of his beer, and I made my way through the house out to my car.

About five minutes later, Brad pulled the back door open. I had already turned off the dome light, so we stayed in the darkness, the only light coming from the front porch of Charlie Matthews's house. Brad had ditched the beer.

"Hey," he said in the darkness. I could smell something minty on his breath and smiled. He had eaten a mint or chewed gum to get rid of the beer taste.

"Hi," I said, and reached over to him, pulling him closer.

Our lips met in the darkness, but I overestimated the distance, and our teeth clacked together.

"Oh, shit." He pulled away, putting his hand to his mouth.

"You okay?" I asked.

"Yeah, you?"

I ran my tongue over my teeth; they were still smooth. "No chips."

"If there were, I could just say I took a puck to the face during a game," he said. "What would your excuse be?"

"I'm an overzealous kisser." Brad laughed in the darkness. "I feel honesty is the best policy when it comes to dental work."

Brad put his hand on my cheek; this time he brought me closer to him. He kissed me gently, his tongue darting across my lip. "I like that about you," he whispered.

Something about the way he said that gave me chills, but I ignored them and pulled him closer. He climbed on top of me, and I wrapped my legs around him. His legs were too long for the back seat, so he braced himself against the floor and ground against me.

In moments, we were both panting, all tangled limbs as our hands moved across each other's bodies. I could feel sweat on his forehead, so I started to push his jacket off.

Pain snapped me out of the heated moment, and I gasped.

"What's wrong?" Brad asked, pulling away from me. I sat up and took out my phone, unlocking the screen and holding it up to my injured fingers. I had used my left hand to try to take Brad's jacket off and wasn't careful.

I paused, staring at the bandage. Waiting to see if I had broken the stitches and my finger was falling off again. The fingers throbbed, matching pace with my racing heart, while my hard-on disappeared to the same beat.

"Are you okay?"

I nodded. No blood on the bandage. "Sorry," I said. I locked the phone and climbed onto Brad's lap, refusing to let the pain ruin this. This was supposed to be cathartic humping, so I wouldn't have to think of Gabe.

But every time my fingers throbbed, an image of him flashed in my head. Gabe and Vic. Gabe and me.

I pulled away from Brad's lips, letting out a frustrated sigh and rolling over to the other side of the back seat.

"What's wrong?"

"My fingers hurt—sorry. It happens now sometimes and just kinda . . . takes me out of it."

"It's okay." He turned his body toward me, and even in the darkness I could see a wry smile on his face. "Remember last summer when I saw you at Tim Costas's party?"

I tried to think back, and all at once the memory returned. It wasn't much of a party, just a bunch of people from school who wanted to use Tim's pool. And I absolutely remembered Brad being there—because he gave me the cold shoulder.

"You mean when you pretended like we hadn't just seen each other fully naked maybe . . . a month before?"

He chuckled. "Yeah. Sorry. I was kind of a dick. I had appendicitis about a week or so before and was still in this excruciating pain. So I understand if you're not feeling one hundred percent right now."

I was taken aback. "Wait, what?"

"Yeah." He leaned back and pulled up his shirt and pointed to his belly. "Here, you can kind of see the scar still."

I leaned across the back seat as he leaned to the side, catching a bit of diffused light through the foggy window. There was a small smile-shaped scar below his belly button.

"What does that feel like?" I leaned away from him and let him pull his shirt back into place. "Every time I get a cramp or stomach-ache, I look up appendicitis symptoms."

He laughed. "I did, too! But, also, none of the symptoms matched up with mine anyway, so I let it go for a little longer than I probably should have."

"Oh my God, you're freaking me out! What were your symptoms?"

His shoulders popped up. "I don't want to tell you. It's embarrassing."

"You *have* to tell me now! I just almost cried in front of you because I jammed my finger on your jacket."

He groaned. "It just . . . felt like . . . I had to fart really bad and couldn't."

I snorted a laugh, which made him laugh. I felt like we were children, laughing at farts.

"So I didn't tell anyone! And I didn't want to go to the hospital and have the nurses all laugh at me because I had gas!"

"Brad! You could have *died*."

"I know! But I didn't. The pain got worse, and I told my mom, so it's all fine. But the appendicitis was nothing compared to the pain after the surgery. They did it laparoscopically, and when they do that, they blow a bunch of air into your abdomen so they, like, have room for the camera to move around and not be blocked by organs."

"Ew."

"Yeah. Afterward they push it all out, but a little is left in there because . . . you know, your stomach has been cut open and all. And for some reason—I googled it, but I still couldn't find an explain-like-I'm-five—the gas created this excruciating nerve pain in my shoulder."

He rubbed at his left shoulder like even the thought of it brought the pain back.

"Why your shoulder if they took out your appendix?"

He shrugged. "I told you I couldn't find the ELI5. It has something to do with the gas and nerves that the shoulder and diaphragm share—I don't know, I'm not planning on being a doctor. Point is, I was a little shit, wincing in pain every time I lay down, or stood up, or moved for over a week. And that was just laparoscopic surgery. I can only imagine how much pain there is having fingers *reattached*."

That felt good. Nice. Outside of my mom, everyone seemed to be trying their hardest to ignore the fact that I'd cut off my fingers, and yes, even this far along into my recovery, I still had pain. It was nice to know that someone else got it.

"So . . ." he said. I thought he was going to ask me if I wanted to keep making out. If he had, I would have said yes. Instead, he said, "Can I get you anything to help? I know you said you're driving, but I can check for some ibuprofen or something in the house."

"I think I'll be all right. Thanks."

He nodded. "Okay. Are you gonna . . ." He thumbed over his shoulder toward the house.

"Yeah, you go ahead first. I'll follow in a bit."

"'Kay." He moved to open the door but stopped. "You don't ha . . ." He continued speaking, but his voice trailed off so I couldn't hear him.

"Huh?"

He was silent for a few moments, then said, "I do know something that might help the pain. Let me see your hand real quick."

I narrowed my eyes at him but held it out. He gently took my wrist and brought his lips down to the exposed tips of my fingers, placing a light kiss on them. The hairs raised on my arms, and something in my stomach did a flip.

"Does that feel better?" He looked up at me in the darkness and I could see his smile.

I pushed him away with my good hand, laughing. "You're so stupid. Get out of here."

He laughed and opened the door, saying he'd see me in there. Once he was gone, I thought about the goose bumps he had given me, absentmindedly running the fingers on my right hand against the tips of the bandaged fingers.

I know he was just kidding, but . . . was that maybe how he showed he cared? I let out another frustrated sigh in the silence of my back seat. Maybe this was just the type of guy I attracted.

Emotionally unavailable. That's my type.

CHAPTER
FORTY-TWO

WHEN AVA WALKED OUT SUNSET ESTATES' EXIT forty minutes early, I had to double-check the time on my phone to make sure I wasn't late to pick her up. But no, she still had forty minutes of work left. Yes, I had gotten there an hour early, but honestly, I was bored at home, and even baking wasn't distracting me. For the past week I had been obsessively checking my phone, waiting to hear from La Mère.

Why I thought sitting in the parking lot of the job I still wasn't allowed to return to would make me check my email *less*, I don't know.

Ava pulled open the passenger-side door and jumped in.

"Did you finish early?"

She shook her head. "I have to reset my entire section still."

"Oh my God, what are you waiting for? Do you not want to leave tonight?"

"What I'm about to tell you isn't about you, but I have to do something tonight and I know you'll ask, so I'm telling you because I care about you, and you should know and not think I'm actively trying to exclude you from something."

"Okay?" I didn't get why she was being so weird, but also I didn't get why I wouldn't be included in something she was doing.

"It's about Gabe."

Oh. That was why.

"What about him?"

"So I didn't tell you, but he and Vic broke up a couple weeks ago."

Wow. That was something I hadn't expected to hear. But I did expect to feel more when I heard it. Like butterflies or those embers of heat that filled my gut when I used to think about him. Instead, I felt . . . nothing? Maybe happy for Gabe?

"Right, good for them, I guess. Why did you feel you shouldn't tell me? And why are you telling me now?"

"I felt like I shouldn't tell you because you're in love with him—"

"Was. Past tense."

She laughed. "Sure."

"No, really, I'm good. You were right: I just kept thinking about him as the first guy I—you know what? Maybe we can unpack all that later? Didn't you say this *wasn't* about me?"

"Right. Which goes to the why I'm telling you now. Gabe was the one who broke up with Vic."

That was even more surprising. I definitely didn't see Gabe being the one who'd choose to break up with him. But still no butterflies for me.

"And Vic didn't exactly handle it well."

My stomach clenched, and I started to worry. Had Vic done something to Gabe? Hurt him?

"First he tried all the nice manipulative ways to win Gabe back, flowers and gifts and shit."

"Sure."

"But when it wasn't happening, and Gabe still wouldn't talk to him, he took some screenshots of their texts, made fake social media profiles, and sent them to Gabe's family."

"Shit." I assumed they were the same family members who weren't exactly okay with who Gabe was. "What kind of texts?"

"Do you really want to know?"

"I think I can assume based on that answer. What a fucking scumbag!" I could feel the blood pumping in my ears, I was so furious. This was the same thing Kevin's brother had done to Gabe! Vic *knew* about the strain Gabe's family put on him and about the trauma of a screencapped text being used against him, and still he did it again. But it was worse, because this time it was Gabe's family.

"There's more. He sent them to Gabe's friends, too, and . . . some more, but we don't need to get into it."

"No, wait, some more how? Is he okay?" The fury in my chest only grew. Yes, I had been pissed at Gabe, but that had gone away over the last few months. I'd never really gotten over my anger with Vic, and why should I?

"Physically he's fine. Vic's warfare is all psychological."

After she let me digest this for a bit, I said, "Okay, so tonight is what? You all just hanging out with Gabe and trying to cheer him up?" I could understand why it might not be the best idea for me to be there for that. I probably also wouldn't be able to keep my mouth shut about what an asshole Vic was.

"Sorta. But also, Morgan and I were talking."

"And?"

Ava grinned. "We're gonna fuck his shit up."

I laughed. Ava had told me they were still being nice to Gabe at work. I had never felt any jealousy because she had always been completely honest with me when she was going to hang out with Kevin and knew Gabe might be there. She'd ask if I wanted to come, but I always passed. Instead, Morgan and I hung out, or I stayed in. But I was glad they hadn't totally iced Gabe out, because now they could do this.

"All right," I said. "What's the plan for this revenge mission?"

She frowned. "I should probably check with Gabe to make sure it's okay that you come. Also, I haven't really told him yet."

"*I* can talk to Gabe. We have some stuff to deal with anyway."

"Still hosting?"

Gabe looked up from the formal dining room host stand, startled. When he saw it was me, he seemed to readjust his posture, then straightened the necktie and purple dress shirt he wore.

"I am." He was still defensive. Probably worried I was here to yell or cut off my other fingers in front of him.

"First male host in Sunset Estates history. Wow. Must be because you had a great trainer. No wonder your aunt wrote a letter of recommendation for that feat." I was hoping the joke would put him more at ease. Kind of me waving a white flag.

His brief smile—no dimples—seemed to prove it did. "You picking up Ava?"

I nodded. "She actually came out and told me what happened. With Vic."

Gabe's shoulders slumped. He didn't seem angry that Ava had told me, but rather more embarrassed than anything. "Does it feel good to be right about him?"

"No, Gabe. I came to check on you, not to gloat. Are you okay?"

"I'm fine." But I could tell that was a lie.

"You don't have to be fine. It's the same shit that happened to you last year, so you're allowed to be completely not-fine."

His eyes were glassy, and he let out a sigh. "I know. But it's actually worse than last year."

"Because it was your family he sent the texts to."

"And a video."

"What!"

Gabe quickly corrected himself. "It wasn't a real video. It was some video he found that happened to be a random Latino dude and a white guy doing it. There's even some fan site watermark in the corner he didn't bother removing, but you can't see their faces, and apparently my family didn't feel like looking that closely at it. Not that I can blame them."

I felt a tiny bit of relief. At least that meant Vic didn't *have* a video of the two of them that he'd use to ruin Gabe's life.

"But it was just another thing for my parents to scold me over. I think I had finally gotten through to them how important it was for me to go to film school. We had a showcase at Murphy—did Ava tell you?"

I shook my head.

"It was a screening for our final film projects. It was . . . kind of the last straw for Vic and me that day. My family showed up, but he didn't. Said he had something with school, but it was a Saturday afternoon. Afterward my dad said he was proud of the film. And my mom even cried. For a few days after the showcase, everything seemed so good. My dad actually asked me questions about USC's film program. But Vic ruined it by sending out those screencaps. I think they're just embarrassed, but they haven't said more than three words to me in days. Which I guess is better than just yelling at me."

"I'm sorry he did that to you. You didn't deserve it."

"I know. Thanks."

"Well, anyway. Has Ava told you about the plan?"

"Plan?"

CHAPTER
FORTY-THREE

ABOUT AN HOUR AND A HALF LATER, James was climbing into the back seat of my car. He tucked the paper bag between his legs and handed us his phone. Morgan had recruited him at work since he was the only one of us who Vic didn't know.

"Phase one completed," James said, his eyes darting around the parking lot. "Babe, Bahama, commence phase two."

"Should we wait for Morgan and Ava to come back?" Gabe asked.

I grabbed his hand, giving it a gentle squeeze. "They'll be fine. Let's go." Gabe and I got out, leaving James to talk to himself in the back seat of my car and hopping into Gabe's car right next to us. It was nestled between Morgan's and mine behind the P.F. Chang's dumpsters.

Gabe looked nervous as he started his car and pulled out of his space toward the shopping center's main parking lot.

"We've got this." I opened the most recent video in James's phone and sent it to our group chat, making sure it went through before I tucked the phone into the breast pocket of my shirt. "Which one is his car?"

Gabe pointed. "Right there."

I nodded, took a picture with my own phone, and sent it to the group text. "Park across the aisle."

Gabe did as I said and turned off the car. I reached across my still-bandaged left hand and grabbed his arm, getting his attention. "It's going to work. I promise."

He nodded and we got out, heading for Oscar's Ice Cream. I checked that the camera lens was just above the edge of my breast pocket and then hit record.

Vic looked up as we walked through the door, his smile dropping immediately when he saw me. There were two bowls of ice cream in front of him. I waved to Grant behind the counter, and we joined Vic at the table.

"Had I known you were bringing a third, I would have gotten another spoon."

I glanced at the Frances McDor-Mint and what I assumed must be the Reese's with a Spoon Sundae—it even came with a dark-chocolate spoon! Adorable!

"I'm more of a Jodie Bananas Foster fan myself," I said.

"So what's up? You wanted to see me?" Vic turned his attention away from me and toward Gabe. But not before I saw his eye flick to the phone sticking out of my pocket.

"I want you to stop contacting me and my family. It's creepy, it's an invasion of my privacy, and if you don't stop I'm going to call the police and tell them you're harassing me."

Vic looked surprised. "*You* contacted me. I never reached out to you or your family. I sent you gifts to apologize, but I never did what you're saying."

Gabe let out a frustrated sigh. "Fine, whatever. The police probably wouldn't do anything anyway."

"But," I said, taking my cue perfectly, "they probably would care that you bought alcohol for Gabe's party. A party full of minors."

And Gabe jumped in with his line. "And *that* is probably a bigger deal for you than just a harassment complaint."

Vic's smile dropped. "I don't . . . No. I really have no idea what you're talking about." He turned to me. His eyes drifted down to James's phone again. Then he looked at both of us, one then the other. Daring us to continue.

He knew exactly what we were trying to do.

I sighed and took the phone out and stopped the recording. His smile returned, and he brought his attention back to Gabe.

"You made me watch that stupid *Veronica Mars* show where she pulled this shit all the time."

"Goddammit." Gabe leaned back in the booth, looking defeated.

"You think I'm an idiot? At least she was better at hiding it than the two of you."

"You're right," I said, giving up.

"So . . ." He put a spoonful of the sundae in his mouth. When he spoke, he spit melted ice cream onto the table. "You boys enjoy the ice cream. Gabe, call me if you ever want to . . . you know. Hang out." He stood up, then stopped himself and pointed at me. "Both of you."

Vic smiled and wiped the ice cream from his mouth with the back of his hand. We watched him walk toward the door.

322

"That went well," I said.

Gabe smiled. "Better than I thought. I didn't think he paid attention during *V. Mars*. Should we go?"

I watched as Vic strode out. "Give it a couple seconds . . . Okay, now."

We got up, apologizing to Grant for leaving the ice cream, and ran to the door. When we burst out into the cool April air, Vic was screaming.

We ran after him, and he stopped a few feet from his car.

Morgan and Ava popped up from behind it, something gloppy dripping from their hands.

"You two couldn't have distracted him a little longer?" Morgan asked. She popped a Sunset Estates prepackaged butter and a margarine packet onto the top of Vic's car, which was covered in different sticky foods.

Ava grabbed an egg from the Trader Joe's bag in her hand and smashed it on the hood. "Seriously, you guys had one job."

"What are you bitches doing?" Vic screamed as he walked around the car, pulling at his hair. As Gabe and I got closer, I saw the discarded cans of sardines, jars of pigs' feet and gefilte fish, and butter packets surrounding the car. Goop dripped off the sides.

Honestly, any more time and I think they would have destroyed their masterpiece. Sensing they were about done, Ava took out another jar of pigs' feet and handed it to Morgan. Then she took the carton of eggs from the bag.

Morgan opened the jar. And together they dumped the contents of their containers on the hood and front windshield of Vic's car. The eggs cracked, their yolks mingling with pickled pigs' feet. I kind of wished it had been noon on a summer day when we did this so it could be baked in. Oh well.

"Next time you decide to fuck with our friend . . ." Morgan said, dropping the jar and letting it roll to a stop at the windshield wipers.

Ava continued the sentence for her. "Just remember the smell of all . . ." She waved her hand over the car. "This." Then tossed the egg carton at him.

Vic batted it away and ripped his phone from his pocket. "I'm calling the cops on you bitches." He turned and pointed at us. "*All* of you!"

My time to shine. "Before you do that, Vic, you might want to think about the incriminating video we have of you."

He threw his hands up in the air, still in character. Which was fine. "What video? The one you guys just tried to take in there? I don't know what you were even talking about!"

I took James's phone out of my pocket. "No, not that one. This one." I opened the video I had sent to the group text before going into Oscar's. As the video started to play, Vic's face slowly fell. Kinda wished I got *that* on video.

In James's cell phone video, a hand knocks on the window of Vic's car. Vic rolls the window down and smiles a friendly smile.

"Hey, man," James's voice says.

"What's up?" Vic asks.

"How you doing tonight?"

"Good, good, you?" Vic in the video asks.

Vic in real life looked me dead in the eye. "What the hell is this?"

"I think you know exactly what this is," I said.

In the video James says, "I could be better, but I was hoping you could help me out with that. Are you over twenty-one?"

Before the video went any further, Vic snatched the phone and smashed it to the ground.

"Dude!" Ava yelled. "That was the only copy! Oh . . . wait." She took out her own phone and the video played again from the top.

As James in the video knocked on the window and said, "Hey, man." I took out my own phone and jumped ahead while Morgan and Gabe started the video on their own phones, James's voice echoing around us, saying, "Hey, man."

I turned my phone back around. It was at the end of the video, when Vic comes out of the Fine Wine & Good Spirits and hands James a bottle of whiskey. James, the goddamned star he is, even pulls out the bottle, showing it to the camera on the phone tucked into the front pocket of his shirt.

"Dude, you're a lifesaver," James in the video says. "Hey, what are you doing tonight? You want to help me drink this? Like as a date with the possibility of consensual sex?"

Vic in the video smiles wide. "Yeah, man. I gotta do something first, but it shouldn't take long. What's your number? I'll call you after."

I stopped the video.

"Vic the Dick!" James said, walking up behind Gabe and me and putting his arms around our shoulders. "You know what? On second thought, never mind. You're not really my type." He planted a kiss on Gabe's cheek, then winked at Vic.

Vic turned to Gabe. "What the *fuck* is this?"

"An insurance policy," he said. "If you ever come near me again, if you ever contact my family again in a way that I can trace back to you, no matter how vague, I will send *this* video to the police. Oh, wait."

He reached into his pocket and took out a receipt. It was dated October 29.

"And maybe you had a hard time remembering it in there, but you *also* bought alcohol for my Halloween party." He squinted at the receipt. "Hey, look, it's the last four digits of your debit card. Probably should have gotten the cash from me first."

Morgan said, "Furnishing a minor with alcohol is a lesser punishment than harassing and stalking, but it's easier to prove. And you're fined *per* incident. And since you did it for a party, you could be fined *per* person at the party."

"And what?" Vic said. "All your friends are going to come forward and say they were drinking underage?"

"The five of us will," I said.

"So that's . . ." James said, ". . . let's see, a thousand dollars, first offense, twenty-five-hundred-per-person second offense." He pretended to do the math, which we had already researched and gone over, in his head. "Carry the one . . . thirteen grand. Dick, dude! That's so much money!"

"And you can't afford that," Gabe said. "Can you, Vic?"

"Not to mention," Ava added, "look at this car. The detailing alone." She shook her head.

Vic looked like he was about to explode. "You know what? Fuck *all* of you!" Tucking his phone away, he turned and grabbed the door handle of his car. He let out a groan and wiped his gooey hand on his leg as Morgan and Ava burst out laughing again.

He used his shirt to open the car and got in. Ava and Morgan walked to the front, getting out of the way as he backed out of the space faster than he needed to. Ava picked up one of the pigs' feet that fell off and started oinking.

"Have a good night, Vic!" She hauled off and pelted the car with the pig's foot as he drove off.

As everyone laughed and cheered, James bent over, picking up his cracked phone. "You owe me a new phone, Tommy."

"I'll get it replaced," Gabe said.

"Nah, I'm just kidding. It adds character!"

"No, seriously. It's the least I can do." He turned to us, tears in his eyes. "Really. Thank you all."

"Of course," James said. "You don't fuck with the Sunset Estates crew."

"Aw!" Morgan pulled us all into a hug that was ruined by Ava's pickled-pigs'-feet hands. She tried to smear them on us, but we ran, picking up leftover butter containers and trying to squeeze what was left out onto her.

I stuck around with Gabe after Morgan, James, and Ava left. We were conscientious enough to throw away the jars and cans, but there was still food surrounding the parking spot Vic's car had been in. Either someone would clean it up, or the birds and insects would get it. Or it would rot until rain washed it all away.

"Are you okay?" I asked, leaning against my car.

Gabe sighed and leaned against his. "Better? But still . . ."

I nodded. I couldn't imagine how awful it must feel, being exposed like that to your family. Even if the video was fake, the texts were real. I was sure I'd sent plenty of texts I wouldn't want my mom to see. I hated Vic. I hoped he got super syphilis and his dick and nose both rotted off.

"Why did you break up with him?" I asked. I had no idea why I was curious, but I had to know.

Gabe slumped. "Because of you."

My stomach lurched and did a weird little buzzy thing that felt new but familiar all at once. "Me? I . . . sorry, I don't think . . ."

"No!" Gabe put up his hands. "No, no, I didn't break up with him *for* you."

And every muscle in my body eased. I felt relief, actually. After everything Gabe and I had been through over the past several months, I had realized that he wasn't the same boy I fell in love with when we first met. He wasn't better or worse in any way. It wasn't like who he was changed on an X-Y axis—or whatever; not the best at math. But he wasn't this perfect dream boy I had put on a pedestal. For a split second there, though—only for a second—if he had said he had dumped his boyfriend for me and asked me out, I might have caved and said yes.

But he wasn't doing that. And knowing he wasn't doing that, I felt relief. Like we could finally move past all our shit. I could take him from that pedestal—hell, I could demolish that pedestal and never put another boy I liked back up on it—and we could be better.

He continued. "It was what you said. You were right, Vic was manipulative. Clearly—look at what he did when I dumped him. He went right to my friends and family and tried to turn them against me so I'd have to come back to him. And I need to apologize to you."

"No, you don't."

"Then I want to, so let me do it. I'm sorry. I knew he was manipulative before, but I wasn't ready to admit it to myself. So when you came along and I started to like you, I think I started subconsciously pushing Vic away and trying to pull you into it. I guess I was hoping Vic would get pissed off and finally be the one to dump me, so I wouldn't have to make the choice. And so I made a bunch of bad decisions because I didn't want to make the one decision I knew I had to. Because at the time I did still like him. And I also liked you."

"I liked you, too. I mean, I'm sure the making out was a dead giveaway."

He laughed. "Sorry I was such a mess."

"Girl, I was a mess, too. Remember when I performed my own amputation?" I held up my hand to him. "Stop being so hard on yourself. I'm not totally innocent, either. I was there and trying to get you to fall for me so you'd dump him. So . . . sorry I was a mess, too."

"So does this mean we're friends again?" he asked.

Did I want to be his friend? It wasn't a want—*could* I be his friend was the real question. I had wanted more than that for months, and then we were nothing. But I did like Gabe, even if that like was now just in a friendly way. Friends was better than nothing. Tonight felt good, helping him. Standing up for him: It was what friends did.

"Allies?" I asked, putting out a hand.

He smiled, and his dimples returned. He pulled me into a hug. "Rule number one: always trust your allies."

When I got home, there was an email notification on my phone:

From: admissions@lmb.edu
Subject: LA MÈRE LABONT—NYC APPLICATION PORTAL UPDATE

CHAPTER
FORTY-FOUR

I DIDN'T RACE INTO THE HOUSE. IN fact, I stared at my phone for a few minutes, reading the email and then just sitting. Though the email didn't provide any answers other than "there has been an update to your application. Click here to open the portal and review your documents."

In all honesty, I should have been so excited to get the email. I imagined myself clicking it and freaking out then and there in the car. But I couldn't click the link.

Maybe I wanted someone to share the excitement with?

So I got out of the car and went into the house, where my mom was on the couch watching TV. I must have looked some type of way, because she asked me what was wrong.

"I got an email from La Mère."

Her eyes went wide. "Did you . . ." Get in? Get rejected? What was she going to say? What were her instincts saying?

When it was clear she wasn't going to finish her sentence, I said, "I didn't open it yet."

She patted the space on the couch beside her and I sat, my phone still unlocked in my hand and the email on the screen. She waited silently, and I clicked the link.

When I signed into the portal, there was a new document link below my application, titled ADMISSION DECISION—DEES, THOMAS.

I put my finger to the screen, and even before the document loaded, I felt different. None of this was how I'd imagined. I'd thought I would be excited, but I think it was more anxiety and worry than anything else. It was like that moment before I took the lid off a Dutch oven—or a bread cloche—to see if my bread had risen properly.

It was a lot of effort for something you'd put together, hoping it all worked out.

But sometimes it didn't.

My mom put her arm around my shoulder, pulling me close to her. "I'm sorry, pumpkin."

I hadn't even read it. Or maybe I had. Because when I finally did comprehend the sentence that said *while we were very impressed by your application, we regret to inform you that you have not been selected* . . . I felt . . .

Relief.

A weight on my chest seemed to lift, and I felt like I could breathe—actual, deep breaths. I didn't feel sad. I turned to my mom, who wiped tears from her eyes. And I laughed.

"It's okay," I said. I laughed again and hugged her.

"But you worked so hard," she said.

I did. But it didn't feel like when I pulled off the Dutch oven lid and my bread was flat—it felt the opposite. Like I had just pulled off the lid and discovered that the bread had not only risen, but was just moments away from the perfect golden brown, crunchy crust. I hadn't gotten into my dream school, but I felt like I was about to have the best bread I'd ever tasted.

Now that I'd been rejected from my dream school—a phrase that was slowly losing its meaning since I seemed to be waking up from the dream—I realized just how many other options I had. There wasn't just one school and one path toward what I wanted from my life. There were hundreds of possible paths.

It felt freeing. I pictured my dad, still alive, saying, *Ah, screw 'em. I already taught you everything I learned there.* I could also picture him buying a bunch of T-shirts from whatever school I did end up choosing and wearing them proudly around the house.

Whatever school I ended up choosing.

That was also a nice thought. Because it meant I was choosing it, not going because my dad went there. Not going because everyone else said it was the best. And not because a famous chef—probably splitting his time between his restaurants and his Food Network show—taught there.

I mean, yeah, I still hadn't gotten into any of the other schools I'd applied to, but it was early. I was also confident that I would get into at least one of them.

My mom still had tears in her eyes when I locked my phone and turned to her. I laughed again. "Seriously, I'm fine. I thought I'd be more upset—I guess I'm kind of disappointed—but also it means I get to pick whatever I want." The pressure was completely off.

She frowned at that. "You could always have picked whatever you want—you know that, right?"

"Yeah. But this is different."

She seemed to get what I meant and patted my knee as she stood from the couch. "In that case, let's have some celebration-and-or-commiseration ice cream."

"Do we even have any?" I followed her into the kitchen.

"There's still that Oscar stuff you brought home." She pulled the black pint container covered with non-trademarked gold statues out of the freezer.

"Ew, that's like four months old."

"Ice cream doesn't go bad." She pulled the lid off, and her face scrunched up. There was a layer of freezer burn across the top.

"Commiseration Oreos?" I asked, reaching into the pantry and pulling out the box of cookies. My mom chucked the pint of freezer-burnt Oscar's ice cream into the trash and grabbed the milk from the fridge instead.

We sat down and talked about the other school options. And a week later, I had acceptances from all the other schools I had applied to—including a personalized letter from the admissions committee at Johnson & Wales complimenting me on the supplemental video.

I really could choose whatever I wanted.

CHAPTER
FORTY-FIVE

"BAHAMA MAMA!" JAMES CALLED OUT FROM THE cracked rear window of the limo. "Lookin' like the Rock in *Red Notice!*"

Ava tried to ask what the hell that meant, but I waved it away as I opened the limo door for her. She pulled up her gold beaded dress and climbed into the limo. I heard Morgan and another girl's voice squeal and compliment her dress as Ava did the same to them.

I waved to my mom, who had tears in her eyes, and she waved back as she turned to talk to Ava's uncle. Then I climbed into the limo.

James and Morgan sat to our right. Morgan's hands were on her cheeks, and her eyes were wide as she was speaking to Ava. "Did you cut it?"

Ava laughed and waved a hand. "Oh, hell no. It's one of my aunt's wigs." She reached up into the wavy, asymmetric bob to check the thousands of bobby pins hidden in there. Beside Morgan, James was in a tuxedo jacket and tails but wearing a kilt and the little kilt purse thingy that hangs in the front. I gave him a skeptical eyebrow.

"Are you wearing that how the Scots wear it?" I asked.

"Dude," Luke warned from the seat by the partition, shaking his head. He had his arm wrapped around a blonde girl I recognized from school. She wore an aquamarine gown, and her makeup looked incredible.

"Bahama Mama," James said. "You gotta stop flirting with me, man. In front of my date and my date's ex-boyfriend?" He put his arm over Morgan's shoulder. Morgan wore a pink dress with a tulle skirt. "And yes, I am wearing it *correctly*." Then he quickly turned and mooned the whole limo.

Everyone groaned, putting up their hands to block the view.

We pulled up to our pre-prom stop at just before five. Perfect timing. We all got out, each guy helping their date. Morgan even stopped to pluck a piece of lint from Luke's date's dress—Ava quietly reminded me her name was Maggie.

We walked two by two through the front door of Sunset Estates.

Gabe was just returning to the host stand when we rounded the corner, laughing. We had been stopped no fewer than seven times on the hundred-foot walk from the front door to the dining room. Gabe clapped his hands over his mouth and let out a squeal I had *never* heard from him.

"You all look so great!" he said.

The door behind him burst open, and George stuck his head out, his jaw firmly unhinged. "Oh my God. Look at all of you. Oh, I'm going to make an announcement. Wait here. Gabe, bring them in when you hear me." He closed the door and ran into the kitchen, then out to the casual dining room to grab the microphone that tied into the sound system.

Gabe looked me up and down, and I gave him the *excuse* me, *friend* eyebrow. He shrugged, but his face reddened.

George's voice boomed over the microphone as he began his announcement.

As we walked into the formal dining room, the faces of even the most cynical residents lit up. Ava and I visited tables of residents we knew, and Luke went around to his own favorites, introducing Maggie. Everyone gushed and complimented Ava over and over, then threw me a nice compliment as well.

"But tonight is more about her, anyway," said Judge Fredericks—back in the formal dining room since I still wasn't back serving. I nodded, though *I* would be the one begging Ava to dance with me. Ava nudged me, probably thinking the same thing.

Ava and I said goodbye to Judge Fredericks before saying hi to a few other tables and making our way into the casual dining room.

She pulled me to her favorites, the ones she called the Golden Girls, only there were six of them. While she talked about the dress and how she'd found it and added some of her own embellishments, I scanned the room, looking for Al and Willa. I spotted Willa first.

Her hands were clasped over her mouth, and her eyes were red. Al was beaming. I excused myself from the Golden Girls and made my way over to them, stopping only six times along the way to respond politely to compliments.

Willa jumped up and hugged me. "Oh, you look so handsome." Her hug was strong, and I almost felt like I was going to cry.

This was the main reason I had pressed for us to stop by on our way to prom, but I hadn't realized it until that very moment. Al and Willa were like my queer grandparents. My fairy grandfather and badass lesbian grandmother. I wanted to share this with them, because I saw them more than I did my own family. When Willa let me go, Al pulled me into a hug, and even his eyes were red.

Al gasped as Ava came over. "Ava, you look fabulous."

"This old thing?" Ava twirled for them as another table across the room was trying to get her attention. She waved and held up a finger. "Would you both excuse me? I've got to say hello to Nan Webber and Rita Fossett."

They nodded and told her to have fun at prom, and she left.

"Oh, here." Al reached into his pocket and withdrew an envelope. I held up my hand.

"Al, you've got to stop. I really appreciated it, but my get-well card was way too much."

"Hey, half of that was me," Willa said.

"See? So I still have a few hundred more." Al shoved the white envelope into my jacket pocket and shooed me away. "Now get out of here before one of these old vampires comes to suck the youth out of you."

I heard a gasp from the salad bar and turned to see George once again clasping his hands in front of him.

Al pointed. "Exactly like that. Run, kid."

CHAPTER
FORTY-SIX

BY THE TIME WE WERE BACK IN the limo and on the way to prom—a little later than we thought—everyone felt high with excitement. Even Luke was grinning. Luke's date had come around and said how cute all the residents had been. She called them "old people," but she was new, so we let it slide.

We still weren't the last to arrive when we pulled up to the Crier's Inn. We made the slow procession past the teacher chaperones, stopping to say hi to our friends and getting in line for pictures.

Ava and I got our pictures, choosing to take two weird poses and one serious one, before heading into the inn's ballroom and finding our table. We were at the same table as James and Morgan, but Luke and Maggie had agreed to sit with Maggie's friends. Our table was rounded out by one of James's friends from ice hockey and his date, Jodie Barnes—a friend of Ava's and mine who didn't work at Sunset Estates—and Lara Guthrie and Helen Fink, the co–photography editors of the yearbook, who had started secretly dating in sixth grade and had been together ever since.

"Lara, Helen, you both look stunning," Ava said. "Those dresses are amazing."

"Thanks, Helen made them!" Lara stood and shoved her hands in the sides of her turquoise gown. "And look, it's got pockets!"

Helen stood and showed her pocketed gown as well. That reminded me about Al's card. I opened it up, hiding the two hundred dollars in the inside tux pocket, and read the message.

Enjoy tonight, kid.
Your friend,
Al

I saw Ava looking at me out of the corner of my eye. I showed her the message, and she smiled.

After dinner I managed to convince Ava to dance with me for three full songs before she started wiping sweat off her brow and begging to sit down. I threw a tiny fit but obliged.

Morgan and Ava were talking about work, and James and his hockey friend were talking about hockey when Brad Waldorf approached. I looked up, surprised to see him, one, in such a sharp black tuxedo; two, talking to me in public when he hadn't been drinking.

"Hey, Tommy."

"What's up, Brad?"

"Whoa!" James shouted from across the table. "Waldorf Salad, lookin' like dirty-blond Henry Cavill."

Brad looked confused for a second but smiled. "Thanks, James." He turned his attention back to me. "You want to dance?"

My face burned hot. I looked around the room, making sure all these people I was seeing weren't just figments of my imagination. A glitch in the simulation tricking me into thinking I wasn't alone. Brad held out a hand, chewing his lip.

I felt Ava nudge my back. "Uh, yeah. Sure." A fast song was playing, so it wasn't like anyone would think anything.

But I took his hand, and he led me across the room. Almost on cue, the song switched from a fast one to a slow one. I stopped, but Brad kept walking to the dance floor. The dance floor that was clearing out slowly. Leaving only couples. Boy-girl couples. And Lara and Helen. Helen nodded in our direction, and Lara's eyes went wide. "It's happening!" she whispered to Helen.

Brad was still holding my hand. He turned back to look at me. "You okay?"

"Are *you*?"

He grinned and gave my hand a light tug. I stepped onto the dance floor as we started slow dancing to a Kacey Musgraves song. He put my hand on his shoulder and put his own hand on the small of my back.

"Is this okay?" he asked.

"Yeah," I said. But my heart was racing. *Everyone* was looking at us now, but Brad didn't seem to care. Shit, was he drunk? Would he regret this as soon as he sobered up? "Brad, are *you* okay with this?"

His smile grew. "I am, yeah."

My heart fluttered. "Is . . ." I glanced around and laughed. "Is this you coming out right now?"

He nodded quickly, like a little kid who was proud of the picture he'd just drawn. My jaw dropped.

"Brad! Congratulations! That's awesome."

"Thanks. It feels . . . fucking exciting!" His cheeks flushed a bit.

I laughed and let him lead me in the dance as he brought me up to speed on his time in therapy and coming to terms with his sexuality. He had told his parents a couple weeks back—they had apparently been *very* supportive and loving—which had been the part he was most worried about.

"That's what I actually wanted to talk to you about when I saw you at the pool hall. But you wanted to hook up. Also, at the hockey rink after you and Lara took our team picture."

I immediately felt guilty. "About coming out?"

"Yeah."

"Shit. I'm so sorry, Brad. God, I'm such an asshole. I just assumed . . ."

He arched an eyebrow and gave me a faux-smarmy grin. "And we all know what happens when we assume." Then he dropped the act. "It's cool, though. I mean, you always seemed so confident after you came out. And I just wanted to figure out how you did it. But my therapist said everyone's coming out is their own thing, so . . ." He shrugged.

I chuckled. "Well, I wasn't out to my mom until I cut my fingers off."

He took my hand and looked closely at the two scars on my fingers. "Looks good. No more pain?"

"Not so much anymore." I took the chance to step a little closer to him. "What made you decide to tell everyone else tonight?"

"I told the guys on the team last weekend," he said. "Everyone was cool with it, but there was less stress because it didn't matter if they shunned me, since hockey season's over. And James spends his time in the locker room loudly rating the other guys' butts compared to the Rock, so he's at least a two on the Kinsey scale. Also, his rankings were all kind of right?"

"Is *that* the way the scale goes?"

"I figured, school's ending, I might never see these people again. What the hell? Sorry, I should have told you first, shouldn't I? I mean, I thought it would be kind of fun to just not tell anyone and have us dance, but I didn't realize that's me pulling you into my narrative."

Wow, he really was in therapy. I shook my head. "No, no, you're good. And I . . ." I lowered my voice. "I was kinda part of your narrative before anyway."

He laughed, and it sounded different from the Brad laugh I had known. He was so much happier, more comfortable than he had ever been. But still so adorable. My heart felt like it could burst, I was so happy for him.

"So where are you going anyway?" I asked. "After all this?"

"I got into Brown!"

"Get the shit out! Congratulations—that's, like, a *really* good school, right?"

He frowned. "You say that like I'm not smart."

"No! I just mean it's Brown University. Ivy League. Shit, that's awesome."

"It is. And I got a hockey scholarship."

"Well, go . . . What's the mascot up there?"

"The Brown Bears."

I smirked. "Very apropos."

He swatted my shoulder gently. "Shut up." He tried to hide a smile, and his cheeks flushed in the light of the mirror ball. "Where are you going?"

"Johnson & Wales. They have a *really* good culinary program. I got word back in April."

Brad seemed to think for a moment. "Was that the one you told me about last year?"

"No, they rejected me."

Brad's eyes clouded, and his jaw dropped. He said, a little too loud, "What!" Everyone around us turned to look, expecting a fight. I laughed, and when one of the lights lit up his face, I noticed his cheeks were a little red. He lowered his voice. "How could they reject you?"

I shrugged. "It's fine." It was actually a lot more than fine. "I probably would have gone if they'd accepted me. But them rejecting me—removing that choice from me entirely—was a surprising relief, if that makes sense?"

"Well, it's their loss," Brad said.

Then everything suddenly clicked. Brown University was in Providence, Rhode Island. So was Johnson & Wales.

Brad and I were going to be neighbors next fall.

The song faded into something upbeat, and I expected Brad to excuse himself, but he took my hand and twirled me, making me laugh, and we started dancing faster.

Brad handed me my soda, then downed his water in three quick gulps before asking the woman at the bar for another one. We had ended up dancing so long even Ava came over to join us. But now we stood by the bar at the far side of the room. A junior girl and her senior boyfriend walked past us, and Brad turned to look at them, suddenly uncomfortable.

"Um," he said, chewing his lip again. "Can we . . . Do you mind if we go someplace quiet and . . . talk for a bit?"

Our code. Oh, he wanted to make out now. And, yeah, I could make out for a bit. Oh no, was that me assuming again?

"Don't take this the wrong way," I said. "And regardless, the answer is yes, but do you mean go somewhere and talk, or go somewhere and 'talk'?" Instead of doing air-quotes, I just put my two index fingers together in the universal signal for *jamming our hot dogs together.*

Brad laughed, and yes, it was his sweet laugh, which he seemed to be so generous with this evening. "Talk! With our *mouths.*"

I made a big show of addressing the imaginary studio audience around us and said, "I really have no idea what he's talking about."

He rewarded me with another laugh, and I let him lead me out to the lobby through the front doors and around the side of the building.

I expected him to pin me up against the wall and start going to town, but instead he shifted on his feet a few steps from me, wringing his hands.

"You good?" I asked.

"Yeah, yeah, sorry, I just." He sighed. "I thought this would have been the easier part of the night."

I chuckled. "What do you mean?"

"I mean I . . ." He took a quick breath. "I . . . like you, Tommy."

Okay. That wasn't what I thought this meeting was supposed to be about.

"And I know I kind of just pulled you into a dance thing and made you part of my coming out. I'm sorry if it made you uncomfortable."

There was something cute about his babbling. Before he had always been quiet, so everything he said felt heavy. Like every word counted for something big just because he was too embarrassed to say anything else. And now it was like every word was getting in the way of what he really wanted to say.

"I wasn't uncomfortable," I said. "Seriously, I had fun."

"I did, too!" He smiled broadly. "I just—I wanted to know if you wanted to go out with me sometime? Like on a date. A real date. Not just sneaking off to make out."

My mouth dropped open. A date? With Brad?

"Uh."

I didn't know what to say. After everything that had happened over the last year, I never expected *this*. I'd gotten so used to guys paying attention to me when it was convenient, not because they *liked* me.

But was this all too soon? And we were going to new schools in the fall—granted, they were in the same city, but still, we'd be leading different lives. Though we'd be out in those lives, neither of us having to hide who we were from the people we loved. Of course, we'd have to come out to our new friends, Brad to his new teammates. That wasn't right now, though.

And maybe planning everything out like it was a recipe wasn't always the easiest way to live your life.

Fuck it.

"Yes," I said. "I would love to go out on a date with you."

I didn't need to wait around when I had a life to live. And there's no use carrying a torch if it isn't going to burn for you, too.

Brad's face lit up. "Really?"

"Yeah. Make an honest man of me."

He pumped his fist in the air and shouted in celebration. He looked like a total nerd, and I couldn't help but laugh.

"All right, calm down," I said. But I was kind of excited, too. I had been on exactly two dates. One with Ava before I came out, which she will never let me live down. And one with Hank Dyer—perpetual drama club lead actor with whom I shared zero chemistry, and we hadn't even kissed. Everything with Gabe didn't count.

"So I'll call you, then?" Brad asked.

"Yeah, call me. Um. But we are going back into the same dance."

"Right, and I will probably come find you to dance again tonight."

My face burned, and my cheeks hurt from my smile. "I'd like that a lot."

CHAPTER
FORTY-SEVEN

WHAT DO I DO AT THE GUARD gate? Make up an old person's name? The text was from seven minutes ago. I chuckled at my phone and typed back.

DO NOT DO THAT. They will arrest you for attempted old person kidnapping.

The reply came back immediately: Too late. Silver alert is out and the fuzz is hot on my tail. But I just filled the tank. With some fuel-efficient driving and a little prayer, I think I can make it to Tijuana. Meet me there, mi amor. I shall be waiting for you.

I laughed but didn't reply back.

"No phone on the floor, Tommy." Morgan dumped off the last batch of polished silverware she didn't need with a smirk. "Who are you grinning and googly-eyed about?"

"I am not googly-eyed."

She flicked her fingers in my face. "Ya googly."

I swatted her away. "Do you need me for anything else? Or am I free to go?"

She scanned the empty dining room, where only Mackenzie and

Katie were folding napkins. The slow brunch service was over, and the other servers were probably at one of the service stations on their phones like me or finishing their chores in the kitchen.

"Nah, you're free to go. See you at Gabe's?"

"Yeah, Brad's waiting to drive me over now."

"Googly."

"You heading there like . . . this?" I frowned and motioned to her hosting outfit. She pinched my arm.

"Shut up, bye."

"Byeeeeeeee." I held the *E* all the way through the salad bar and past the servers on their phones at the FDR service station.

I'd managed to get a doctor's note saying I could return to work earlier than planned since my physical therapy was going well. It was mid-June and my seventh shift back, and while my fingers were still tight, and trembled when I tried to make a fist, they were perfect for holding trays. Also, I looked super classy when I kept the ring and pinky finger up while placing dishes and removing utensils.

I still wasn't able to work in the kitchen and probably never would be here. They weren't even letting me KS, and the lemon cutting was now a kitchen job, so I'd ruined that for everyone. The kitchen support staff was one second-degree oil burn away from not being able to fry the frozen French fries anymore.

I waved goodbye to everyone in the kitchen and made my way out to the loading dock, but Brad's car wasn't there.

I called him.

"Hello, darling?"

"Are you really driving to Mexico?"

"No, I'm out front."

"Ugh, go around back. I'm at the loading dock."

"Come around front. I'm at the front."

"I've been on my feet all day," I whined but was already heading back into the building.

"Tommy, it's three p.m."

"You're the worst non-boyfriend-boyfriend I've ever had."

"I'm the only non-boyfriend-boyfriend you've ever had."

"Oh, honey . . . if you only knew."

"Wait . . . What?"

Non-boyfriend-boyfriend was our pseudo title. We weren't officially boyfriends yet, but we weren't not-boyfriends, either. I hung up with a smile on my face as I headed through the private dining room and ran right into Willa and Al. My smile grew.

"Where are you folks off to?" I asked.

Willa and Al shared a look. Willa spoke first. "Gabriel invited us to his graduation party."

"Really? Aw, that was sweet of him." I knew that since I had been gone, Gabe and Al had bonded over their love of movies. The few times I saw them together, Willa would roll her eyes, excuse herself, and know enough to never come back. "So we're all heading in the same direction."

The tension in their faces eased, and they walked out with me, asking how the brunch shift had gone and how my hand was adjusting—they asked about my hand more than Natalie and George did.

Brad was parked in the roundabout just outside the automatic front doors. He popped the trunk and got out of the car.

"Come here," I said to Al and Willa. "I want you to meet some-one."

They shared another look and followed me as Brad handed me the backpack I'd asked him to hold when he dropped me off for my shift that morning.

"Willa, Al, this is my friend Brad Waldorf. Brad, this is Willa Vaughn and Alvin Turner."

Brad put on his most charming smile and held out a hand to both. "Nice to meet you."

"Hello, *Brad*," Al said in a flirtatious voice that made Brad's cheeks flush.

"Always nice to meet a *friend* of Thomas's," Willa said.

I gaped at her. "*You're* doing it now, too?"

She shrugged as if she didn't know what I was talking about.

"All right, let's go. Say goodbye, Brad." I pushed him gently toward the car as Willa and Al said at the same time, in the same overly friendly tone, "Goodbye, Brad." I turned on them both, clenching my teeth at them. Willa gave me the quickest of winks, and they headed off to her car.

"Aren't you going to change?" Brad asked, looking at the back-pack in my hand.

"Yeah, I'll just do it on the way there." His cheeks flushed again, and I smirked. "What? This isn't breaking any rules. You've seen me in my underwear before." Our rules were very simple: we were taking it slowly because of our history together. We were dating and doing all the things we had jumped right over that first night we got drunk and gave in to our *secret desires* almost two years ago.

His cheeks grew redder as he started the car and began to drive. I unbuckled my belt and gasped.

"Oh, shit. I forgot! I didn't *wear* any underwear today!"

"You better stop it." He was grinning ear to ear. But I caught him glancing over during a red light, and there might have been a bit of disappointment to see that I had in fact remembered to wear underwear.

It was a ten-out-of-ten day. Barely seventy-six degrees, with huge fluffy clouds drifting across a bright blue sky. My graduation celebration—I didn't want a party—had been on Friday, and it was rainy and gross. My mom and I went into the city to an expensive restaurant owned by one of the former *Food Network Star* chefs. I don't know how my mom even got a reservation, because it was packed, but my God, was that food good. They had this Portuguese chickpea dish that, had you drowned me in it, I'd have died happy.

Meanwhile, Gabe's graduation party couldn't have come on a better day. When we arrived—parking right near the same spot Ava, Morgan, and I had parked on Halloween—there was a massive tent in their side yard and people walking around in tux shirts and vests passing hors d'oeuvres. I started to wonder if Gabe's parents had paid for this perfect weather.

Brad grabbed a mini quiche off a tray and popped it into his mouth. The server held the tray out to me, and I waited for Brad to finish chewing to ask how it was.

"It's the best mini quiche I've ever had." He took four more, and I took one as well. And, yeah, it was pretty damn amazing. Buttery crust, fluffy egg, and *real* bacon, not freeze-dried then rehydrated.

We separated as Brad headed for the tent to see what food stations were there, and I went to the bar to ask for two sodas. That's where Gabe found me.

"What did you do to piss off your parents into spending your college fund on a party?" I asked.

He frowned. "It is pretty ostentatious, isn't it?"

"'Ostentatious' is your middle name. Oh, wait." I set the sodas on a table and took out my phone. He peeked over my shoulder as I opened the contacts app and changed his name to "Gabe Ostentatious De La Hoya." Out of respect, I had corrected "La WHORE-a" to "La Hoya" after the Vic-pigging.

He chuckled. "Perfect."

Brad joined us, his hands full of small plastic fishbowls filled with rice, veggies, and tuna tartare.

"There's a poke station!" he said, setting the bowls down on the table. He turned to Gabe. "Hi. I'm Brad." He held out a hand.

"Gabe, nice to meet you. Thomas has told me a lot about you." Gabe's smile was genuine. If he was nervous or jealous or feeling really any other emotion other than contentment, he wasn't showing it.

"Oh, hey! Yeah, you too! Your house is beautiful. I was actually here for the Halloween party."

"Thanks. I thought you looked familiar. You're friends with James and Xavier, right?"

"Yeah, we played hockey together." He grabbed one of the poke bowls. "This spread is amazing, by the way. Sushi station, charcuterie board, raw bar."

"They're going to barbecue later. There's also a chipwich station where you choose what cookie you want and what kind of Oscar's Ice

Cream you want inside."

Brad's eyes went wide with excitement. He turned to me. "A *chip-wich* station? Would you excuse me? Nice to meet you, Gabe. I'll be right back. Want anything?"

"I'm good with the poke for now."

He gave us a thumbs-up and left in search of the chipwich station. My heart gave a little flutter. I tried to hide my goofy grin and failed miserably, because Gabe gave me a knowing look.

"He's adorable," he said.

"He is."

"Are you still not-boyfriend-boyfriends or have you evolved to not-not-boyfriend-boyfriends?"

"Shut up." I took a bite of the poke bowl, and damn, was it good.

Brad wanted us to move slow. It was his therapist's suggestion, to make sure we managed to hit all the stages of dating and relationships Brad wanted to hit. He also discussed all of them with me, making sure I was okay with them and asking what I wanted.

It had been weird at first. But the more I thought about it, the better it was. I didn't want to just assume things with Brad like I had with Gabe. That had bitten me in the ass—or, well, fingers. We took things in steps. It was like baking—measuring everything and making sure enough time was put into each step before moving on to the next. It was nice, knowing someone was on the exact same stage of the recipe as me. If something went wrong, we agreed to talk about it. But we also agreed that our dating now didn't guarantee our dating when we got to Rhode Island. Fate had managed to keep putting us together, but we still each had our own plans for school.

That part made me a little nervous if I thought about it too long, and I felt like the same happened to him, too. But that was all later, not something we had to worry about now.

"You know you could have had a boyfriend-boyfriend," he teased. Four months ago, a joke like that would have felt like a dagger to the heart. But now we had our own friendly gallows humor. Our own Sunset Estates nuance humor.

"Because you were *so* available." I rolled my eyes.

"You could make a huge scene here and dump him and run away with me. My parents will break into my trust fund and buy a fleet of new cars."

"Run away to Los Angeles? That's a big commute to Rhode Island." Gabe had gotten into film school at USC. He was off to become a famous Hollywood director completely against his parents' wishes. Good for him.

"Why would I commute to Rhode Island?"

I rolled my eyes and finished off the mini poke. Thank God Brad had brought more.

"Seriously, though," Gabe said. "I like him for you."

My face burned, but I played it off. "Thank you for your approval. It means so much given your stellar track record with men."

He laughed, and his face brightened. "Al and Willa came!" He waved, and I followed his gaze to see them wave back as he left to go say hello. I sent Ava a text. She was at her own graduation party, which was strictly family—I could have gone, but she said it was still going to be her family trying in vain to talk her out of a gap year. I told her about the food stations and that we should have gone to her party instead because now Brad was going to leave me for Gabe.

No way, my stuffy family are dragging me down, and my

aunts are still arguing about their potato salads.

We settled this. Aunt Ruby, hands down.

I KNOW! Tell Richie Bitch I'm hitting that sushi station hard when I'm done here. See you at five.

"I panicked." I looked up from the text to see Brad with a plate with four different chipwiches. Each chipwich had one cookie flavor on one side and a different flavor on the other. They were all cut in half, so there were eight different ice cream flavors sandwiched between each half of a cookie.

I laughed. "You have to eat all of those now."

"That's not a problem, but I did plan to share one. They also have candy and stuff you can dip them in—you know, like, to line the ice cream—but that was too many choices." He handed me half a chipwich. It was an oatmeal raisin cookie with what looked like a peanut butter chocolate chip cookie sandwiching . . .

"Is this Scoop-ita Nyong'o?"

Brad spun around, looking at everyone, his mouth full of chipwich. "Is *she* here, too?" Before giving me a goofy grin.

"You're such a goober!" I gave him a kiss that tasted like Barbara Straw-Barrie.

That was allowed at this stage of our non-boyfriend-boyfriend recipe.

By the time Ava arrived, most of Gabe's extended family—and Al and Willa—had cleared out. The people left were a few of Gabe's Murphy friends—the ones who hadn't shared or didn't care about the video—and the Sunset Estates crew. Luke, Morgan, James, Ava,

Brad, and I sat at a wooden picnic table that had never been here before and was probably rented. Gabe was off talking to a few Murphy guys. Brad got up to grab more food before they started breaking down the stations, and Morgan shook her head.

"He's going to marry you," Morgan said, watching Brad fill up his plate again.

I frowned. "We should probably become boyfriends first."

"Yeah, but once he figures out how well you can cook, you're done for."

He knew exactly how I could cook. He'd come over to meet my mom two weeks before, and I'd made dinner. And dessert. He had two helpings of the crab cakes and elote salad I made, as well as two pieces of blueberry pie. Plus, I gave him the rest of the pie to take home. He said it was the best pie he had ever had—which, yes, that's probably true. I think I've finally got my pie crust recipe down perfectly, and it will die with me . . . or maybe my children. I was already secretly excited for him to try my pumpkin pie at Thanksgiving. *That* was where the magic really happened.

"So when's everyone's last day?" I asked, changing the subject. We had all given George and Natalie our final shift dates. That was, of course, depending on whether we all decided to come back to Sunset Estates during breaks. The thing about working there is you never actually get taken out of the system. After we went off to school, we could call a couple weeks ahead of time if we were going to be home for the weekend or for a break and wanted to pick up shifts. I'd be doing that. At least until I got a job at a restaurant in Providence— which, yes, I had already been checking which ones looked like good places to work.

"Never," Luke said, taking a bite out of a chipwich. He was still figuring out what he wanted to do.

"I'm done the weekend before July Fourth," Morgan said. "Gabe's taking over hosting my shifts after that. At least until he goes to LA." Morgan would be at University of Wisconsin in August.

James called to Brad and told him to get some potato salad. "I'm still working weekends through the school year. Till something better comes along. Or I get an internship." James was going to Drexel in Philly and planned to commute.

Ava and I had decided on the same end date. August 15. It was going to be Sunday brunch, a nice, relaxing final shift. And then we had about a week or so before I had to leave. Ava's uncle had agreed to let her take her gap year or two and unlocked her trust for her. I'll be honest, the idea of a gap year still made me feel anxious. But I knew she wasn't. Ava was the smartest person I knew, and whatever she did, she'd be amazing at it.

"You know," Morgan said. "there's going to be a whole bunch of shadowing over the next few months. Lots of new people."

But all that was later. For now, there was nothing pressing in our lives. The drama and excitement of the past year had dissipated, and everything was starting to seem peaceful. Take today—all hanging out, laughing, eating great food.

Like, *really* great food.

Maybe all this would be over tomorrow or the day after the first hiring wave of the summer, and all the new brats would be selfish, entitled little shits. Or maybe next year at Johnson & Wales would be awful and I'd never get full motion back in my fingers and never be able to bake intricate little French pastries and—

But that was spiraling. Whatever bad happened would happen, or it wouldn't. The year my dad died was the worst year of my life. But the rest of us were still here.

Ava gave me a look like she knew I was in my head about something, but she didn't say anything.

I turned to Gabe, who was laughing, *actually* laughing, despite what had happened to him just a few months ago. Having to relive the worst thing that had happened to him all over again, but this time from someone he trusted.

We all have bad weeks or years. Moments when it seems like everything is so overwhelming that you don't know what to do or where to start. It's like being in the weeds during a shift. Everything feels like it's all happening at once and you can't get ahead of it. But there's always a way. A way to figure it out and roll with it. Or you do flounder and struggle, and you need help from your friends. But eventually there's a lull.

Brad sat back down, handing James his potato salad, and offered me his plate. I smiled and popped a rolled-up piece of Jamón Ibérico into my mouth. I *could* worry about Brad and me starting something before going to college, where everything would change, but . . . I wasn't.

I was happy with right now, sitting there with my friends and my not-boyfriend-boyfriend—who, yes, I was very much hoping was going to turn into my not-not-boyfriend-boyfriend . . . boyfriend?

I was enjoying the lull. And the *really* good food.

Acknowledgments

I WROTE THE FIRST DRAFT OF THIS book in April of 2020. Do you remember April of 2020? I mean, I remember it happened. But every day seemed to be glommed together into one long never-ending Wednesday, and nothing was certain. I kept expecting an email from my publishers saying they had decided not to publish my debut, *All That's Left in the World*, because the pandemic had become worse than they expected and there was no way they were publishing a pandemic romance anymore! I was also working in commercial real estate, which obviously had screeched to an immediate halt and had no clear future.

My partner was working in my office upstairs while I was writing in the dining room. Instead of worrying about the uncertainty of my future, I focused on Tommy, Ava, Gabe, and suddenly also Brad— who started out as a nonspeaking background character who I slowly realized I wanted to have a happy ending as well. I focused instead on how their futures were uncertain, too. But in a totally different yet equally uncontrollable way.

I went to school for film—I'm sure you can tell based on the fact that at least one of my characters is always obsessed with movies—but when I graduated there was no job in film or television for me. Years of preparation and planning—and about forty grand in student loans—all for nothing! At least it seemed that way at the time. I got a job at a bank but continued writing in my free time. My day job changed, but I still wrote. It took ten years before I even found representation for my writing. Which is why I will always be so very grateful to my agent, Michael Bourret, for being a wonderful sounding board, a brilliant business partner, and a well of knowledge who I appreciate so very much.

Lose You to Find Me was also not what I had originally planned to be my second book with Balzer + Bray. I sent over a few options to choose from and to my surprise my editor, Kristin Rens, and her wonderful team chose this one. Where I saw a directionless, rambling series of vignettes, Kristin saw . . . well, actually the exact same thing. BUT! Beneath that, she knew there could be something great in *Lose You to Find Me.*

My UK editor, Tig Wallace, was another surprise. I thought, *There's no way the UK is going to want something I pitched as* "Empire Records *in an old folks home*," and yet, Tig absolutely wanted to work on this story with me. It's not easy to find people who work well together, but Tig and Kristin were always on the same page and really helped me turn Tommy's story into something special. I hope you are both as proud of this book as I am!

You know that saying "There's too many cooks in the kitchen"? That cannot be more wrong in publishing. There were a lot of cooks in this kitchen, and I needed every single one of them to get this book into your hands. So more thanks must go to the rest of the teams at Harper-Collins and Hachette. At HarperCollins: thank you editorial assistant Christian Vega, production editors Caitlin Lonning and Alexandra Rakaczki. The design team Chris Kwon and Alison Donalty. My wonderful cover illustrator, Alfredo Roagui, brought Tommy and Gabe to life in the most gorgeous, vibrant way, and I cannot thank you enough! Allison Brown in production, Michael D'Angelo in marketing, Lauren Levite in publicity, Patty Rosati and team, all of whom focus on school and library marketing, and of course Andrea Pappenheimer and team in sales.

On the Hachette Children's Group front I want to thank my newest editor, Naomi Greenwood, who introduced herself to me along with a mountain of wonderful news (that somehow keeps on coming?). I am so excited to work with you on our next projects! Desk editor Laura Pritchard. The wonderful marketing team, Beth McWilliams and Alex Haywood; Lucy Clayton in publicity; Michelle Brackenborough in design; Joelyn Esdelle in production; and Nicola Goode and her entire team in sales.

I also need to thank the entire Dystel, Goderich, and Bourret team including Michaela Whatnall, foreign rights director Lauren Abramo, foreign rights assistant Gracie Freeman-Lifschutz, and Andrew Dugan and Nataly Gruender for taking care of financials, and Anna Carmichael at Abner Stein for representing me overseas.

Once again, thank you, the reader, who has purchased this book, received it as a gift, borrowed from a friend, or checked it out from a library. You've helped all the people above continue to do the jobs that they love.

As a Lambda Literary fellow, I submitted the early, messy, meandering draft of this book for workshop, so I absolutely have to thank the Young Adult Cohort in the 2021 Lambda Literary Emerging Writers Fellowship. Starting with our incomparable leader Robin Talley, and the rest of the fellows: Guthrie Blechman, Elizabeth Evers, Isaiah Holbrook,

C. Julian Jiménez, Leah Johnson, Mary Maxfield, medina, Stephan Nance, Dionne Richardson, Nik Traxler, and Joni Renee Whitworth, thank you all so much for sharing your work, and I'm so excited for the world to read your words. Stay hydrated for the revolution!

Jennifer Dugan, Jason June, and Amy Spalding, thank you all so much for reading and blurbing this book. It's such a wonderful feeling having people you admire read and enjoy your work!

To the authors I'm lucky enough to now call friends: Brian D. Kennedy, Naz Kutub, Susan Lee, Anna Gracia, Steven Salvatore, Zachary Sergi, Charles A. Bush, Amy Ignatow, Kristin Dwyer, and Dante Medema and more, I'm so thankful for you all.

My after-school job in high school was as a server in a retirement community, so I absolutely have to thank my own "Sunset Estates Crew" and residents for the wonderful years we spent together and for inspiring this completely made-up place. Also, my lawyers have instructed me to put in writing that the events and people in this novel are all one hundred percent fictitious and any similarities to real places or people, living or dead, is purely coincidental.

I'm just kidding; I can't afford lawyers. But the rest of that is true.

To be fair, though, some of the people in this book are real. When I wasn't writing *Lose You to Find Me* or working on *All That's Left in the World* edits during 2020, I was watching YouTube cooking videos and *UNHhhh*. So thank you to the internet personalities who never met me but still managed to provide me with much-needed comfort and inspiration: Sohla El-Waylly, Rick Martínez, Andrew Rea, Claire Saffitz, Trixie Mattel, and Katya Zamolodchikova.

Thank you, Katie Fehlinger, for creating the "Reese with Her Spoon" pun that inspired a whole list of Academy Award–winning and ‑nominated actress ice cream flavors that I've been trying to include in a book for *years*.

Once again, thank you Dr. Benjamin Clippinger for answering my medical questions, including the nightmare-fuel tidbit that leech therapy is still effectively used in reattaching severed body parts. If anything is wrong it's because I failed to ask him the right question, so just ignore it.

My friends pretend to care when I'm talking about writing-related stuff, and I cannot thank them enough: Brandon McMullin, Kellie Clark, Brittany Young, Maureen Belluscio, Bob Gurnett, Allie Beik, Tim Davis, Nick Biddle, Matthew Kelly, Sheryl Fields, Jesse Hein, Patrick Vacca, and CJ Moore. And thank you, Erika Kincaid, who remains my biggest cheerleader but has now recruited everyone in the Kincaid/Von Tiehl family onto the squad! And to Jon Keller . . . I forgive you.

Thank you to my supportive family: Ann Marie Brown, John Brown, Sean, Jamie, Ryan, Ethan, Nolan, and Dylan Brown, Sean McLean (for watching *Empire Records* with me every single night for an entire summer when we were kids), Stephanie Sullivan, and my aunts, uncles, and cousins too numerous to mention!

I dedicated this book to my grandparents, who I am eternally grateful for. I think I managed to adopt all their best personality traits, so I especially thank Margaret and Aaron Keels, and Ann and John "Jack" Brown, from the bottom of my heart.

And finally, as always, to my wonderful partner, Michael Miska. I thank you for your love and support, but also for always knowing exactly what I'm thinking. You are the best surprise that life has given me.